SAWDUST

PD Scullin

Published by
Lint Screen Publishing
lintscreenpublishing.com

Cover illustration, design and typography by Rohit Ashrao
Formatting by Polgarus Studio
Author photo by Torrance Patrick

ISBN 978-0-9980279-0-6 (paperback)
ISBN 978-0-9980279-1-3 (eBook)
ISBN 978-0-9980279-2-0 (hard cover)
ISBN 978-0-9980279-3-7 (audiobook)

Dedicated to my mother Mary and my wife Donna,
two women who have kept the three rings of my life in order.

"Damn everything but the circus."
—*Sister Mary Corita Kent*

CHAPTER ONE
Happy

"Was this how it ends— my fate in the hands of a madman? I was testing God's mercy, and He was testing my courage."
— *Paul Driscoll's notes, 28,000 ft. over Pennsylvania, December 3, 1982*

A butterfly flaps its wings, and someone eventually pays the price.

Greg Cartwell, the pudgy creative director of Jepson Advertising Group, looked up from his desk. "Have a seat," he said. Behind him stood a shelf with Akrie Awards— tire-shaped statues given by the Akron Ad Club for the best local ads.

Paul Driscoll smiled and sat as Cartwell lit a cigarette. "Paul, I know you're not happy here."

"I'm happy," Paul lied.

"No, you're not, and the shit you pulled last week proved it. When Larry Jepson gives you copy revisions, just do them. Don't try to make him look stupid."

Jepson had marked up Paul's copy for an Alumi-Shield Siding ad. The twenty-three-year-old copywriter defended his work by writing a note quoting advice from advertising legend, David Ogilvy. He placed the note on Jepson's desk after hours, thinking the agency president would agree his copy was best.

The ad ran with Jepson's revisions.

"I wanted Larry to know why I wrote the ad the way I did."

"That was stupid. Then, you have the balls to ask me for a raise. You expect me to support you after you go over my head and piss off the old man? No, Paul. This isn't working. We're making you available for new opportunities."

"You're firing me?"

"Laying you off."

"Isn't that just a nice way of saying 'fired'?"

"Look, you're a good writer, but you can't take constructive criticism. This is a collaborative sport, and you've got to play the game."

"I played the game, Greg. I did everything you asked of me. I even worked my ass off after my dad was killed. I pulled all-nighters and weekends working on the Goodrich pitch."

"I'm sorry we didn't get the account, and I'm sorry about your dad, too. It's awful what happened to him. I'm also sorry we're cutting you."

"You're supposed to have my back."

"I can't protect you when your attitude sucks. You debate every revision and act like every word you write is precious. This is advertising, Paul. We sell shit. It's hard work, and no one wants to be around unhappy people."

"But I am happy, Greg. Really." He smiled.

"Sorry. The decision's made— straight from the top."

"What if I apologize to Larry—"

"No, don't. He's pissed."

"Because I questioned his revisions?"

"That, plus he knows you're banging his daughter." Greg crushed his cigarette into a tire-shaped ashtray.

Amy Jepson was an assistant account executive on the aluminum siding business— her qualification being her father owned the agency. She was an only child who craved attention and got it. Amy was attractive and liked sex without romantic attachments. Paul had been seeing her for months and wanted a steady relationship, but she insisted they keep it casual and secret. At work, they were all business. Outside the office, she called the shots, deciding if, and when, they saw each other.

"That's none of Larry's business," Paul said.

"Screwing the boss's daughter is never a good idea, unless you're going to marry her. And I doubt Amy's the marrying kind. Paul, collect unemployment, hit the reset button, and get on with life."

"When's my last day?"

"Today. Now. Avoid Larry, and stay away from Amy. She's trouble."

"What about severance?"

"You were here, what, two years?"

"Yes."

"You'll get a couple weeks' severance. Pack up. Larry's in a meeting, so move fast." Cartwell stood and put out his hand. "Let me know if I can help."

"Thanks." Paul noticed Advertising Age magazine on Greg's desk. "Can I have your Ad Age?"

"Take it."

On the way to his cubicle, he saw Amy flirting with Jack Lunkorm, the production manager. She looked at Paul, smiled, and returned her attention to Jack, laughing. Paul knew that laugh— her flirty laugh. He wondered if she knew he'd been fired.

He packed his office. Most people ignored him; a few wished him well. On his last trip to his car, he saw Greg's empty office. Paul walked in, grabbed an Akrie Award for an ad he'd co-written, and placed it in his box.

He was ready for new opportunities.

⤳

Paul picked up the mail and opened his apartment door. Sunlight flooded the white walls in the hallway. The living room contained threadbare plaid furniture from Goodwill. Scattered across the floor were albums by The Beatles, Devo, The Clash, Springsteen, Elvis Costello, The Dead Boys, and copies of Rolling Stone magazine. Off the living room was a small sunroom, where a green 1957 IBM Electric typewriter sat on a desk in front of a window.

He opened Ad Age. There weren't many want ads. The 1982 economy was bad. Most want ads requested more experience than his two years. One ad caught his attention: "WANTED: CIRCUS MARKETING DIRECTORS!!!"

Three exclamation points translated into urgency and desperation— two qualifications Paul had.

The ad copy painted a colorful portrait of life on the road promoting Finnion, Barton & Powell Circus, "Tops in Big Top Splendorama!" The position required a college degree and two years of sales or marketing experience. Paul fit the bill. He liked the title "Marketing Director"— it sounded more important than "Copywriter."

He tore out the ad, stuffed it in his pocket, and opened his bank statement. $346.35. The phone rang.

"Heard you got laid off," Amy Jepson said.

"I got fired, because your dad found out we're seeing each other and is pissed. Did you tell him?"

"You think I'm daddy's little tattletale?"

"Someone told him."

"It wasn't me. And we're not seeing each other. Christ, you make it sound like we're in high school."

"Sorry. You want to grab a beer tonight?"

"Can't. Got plans." Paul wondered if her plans were with Jack Lunkorm.

"How about tomorrow?"

"No. Look, Paul, I can't see you anymore. It's nothing personal, but it's over."

"Because your dad doesn't like me?"

"No. I don't care what he thinks, I just don't want to see you. We had some good times, but it's time to move on. No hard feelings, okay?"

"Sure."

"But we can still be friends, right?"

"I guess so." Paul knew he couldn't be friends with someone he wanted as a lover.

"Great. I got to run. Bye." The phone clicked. He put the receiver down and realized he'd been fired again.

It wasn't even noon yet.

Frank Sullivan waved as Paul entered Angel's Place, a dark dive bar clouded by a fog of smoke. Behind the bar stood rows of liquor bottles and a jar of pickled eggs in iridescent purple liquid, sitting beside an old cash register.

Frank was an account executive at Jepson, and Paul's best friend. He was tall, athletic, handsome. He supervised Amy, and was the only person Paul had told about their relationship.

"Greg said I got fired because Larry found out I was sleeping with Amy," Paul said. "He said I was stupid for screwing the boss's daughter."

5

"Greg should talk," Frank said. "I heard he's banging Amy, too."

"Really? Why would she go for a balding old guy?"

"Who knows? It's a rumor."

"He better hope Larry doesn't hear it, or he'll get shit-canned."

"Greg better hope his wife doesn't hear it. Are you finally going to write your great American novel?"

"I wish," Paul said. "I've got to find a job before my money dries up. I saw something interesting though." He showed Frank the want ad. "Wouldn't it be hilarious if I ran away and joined the circus?" They laughed and sipped their beers.

"You should apply."

"I should."

"You won't. You're all talk."

"Bullshit."

"Bet you a buck you won't apply." Frank grinned. "You're chicken."

"Make it five, with odds. Five bucks if I apply, four-to-one if I get the job."

"You're on." They shook. "I see your future, Paul. It involves elephants. And a broom."

"Elephants are less dangerous than Larry."

When Paul returned home, he sent a letter with his resume to the circus P.O. Box in Sarasota, Florida.

Three days later, a woman named Beverly called and asked if he was available the following evening in Norristown, outside of Philadelphia, for an interview with Tom Burnett, V.P. of Marketing and Promotion.

"Yes," Paul said. He felt his heart thumping.

He drove four hundred miles to the Liberty Trail Hotel. The desk clerk gave him a note from Tom Burnett, asking to meet in the bar at six. Burnett wrote he'd be wearing a blue pin-striped suit and bright red tie. His signature was fluid, elegant— as if it belonged on the Declaration of Independence.

Paul showered and dressed in a burnt orange three-piece suit with a yellow dress shirt and a brown and beige-striped tie.

At 5:55, he went to the bar and walked up to a man in a blue suit. "Excuse me, are you Tom Burnett?" The man stood and smiled.

"You must be Paul Driscoll. Glad to meet you." Burnett gave him a bone-crushing handshake.

He was six inches shorter than Paul, in his forties with a slim build and slicked jet-black hair parted to one side. His deep tan set off a smile of perfect white teeth. He looked as if he could run five miles in a suit without breaking a sweat.

"Have a seat, Paul. Pull up a drink." Paul smelled musk cologne and noticed Tom Burnett's monogrammed shirt, a crisp white cuff that read "TRB" in bright red thread. Paul thought monograms were pretentious— a person marking his territory with thread.

He ordered a draft.

"A beer man," Burnett said. "Beer is everyman's drink, and Finnion, Barton & Powell Circus is for every man, every woman, and every child."

The bartender delivered the beer. Burnett clinked his glass of whiskey against it. "Here's to you, Paul, and pursuing a life of excitement with Finnion, Barton & Powell Circus: Tops in Big Top Splendorama!"

"Thanks." He sipped his beer as Burnett drained his glass and motioned the bartender for a refill.

"I like what I saw on your resume, Paul. Working your way through college tells me you're a go-getter."

"Thanks."

"What do you know about circuses?"

"Not too much, I saw one when I was a kid." Burnett nodded his head and took a slurp of whiskey.

"The circus dates back over four thousand years. Before Jesus was a twinkle in his father's eye. How many jobs have a history that rich?" Burnett smiled a thousand-watt smile. "Tell me what you like and don't like about being a copywriter."

"I love writing and being creative. But I don't like office politics."

"Paul, this job will let you write all you want. And there's absolutely no office politics."

"I'll write circus ads?"

"No, they're already written. You'll write ad tags with the show dates, location, and sponsor information. I meant you'll have lots of time to write what you want. I saw on your resume you write fiction."

"Yes, I want to write novels and screenplays someday."

"Isn't today some day? Being a marketing director will give you the experience and freedom you need to write." Burnett smiled, and Paul smiled back. "But let's not rush to the altar. We'll grab something to eat, see the show, and get to know each other."

He raised his glass. "Here's to you, Paul. To your dreams, your writing, your life!" Burnett gulped his whiskey and settled the tab.

Tom Burnett drove a 1982 dark blue Cadillac Sedan DeVille that smelled of freshly oiled leather and musk cologne. He looked like a child behind the ship-sized steering wheel. The bench seat was adjusted close to the dashboard.

It was a quick drive to the field where the circus was set up. The large red and white-striped big top tent stood erected by dozens of poles and miles of strong rope.

"Our big top can cover an entire football field," Burnett said. "And our show's a hell of a lot more exciting than any football game."

Four enormous aluminum poles spaced throughout the length of the big top acted as foundations for the massive tent. Atop each pole, a bright blue "FB&PC" flag flapped in the breeze. The circus personnel directing traffic waved Burnett through. He docked his Cadillac close to the big top.

"V.I.P. parking's a perk," he said.

They walked onto the circus midway, which was formed by the ticket sales trailer at one end and the big top at the other, and was flanked by a sideshow tent. Concession and souvenir stands lined the path from the ticket sales trailer to the big top.

As the crowd milled through the midway, Tom and Paul ate hot dogs, greasy fries, and watery sodas.

"I've been with the show since I was twenty-two," Burnett said. "My first job out of Southern Illinois University. I had a management degree and no clue. So, I did what you did, and answered an ad for marketing directors with Finnion, Barton & Powell Circus."

"Really?"

"Absolutely. I interviewed, saw the show, joined up, and never looked back. Guess I was pretty good at it because I kept getting promoted. Before long, I was supervising all the other marketing directors and developing ad campaigns, promotions, publicity stunts— you name it. Now I'm part of the management team and can't imagine doing anything else. Just like that," he said, snapping his fingers, "it's twenty-two years later, and I haven't regretted a single day. And, Paul, you remind me of myself."

"I do?"

"Yes. I've got a good feeling about you. Look around." Burnett waved his arm holding a hot dog toward the walking crowd. "Look at the kids smiling, the pride on their parents' faces— pride for bringing them here. It's magic, Paul. Everyone remembers their first circus. It's like having sex for the first time, you never forget it. Seeing the circus is a rite of passage, a milestone. And marketing directors make it possible."

Paul remembered his only circus experience. He was five or six, and his parents took him and his five siblings to see a circus playing a Youngstown, Ohio arena. Their seats were high in the rafters; the three rings appeared small in the distance.

He recalled the circus smells more than its sights. The aromas of popcorn, hotdogs, and the pungent smell of wild animals and their turds— smells he wouldn't experience again until he visited a zoo. Wild animals had a threatening stench that screamed, "Run! Run fast! Now!"

Little Paul didn't like the clowns. They weren't funny. They were creepy and grotesque.

He thought the elephants would be larger. From his seat, they were less impressive than he'd imagined.

He liked the high wire act— walking and riding a bicycle on a high wire was amazing.

But the rest of the show didn't register. It was either a bad circus, or he had greater expectations than a circus could fulfill.

He did remember it, though.

Burnett nudged him and gestured across the midway. "Paul, yesterday this was an empty field. Today, it's a vibrant community. Finnion, Barton & Powell is a city that travels by night, with hundreds of dedicated professionals, incredible performers, and a menagerie of animals second-to-none. And in two days, everything you see will be gone, moved down the road— where a new city of wonders will be erected, thrilling new crowds. But what happens in this field tonight and tomorrow under our big top, will live in the memories and imaginations of these people for the rest of their lives.

Think about that, Paul. We're in the unforgettable memory-making business."

"That's amazing."

"The circus has lasted thousands of years for one simple reason. People want it. They need it. Circus is like religion." Paul hung on every word. Burnett was evangelical, passionate, persuasive. "Circus people have a saying when someone's circus through and through, we say they have sawdust in their veins. I've got sawdust in my veins, and Paul, I suspect you do, too." He smiled his charismatic smile and winked.

They finished their concessions and headed into the big top. Circus people greeted Burnett with enthusiasm. Their seats were in the front row by the center ring.

The big top was almost three-quarters full. "Pretty good crowd," Burnett said. "Capacity's five thousand, so every show's an opportunity to open ten thousand eyes to our circus wonders. Marketing directors play the starring role because it's their job to put butts in seats."

The lights went down as a spotlight illuminated a large man in a bright red topcoat and tails, trimmed with gleaming gold piping. He wore a black top hat and carried a small black riding whip as he stepped into the center ring. The ringmaster raised a gleaming gold microphone as his silky baritone voice boomed over the P.A.

"Ladies and gentlemen, boys and girls, children of all ages, welcome to the fantastic, fantabulous sixty-fourth edition of Finnion, Barton & Powell Circus: Tops in Big Top Splendorama!"

Colorful lights crisscrossed the roof of the enormous tent as a drumroll played, increasing in intensity. Cymbals crashed. At the far end of the big top, lights illuminated a twelve-piece band playing lively music. The circus cast and performing animals entered the big top, parading on the sawdust track surrounding the three rings.

Performers smiled and waved at the crowd.

There were a dozen elephants with sad, soulful eyes, three pristine white horses, dogs, a gaggle of clowns, acrobats, jugglers, a lion tamer, trapeze artists, stilt walkers, daredevils and a cast of pretty women in sparkling, tight-fitting outfits that amplified their generous breasts and long legs. The women wore heavy rouge, mascara, and eyeliner, they flashed bright smiles like lighthouses on a moonless night.

The big top was a spectacle of colorful lights. The din of the band melded with the cheers and applause of the audience.

"Feel that, Paul?" Burnett shouted. "That's tradition mixed with anticipation, electricity, sex appeal, and danger! You can't get this excitement working in an office!"

Paul wasn't sure if it was the beer, the hot dog, the greasy fries, Burnett's cologne, or the magical allure of the circus, but he felt something stirring inside.

The idea of working for a circus was appealing.

After the show, the two men went back to the hotel bar. "The circus I saw as a kid didn't compare to yours," Paul said.

"We call ours 'Tops in Big Top Splendorama!'" Burnett said. "Those happy faces you saw prove it's not hype."

"Your lion tamer's incredible."

"Not lion tamer— wild animal trainer. Chuck Gund is the best ever."

"I loved the bear act."

"The Komoskoff Family from Russia. They're world-famous."

"The guy shot from the cannon was great, too."

"Rocket Baxfree. Consummate pro."

"I also liked the trapeze act, the daredevils, and acrobats. I even liked the clowns."

"I'm glad. Look, Paul, I'm going to cut to the chase. My gut tells me you've got sawdust in your veins. I think you're one of us, and I want you to join our family."

"Really?"

"Absolutely. Come see a world few people ever do. Discover who you are, and who you could be. What do you think, Paul?" Burnett smiled.

"It sounds very interesting. Can I take a day or two and think about it?"

Burnett's smile collapsed. "Think about it?"

Paul felt guilty. "It seems like a great opportunity, and I'm really interested, but it's such a different career path from where I've been—"

"Cooped up in an office, writing ads."

"I know that's not as exciting as—"

"Paul, I thought you wanted to be a real writer."

"I do."

"Exploring America and promoting the world's best circus will give you more stories to write about than any copywriter job ever will."

"I'm sure you're right. Can I just have a day to think about it?"

"Fine. You need a day, take a day. But hurry. I have two immediate openings to fill."

"I will. I promise."

The men drank as Burnett regaled him with road stories. Paul thought the job sounded exciting, like traveling with Jack Kerouac and Neal Cassady across America. Or being with Hemingway and Fitzgerald in Paris in the twenties.

The bartender announced last call and they ordered. Burnett appeared fresh and crisp. Paul felt woozy, sweaty, exhausted.

"I want to join," Paul said.

"You're serious?"

"Yes."

"It's not the beer talking?"

"No. I want to join Finniman, Bartly & Powell Circus."

"It's Finnion, Barton & Powell Circus."

"Right. I want to join."

"Fantastic. You're going to love it, Paul" Burnett said, giving him a firm handshake. "When can you start?"

"Give me a week."

"You got it. Call the home office tomorrow, and Beverly will set up your training with Barb Siegel. She's our marketing director supervisor. You'll love her. Welcome to our family, Paul."

They clinked glasses and gulped.

The next morning, hungover, Paul telephoned Frank Sullivan. "You owe me twenty bucks."

CHAPTER TWO
Training

"Jesus preached to love one another. Jesus never met Brian Munyard."

— *Paul Driscoll's notes, Oneonta, NY*

Paul packed his apartment and stored items at his family house. There was a going away dinner, and Paul sensed everyone was wondering why he was joining a circus. No one talked about it though, or asked why he'd lost his copywriting job.

A shroud of unasked questions lingered, in the traditional Midwestern way.

The next morning, he shook hands with his brothers, hugged his sisters, and kissed his mother.

"Drive carefully," she said. "Watch the semi-trucks. They drive like maniacs. Let us know where you are. Be careful."

"I will."

Backing his Chevy Nova out of the driveway, he saw his mother's brown eyes fighting back tears.

As he drove, Paul thought of his mother's eyes during his father's funeral, four months earlier. She sat tranquilized, staring vacantly ahead. Her gaze was one of longing for the past, resentment of present, and pain and worry for the future.

His father's picture was plastered in the media. The tragic story was sensational news: a small-town man on a business trip in Cleveland, shot and killed in a convenience store robbery while coming to the aid of the owner who refused to open his cash register.

The owner lived. William Driscoll bled-out and died, leaving six children and his bride of thirty-one years. The incident was shocking and heartbreaking. Proof of life's fragility and death's randomness.

The shooting was hot news for a week, then a drunk driver ran over two kids— a brother and sister, and that became the media's tragedy du jour.

His father's killers were still at large. The police had no leads. The Driscoll family had given up hope for justice.

Paul had given up on God.

He missed his father. Here. Then gone, forever.

He thought of him often, and fought back tears during emotional songs or movies.

Paul wondered what his dad would have thought of his joining a circus. He thought he'd understand it was what Paul felt he had to do.

An eighteen-wheeler quickly changed lanes in front of him, snapping Paul back into the present. He wiped his eyes as he heard his mother's voice in his head, warning him about semi-trucks.

He concentrated on driving.

Paul arrived at The Sunshine Inn in Bridgeport, Connecticut, where he was sharing a room with Brian Munyard, another new marketing director.

Brian was twenty-four, short, with a belly that looked seven months pregnant. He wore gold wire-frame aviator glasses on his acne-scarred face.

"The friggin' Bee Gees are better than the Beatles," Brian told Paul over a pepperoni pizza that night. "The Beatles never created disco masterpieces like the Bee Gees. Saturday Night Fever nails Sgt. Pepper's Lonely Farts to the wall!"

Paul hated disco and loved the Beatles. He debated Brian, but he dismissed it all. Brian's world was closed, his word scripture.

Paul decided to agree with whatever he said. He'd suffer the fool for a couple of days, then they'd go their separate ways.

His first morning in the motel, Paul's crotch itched. It had been itchy for a few days. He thought it was a heat rash and hoped it would pass.

He showered and rubbed his crotch with a towel. The scratching of the rough cotton pile brought relief. Paul noticed brown specks in the towel.

They moved.

He inspected. The specks were creatures moving with determination over the cotton piles. His heat rash was crabs.

"Shit."

Paul folded the towel, and carefully patted his body dry. He didn't use the fresh towel on the rack. Even though he didn't like Brian, he didn't want to infect him.

He wrapped his washcloth in the crabby towel and wadded them together, placing the bundle in the corner.

He stepped into his white briefs, moving deliberately, not wanting to upset his crotch population. The elastic band on his underwear would keep the crabs confined to maximum security BVDs.

Paul thought the crabs were souvenirs from Amy. She was the only woman he'd slept with in the past year. Were they part of his severance package? Did Greg Cartwell share her gifts?

That would be poetic justice.

Maybe Greg gave them to Amy. Perhaps they were chain of command crabs, traveling down from management.

Or, maybe they were from Jack Lunkorm. Amy was also friendly with him.

Or were the crabs God's punishment for his cavalier attitude toward premarital sex? He grappled with the hard wiring of Catholicism he had received in eight years of parochial elementary school. God sent a hungry army to extract justice for succumbing to temptations of the flesh.

Message received, God, Paul thought.

"Almost done?" Brian shouted, pounding on the door. "I frickin' gotta go!"

"Just a minute."

Paul hoped crabs had a short life span. He couldn't travel the country with freeloaders in his pants.

Thanks, Amy.

Or, Greg.

Or, Jack.

Thanks, God.

Paul opened the door. "About time," Brian said, rushing into the bathroom, stationing himself at the toilet and peeing. "Want to get some breakfast?"

Paul considered saying he was starting a hunger strike. "Sure."

They sat in a vinyl booth at the 3-Squares Diner. Brian sopped gooey egg yolks with a piece of toast, and crammed it into his mouth. "Tell you one thing— I won't be long in this freakin' job." Brian spoke while smacking his lips.

"Why?" Paul asked.

"My cousin's making a killing selling Amway, and says he can set me up, too. Sounds great, right?"

"I guess so," Paul said, lifting a strip of bacon to his mouth with his right hand, as his left scratched his crotch.

"'Guess so?'— I frickin' know so!" Brian said, shoveling hash browns into his mouth. "But first, I'll do this circus thing."

Paul wondered what Tom Burnett had seen in Brian. The fat man must have acted normal in his interview. Paul had a headache, a nauseous stomach, and body lice. He pantomimed signing a check to the waitress.

"What do you think?" Brian asked, mopping the remains of his plate onto his last slab of toast.

"About what?"

"The waitress. Think she's worth a fifteen percent tip?"

"Sure."

"I could have used more coffee. She's a seven to ten percenter."

"Waitresses don't make much. Tips are pretty much all they get," Paul said. His sister, Kate, was a waitress, and he knew the job was tough because of cheapskates like Brian.

"I leave a good tip for a bottomless cup, but I've been staring my cup bottom for ten minutes." Brian pulled a calculator out of his pocket. "I'll figure out the tip, and we'll split-skis."

"I'll leave the tip."

"We need to figure out halfsies, mister moneybags."

"I can do that without a calculator."

"Now Rockefeller's an Einstein, too. Figure it out. I'll check your homework. Dealio?"

"Dealio." Paul was ashamed he repeated a Brian-ism. The waitress delivered the $8.50 check. "It's four and a quarter each."

Brian wasn't listening. He worked his calculator, punching keys, talking to himself. "Eight point five zero... divided by two...

equals… four point two five. It's four twenty-five each."

"I know."

"Got change?" Brian pulled a five out of his wallet.

Paul gave him three quarters and left two singles on the table. He walked to the register as Brian continued poking his calculator.

～

When they returned, Brian went to the bathroom, closed the door and began making noises like a walrus delivering a baby. Paul called Amy.

"Hello," her recorded voice said. "You have reached the office of Amy Jepson, assistant account executive with Jepson Advertising Group. I am not in right now. Please leave your name, number and a message, and I will call you back as soon as possible. Thank you, and have a great day!" At the beep, Paul cupped his hand and whispered.

"Hi, Amy, it's Paul. I'm in Bridgeport, Connecticut, for my new job and I discovered something you should know about. Please call me. It's important." He gave his number and hung up, breathless.

～

Barb Siegel from Long Island was twenty-eight, single, and overweight, with a pretty face and dazzling smile. She was a ten-year veteran of Finnion, Barton & Powell Circus.

She attended New York University for two semesters as a theater major, then answered a circus marketing directors ad. Tom Burnett was impressed by her confidence, and hired her on the spot.

She was an excellent marketing director, and when Burnett got promoted, Barb became the supervisor of all ten marketing directors.

Marketing director was the modern term for 'advance man' or

woman. The job consisted of traveling ahead of the circus and living in a city for three weeks or so, blitzing the media promoting the upcoming shows. Even if someone was blind and deaf, they'd know the circus was coming.

Barb introduced herself to Paul and Brian and began their training. There was a card table with three folding chairs in a small living room next to her bedroom. Each student received a set of three-ring binders, detailing the marketing director tasks: selling and supervising circus promotions, publicity, advertising media negotiations and buying, public relations, arranging for a sewage company to flush and clean "donikers"—portable toilets mounted on flatbed trucks, ordering the delivery of twenty bales of timothy hay for the elephants, and running a newspaper classified ad for general laborers, or roustabouts.

The binders also contained standard circus contracts, along with examples of successful circus promotions, many created by Barb.

She was dressed in black; her size could not be ignored, and her sandalwood perfume assaulted nostrils and lingered long after she left the room.

Her voice blasted a distinct Long Island accent, and she smacked arms for emphasis.

Her aggressive demeanor was unsettling to Paul. In his Ohio upbringing, one was polite and indicated in roundabout ways what he was after, with equal measures of passivity and hopefulness. One 'hoped' things would happen, and was 'lucky' if they did.

Barb Siegel asked for the moon, and settled for nothing less, taking pride in negotiating well.

"Always, always, always ask for more," she said. Barb believed in her product and couldn't imagine why anyone wouldn't buy. If refused, she'd re-state her case and come again and again until she achieved surrender.

21

"Don't wait— castrate, then skate!" was another maxim, meaning, close the deal and beat it. After an hour of lectures, Paul thought he may be too passive for the job. He was shy by nature and hated aggressive sales people.

"Don't forget," she punched their arms, "if you don't ask, you won't get!" She smiled. "Let's see if you've been paying attention. What happens if you don't ask?"

Brian looked at Paul, both looked at Barb. "You won't get," they said in unison.

"You guys don't sound very confident!" she barked. "Try again. If you don't ask—"

"You won't get!"

"What?!"

"You won't get!"

"Now, the whole thing!"

Their volume and confidence grew. "If you don't ask, you won't get!"

She smiled. "Good."

Throughout the morning, Brian peppered her with questions:

"Barb, should we sell a lot of promotions?"

"Is it good to get tons of press coverage?"

"Should we try and sell-out every show?"

Brian lobbed softball questions, kissing her ample ass, and she sent them far over the fence.

"Paul, you feeling okay?" Barb asked, in the afternoon.

"I have a headache."

"Want some aspirin?"

"No, thanks."

"If you have any questions, speak up. This is your time, too. Maybe Brian will let you get a word in." Brian honked a laugh.

"You're funny, Barb. The funniest thing since sliced bread."

"Since when is sliced bread funny?"

"Good one, Barb. You're cracking me up!"

She announced a break. "Great idea, Barb," Brian said. "Got to stay sharp to stay sharp."

"Can I have some aspirin now?" Paul asked.

"Sure. Bottle's on my bathroom sink."

"Thanks." Paul opened her bedroom door, the room was littered with clothes, newspapers, empty chip bags and soda cans, scrunched candy wrappers, and Post-It Notes filled with illegible handwriting stuck to windows and walls.

The bathroom was cluttered with used tissues crumpled like tumbleweeds, and assorted makeup jars, bottles, and tubes on the countertop. The sink had long strands of black hair and a squiggle of toothpaste. A plastic razor with stubble and dried shaving cream sat on the tub's edge. In the toilet, a wad of toilet paper floated like a dead body in murky waters.

Paul flushed, idly scratching his crotch, and wondered how anyone could live like this.

He peed, washed his hands and dried them with tissues, not trusting her towels.

When he returned, Brian was babbling to a bored Barb.

"Seriously, Barb, we should have a graduation blowout after we finish tomorrow. Go to a disco, drink, dance, let the old hair down."

"I have to be in Asbury Park early Saturday to meet the show," she said.

"Come on, you only go around once— am I right, Paul?"

"I think so," Paul said. Going to a disco with Brian and Barb sounded hellish.

"I'll find the best disco, and first round's on me! What do you say, team?"

"Okay," Barb said. "But it's an early night for me." She spoke with the enthusiasm she'd give someone requesting her to sit in an electric chair.

"Fan-frickin'-tastic! I closed the sale. I did ask, and I did get— see, Barb? I'm a natch."

"A what?"

"A natch— short for natural. I like to 'breviate, Bar. 'breviate, that's short for—"

"Got it."

"You got it all right," Brain said, striking a Travolta disco pose with his right fist thrusting into the air.

Paul felt his head contracting, hoping it was a brain aneurysm.

Barb finished her lesson and told her students their first assignments: Paul would handle shows in Haverhill, Massachusetts, and Brian, Bangor, Maine.

Brian invited her to join them for dinner; she declined, saying she had work to do.

The trainees returned to their room; Paul phoned the front desk and checked for messages. There were none. Amy hadn't called. He imagined her with Jack Lunkorm, or Greg Cartwell, in a seedy Akron motel. If with Greg, he'd no doubt have brought a few of his Akrie Awards for foreplay.

They had dinner at Durstun's, a restaurant with wood-paneled walls lined with vinyl booths, a sea of four-top tables, and an aroma of stale frying oil and disinfectant. Brian asked the wait people the name of Bridgeport's best disco.

"Disco sucks," said one waiter.

"I hate disco," said another.

"The Hammer," said a young waitress. "The Hammer's the hottest disco around. I love it."

"Great, we'll go tomorrow night," Brian said. "Come join us."

"Can't. I have an algebra test Monday. I'm flunking, so I've got to cram all weekend. Thanks, anyway."

"Stupid algebra," Brian said. She giggled. "What's your name?"

"Wendy."

"Wendy, you'll never use algebra when you're older." She laughed. "Meet us at The Hammer tomorrow."

"I don't know—"

"We'll show you a good time, drinks on me."

"Maybe."

"You'll have a great time." She blushed, and returned to work. Brian watched her as she walked away. "Would you do her?"

"She's barely sixteen," Paul said. "She's jailbait."

"She's old enough to know better."

"Old enough to get you a cellmate."

"I'll bet she can disco down."

"You're serious?"

"Disco's all about action, Paulie. That beat gets going and starts stirring your loins, your jungle instincts take over— next thing you know, you're horizontal bumping! I know what I'm going to wear tomorrow."

"Going to wear— are you a girl?"

"You don't just walk into a freakin' disco without planning your wardrobe. I hope you have something decent. Don't embarrass me in front of Wendy."

"Jeans and a tee-shirt?"

"No girl's going to go for some joker in jeans and a tee. Do you have a floral silk shirt, tight black or white pants, anything dressy?"

"I have a couple suits." Getting dressed-up was another reason to hate disco.

"Okay, but don't wear a tie. And put your shirt collar outside the jacket."

"Yes, mister disco fashion."

The two marketing directors ate large portions of mediocre food. Brian talked throughout, telling Paul his dream of being a disco star, touring with the Bee Gees. "I'd be Brian Gibbs." He talked about making millions and buying his parents "a new car and a friggin' mansion."

After dinner, Brian suggested they grab a beer. Paul agreed.

A bar was a better place to ignore Brian than a cramped motel room.

The Amberjack Tavern was a long, narrow room reeking of cigarettes, beer, grease, and wet dog. Five middle-aged men sat at the bar; two young guys played pinball.

The bartender was a sixty-something thin woman in skin-tight jeans and a shimmering red blouse. Paul and Brian sat at the bar and ordered drafts. Each reached for his cigarette pack and lighters. Bob Seger sang "Night Moves" on the jukebox.

"Love this frickin' song," Brian said, lighting a Winston. "Reminds me of Cheryl." He exhaled smoke slowly. "Good old Cheryl— that's who this song reminds me of."

"Who's Cheryl?"

"The one that friggin' got away." Brian shook his head. "The one... that... friggin'... got... away."

"Want to tell me about her?"

"Okay, if you insist. She was my first and only love. We dated four years and were talking marriage— white dress, monkey suit, big cake, honeymoon—the whole package." He snubbed his Winston into a metal ashtray, took a slurp of beer, and stared at the crushed cigarette butt.

"What happened?"

"She fuckin' dumped me; that's what fuckin' happened." It was the first time Paul heard Brian say 'fuck' instead of a sanitized variation of the word.

"Dumped you?"

"Like last week's garbage. One day she's wearing my frickin' class ring, next day's she's giving me the friggin' finger." Paul was impressed with his wordplay.

"Why?"

"She fell for a guy in a rock band."

"At least she didn't dump you for a ukulele player," Paul smiled.

"Not fucking funny." Brian waved the bartender for another round. "She stole my heart, then smashed it into a million fucking pieces. Goddamn bitch."

"Sorry."

"Doesn't matter," Brian said, lighting another Winston. "Plenty of frickin' fish in the sea, right?"

"Right."

They drained their glasses as the bartender delivered fresh beers. Elton John's "Bennie and the Jets" played on the jukebox.

"Cheryl's why I joined the circus," Brian said. "I couldn't stand seeing her with her new boyfriend. I had to get away, so, I took this job. That's my story. What's yours? You said you were in advertising, right?"

"Yeah. A copywriter in Akron."

"You running from something, too?"

"No." Paul scratched his crotch.

"You're lucky."

Paul didn't feel lucky. His father had been murdered, and he was fired for sleeping with the boss's daughter who gave him crabs, then, dumped him.

Some luck.

Brian ordered a pitcher and told Paul he'd been an accounting major but dropped out after the breakup. He got a sales job with a radio station where his uncle was the manager.

"I made almost six figures," he said, gulping beer and pouring another. Paul knew this was a lie. Their pay was $360 a week, plus mileage. Marketing directors paid living expenses out of their salary. If Brian earned close to a hundred thousand and left to work for circus peanuts, no wonder he needed a calculator to figure out tips.

Paul let Brian talk, and sipped his beer and nodded. Before the night was over, they shared three pitchers and shots of peppermint schnapps for breath mints. They somehow made it back to the Sunshine Inn.

Paul crawled into bed and it spun like a Tilt-A-Whirl. He kept one leg on the floor until the spinning stopped. He heard Brian in the bathroom vomiting gushes into the toilet.

Paul passed-out to deep sleep.

Morning came early— unannounced and un-welcomed. Paul's head throbbed, amplifying every heartbeat with bursts of sharp pain on the right side of his skull. He needed aspirins, water, Coca-Cola, and sleep.

He heard Brian in the bathroom, singing off-key. Paul scratched his crotch. The crabs were enjoying a breakfast buffet.

"You freakin' awake, sleeping beauty?" Brian yelled. "Rise and shine to dine before Barb time!" He laughed. "I'm a friggin' poet and you know it!"

Paul knew he'd been drunk last night to think he'd witnessed wit and humanity in Brian. His blubbery roommate stood in the bathroom doorway drying himself. He draped the towel over his shoulder and walked naked toward Paul's bed, looking like the Pillsbury Doughboy.

Paul was uncomfortable around naked men. In Catholic school gym classes, he hated the locker room because he was a late bloomer. While other boys strutted and displayed pubic patches, he kept his bald privates covered. Even after puberty, Paul was uncomfortable in locker rooms with naked men walking about, their dicks flopping like elephant trunks.

"Get movin', buddy," Brian said, twirling his damp towel. "Don't make me snap your lazy butt into gear!"

"I'm coming."

Brian squirmed into tight white briefs as his belly and love handles flopped over the elastic band.

"Aren't you hung-over?" Paul asked.

"Hung-over?"

"We got pretty wasted last night— remember?"

"You must be a freakin' lightweight, Paulie." Brian grinned. "Did baby have too much ba-ba?"

"I wasn't barfing my guts out last night."

"My Salisbury steak was bad. The meat turned, or something." Brian wound-up his towel and snapped it.

"Stop it! I'm not in the mood for your shit, Brian." Paul's words sounded angrier than he'd intended.

"The lightweight's got a hothead. No problem-o. I was just jokin'. Jeeze la freakin' la-wheeze." Brian tossed his towel across the room and walked toward the dresser, his belly jiggling like Jell-O in an earthquake.

Paul went into the bathroom, closed the door, and downed two aspirins with water. He grabbed a clean washcloth and towel, and showered, attending to his crotch.

Barb Siegel looked like she was wearing the same outfit as yesterday. She told the students she needed a few minutes, went into her bedroom, and closed the door.

"Looks like she got wasted last night," Brian said.

"We all did."

"I'm fresh as a friggin' daisy!"

When she returned, Barb's face was made-up with thick mascara, eyeliner, rouge, and lipstick. She had doused herself with flowery perfume. Her lesson was about media negotiations. "Don't forget—if you don't ask, you won't get!"

Brian took copious notes, even though it was a repeat from yesterday. He asked suck-up questions, and Barb gave obvious answers.

"Yes, Brian, it's good to get the most media for the least money. For God's sake, are you even listening?"

Paul's head was splitting. He asked Barb for aspirin, and walked through her littered bedroom. On the desk was a bottle of Meyer's Rum with an inch of brown liquid.

On the bathroom countertop were prescription bottles and aspirin. Her sink was filthy. Lipstick was on the drinking glass.

He bent over the faucet and washed the aspirins down. His crabs were restless, and Paul gave them a brisk massage outside his pants. He stared at his exhausted face in the mirror. Once he made it through this day and night, he'd be far from Barb and Brian.

And "far" had to be a much better place.

CHAPTER THREE
Graduation

"They say we're all the same. Maybe so at birth, but we become very different people. The soil, the climate, the conditions we're raised in, all create distinctive organisms— some we're naturally attracted to, some we're repulsed by. Mother Nature's a real bitch, but she's all we got."

— Paul Driscoll's notes, Greenwood, MS

Barb bought her students dinner at an Italian restaurant. Afterward, Paul rode with Brian to the disco and she followed.

The Hammer's music was rocket engine loud. The circus crew got a table and ordered drinks. Brian's head bopped to the heavy bass beat. He looked around the club like a hungry lion prowling. When the drinks arrived, Brian toasted, "Here's to the best damn marketers in the history of Finnion, Barton & Powell Circus— and here's to disco!"

They clinked glasses and drank.

"I don't see her," Brian said, to Paul.

"Who?"

"Wendy, that cute waitress."

"Maybe she's grounded."

"She wasn't that young."

"She's jailbait."

Brian invited Barb to dance and she declined. She sipped a wine cooler and looked bored. Brian gulped his beer and ordered another round.

Paul looked around and felt sad. The fog, lights, pounding music, disco wardrobes— it was a Halloween party with a "Saturday Night Fever" theme.

Strobe lights flashed. More fog poured from the ceiling and floor as the dance surface flashed bright colors in rapid patterns. The opening chords of the Bee Gees' "Stayin' Alive" blared. Brian bolted from his seat, turned to Barb and Paul, and shouted, "We're friggin' Stayin' Alive! Who's with me?"

Paul shrugged. Barb said, "No thanks."

"Party poopers. I'll show you how it's done." Brian danced onto the dance floor and joined two girls in the crowd. For a fat man, he was spry, dancing in tempo to the music, twirling his arms and body. He executed half splits, strutted, and moved like a wet John Travolta on an electric fence. The girls dancing with him were amused.

Barb and Paul watched. "He takes disco seriously," she said.

"He loves it. I think disco sucks."

"I like the music, but don't like dancing."

The drinks arrived, Barb looked at her wine cooler. "I don't think I can drink this. I'm leaving soon, I've got to drive to Asbury Park first thing."

"Would you take me back? I don't like this place."

"Sure. What about Brian?"

"He'll be fine."

When "Stayin' Alive" ended, Brian returned. His white suit had huge wet spots beneath the armpits; the front had splatters of marinara sauce from dinner. His hair was sopping. He dabbed his sweaty face with cocktail napkins. "This place is freakin' great!" He saw his new beer and chugged half.

"I made it!" a girl's voice shrieked.

"Wendy!" Brian hugged the young waitress. "You were right— this is disco heaven!"

She wore a red dress, cut low to display her under-developed breasts. Her makeup was heavy, like a child who played with her mother's cosmetics. She was with another young girl, further along the puberty curve, in a tight blue dress.

"This is my friend, Jane," Wendy said. "She drove. My parents think I'm studying at her house, so I can't stay late. I have a strict ten o'clock curfew."

"I've got to go," Barb said. "Got an early morning."

"I'm going with Barb," Paul said. "I'm beat."

"What a couple friggin' wet blankets," Brian said.

"You guys have fun," Barb said.

"Don't stay out late, Brian. It's a school night," Paul said, smiling.

"Thanks, Dad."

In the parking lot, Barb asked Paul about the girls. He told her about Wendy.

"She's kind of young, isn't she?"

"I told Brian that."

"He'd better watch himself. When you're a stranger in town, it's easy to get into trouble."

"Brian's harmless."

Barb opened her car door. "I've got to clean this thing out." She grabbed clothes, trash and files, and tossed them on the back seat. Paul got in, assaulted by the aromas of flowery perfume and pine. A pine tree air freshener hung from the rear-view mirror.

Barb lit a cigarette and drove. "I should have talked to you guys about road conduct."

"Road conduct?"

"A marketing director is the only circus representative in town. You don't have any back-up. Everyone's local except you. Naturally, people are suspicious, and some people don't trust circus people. It's not fair, but it's true. Over the years, we've had marketing directors get into trouble because they weren't careful."

"What kind of trouble?"

"You name it. Bar fights, getting jumped, busted for being drunk and disorderly— anything you can imagine. Townies are cliquish. They don't like outsiders. They think circus people are con men and carnies. No one likes carnies. And playing around with underage girls is never a good idea."

"Brian's more bark than bite."

"Barking leads to trouble. He needs to learn that the road can be dangerous."

"He'll probably learn the hard way. And thanks for the ride. And dinner and training."

"That's sweet. You're welcome." She smiled at him. "Let's have a nightcap in my room." That was the last thing Paul wanted to do, but she'd be disappointed if he refused.

"Sure— a quick one before bed."

"Or, a quick one, then a quickie in bed." She smiled, and winked. Her garish mascara made the wink look like a bat falling from the sky, crashing and rising again. Paul laughed nervously.

Barb asked Paul to fill her ice bucket. The ice machine down the hall made loud grinding noises and spat ice cubes into the bucket. Thunk… thunk… thunk… thunk.

When he returned, Barb was sitting on the love seat. A half-full bottle of Meyer's rum, can of Coke, and two drinking glasses were on the side table. She had applied a fresh coat of makeup and flowery perfume. She patted the seat next to her.

"Let's have a drinkie-winkie." She gave a girlish giggle. She scooped ice from the bucket into the glasses and poured rum. She opened the Coke and topped each glass, using her index finger to stir the drinks. She seductively licked her finger. She looked at Paul with full moon pupils. "Ummm." She handed him a glass and clinked hers against it. "Cheers!"

"Thanks." Paul sipped, and yawned.

"You tired?"

"A little. Been a long week."

"I'll get you to bed soon." She smiled and poked his arm with a fist, then giggled and sipped. "Remember when I said it's hard being a stranger in town?"

"Yes."

"It also gets lonely." She snuggled closer. Paul resisted the urge to scratch his itching crotch.

"I don't mind being alone."

"Loneliness gets to you. I tell marketing directors to remember the advice of Crosby, Stills, and Nash."

"What's that?"

"'Love the one you're with'— excellent advice for road life. You don't know where or when your next relationship will be, so if there's an opportunity, take it. Love the one you're with."

"I'll remember that." He squirmed— the crabs were feasting.

"I like you, Paul, and since I won't be seeing you for a while, I thought we could spend tonight getting to know each other." She winked, emptied her glass, and began pouring another cocktail.

"I like you, too, Barb, but I have a girlfriend in Ohio and—"

"A girlfriend?! You're in a long-distance relationship with this job? Seriously? Paul, you're on the road until November. That's an eternity to be faithful."

"She's worth it. I think she's the one."

"So your job's like a prison sentence? You'll be true to her, and she'll be true to you until you get paroled?"

"I guess so."

"Paul, you're sweet, but naïve."

"I can do it," he said, feeling phantom guilt about his imaginary girlfriend. "I'll be faithful."

She leaned in closer. "Don't worry, I won't rape you." She laughed. "I won't tell if you won't. It'll be our little secret."

"Thanks, Barb, but no thanks."

"I get it. You've got morals. Fine. Good for you, Paul. If you change your mind, I'll keep a pillow fluffed for you."

"Thanks for understanding."

"We'll be seeing a lot of each other down the road. Take a rain check."

"Thanks."

"Tonight, I'll just reintroduce myself to Mr. Buzzjoy."

"What?"

"My vibrator, Mr. Buzzjoy. He never lets me down— except when his batteries die." She laughed. "Tell me about your girlfriend."

"Her name's Amy, in Akron."

"And Akron Amy let you take a traveling job?"

"She thought it would be a good test for our relationship."

"Brave woman. I'm sure she has a Mr. Joystick. And you'll have blue balls. If you take a chastity detour, I'll be here with open arms, and legs."

"Thanks." He yawned. "I better go. I've got to get to Haverhill first thing."

"Haverhill's a good circus town. You'll do great. Just don't forget, if you don't ask—"

"I won't get. I know. I'll ask, and I'll get. I'll do you proud, Barb."

"I wish you'd do me proud tonight, Paul. Do me good and hard—that'd make me proud." She smiled. "But you will, soon enough."

She leaned over, opened her mouth, and clamped it over his. Her warm liquor breath was on his lips as her pointy muscular tongue forced itself past his teeth, jabbing his tongue. He pulled back.

"I better get going."

"Suit yourself." She wiped her mouth. "You'll see, Paul. Loving the one you're with makes life on the road easier."

Paul was in bed watching Steve McQueen in "The Great Escape". It seemed appropriate. He had escaped Barb Siegel, and would soon escape his roomie.

Brian entered, slammed the door, and slid the security chain lock in place. "What a frickin' night! Holy crappola!"

"What happened?"

Brian stood in front of the TV and removed a wadded bloody cocktail napkin from his nose. "Jane's older brother showed up, and the prick sucker-punched me."

"You're kidding."

"It look like I'm friggin' kidding? I think he broke my nose. My suit's ruined. Spaghetti sauce comes out, but blood's impossible." His white suit was a canvas of splotches, splatters, and drips of red mixed with patches of varying shades of yellowing perspiration stains.

"I'll take you to the emergency room."

"No. If my nose is busted, they'll just put friggin' tape on it. I can do that."

"What happened?"

"I was dancing with the girls, we took a break, and this guy comes up and starts yelling at Wendy's friend, Jane. It was her big brother. I tried to calm him down, and he gets mad at me and says the girls are too young to be there, and I shouldn't be buying them drinks. Then, the frickin' guy sucker-punches me. I got so P-O-ed, I was about to kick his ass, but, lucky for him, three or four big guys held me back. Then the brother takes the girls home. And I end up with a busted nose, no date, and a big bar tab. Un-frickin'-believable."

"I warned you young girls were trouble."

"They're old enough to study algebra for freak's sake. That's adult math." Brian looked at his splattered suit. "My friggin' Bee Gees' suit is ruined!"

"Dye it red."

"Not funny. What'd you and Barb do?"

"Had a drink in her room, and called it a night."

"Drinking with the boss— nice move. Barb's cute. I could imagine waking up to that notch on my belt."

"She's all yours. Not my type."

"You're way too picky, Paulie. Everyone's too young or not your type. Any port in a storm, I say. Live a little."

"Right, lover boy, I'll take dating advice from the guy with a busted nose in a bloody suit."

"Barb says, 'you don't ask, you won't get.' This job is all about closing sales. I plan on closing, and enjoying myself."

"Looks like you're having a hell of a good time, Brian."

"Shut the frick up."

In the morning, Brian bounded out of bed naked, and stood over Paul. He displayed his pillow with dried blood. "I'm leaving the maid a souvenir of the Bri-monster."

"Better that than yellow sheets. Put some clothes on."

"The human body's a beautiful thing."

"Not yours. Get dressed."

"Someone's grouchy. Let's grab breakfast."

"No, I want to get going."

"Come on. One last meal before we become marketing director legends." Paul looked at the pathetic naked fat man with a crooked blood-encrusted nose.

"All right. Let's make it quick."

"You gotski!" Brian said, disco dancing into the bathroom.

Paul suffered through breakfast as Brian talked about his glory days fighting Golden Gloves in Philly. "I was exactly like Rocky. Maybe better."

After breakfast, they packed, settled their hotel bill, and walked to their cars.

"Well, Paulie, it's been fun," Brian said.

"Yeah. Good luck in Bangor."

"Good luck in— where you going, again?"

"Haverhill, up by Boston."

"I'm sure we'll see each other down the road, roomie." He smiled.

"Right."

"Take care." Brian shook Paul's hand.

"You, too." Paul looked at Brian's crooked nose. "Be careful. Stay out of trouble."

"Trouble's my frickin' middle name." Brian laughed.

Paul smiled, walked toward his car and didn't look back; he only wanted to look ahead.

CHAPTER FOUR
Katherine

"Humans think we're resilient like cockroaches, but at any moment, we can get crushed. That's how God keeps his roaches in check— scared, and praying."

— *Paul Driscoll's notes, Port Arthur, TX*

Paul exited I-495 for Haverhill, driving one-handed, and scratching with his other. He vowed to see a doctor, but since it was Saturday, he'd have to wait.

Haverhill had a population of fifty thousand. With four shows over two days, there was the potential of twenty thousand people packing the big top. Paul was confident he could sell out his shows. He had twenty-three days to become a hero and move on ten towns down the road. The ten marketing directors leapfrogged one another across America.

He headed to The Essex Mall to make sure everything was in place for the circus setting-up in its parking lot.

The mall was well-worn, with many closed stores and not many shoppers. The food court was busy with overweight people greedily scooping food with plastic utensils and slurping sodas. Paul entered the mall management offices. There was a counter with sliding windows and a chair behind it.

"Hello," he said. "Hello! Is anyone here?"

"Just a minute," a woman's voice called.

Paul looked at a framed photo of the mall with beautiful landscaping and a full parking lot. A plaque beneath it read, "The Essex Mall, Opening Day, April 3, 1970."

"Can I help you?" a female New England accent asked, snapping Paul back to 1982. In the opening of the counter glass was an attractive woman in her mid-twenties, with light hazel eyes with bluish tinted stars around her pupils. Her shoulder-length auburn hair had reddish highlights, and slight dimples punctuated her easy smile.

"I'm Paul Driscoll with Finnion, Barton & Powell Circus. I'm here to check with the mall manager and make sure everything's set."

"You're with a circus?"

"Yes. We're playing here in three weeks."

"Here? Inside the mall? Must be a pretty small circus."

"No, it's a big circus, with a big top, and hundreds of people and animals. We'll be in the parking lot."

She smiled. "I was kidding. I didn't think you worked for a flea circus."

"Oh." Paul gave an awkward laugh. "Our circus is big." She giggled, and they looked into each other's eyes. "With a big top and everything."

"Uh huh. The manager's out to lunch."

"I can wait."

"I'm not sure when he'll be back. Sometimes he goes to the food court, and sometimes he leaves. It could be over an hour, and I have work to do so I can't keep you company."

"Then, I'll grab lunch and come back."

"I wish you wouldn't," she smiled. "I'd much rather talk to a circus guy than do filing. What's your name, again?"

"Paul Driscoll."

"I'm Katherine Flynn-Ryan."

"Well, Katherine Flynn-Ryan, it's a pleasure meeting you." He stuck his hand through the opening of the counter glass. Her hand was warm and soft. "I'll return in an hour or so."

"Good, Paul Driscoll. I have something to look forward to."

When Paul returned, Katherine was sitting behind the counter. "Hello, Katherine Flynn-Ryan."

"He's still not back," she said.

"I'll wait."

"Excellent, Paul Driscoll. I like having company." They smiled. "Did you always want to run away and join the circus?"

"No. I never liked circuses as a kid."

"Then, why are you working for one?"

"I was an advertising copywriter in Akron, and got laid-off. I saw an ad for circus marketing directors, and a friend made a bar bet that I wouldn't apply for it. I did, got the job, won the bet."

"You work for a circus because of a bar bet?"

"Yes."

"That's strange."

"I love writing, and figured spending time on the road would give me lots of stuff to write about."

"What do you write?"

"I want to write novels and screenplays. I write short stories."

"And the circus will help you?"

"I hope so."

"You're James Joyce in the making."

"I wish I was a tenth that good."

"I have a good feeling about you, Paul Driscoll. You're a bit of a dink, taking jobs because of bar bets, but I suspect you've got some talent."

"Thanks, Katherine." An overweight man walked into the office.

"Mr. Bailey, this is Paul Driscoll with the circus to see you," Katherine said. The fat man shook Paul's hand.

"Tom Bailey, glad to meet you. A package came for you yesterday. Got it in the back."

"Great. Is everything set for our shows?"

"Yes, and we're excited to have your circus. We could use the traffic."

Bailey went to his office and returned with a folder containing the signed circus contracts and site selection map for the big top and equipment. He gave Paul the package from the home office in Sarasota. Inside was his master plan, and a three-ring binder labeled "Haverhill, Mass., June 14, 15, 1982." It contained all the vital show information and would be the permanent record, with site details, costs, expenses, ticket sales, ticket comps, promotions, media buys, publicity coverage, circus suppliers, their costs, and delivery dates. The binder would live on in the Finnion, Barton & Powell Circus archives, a testament to Paul's virgin voyage. In training, Barb had stressed the importance of the master plan. "Serve the master plan and it will serve you."

The phone rang, Katherine answered it, and gave it to Bailey. "Yes, uh-huh. Oh, no. Not again. Unbelievable. Okay, I'll be right there. Goodbye." He handed the phone back to Katherine. "I've got to run. There's an emergency at The Gap store— more plumbing problems. Katherine, show Paul his office, and help him get set up. Thanks." Bailey left.

Troubles at The Gap?" Paul asked. "A jeans emergency?"

"Toilet trouble. It's been a problem ever since a kid flushed a cherry bomb last year."

"Cherry bombs aren't good for plumbing."

"Impressive, Paul Driscoll— you know plumbing and circuses."

They laughed.

"I drove through Boston on the way, what's it like?"

"You've never been?"

"It's my first time in New England."

"Well, me and a couple girlfriends are headed to Boston tonight to partake at Irish pubs. Would you like to be our escort?"

"How do you know I'm not a homicidal maniac?"

"You look harmless. Plus, you've told me you work for a circus— how much worse could you be?"

"I'd love to be your escort. I don't know a soul here, and my social calendar's open."

"Great." She wrote down her address and phone number. "Come by my house at seven-thirty."

"I will."

"You better." She smiled.

The Shamrock Motel was owned and operated by an elderly woman the size of a tall garden gnome. Her white hair was braided in a ponytail, and she spoke in a thick Irish brogue. Paul asked the weekly rate, she asked his name.

"Paul Driscoll."

"Driscoll. Good Irish name. I'll give you a room for a hundred twenty-a-week. From one Irishman to another. You won't find a cheaper, cleaner place. My girls do good work." Paul booked it. The Shamrock was the fourth motel he'd checked out, with the lowest price.

His room was small and clean, with well-worn carpets, an old TV, and a bed with a slight valley a flowered bedspread couldn't hide.

He unloaded luggage from his car, his electric typewriter, and a small orange hard plastic suitcase packed with copies of Playboy, Penthouse and Hustler magazines. To celebrate meeting Katherine, he leafed through a Penthouse and found a brunette preening nude in high heels. He imagined she was Katherine and...

He took a long shower, tending to his crabs with a thin washcloth and towel. He returned the orange porn suitcase to his car trunk.

The cleaning woman didn't need to know his dark secret.

After a Kentucky Fried Chicken dinner, Paul drove around Haverhill.

It was an old mill town, once renowned for shoe manufacturing. Now it had closed factories and boarded-up businesses. He knew the look of a town struggling to survive. He grew up in Ohio steel country, where plumes of black smoke billowing from mills signaled prosperity, and clear blue skies indicated economic catastrophe.

Paul drove to Katherine's house and parked his '77 Chevy Nova. It was the nicest car in the neighborhood.

She lived in an old wooden frame house, with peeling paint and concrete front steps cracked from harsh winters. Paul knocked. A fifty-something woman with tired eyes looked him up and down. She shouted upstairs, "Katherine, your circus friend's here." She turned to Paul. "Don't just stand there, come in. I'm Eileen Flynn, Katherine's mother." She stuck-out a blue-veined hand of translucent pasty Irish skin.

"Paul Driscoll, pleased to meet you." He walked into the house; it smelled of cooked cabbage, burnt toast, and coffee.

"Is it Driscoll, or O'Driscoll?"

"Driscoll."

"Then, your people are from County Cork. Salt of the earth,

those people. Always remember from whence you came, that's what my sainted husband used to say. Always remember from whence you came."

"I will. County Cork." New Englanders seemed to be big on being Irish, he thought. If 'Flynn' was Katherine's maiden name, 'Ryan' must be her married name, but she hadn't mentioned being married or divorced.

"Tell him I'll be down in a minute, ma!" Katherine's voice shouted from upstairs.

"Typical woman. Always keeps you waiting. Come into the kitchen. It may be awhile."

A somber young man with a ruddy complexion and red hair sat at the kitchen table drinking a Budweiser.

"Who's he?" he asked Eileen. He had watery blue eyes that betrayed too many beers, with a stiff chaser of anger.

"Katherine's friend. He's our guest, Tommy. Behave yourself."

"Does it have a name?"

"Paul Driscoll. And I said be good. If you can't, then leave. I won't stand for your antics tonight."

"Hi," Paul said, extending his hand to Tommy, who looked eighteen. He glanced at Paul's hand and ignored it; raising his Bud, he took a long swallow.

"Those hands have never seen an honest day's work," he said, looking up at Paul.

"Tommy, I've warned you. If you're going to be contemptible, you can leave."

"Suit yourself, ma." Tommy pushed his chair back and stood up with his beer. He stared at Paul. "Pleased to meet you, Katherine's new boyfriend; probably soon to be ex-boyfriend." He walked to the refrigerator and removed three cans of Bud in a six-pack plastic collar. He looped his long fingers through the plastic rings. "I'm going to

Mikey's. He's having a party."

"Drive carefully," his mother said. "Cops are everywhere. You don't need another D.U.I. You hear me?"

"Yeah, ma, I heard you. I think the whole damn neighborhood heard you." Tommy wobbled out the back door just as a little boy, aged three or so, ran into the kitchen and hugged Eileen's legs.

"Come here, little angel." She scooped up the child and kissed his face. "I could just eat you up." The boy giggled. He had red hair, a freckled face, bright blue eyes, and acorn-sized dimples. "Robbie, meet Mr. Driscoll. He's a friend of your mother's." She hoisted the child toward Paul. He shook hands with the child who bore a striking resemblance to Katherine. Robbie giggled, Eileen placed him on the floor. "Go tell your ma her company's waiting." The boy ran upstairs.

"Cute kid," Paul said. Katherine never mentioned being a mother. He wondered where the father was.

"Robbie's a treasure. I apologize for Tommy. He's been a lost soul since his father passed."

"That's all right. My dad died four months ago, so I know how shocking it is."

"Four months? What date?"

"January twelfth."

"Lord have mercy, that was the day my Robert was called." She made a sign of the cross.

"I'm sorry for your loss."

"Thank you, Paul. And you for yours. It's no excuse for Tommy's rude behavior. He's angry at the world. When he was Robbie's age, he was sweet as anything. But that's life. We go from the pure innocence of childhood into the troubles of adulthood. Some stay happy, some get angry, and some crawl into a bottle and drink their death. I pray Tommy comes back from the dark patch he's in." She made the sign of the cross, lifting her crucifix necklace and kissing Jesus.

"I'm sure he'll come back." If the welcome-wagon reception Paul received was any indication, Tommy was headed to a hospital, prison cell, or morgue.

"I pray you're right. Well, look who's here." She turned. "My Katherine."

Katherine was holding Robbie, smiling as her son kissed her face. She looked beautiful in jeans and a shimmering gold top. Her face was luminescent, her lips luscious, her eyes bright.

"Hello, Paul Driscoll, circus man," she said.

"Hello, Katherine Flynn-Ryan, mall management lady." They laughed.

"Ma, we're running late— would you put Robbie down before nine? I don't want him being a cranky-butt in church tomorrow."

"I will. Run along and drive safely. There's all kinds of nuts out there."

"Thanks, ma." She smothered Robbie with kisses and passed him to his grandmother. Katherine grabbed Paul's hand. "We've got to go, Paulie." He had hated the name 'Paulie' coming from Brian, but from her lips, it sounded like poetry.

In the driveway, Katherine opened the door of a dented, rusted blue 1972 Ford Maverick. The inside was littered with fast food wrappers and empty soda cans.

"Shove them under the seat. Sorry, I'm usually not this much of a pig, I swear."

"I'm not exactly a neatnik myself," Paul said. The car engine cranked and started.

"The battery's on its last legs." She backed her car out.

"Mind if I smoke?"

"Sure, if you give me one." He lit two cigarettes. "We'll pick up my friends, Maggie, and Colleen."

"Great." He contemplated asking about her child and marital status, but looked out the window instead.

"I'm glad you met Robbie."

"He's very cute."

"He's my everything. His dad and I divorced last year. I'm working with our parish priest to get the marriage annulled. I don't want to be divorced in the eyes of the church. Robbie's supposed to see his dad every other weekend, but the bum hasn't been around for over eight months. A boy needs a father. He also hasn't paid child support for six months."

"Sorry to hear." There was a long silence.

"He's an asshole. Patrick Ryan's a shit of a father, and was an even worse husband." Paul felt uncomfortable.

"Do you go to Boston often?" he asked.

"About once a month. I go to keep my sanity. You'll love the pubs. They pour a proper pint of Guinness." Katherine talked about her friends. "Maggie's my oldest and dearest friend, I've known her since kindergarten." She met Colleen in second grade at St. Vincent's Catholic School. The three women were "thick as thieves" and had been through a lot together. "There's a bunch of bad relationships between us," she said, with a smoker's laugh.

Colleen lived in a tidy neighborhood with small homes built in the 1950s. She was waiting on the front porch and ran toward the car as if escaping prison. She opened the door, leaping onto the back seat. "Go! If I spend another minute in that house, someone will die!"

Colleen introduced herself in a loud New England accent. "That woman's crazy. She thinks all I do is go out and get drunk and that I'll get knocked-up and marry some loser. Just because that's what she did, doesn't mean I will. This apple's falling far from that goddamn tree, I promise you! Katherine, can I bum a smoke?"

"I got mine from Paul." He reached into his pocket, and passed a cigarette to Colleen.

"Thanks. Got a light?"

"Sure." He flicked his lighter. As she leaned into the flame, he noticed she looked much older than Katherine.

"I need this like I need oxygen," she said, exhaling. "I have to come down after being with that bitch."

"Relax. We're having fun tonight," Katherine said. She pulled in front of a two-story brick house. "Coll, would you get Maggie?"

"Hold my cigarette, Paul. I don't need Maggie's parents telling mine I'm smoking." Colleen jumped out and ran up the porch steps.

"She's a pistol," Katherine said. "Deadly when loaded."

"I'll bet."

"Her car's in the shop. She got wasted last weekend and hit a tree. She can be moody when she drinks, but she's a great friend. I'd take a bullet for her, or Maggie. They're the best."

Colleen and Maggie climbed into the backseat. Paul introduced himself to Maggie. She was short and overweight, with a pretty face.

"So, you're the circus guy," Maggie said, in a soft voice.

"Paul Driscoll, pleased to meet you."

"Maggie Kincaid."

"Margaret Teresa Kincaid," Katherine said. "Teresa was her confirmation name. Mine was Brigit. Colleen's was Rita."

"I'm Paul Stephen Driscoll."

"We've got a carload of Christ's soldiers," Katherine said. "Tonight, let's drink to our patron saints. They're probably thirsty."

The soldiers laughed.

During the ride they shared details of their lives:

• Colleen had a failed marriage to "a no-good drunken asshole shit of a man." He and Katherine's ex were drinking buddies, and worked for a moving company. "They deserve each other," Colleen said. "Two turds on four legs."

• Maggie had recently been in a long-term relationship with "a noncommittal man-child." Maggie choked back tears saying she hoped, "he'll grow the fuck up and realize the good thing he had."

• Colleen's mother had "a fucking toxic voice that could peel paint," Colleen said, in her air horn voice.

• Katherine said she "couldn't imagine life without Robbie," and was "determined to make sure my asshole ex doesn't screw him up."

• Paul admitted he'd only had Guinness once and didn't care for it. The women laughed, and said he hadn't tasted Guinness until he'd tasted "a proper pint."

• Maggie said she was "on the hunt and ready to play— my kitten's lonely and needs some company."

• Colleen seconded that.

• Katherine laughed and called them "horn-dog sluts," and added, "the nuns would smack your loose asses for impure thoughts." Everyone laughed.

Throughout the ride, the women smoked Paul's cigarettes, as he discreetly tended to his active crotch critters.

In Boston, they went to O'Brien's Pub, a dark dive packed with a rowdy crowd. They worked their way to the ancient wooden bar. Paul waved a $20 bill trying to get the bartender's attention. Katherine nudged him. "Step aside, rookie." She shouted, "Hey, Moran— get your ugly Irish ass over here!" A lanky, young, freckled-faced bartender saw Katherine and smiled.

"Hold your horses, lassie. Be there in a minute."

She smiled and turned to Paul. "I went to high school with him. He's a friend."

"You seem to know everyone."

"Who I don't know, I know someone who does. In the Irish mafia, it's good to be connected."

"I'll buy the first round."

"Four Guinnesses," Katherine told Moran.

One round led to another, and another, followed by cheap whiskey shots compliments of Moran.

"One for the ditch," Katherine said. They ordered another round of Guinness. She and Colleen struck up a conversation with two Irishmen from Galway, studying at Boston University.

At closing time, the pub manager began herding people outside. The girls kicked in some money and Paul settled the tab. It was a fun, expensive night.

Katherine was talking with the Irish students as they walked to the car. She said she had people back in Ireland fighting for the cause. "Never forget from whence you came."

The students said they loved Boston. She got angry. "Never forget from whence you came!"

The young men said they wouldn't, and walked away. Katherine opened her car and Paul, Maggie and Colleen piled in.

"God, Katherine," Maggie said, "you were hard on those boys. The tall one was cute. I wanted to give him my number."

"I wasn't hard on them. And you shouldn't be fishing in the tadpole pond, Mags. They were kids. All I said was never forget from whence you came."

"It's their country. You didn't have to insult them."

"I'm sick of these Irish wimps coming here to hide. My family's spilled blood over there, and these guys are hiding in their cozy B.U. dorms, pub-crawling at night. They're chicken-shits."

Colleen arbitrated a truce. Paul sensed this situation was probably routine— Katherine and Maggie fighting, Colleen holding the peace.

Katherine dropped her friends off. The women embraced and said, "I love you."

Katherine invited Paul into her house. Tommy sat at the kitchen table. A cracked eggshell and raw egg in a glass sat before him, along with an open can of Bud and a half-eaten PB&J sandwich.

"Katherine and her new man are back," he slurred. "I think he's more boy than man." Tommy grinned and gulped the raw egg with dramatic flair. He wretched, smiled, took a long swig of beer, and burped.

"Be nice," Katherine said. "Or go to bed."

"Fighting your man's fights already? Not a good sign."

"Shut up, Tommy. You're drunk. Go sleep it off."

"I'll finish my beer and sandwich and won't bother you and your boyfriend. And I do mean boy-friend."

Paul wasn't sure what to do. He wasn't a fighter. The last time he hit someone, he was eleven at a Little League game. The brother of a girl who had a crush on Paul wanted to fight him. They squared off and he punched the girl's brother in the stomach. He doubled over, and began spitting up blood. The fight was over. Paul felt like a tough guy, until he learned the kid had intestinal troubles.

"Finish up and go to bed before you wake up mom and Robbie." Katherine's voice was stern.

She led Paul into the living room. Tommy stumbled upstairs, muttering as he went.

"Ignore him," Katherine said.

They went into the kitchen. Katherine apologized for her brother, and said he had taken their father's death hard. "Tommy's been an alcoholic since he was fifteen. He's been spoiled his whole life, treated like royalty because he has the family jewels. Mom can't take his drinking anymore and has given him two weeks to clean up or move out."

There was a crashing noise upstairs. Tommy had thrown a chair through his bedroom window. He stumbled downstairs. "Dad wouldn't allow it, Katherine," he said, in a spittle-punctuated burst. "Dad wouldn't allow it!"

"Dad wouldn't allow what?"

Eileen came down the stairs in a well-worn bathrobe. "That's the last straw, Tommy," she said. "I can't have you busting up the house. You're getting out tomorrow."

"But, ma, dad wouldn't allow it. Katherine's divorced and she's dating again," Tommy said, walking toward his mother. She began crying.

"You've got to leave Tommy, until you get back to your senses. I pray you lay your demons to rest, but I can't have you and your troubles under my roof."

"You want me to leave, I'll leave. But you know dad wouldn't allow it. Katherine's dating after her divorce— she's sinning!" Tommy opened the refrigerator and grabbed a beer. "I'll sleep in my car. Sorry, ma." He walked out the back door. Eileen's face showed worry.

"I apologize for his behavior."

"That's all right," Paul said. "He's drunk."

"He has the Irish curse, and it has the better of him. It was a pleasure meeting you, Paul. Goodnight." Eileen went back upstairs.

"You better go," Katherine said. "I'm sorry."

"That's all right. I had a great time tonight. Thanks for inviting me."

"You're sweet, circus man," she said, giving him a quick kiss on the cheek. "Go now. Hurry, in case Tommy erupts again."

Paul saw tears welling in her eyes. He wasn't sure if they were a result of her embarrassment for her brother's behavior, or her fear of Paul getting pummeled. He gave her a quick kiss.

It felt natural.

CHAPTER FIVE
Passion

"I thought love was ego, a projection of ourselves onto others in a grubby grab for affirmation. That's love at its best. But at its worst, love leaves a scar from rejection, a scab we can pick at endlessly."

— *Paul Driscoll's notes, Bluefield, WV*

Paul woke Sunday morning with a hangover, relieved Brian wasn't there to aggravate it.

He asked his brain to discern the day of the week. The report came back: Sunday— the day good Catholics go to Mass, pray, worship God and ask for absolution for their sins, then accept the body of Christ to scour their souls clean.

He thought about attending Mass, but decided against it. Not in his current condition— infested by crabs, suffering Guinness flu.

Although God was forgiving, even God had limits.

Paul spent the morning at a diner drinking weak coffee, eating spongy toast with crispy bacon, and reading the "Boston Herald". He thought about Katherine's teary goodbye. He'd call later, after she got back from mass, and find out what happened after he left.

Paul imagined the priest at her church as an elderly Irishman who said things like, "Jesus died for your sins, but ye cannot give even an hour of your precious time each week to honor His eternal sacrifice? Him— who was nailed to the cross for your sins. But ye are so busy! And some here will leave His house after partaking of His flesh— a snack for salvation. Stealing ten minutes from our Holy Redeemer, who made the ultimate sacrifice on your behalf. Surely ye are mightier and more important than Christ our Lord, Himself!"

No. Catholic church was not the place for Paul today.

He returned to his room and watched cartoons, attending the church of Looney Tunes. His phone rang.

"Hello?"

"You're awake."

"Katherine— hold a second?" Paul dropped the phone and turned down the TV. "Sorry. How are you?"

"Fine. And you?"

"Good. I had some breakfast, read the paper and now I'm just doing circus paperwork. I was going to call later, but I figured you were at church."

"We went to the 9:15. What Mass did you attend?"

"I'm not much of a churchgoer."

"You're pitiful, Paul Driscoll, I'll pray for your eternal soul." Katherine laughed.

"I'll take all the prayers I can get. Did anything happen last night with your brother?"

"He slept in his car, and this morning mom told him to find a place to live. She's going to a judge tomorrow and getting an injunction against Tommy from coming to the house. He's too destructive. He got angry and left, saying he'll stay with a friend."

"Sorry, it's come to that. But, it was a fun night. Thanks for taking me."

"What are you doing today?"

"I was going to ask if you wanted to go to a movie, dinner, or something."

"Sure. Mom's watching Robbie, so I'm free."

"Great. What would you like to do?"

"It'd be a shame to spend this beautiful day in a movie theater. There's a pretty big beautiful body of water close by called The Atlantic Ocean. We could see that."

"I've heard of it."

"I'll pick you up at one o'clock."

"Great."

"See you then, circus man."

"Okay, mall management lady."

Paul and Katherine spent the day walking the beach in Seabrook, New Hampshire. Green waters washed the brown sands in peaceful rhythm. Since he was a child, Paul was attracted to ocean water, but feared it. He knew beneath the waves lurked muscular undertows that could take him to his death.

They sat on the beach and watched the surf.

"Your mother said your father died on January twelfth," Paul said. "That's the same day my dad died."

"That's a spooky coincidence."

"How'd he die?"

"Lung cancer. He was diagnosed a year ago, did chemo, and we watched him wither away. Tommy's drinking got worse."

"I'm sorry."

"Dad had a good life. Short, but good. What about your father?"

"He was out of town on business, went to a store for cigarettes, and got killed during a robbery. The store owner was shot, my dad went to help him, and he got shot."

"My God, that's awful." Katherine made a sign of the cross.

"Smoking kills, I guess." Paul's mouth attempted a smile but failed. "They still haven't found his killers."

"I'm so sorry. I guess God needed him."

"I think his family needed him more."

"You've got to have faith, Paul."

"Why?"

"Things happen for a reason. We'll never know why our fathers died, but I know they're in a better place."

"I wish I had your faith. Do you have faith Tommy will straighten up?"

"Yes, when he adjusts to the world without dad. He favored Tommy."

"My parents had six kids, and tried hard not to show favoritism."

"Dad showed me love, but he knew someday I'd marry and change my name. But Tommy would always be a Flynn, and he could father male children to carry on our family legacy. Mom treated us equally. There's no bottom to the well of an Irish mother's love."

"There's just you two?"

"Yes. They wanted a big family, but that wasn't in God's plan. When Robbie arrived, he was a taste of salvation. Even though he didn't have the Flynn name, he had Flynn blood. And if Tommy ever straightens out, he could continue the Flynn line. That'd give my mother relief, she's worried sick about him."

Katherine told Paul about the Seabrook nuclear power plant under construction in the distance. The locals lived in fear of it, following the 1979 Three Mile Island facility meltdown in Pennsylvania. Officials assured residents the power plant would be safe, with the latest technologies and safeguards ensuring problem-free operation, but locals were skeptical and protested.

As they walked, Katherine held Paul's hand. Its warmth was comforting. The surf and seagulls made a pleasant soundtrack. The couple spent hours talking along the beach. Their conversation natural, like waves lapping the shore.

They stopped at a pizza place and shared a pitcher of beer, talking and laughing as if they'd known each other for years. Afterward, they bought a six pack and returned to Paul's room.

It was a beautiful evening, and they sat in metal chairs in front. After two beers, they went inside and began kissing. Their attraction and passion fed off each other.

He knew he should tell Katherine about his crabs, but his hormones silenced his conscience. They began stripping each other, exploring their bodies. Curiosity fed excitement, fueled passion, and hormones obliterated guilt.

Paul had convenient amnesia; he'd tell her about his condition later.

They returned to Katherine's house, she tucked Robbie into bed and joined Paul on the front porch. "Katherine, there's something I meant to tell you earlier."

"What?"

"I, I think maybe I might have crabs."

"What do you mean you think you might?"

"I've had some itchiness in my groin—"

"My God, you're serious!" She stared at his guilty face. "Please tell me you're kidding."

"I don't know for sure."

"And since you weren't sure, you thought it'd be a good idea to screw me, is that it? What's wrong with you?"

"I'm sorry. I meant to tell you, but I got caught up in the heat of the moment. I'll make a doctor's appointment tomorrow, I promise."

"Great idea, Paul, see a doctor about crabs— after you've slept with me. And if you have crabs, you'll build a time machine and not sleep with me. Is that your plan? Christ Almighty!"

"I'm sorry, Katherine. I just wanted you so much—"

"That's your excuse— you were horny?"

"I know I should have told you—"

"Yes, you should have." She lit a cigarette, and he noticed her hands were trembling. "Very chivalrous, circus man. You're a real prince." She mashed her cigarette into the ashtray. "Unbelievable."

"If I do have crabs, I'll get extra medicine and share it."

"You'd better." She lit another cigarette. "You sure know how to sweep a girl off her feet. Some girls get flowers, chocolates, jewelry— but me? I get crabs medicine."

"Please, Katherine, I couldn't feel any worse."

"And how do you think I feel?"

"I'm so sorry."

"It's my fault. I thought you were a decent guy."

"I am, I swear to God. But I'm so lonely with this circus job—"

"The one you just started?"

"I'll make it up to you. I promise."

"Right."

"Whatever it takes."

"I don't want to see you again."

"Please, Katherine, don't. I'll see a doctor first thing tomorrow."

"Do you even know a doctor here?"

"No. Can you recommend one?"

"Yes, but I'm not going to. Haverhill's a small town, and people talk. There's a free sex clinic downtown. Go there, but keep my name out of it."

"Do you know where it is?"

"Yes, Paul— I go there all the time. I'm a regular for my herpes, syphilis and crab treatments." She gave him a piercing stare. "Wait, crab man. I'll get the address and phone number."

She went inside, looked in the phone book, wrote down the information, and returned. "Here's your get out of jail free card."

"Thanks. I appreciate it."

"Let me know the minute you know something."

"I will. I'm sorry, Katherine."

"Go. I don't want to look at your puppy dog eyes begging forgiveness. I thought you were different, Paul, but you're just another guy who does all his thinking with his little head. Typical man."

"Please, don't hate me. I'll make it up to you, Katherine, I swear to God."

"God will forgive you long before I do, Paul Driscoll."

She walked inside and closed the door. Paul slipped the paper she'd given him into his pocket and drove back to the scene of his crime. His imagination served a vision of his dad in heaven smoking a cigarette as Katherine's father approached and asked, "What the hell's wrong with your son?"

The Haverhill Free Clinic was on the second floor of an old building in a dicey part of town. Paul arrived five minutes after the clinic opened, surprised to see it was crowded.

"Help you?" a black woman asked at the counter.

"I need to see a doctor about a condition I might have." The woman looked bored.

"Fill out the paperwork," she said, handing him a clipboard with forms and a pen. "And put your name on the list," she pointed to a sign-in sheet. There were thirteen people ahead of him. Paul signed-in as Tony Kolirew.

He looked around the waiting room for a seat. A young couple looking strung-out on drugs huddled in a corner. The woman was crying; the man stared straight ahead with arms folded. There was an empty seat next to them.

Paul continued searching.

There was a vacant seat next to a young woman with red facial blemishes. She twitched, her nose running. Paul kept looking.

An old black man mumbled to himself. There was an open seat by him. The man wretched, held it in, and swallowed hard.

Paul crossed the room and sat next to the twitching blemished girl, being careful not to touch the armrests.

On the form, Paul created his fictional self: Tony Kolirew, 112 Main Street, Haverhill, MA. In good health. He listed the reason for his visit: *I think I might have crabs.*

He completed the mandatory questions.

After forty minutes, a nurse opened the door leading into the back and called, "Tony Kolirew."

No one stirred.

"Tony Kolirew," she shouted. "Last call for Tony Kolirew."

"Here I am," Paul said.

"This way, Mr. Kolirew." The nurse led him into a small office. "Are you related to Mike Kolirew? He was in my biology class."

"I don't think so. Must be a different branch of the family."

"Right." The nurse smiled. "The doctor will be with you shortly." She exited.

In ten minutes, she entered again with a sixty-something short, stocky, balding doctor with a stethoscope slung around his neck. He wore wire-frame glasses, dark slacks, a white medical coat, white sneakers and a head apparatus with a lighted magnifying viewer.

"Mr. Kolirew, I'm Doctor Walsh," he said, making brief eye contact, then glancing down at the clipboard with the form Paul had filled-out. "Says here you think you might have crabs." The doctor looked up with piercing blue eyes. "And why do you think that, Mr. Kolirew?"

"I have itching in my groin…"

"For how long?"

"A week or two."

"You've been itching for over a week and you're just now getting medical attention?"

"I started a new job and have been traveling."

"Has the itching gotten worse?"

"Yes."

The doctor sighed. "Let's have a look. Pull down your pants and underwear."

Paul unbuckled his pants, and slid them with his underwear down to his knees. The doctor placed his magnifying apparatus in front of his eyes and crouched to his crotch. Paul looked away.

"Yep, you've got crabbies. An excellent case. You can get dressed." The doctor stood.

"How do I get rid of them?"

"Kwell, it's a lotion that kills crabs fast. You should have seen a doctor when you first started itching." The doctor gave a stern stare. "Have you had sex with anyone since your itching began?"

"Once."

"When?"

"Last night."

"You had sex last night?"

"It was accidental. In the heat of the moment."

"Did you tell the woman you thought you had crabs?"

"Yes."

"And she still had sex?" Paul felt as if he was in a confessional being grilled by a priest.

"I told her after that."

"You're quite the catch." Paul felt ashamed. "She the only one?"

"Yes, sir. Just her."

"Mr. Kolirew, I'll give you a prescription for enough medicine for both of you. Share it with the lucky woman."

"Yes, doctor."

"Kwell is a topical lotion. Wash completely, dry and apply it to your pubic area. Wear loose fitting clothes. Leave the medicine on for eight to twelve hours, then, wash the area thoroughly. One application is usually enough, but I suggest you do it twice. If itching persists, repeat. And do not engage in any sexual activity for a week, not until you both are certain you're crab-free."

"Yes, sir. Thanks."

"And the next time you think you have crabs or any sexual disease, get medical attention immediately. And for God's sake, if you suspect something, don't sleep around." The doctor's eyes narrowed. "Is that understood, Mr. Tony Kolirew?"

"Yes, doctor."

"To save you embarrassment at the pharmacy and avoid you returning and wasting my valuable time, I suggest that if your driver's license does not read Tony Kolirew, you tell me the name on it. Pharmacies require identification."

"It's Paul Driscoll."

The doctor scribbled on his prescription pad and looked over the top of his glasses.

"Mr. Driscoll, you and your lover should take care of this immediately." He handed him the prescription.

"We will. I promise."

"And keep your last name. Driscoll is much better than Kolirew. It's more Irish." The doctor left, and the nurse smiled at Paul.

"If you see Mike Kolirew, tell him I said hello."

Paul submitted his prescription at a pharmacy and went to the pay phone booth.

"The Essex Mall," Katherine said.

"Hi, Katherine."

"Did you go to the clinic?" she whispered.

"Yes. I'm at the pharmacy waiting for the prescription."

"Did you test positive?"

"Yes, but the good news is the medicine will kill the crabs fast. In a day or two. And the doctor gave me enough for both of us."

"His and hers crab medicine, how romantic."

"I'm sorry, Katherine, I feel horrible."

"You should."

"I'll make it up to you—"

"Yes, you will."

"You'll see."

"Uh huh."

"The doctor said no sex for a week."

"That won't be a problem."

Paul looked out the glass door of the closed phone booth. There was silence on the phone, a long silence that blew cold.

"Is the medicine pills?" Katherine asked.

"No, it's a lotion. The doctor said to shower, dry, apply it to the pubic area and wear loose clothes. Then, after ten or twelve hours, shower again and the medicine should kill all the crabs. He said to use it for two days, but wait a week before sex to be sure they're gone."

"We should apply it as soon as possible."

"Right."

"Let's meet at your hotel in a half hour. I'll shower first, put the medicine on, and get back to work. Then you can handle your dirty business."

"Okay. See you at the Shamrock in a half hour." He was aroused at the thought of Katherine naked in his shower.

"Are you coming into the office today? I've had a couple of calls for you."

"Yes. I'm really sorry, Katherine."

"So you've said, a million times. I've got to go."

She hung up. Paul left the phone booth, picked up his medicine, and exited, scratching himself on his way to the car.

"See you in hell, crabbies!"

On his way to the Shamrock, Paul bought a bouquet of flowers. At the motel, he put the flowers in an ice bucket with water and studied his circus master plan. He had already blown half his first day on the job and knew Barb would call soon to check on his progress; he needed something to report.

There was a knock, he grabbed the bouquet and answered. It was the maid. Paul put the flowers back in the ice bucket and carefully handed the woman his soiled linens, requesting fresh towels and washcloths. He tipped her two dollars and asked her to return later to clean the room and leave more fresh linens.

His Haverhill stay was expensive: the Boston trip, a pizza date, beer, crabs medicine, flowers for forgiveness, and tipping.

Katherine arrived looking frazzled; he answered the door offering flowers. "First crabs, now flowers," she said. "You really know how to treat a girl." She smelled the flowers.

"Katherine, I feel awful. I barely got any sleep last night."

"Did you try counting crabs instead of sheep?"

"Very funny. I know I've probably blown it with you forever."

"Don't give me your pitiful puppy eyes, Paul. Give me time. Who knows, you might win me over again. Eventually. Keep the flowers coming, the wining, dining, bowing and scraping for forgiveness— we'll see. But first, I need a shower and your medicine."

"It's on the sink. Shower, dry off, then apply the lotion." Katherine nodded, put the flowers in the ice bucket and grabbed a fresh towel.

"My hero!" she swooned in a southern belle accent. As she walked by, Paul whiffed the light scent of her perfume. He liked her smell and loved her smile and sense of humor. She said he could win her back. There was hope.

Katherine was out of the bathroom in twelve minutes. She gave Paul a kiss on the cheek and grabbed her purse. "That medicine has a funky smell. I hope it kills the crabs before it kills me."

"I'll see you after lunch."

"Good. I've got lots of messages. Two from some pushy lady— Barb-something."

"Barb Sigel?"

Katherine nodded. "Who's she?"

"My boss. I'm sure she wants to know what I've been doing."

"Tell her you've been spreading crabs. That might get you a promotion."

"Not funny. Take your flowers and please find a way to forgive me."

"We'll see."

When Katherine left, Paul called Amy Jepson's office to let her know his diagnosis. He got her voicemail. He left a message: "Amy, this is Paul Driscoll. I'm on the road with my new marketing job. Please call me, we need to talk." He left his number.

CHAPTER SIX
Working the Master Plan

"They say guilt and shame are wasted emotions. I feel guilty thinking people who say that are full of shit."

— *Paul Driscoll's notes, Bluefield, WV*

Paul arrived at the mall offices with his master plan.

"The messages are on your desk," Katherine said. "Tom Bailey was looking for you, too, but he's out."

"What's he want?"

"Something about inspections."

"Your flowers look great," Paul said, noticing the vase on her desk.

"Thanks. Get some work done, circus man, Barb called again. She's not good with phone manners."

"No, she isn't."

Paul went in the back to his small office with no windows, a desk, two chairs and phone. Four pink message slips were lined up on the desk, three from Barb Sigel marked "URGENT". One was from Brad Lunky with WIOM-Radio. Paul dialed Barb— who answered midway through the first ring.

"Hi, Barb, it's Paul, returning your—"

"How's it going?"

"Good, good."

"Have you started meeting media reps?"

"No, but I have some meetings lined up."

"Hurry, Paul. You've got to get on air and blitz the market. Business was soft in Asbury Park. We need New England to be killer."

"Okay."

"And remember, half-cash, half-trade on media buys. And sell a ton of promotions. Don't forget— if you don't ask, you won't get!"

"Yes, Barb."

"Don't wait! Castrate, then skate."

"Castrate, skate. Right."

"We're counting on you, Paul," Barb said, as if the circus would fold its big top should he fail.

"Yes, Barb."

"If you need help, call. I'll be there next week. Until then, I'm working with the marketing directors handling the Connecticut dates. I know you can do it, Paul. Serve the master plan and it will serve you."

He was comforted when she said her mantra. The world was on its axis. "Got it, Barb. I'll ask, and I'll try to get."

"Don't say 'try.' Try is negative thinking. You will get, Paul." She paused. "I'm at this number through tomorrow. Then, I'll be in New Haven. I'll leave you my new number."

"Okay, Barb."

"We're counting on you, Paul," she said one last time to boost his confidence with a cattle prod.

"Right, Barb." He hung up. His heart was racing. He had work to do, crabs to kill, romance to rekindle, a circus to save.

He opened his master plan and began serving it.

His first assignment was to meet with all the local media

representatives, collect ad rate cards and begin negotiations and sell additional promotions. The master plan had a list of the local media. WIOM was listed. He picked up the message from Brad Lunky and called to schedule a meeting.

"I can be there in fifteen minutes," Lunky said.

"I think I can squeeze you into my schedule," Paul said.

"Great, I'll be right over."

Brad Lunky was twenty-five, with short curly dishwater blond hair, blue eyes, and pink ears poking out from the sides of his narrow head that slumped to his chest as he walked. His gait was awkward, like a foal testing its legs. His brown polyester three-piece suit was a size too small. The hem of his pants fell above his ankles. He wore a yellow shirt and a vivid red-and-blue striped tie in a loose half-Windsor knot. His face showed signs of an ongoing war with acne; and a field of pockmarks revealed the acne was winning. Paul sensed Lunky was more nervous than he was.

Brad Lunky's handshake was limp and clammy. His cheeks puffed into a taut smile revealing a haphazard arrangement of yellowed teeth. He had facial tremors as if receiving mild electrical shocks.

"Mr. Driscoll, I'm glad to meet you—"

"Call me Paul, Brad" he said, sitting. He felt at ease with Lunky's obvious discomfort.

"Paul, I want to tell you about the incredible reach of WIOM-AM Radio, the authentic voice of Haverhill," he said, in a high-pitched voice. "We're the number three adult contemporary station in the metro area, rising fast in the ratings. In fact, we're number two in the crucial twenty-five to thirty-four-year-old female head of household demographic."

"Very impressive." Paul nodded. Lunky pulled graph charts from his briefcase and showed them.

"I think we'll post even stronger numbers in the next rating book." He gave a nervous smile, Paul smiled back. "And we have a new drive time DJ— Crazy Cunningham. I don't know if you've heard his unique brand of zaniness, but he is something else. Crazy Cunningham is a one man laugh riot! Listeners can't get enough!"

"Brad, your station sounds perfect for Finnion, Barton & Powell Circus," Paul said. Brad Lunky smiled with quivering lips. "And I'd love to buy a heavy schedule on your station, if it meets our criteria."

"Criteria?"

"I'm only authorized to purchase media on a half-cash, half-trade basis."

"Half-trade?" Lunky looked confused.

"We pay half-cash for the media value, and the other half in circus tickets your station can use for listener promotions. Our tickets are like gold for promotional prizes. People love them."

"Half is paid cash, the other half's tickets?" Lunky frowned, his commission cut in half.

"Right," Paul smiled. "It's best for you, giving your listeners the opportunity to share the excitement of Finnion, Barton & Powell Circus. It's a win-win-win for everyone!"

"I'll have to check with my station manager."

"I understand. I'd love for your station to be a key promotional partner."

"I'm glad," Lunky said.

"Can I keep your rate card and ratings materials?"

"Of course," Lunky said, handing over his sales package.

"And one last thing." Lunky looked at Paul with concern.

"What?"

"Brad, any station we buy, we also want as a featured promotional partner. It doesn't cost your station a thing. You just agree to sponsor a circus promotion, like a 'tell us an elephant joke' contest. Your station produces a spot with on-air talent— your crazy new DJ sounds perfect, and we'll give you more circus tickets to give away as prizes. They're free! The promotional spots are rotated with our regular spots."

"Elephant jokes?"

"That's one example. We have lots of great promotional ideas. It could be having listeners talk about their favorite circus animal, or circus memories, first time seeing a clown, or anything circus-related. These promotions get listeners excited, and give them a chance to win tickets."

"So, half-cash, half-trade on the media buy, plus circus promos with free tickets."

"Right. We've found this formula works best for our partners, Brad, and we want to help make your station shine." Lunky seemed nervous. Paul smiled.

"I'm pretty new, but I'll tell my station manager what you said. He might want to talk to you. Is that all right?"

"That's fine— whatever it takes to get WIOM on our team. I have a limited budget, though, so I'll have to make some tough choices." If Paul could keep all buys half-cash, half-trade, he could afford the top three stations. He wanted Lunky to know he'd push away from the poker table if negotiations got testy. Barb taught him this strategy.

"I'll let my manager know." Lunky extended his hand. "WIOM will work great for you, I hope it works out."

"I agree." Paul shook his sweaty hand. "Brad, it's been a pleasure."

"Thanks, Paul." Lunky exited, and a minute later, Katherine entered. "What kind of dink was that?"

"A tall, nervous one." Paul felt confident.

He spent the afternoon scheduling media rep meetings. Lunky had been good practice. Barb said some stations wouldn't go for half-cash, half-trade, so it was good to have back-ups. Paul would talk to five stations for insurance. There was only one local newspaper.

The TV stations were in Boston, a market too expensive to buy. He'd reach out when the show was in town and try to arrange news coverage. According to the gospel of his master plan, a TV anchor riding an elephant was video catnip for stations.

By the end of the day, Paul felt good. If Barb called, he could report progress.

Katherine refused his dinner invitation, but invited him to her house later and suggested they could go out for a beer.

Since it had been a productive day, Paul treated himself to a steak dinner at The Steak-A-Torium chain restaurant. He found four typos in the menu: 'Potatos', 'Porterhose', 'Brocolli' and a French Dip Sandwich 'served aw jew'. He imagined the sandwich served by Saul Steinberg, who'd gush, "Dip— take a bite. You like? Dip, again! Oy vey, such a sandwich! Eat, eat!"

When he arrived at Katherine's, she said she saw no sign of dead crabs. She had bought some beer and wanted to stay at home in case her mother needed her. "Tommy moved out today. I don't want mom to be alone."

Robbie had been put to bed, and Eileen was in her bedroom. Paul and Katherine sat on the porch and drank beer. It was a beautiful night, with a full moon as yellow as warm cheddar cheese.

Paul apologized again for not warning her about his potential crabs. "What's done is done," she said, in a fatalistic Irish tone. "It's hardly the end of the world."

"Have you had any itching?"

"No."

"You probably didn't get crabs, and if you did, the medicine killed them. I have more lotion if you need it."

"I'll let you know."

"Can we start fresh?"

"Okay. I just need to remember you're a man, and be careful."

"Please, Katherine, don't lump me in with all the bad guys you've known. I'm different."

"We'll see. Frankly, I'm more concerned about mom than crabs. Family comes first."

They talked through a six-pack. Talked of their families, the tragedy of losing fathers, surviving Catholic schools, expectations, disappointments, hopes, and dreams. Paul made her laugh, and Katherine's spirits lifted like a light fog in bright sunlight. He told her he cared about her and wanted to pursue a relationship. She smiled. "Uh huh. Until your circus comes to town and you leave."

"We can still write and talk."

"Right."

The night ended with a cautious kiss. Paul was hopeful. He showered at the motel and checked his crotch for casualties. He applied another coat of lotion, slipped into his briefs, and had his first good night's sleep since his travels had begun.

Paul was at The Essex Mall offices first thing Tuesday morning, dressed in a burnt orange three-piece suit, white shirt, and brown striped tie. Katherine smiled.

"Don't you look nice? All gussied-up for your circus chores."

He smiled, thanked her for last night, and told her his crabs were dead. She swooned, "My hero, noble slayer of crabs! Your lady's privates are also vermin-free. No itching or signs of the enemy."

Paul laughed, went to his office and studied the master plan. The other salespeople were not rookies like Brad Lunky. They were sharks who looked at Paul as fresh meat.

When he explained the half-cash, half-trade policy, they replied that even if their station's management agreed, they'd demand one-hundred-percent cash payment up front. Paul explained circus policy was fifty-percent cash up front, fifty-percent on circus arrival. But he'd ask his management for one hundred percent.

He said he was talking to many stations, and while that particular rep's station "sounded perfect"— he could only afford three. And, he needed promotions with each.

The reps agreed to float the idea of promotions to management. Paul collected rate cards, placing them in a folder. He had a five-card hand, waiting to see which three stations would play half-cash, half-trade, and circus promotions. With luck, it would be the top three-rated stations.

Paul met with Lloyd Bixton, the newspaper rep. He was in his sixties, with short white hair, a white mustache, coffee-stained teeth and breath smelling like a corpse who'd smoked and drank his way to death. Bixton wore red-and-black plaid pants, a pink short-sleeved shirt, and a blue polka dot bow tie. Paul had seen circus clowns with better taste.

Barb Sigel said monopoly media companies usually didn't go for half-cash, half-trade, but marketing directors should always ask. Paul made his pitch to Bixton, who leaned back, listened, and raised his right hand.

"Okay, I get it. Your circus is coming." He leaned forward. "You need ads, we need sales. Scratch my back, I scratch yours. Got it. Well, Mr. Driscoll, we don't do trade deals. Newspapers need legal tender for ink and paper. And from circuses, we need cash up front. We've been burned before."

"Our circus is legitimate."

"I'm sure it is," Bixton said, lighting a cigarette. "But cash up front is our strict policy."

Paul would tell Barb he asked, but didn't get.

He began pitching the seasoned salesman on the 'color the clown' contest. "Your paper runs a full-page ad with an outlined drawing of a clown, and kids color it in, and send their masterpieces back to the newspaper to judge. The ad also contains the circus logo, show dates, times, and location. And twenty winners receive a pair of circus tickets. We'll give you free prize tickets in return for ad space."

"Yeah, yeah— color the clown promo," Bixton said, bored. "We've done that one, and it was pretty successful. But we'll need more than twenty pairs of tickets, though." He inhaled his Pall Mall, exhaling little smoke. Paul said he'd check with management about extra tickets.

Lloyd Bixton was good. Willie Loman in his prime.

The men agreed to talk again after they'd spoken with their bosses. Bixton said, "We're the only game in town. Anything that happens in Haverhill, happens in our pages. Mr. Driscoll, you need us if you want to succeed here." He slid his rate card and business card across the desk. "Let's talk tomorrow. Any questions, call." He mashed his cigarette in the ashtray, stood up and shook Paul's hand. "Pleasure meeting you, Mr. Driscoll."

Paul smiled nervously, feeling like Brad Lunky. He wondered if the old guy called him 'Mr. Driscoll' as an intimidation technique. It worked. He felt like a card hustler who'd been caught bluffing.

After Bixton left, Katherine gave Paul a message slip from Kirby Tooby, with the Haverhill city services department. "Watch your wallet, circus man," she said. "City bureaucrats will rob you blind."

She said New England politics were notoriously corrupt. Everyone had his hand out. Her father had some dealings with the city when he was supervising commercial real estate construction jobs. "Be careful. They'll be on you like crabs." She smiled. "And your magic medicine won't work— they're professional parasites."

He called.

"Tooby, city services manager," a gruff New England accent said.

"This is Paul Driscoll, with Finnion, Barton & Powell Circus, returning your call."

"The circus— right. I understand your circus will be setting up at The Essex Mall on June fourteenth and fifteenth."

"Yes."

"Have you secured your electrical inspection yet?"

"Electrical inspection?"

"Haverhill requires an electrical inspection for traveling amusement shows. We'll be happy to send an inspector for a hundred-dollar fee."

"I didn't know we needed an electrical inspection."

"It's the law."

"I'll have to talk with my management about this."

"Talk all you want, but no inspection, no certificate. And no certificate, no circus. You also need a city electrician on the site any time you operate electric generators."

"Oh?"

"An electrician is two hundred-eighty bucks a day. Two days is five hundred-sixty dollars. You'll also need Haverhill city police protection."

"Police? We have circus security people, plus mall security."

"That's fine, but our law states that you have at least one cop, preferably two, on duty each show date. Better safe than sorry."

"Do police cost money?"

"Well, now, Paul," Kirby Tooby said, with a smoker's laugh, "you don't think cops work for free, do you? It's two hundred-forty bucks per officer, per day. That's four hundred-eighty for one cop, nine-sixty for two on both days."

"But I only need one?"

"Preferably two, but yes, at least one cop. It's the law and we enforce it. We must protect our citizens. I'm sure you understand."

"All right, Mr. Tooby. I'll get back with you after I check with my management."

"Hurry up, I'd hate to see your circus get cancelled for noncompliance. My kids love a circus. Speaking of which, if you could see your way to five tickets, I'd appreciate it, Paul."

"Five tickets?"

"Two adults, three kids. One hand washes the other. I'll make sure your paperwork gets expedited."

"Okay, Mr. Tooby, I'll ask and get back to you."

"You do that. We're looking forward to having your circus here."

"Thanks."

Tooby hung up. Paul looked at his notes. It had been a good day, until he ran into the twin blades of Lloyd Bixton and Kirby Tooby.

He went to scratch his crotch and realized it wasn't itchy. He looked through his master plan for information about electrical inspections or police protection. There weren't any.

Welcome to New England politics.

That night, he treated Katherine to dinner at a local bar. She was in a good mood; her mother's spirits had lifted with Tommy out of the house.

Paul told her about his day playing poker with media reps. They laughed about Lloyd Bixton's garish outfit. Katherine laughed when she heard about Kirby Tooby's conversation.

"Electrical inspection and police protection? Really? They see you coming a mile away, circus man. You're the fatted calf being led to bureaucratic slaughter."

He invited her back to his motel room. "No thanks. I know where that ends up. And the doc said no sex for a week, remember?"

"We'll just watch TV."

"I don't trust you, or me."

They returned to her house. Robbie and Eileen were asleep. They sat on the couch making-out like hormonally-charged teens, finding their rhythm kissing and caressing, which would have to suffice until their prescribed week of abstinence ended.

Paul returned to the Shamrock. A pink message slip from Amy Jepson was taped to the door marked "URGENT". It was too late to call; he'd do it tomorrow.

CHAPTER SEVEN
Falling

"Lust takes the civilized refinements of humanity and has its way. We try to rise above, but ultimately our animal instincts prevail. We're no match for the beasts within."

— *Paul Driscoll's notes, Greenwood, MS*

Paul heard the phone ringing as he got out of the shower the next morning.

"Paul, it's Barb. You awake?"

"Yes." He cradled the phone on his shoulder, wrapping the towel around his waist.

"How's it going?"

"Good. I've met with all media reps."

"How many?"

"Five radio stations, one newspaper."

"We can't afford five stations, we have a tight budget."

"I talked to five knowing I can only afford three. I want backups in case the top stations won't go for half-cash, half-trade."

"Oh. Good idea." He sat on the bed knowing it would be a long conversation.

"The newspaper guy said they won't go for half-cash, half-trade..."

"Did you ask?"

"Yes. That's how I know they won't go for it." He wondered if she ever listened. "They want a hundred percent cash up front."

"That's crazy."

"I told him I'd check with my management. He said they'd been burned by circuses before—"

"Were they burned by us?"

"He didn't say." Paul wondered if Finnion, Barton & Powell Circus had ever not paid up.

"Probably a fly-by-night circus."

"He said he'd check with his management. Not sure if he's bluffing or not."

"Wait and see what he comes back with. The show doesn't like advance payments."

"I told him that."

"And you did ask for half-cash, half-trade?"

"Yes, Barb."

"You're sure?"

"Yes. I was there. I think I can get three out of five radio stations to go for cash-trade deals."

"What about promotions? Did you sell everyone a promotion?"

"I told everyone about promos. They said they'd have to get management approvals. I have follow-ups today."

"When will you know?"

"Later today, maybe."

"All right, Paul. Remember— half-cash, half-trade. With promotions."

"I know, Barb."

"Play hardball. Haverhill has to be a blockbuster. Business is soft in Connecticut. We need you!"

"I'll do my best."

"Do that. We need big shows, Paul. Don't forget— if you don't ask, you won't get."

"I know, Barb. There's one other thing…"

"What?"

"A city official told me we need an electrical inspection for a hundred bucks, plus a city electrician on duty on show days, plus at least one city cop for security. And we have to pay for all of them."

"Pay? How much?"

"I can't remember. I'll check my notes and get back to you."

"Goddamn locals. They're always trying to screw us because we're the circus. Let me know how much extortion money they want, and push hard on the reps for half-cash, half-trade— with promotions. Now we really need huge sales to pay for all the added expenses."

"I'll do my best."

Paul hung up and heard his heart thumping. Her anxiety was contagious.

He took some deep breaths and calmed down knowing he had a master plan to serve. The fate of the circus was on his shoulders. Otherwise, he'd be the scapegoat on his first show.

He rubbed his crotch with the towel and inspected it. Clean. No specks. The phone rang. "Hello?"

"Paul, it's Amy."

"Hi."

"Where are you?"

"Haverhill, Massachusetts. Up by Boston."

"What are you doing?"

"Working my new job, show business marketing."

"Show business. Really?"

"Live entertainment."

"Rock concerts?"

"Sort of. The reason I called is—"

"Glad you called, I was going to call you."

"Oh."

"Yeah. I'm late."

"Late?"

"My period. It's late."

"What?"

"Didn't you learn anything in sex ed? My period's late."

"You're pregnant?"

"I don't know. I'm seeing a doctor this afternoon."

"I thought you were on the pill."

"Usually, I am."

"You think the baby's mine?" Paul thought about the rumor of her and Greg Cartwell sleeping together. He also wondered about Jack Lunkorm, who she was so friendly with.

"If I am pregnant, I'm sure it's yours." Paul's chest ached. There was silence. "Don't worry, mister show biz, I don't expect anything from you. I'll get it taken care of."

"I'll come back. We'll get married and—"

"Get married? Don't be ridiculous. I told you, I don't think we're good together. A baby won't change that. I don't want your baby, or anyone else's. It's my body, not yours. It's my problem, and I'll take care of it." Paul was guilt-ridden and remorseful. She sighed. "What were you calling me about?"

"Well, my crotch has been itchy for a while, so I went to a doctor and, well, I have crabs."

"Crabs!"

"Yeah. And I think you might have crabs, too."

"You're saying I gave you crabs— you're serious?"

"You're the only person I slept with in the past year—"

"So it has to be me, is that it?"

"You, or someone you slept with."

"Oh, I get it— now, I'm the slut who gave you crabs. God, Paul, you don't have to create a big drama; I'm not blaming you if I'm pregnant."

"I just wanted you to know about the crabs."

"Thanks. Your concern's very touching. You're a real saint, so I'll confess everything— the kid's not yours, Paul, could be anybody's. And I gave you crabs that I got from one of the several hundred guys I've screwed. There. Happy?"

"I thought you might want to have a doctor look into it, if you've been itchy."

"Thanks for the medical advice, Doctor Driscoll."

"I'm sorry, Amy. I'll do whatever you want if you're pregnant. Money, marriage, whatever. Just let me know."

"Here's what I want, Paul. I want you to shove this entire conversation up your ass. In fact, shove your new glamorous show biz life right up your ass, too!"

"I'm sorry, Amy. Please, let me know what happens with your doctor."

"Fuck you."

Paul listened to a dial tone and hung up. Then he did something he hadn't done in a long time, he prayed. He asked God not to create life.

Then he felt guilty about that, and prayed for forgiveness.

When he entered the mall office, Katherine smiled with a fistful of pink message slips.

"You're popular, circus man." She handed him the messages.

"Apparently."

"How'd you sleep?"

"Pretty good." He began reading his messages, a distraction from imagining his and Amy's baby.

"You seem tired."

"I'm okay. Got a call from my boss and she dumped a lot of crap on me. I need coffee."

"I made a fresh pot." He noticed how beautiful she looked in her green dress. Her green eyes sparkled as she flashed her dimples.

"Sorry if I'm distracted. I've got to get my media schedule and promotions firmed-up before my boss crawls up my ass."

"Sounds painful."

"She is. How about you, are you okay?"

"Yes."

"I mean, down under?"

"Down under? Oh, you mean, do I have crabs?" She laughed. "No. No creatures have surfaced down under."

"Great. I'm clean, too."

"Disease-free, that's what I like in a man."

"Could we get together tonight?"

"Okay. But no romping, stud-boy. Doctor's orders."

"Right."

"You've got a lot more wining and dining to get back in my good graces. Now, get your butt to work before your boss crawls up it."

"Yes, ma'am." He kissed her and found momentary peace.

In the late afternoon, Paul called Amy. Her voicemail answered and he spoke after the beep: "Amy, it's Paul. Sorry about our conversation earlier, I just wanted to know what happened at the doctor's office. Let me know. I'll do whatever you want." He left his phone number.

Over the next two days, Paul left six more messages for Amy, with no reply.

He imagined holding and cuddling their baby. Was the child the spirit of his father coming back? He had left Earth so abruptly, it made sense he'd return in an unexpected manner.

Maybe God does those kinds of things.

Paul felt guilty thinking about reincarnation. It wasn't part of the Catholic doctrine he was taught, and wasn't what his father believed.

He prayed. If Amy was pregnant, he would try to talk her out of an abortion. That was against the church. He wasn't sure if it was a mortal sin, but it had to be major.

He'd return to Akron and marry her. He'd get a job at another ad agency, certain that Larry Jepson would give his son-in-law a good referral.

Although Amy said they weren't meant to be together, maybe the baby would be the epoxy to bind their relationship.

Maybe fatherhood, not the circus, was the journey Paul Driscoll was meant to take. Fate dictates life, and fighting fate leads to a miserable life.

But what if the baby wasn't his? He knew Amy would be offended if he asked for a blood test before marriage.

He tried not to think about the baby. Nothing was real until he knew something, and he wouldn't know anything until Amy called back.

He asked God to make her call. Until then, he had circus work to do.

The top-rated station insisted on an all-cash media buy. Paul declined. But the second, third, and fourth-rated stations agreed to half-cash, half-trade with circus promotions. He booked them. Each station would be running a minimum of twelve spots per day, plus an additional eight promo commercials. Finnion, Barton & Powell Circus would own the Haverhill airwaves for the next two-and-a-half weeks.

The stations also agreed to do DJ endorsements and conduct interviews with Blippo the Clown. Blippo was the circus's advance man in makeup and comically oversized shoes. Paul was responsible for using him to get as much publicity as possible.

Lloyd Bixton, the newspaper rep, had the circus by the short hairs, and got his all-cash buy. The show had to have ink in a one newspaper town. Paul considered it a victory the paper agreed to fifty percent cash up front, and fifty on show arrival, instead of a hundred percent cash up front. The newspaper also agreed to run a 'color the clown' contest for thirty free tickets instead of twenty.

Barb Sigel approved all contracts begrudgingly over the phone. Even though Paul was within his budget, she asked if he could go back and ask for more. "If you don't ask, you won't get." Paul insisted he drove hard bargains, and his deals were the best the media would do.

She was furious that Kirby Tooby, the Haverhill city official, was extorting the show. Having a city cop and electrician on show dates would be a $1,200 expense. Plus, the city flimflammer wanted five comp tickets. She asked Paul if he tried to negotiate the number of free tickets. He lied and said he did, but Tooby was adamant.

"Son of a bitch," Barb said. "These crooks are killing us. We need huge business."

His stomach tightened. "I'm giving a hundred percent, Barb."

"Give a hundred-ten-percent, Paul."

"Right. A hundred-ten-percent." With those reassuring words, Barb hung up.

After two days of hard work and hard worrying, Paul returned to his room one evening and found a pink message slip from Amy taped to his door: "False alarm. Leave me alone. Drop dead."

Paul thanked God, then thought of Katherine. He wanted her more than ever.

God had spoken: Amy was history, Katherine was today— maybe she was the one.

For the rest of the week, Paul served his master plan trying to sell circus promotions to mall retailers. None bit.

The promotions were one-sided. Retailers had to give up space in their ads to promote the circus, and in return, received free tickets to give away.

Although he pitched the promotions with mustered enthusiasm, store managers saw the deals were bad. Paul knew when Barb came to town, she'd look through his master plan checklist to make sure he had served it well.

He had to ask, even if he didn't get.

For the rest of the week, Paul served his master plan trying to sell

Paul and Katherine did not make it a full week before getting naked. After five days of abstinence, they shared an evening drinking at O'Callahan's, an old bar downtown, then went to his room collapsing on the bed and making out as if they'd been separated for years.

Katherine told Paul before their first coupling that she was on the pill, but since his Amy scare, he asked again if she was taking precautions. She reassured him she was, and his libido shifted from yellow light to green.

They groped and stroked and explored and discovered one another again. Their reunion felt natural, thrilling, and exhausting. They collapsed into each other's embrace. She awoke at 2:30 a.m. and requested a ride home.

"I don't want Robbie to miss his mommy in the morning."

Paul drove her home, and they kissed passionately.

The moment she left his car, he missed her.

They spent Saturday on the Atlantic coastline, walking the beach hand-in-hand.

"Tommy hasn't been home since the court order," Katherine said. "Mom's doing pretty well. She comforts herself thinking about how sweet he used to be."

"People find what they need when they need to find it."

"You're wise, Professor Driscoll."

"That's why religion's so popular. We need beliefs to get through the day. When I was a kid, I obsessed over the death of my parents. That was the most frightening thing imaginable. I'd pray to God to protect them."

"You were being a good Catholic."

"I was, but when I got older, I fell away from the church, not sure what I believed. Then my father got killed."

"That's so awful."

"I prayed hard for his soul. But in the back of mind, I'm not sure there is a God. And if there is, why did He have my father killed? Was that my punishment for falling away?"

"You can't think like that."

"I didn't know if prayer worked, but I figured it couldn't hurt."

"Prayer's always good."

"I wish I believed that."

"I don't know why God took your father, or why He called mine. No one knows. You need faith, Paul, that things happen for a reason. Accept that there are greater powers and mysteries we'll never know. That's faith. And take comfort in your faith."

"I don't know."

"I do. Join me for the nine-fifteen mass tomorrow. Come to our house, I'll drive."

"Will you protect me, Katherine?

"From what?"

"From the church falling when I enter." She smiled.

"Yes, circus man, I'll protect you." Paul stopped and looked into her eyes. Her pupils were black pools with thin rings of irises.

"I have faith you will," he said. He kissed her softly. "I'll go."

"Great. God always welcomes back the prodigal son."

"Even if he's had crotch critters?"

"Save that story for the confessional. Someone has to save your soul; it might as well be me." He kissed her again.

"One step at a time, Saint Katherine."

That night, Paul drove Katherine and her friends Colleen and Maggie to Boston for an Irish pub crawl. Musicians played and sang sad Irish songs of longing for freedom, healing the pains of love gone bad, abuses from evil British bastards, and the heartbreak of not being on one's native soil. These sorrowful dirges were interspersed with songs celebrating the joys of whiskey and comforts found in a bottle. The fog of Irish sentiment lay heavy over the crowd as they drowned their sorrows in oceans of Guinness and Jameson.

Katherine saw a friend of her ex-husband and became nervous. They settled the tab, and slipped out of the pub.

"I don't think he saw me," she said.

"Why are you so concerned about your ex's friend?" Paul asked.

"I don't want anything to do with Patrick Ryan. He's trouble, Paul. Pure trouble."

He let the subject drop, but thought it odd that with all

Katherine's talk about the importance of family, she could dismiss the father of her son. Paul didn't know the full story, and perhaps never would. He rationalized that some questions are best left unanswered, and some answers left unquestioned.

CHAPTER EIGHT
The Prodigal Son

"Jesus had God as his Father, and the Holy Spirit as his brother. I was taught all three of them were one, and I still can't comprehend that. All three Gods took my father, and ganging up isn't fair— especially when you're Gods."
— *Paul Driscoll's notes, Bridgeport, CT*

Italian immigrants built St. Patrick's Church in 1908. Stained glass windows lined the structure depicting pious saints being tortured, the Virgin Mary holding baby Jesus, surrounded by adoring angels, and the sad face of the adult Jesus Christ suffering beneath a crown of thorns. Along the sides were the fourteen Stations of the Cross graphically depicting the tragic end of Jesus's life, along with four confessionals where Haverhill's sins were whispered, and just penances dispensed.

There was an ornate altar constructed of mahogany, polished marble, and gleaming brass railings. Suspended above was a wooden crucifix with a four-foot-high Jesus nailed to it. Painted blood dripped from His forehead, side, hands, and feet. His face had a sallow expression of anguish, pain, and sorrow. He wore a small swath of white cloth around His waist.

When Paul saw this Jesus, he thought of baby Jesus wrapped in swaddling clothes in the manger. There wasn't much difference in Jesus's fashions upon entering and exiting our world.

To the right of the altar was a sturdy wood lectern with a microphone. From this elevated perch, scripture was read, and homilies delivered.

St Patrick's had the scent of candle wax and incense, the distinct aroma of Catholic churches broadcasting a sacred space of begging for forgiveness for past sins, and pleading for strength in battling future sinful transgressions.

An organist played a mournful dirge as Paul, Katherine holding Robbie's hand, and Eileen walked down the aisle. Each genuflected and made the sign of the cross acknowledging the immense sacrifice Christ made for humanity's godforsaken sake. They entered the pew, placed the hardwood kneeler on the floor, knelt, and reflexively made signs of the cross and prayed silently.

As Paul knelt, he wondered what he should do at Communion time. He knew he shouldn't take Communion since he hadn't said a good confession in ages, and so, was in a state of sin; but if he didn't take the body of Christ, he would look like a serious sinner— not a good message to send Katherine, Eileen, or Robbie. He prayed God would allow him to receive Communion and not hold it against him on judgment day. His Communion would be for show only. A stunt host.

Paul thought about the sins he'd committed over the years since his last confession. He knew if he ever did make another confession, his penance might be triple digit Hail Marys, Our Fathers, and Acts of Contrition.

Even though Paul hadn't been to Mass in years, it came back to him. The responses to prayers, the choreography of Catholicism was coming back— when to kneel, sit, stand, make the sign of the cross, genuflect, and shake hands with surrounding parishioners. Paul loved the shaking of hands. It was the one Mass moment when somber Catholics smiled goofily, and connected with others.

Once done, they resumed their repentant, solemn modes.

The priest gave what Paul considered to be a typical Catholic homily. It began with a simple premise, then meandered into boring babble. The priest rambled on for twenty-four incoherent minutes. Paul fought heavy eyelids and thought about how he'd improve the mass.

Since the homily was the only part of the service that was new, and most priests were lousy at writing coherent and compelling homilies, Pope Paul Driscoll would have masterful writers craft concise, inspirational messages and distribute them to priests worldwide. They'd be commanded to give these texts, and nothing more. Consistency would be the key to his holy church. The principle worked for McDonald's restaurants, why not the Catholic church?

He wondered how he'd look wearing the big Pope hat. He liked hats— especially ones that gave height.

He caught himself. This kind of sacrilegious thought would not do well at heaven's gates. He wondered how long it would take St. Peter to cast him into hell's lakes of fire. He'd have to die wearing asbestos.

When the homily finally grinded to a halt, the priest walked from the pulpit and sat. Paul wondered what the point of his homily was. He imagined others were contemplating the same. The priest had delivered empty spiritual calories.

When it was time for sharing a sign of peace, Paul shook Katherine's hand and Robbie's. Good kid, thought Paul. He shook Eileen's hand, receiving a soft grip and awkward smile. He wondered if she liked him.

He was on a roll granting peace, so he turned and began shaking the hands of parishioners. The elderly man seated behind Paul looked at him, and his eyes widened. It was Dr. Walsh from the Free Clinic, the man who granted his miraculous Kwell cure. The Lord did indeed work in strange and mysterious ways. The doctor put his hand out, lowered his head and peered over his bifocals. "Peace be with you," Paul said, smiling.

"Peace be with you."

"I'm okay, doc," Paul whispered. "The Kwell worked great. Thanks."

Dr. Walsh gave him a stern look and nodded. Paul turned and faced the altar.

At Communion, Paul stood behind Katherine in the slow procession to the altar. He recalled his First Holy Communion in first grade. He wore a hand-me-down blue suit from his brother, Tim. The suit was too large for Paul, so his mother tightened his belt. The nuns and priest had lectured the children repeatedly about proper etiquette for receiving the Holy Eucharist.

He understood that the Host was literally 'the Body of Christ' and shouldn't be touched under any circumstances. But when the priest placed the First Communion Host on Paul's tongue, he closed his mouth and the Body of Christ adhered to the roof of his mouth.

He walked up the aisle to the back of the church fearing Christ would stay stuck. He unclasped his praying hands and used his right index finger to pry the Host from his mouth's roof. In the back of the church, Sister Angelina grabbed him and shook him.

"What do you think you're doing, Driscoll? Didn't I tell you never to touch the sacred Host?"

Paul stammered as he explained sticky Jesus, but the nun would hear none of it. "No talking in church, Driscoll. Return to your seat. I'll see you after Mass."

He obeyed, feeling shame, guilt, and remorse for poking his finger into the Body of Christ. Young Paul knelt and begged God's forgiveness.

He was afraid— he knew God was not one to anger.

After Mass, Sister Angelina admonished him. She was well into her sixties, or seventies, and would have stood five feet tall, if she ever wore high heels— which she never did, because she thought "only whores wear heels."

She explained what happened to Father Dave, a young priest with a pudgy face and strawberry blonde mustache. He spoke to Paul in a soft, stern voice about the terribleness of his action. He told him he must make a full confession. Paul knew a full confession was the only way to clear a major sin from his permanent record.

He asked Father Dave if he could give his confession now. The priest raised his eyebrows.

"Mister Driscoll, the holy mother church does not revolve around you. You must conform to her schedule, her rules, her regulations. You know the hours for confessions. See me then. And when you do, Mr. Driscoll, confess the sin of selfishness for asking me to hear your confession in off-hours to suit your convenience."

Young Paul hung his head. What hope did he have for eternal salvation after botching his First Holy Communion?

When adult Paul arrived at St. Patrick's altar, a young priest held the sacred Host before him and said, "The body of Christ."

"Amen," Paul said. The priest placed the Host into his cupped hands. He placed it in his mouth and ate, tasting the irony that now priests dealt Hosts like cards into open palms.

He declined the opportunity to drink from the chalice of wine consecrated into the Blood of Christ. He didn't think it sanitary to share a cup sipped by strangers. He hoped God would understand his hygienic concern and not take offense.

Returning to the pew, Eileen, Robbie, Katherine, and Paul knelt, bowing their heads in prayer.

"*Oh, dear Lord,*" Paul prayed, "*Thou art great and wonderful and I am truly sorry I have partaken of Thy Communion in a state of sin without having made a good Confession of the many sins I have committed against You and Your glory. I ask Your forgiveness for I am weak of the flesh, and Thine is the kingdom, the power, and the glory forever and ever, amen. Please, help me be stronger and act more Catholic to resist the many temptations that evil Satan lays before me. Help me, Lord, to be the person You want me to be. The person You made me to be. And please, dear Lord God, Savior and Redeemer, protect those I love and keep them safe, especially my family and friends. Plus, Katherine and her family and friends. And bless my father in heaven and keep him close to You. Protect him throughout eternity. Bless Katherine's dad, too. Please grant me success in my new job. Bring large circus crowds, so more people will see the wonders of Thy eternal glory through the performances of the great men, women, and beasts Thou hast made. Please grant me safe travels and help me do Thy will as a strong soldier of Christ. Please, dear Lord, help me worship Thee more often, and bow to Your eternal greatness and make You proud of me, even though I am but a wretched sinner. But, I am the flesh Thou hast made and with Thine help, let me fill you with pride. Help me, dear Lord, be worthy of Thine eternal love. Forever and ever, amen. Oh, also, thanks again for not letting my seed take root in Amy Jepson, and ridding me of crabs. Amen.*"

He looked up at sorrowful Jesus on the Crucifix and wondered if He had heard his prayers. Should Paul have addressed his prayers to Jesus instead of God? Would Jesus on the crucifix answer the prayers Himself, or act as an antenna broadcasting Paul's requests to His Holy Father in heaven? Wasn't every identity of The Holy Trinity one in the same? Did They talk, or was it better to just pray to God and let Him sort it out with Jesus and the Holy Spirit? He wondered who was really calling the shots. Paul caught himself, knowing it was probably a sin to question the mysteries of the Lord.

Katherine turned and smiled. He caught a whiff of her light perfume and felt a stirring in his pants. Robbie knelt with eyes closed, hands in prayer like an angel. Eileen was deep in prayer, moving her lips. He felt at peace.

Paul realized he had an erection. Popping boners in church had been a problem throughout his Catholic career. He closed his eyes and prayed.

"Oh, dear Lord, please forgive me my weakness of mind and stiffness of flesh. Help me keep my beastly, sinful desires under control and resist Satan's call. Please dear Lord, I pray and beseech Thee, for Thine is the kingdom, the power and the glory, forever and ever, amen."

It didn't work. His erection was evident in his dress pants. Paul thought of his circus duties and Barb Sigel and elephants walking and clowns juggling and roaring lions and that nitwit Brian dancing his awkward disco dances in a spaghetti-sauce-stained white suit.

He turned his attention to the priest performing his post-Communion chores at the altar: cleaning the chalices and gold patens, and returning the leftover Eucharist wafers to the ciborium.

God heard Paul's prayer and his erection waned.

The congregation moved in unison from knees, lifted kneelers, and sat. Paul gave thanks to the glories of God for helping him defeat his untimely excitement.

Take that, Satan!

After Mass, Paul drove the family home, and Eileen made a breakfast of scrambled eggs, link sausages, blueberry muffins, orange slices, and coffee.

"It was a lovely service," she said.

"Yes, it was," he said.

Paul drove Katherine to the White Mountains in New Hampshire.

"You were good in church, circus man," she said.

"Thanks. It all came back to me. The Mass must be imprinted in my genes."

"The church never leaves you. It's like family, and family always accepts you back again."

Paul wasn't sure God wanted him back if he had doubts about his belief. He was angry God took his father. Why did his Heavenly Father need his earthly one?

If God sent a sign, that would make it easier to believe.

Then Paul heard a possible sign— a commercial for Finnion, Barton & Powell Circus.

"Hey, that's my spot," he said, turning up the volume. Cheerful calliope music played as a baritone voice boomed: *"... children from one to one hundred will love the incredible excitement and fantabulous sights and sounds of the amazing, incredible, stupendous Finnion, Barton & Powell Circus! See a dozen elephants— ponderous pachyderms— as they dance and delight. Experience the thrills and chills of amazingly agile, athletic acrobats flying and defying gravity. Marvel as Chuck Gund, the world famous wild animal trainer, enters a steel cage and tames ferocious, carnivorous, ravenous, man-eating lions and tigers— making the killer beasts act like cute kittens. Experience all this, plus a gaggle of the goofiest, most hilarious clowns who ever squeezed into an itsy-bitsy car! Finnion, Barton & Powell Circus features over two hundred animals, amazing death-defying acts, breathtakingly beautiful women and unbelievable sights performing beneath a Big Top bursting to contain three rings of explosive excitement! Don't miss Finnion, Barton & Powell Circus, coming to The Essex Mall in Haverhill, Monday, June fourteenth and Tuesday the fifteenth. Tickets on sale now at The Essex Mall. Hurry! Get your tickets today! Don't miss the incredible Finnion, Barton & Powell Circus, Tops in Big Top Splendorama! Don't miss it!!!*

"Wow," Katherine said, turning down the radio. "Your commercial's a little over the top."

"I didn't write it, I just bought the media. I hope it gets people excited to see the show."

"It'll work. That commercial makes your circus sound like the second coming of Christ."

"Maybe I can add that to the script. Jesus would be a great draw. He could handle the loaves and fishes concessions."

"I better get you back to church, circus man. You're returning to your evil ways."

The White Mountains were beautiful. As they walked the trails, Paul said he could see himself moving to New England. "There's a lot of great ad agencies in Boston, and I could probably find a job when the circus season's over."

"I'd like that," Katherine said.

"So would I. We could be together." They spent the afternoon talking, laughing, and sharing feelings.

As they drove back, Katherine said, "I heard some big news yesterday."

"What?"

"My cousin Sean's returning to Haverhill next week."

"Where's he been?"

"It's a family secret."

"A secret?"

"Promise you won't tell?"

"Who would I tell? I don't know anyone in town except you and your friends."

"Promise you won't tell your family and friends, or circus people?"

"I'll keep quiet. I know how to keep my yap shut, sister," he said, in a bad Bogart impression.

"Don't joke. I'm serious."

"Okay, I swear to God, I won't tell."

"Very reassuring, coming from a guy who questions the existence of God."

"Come on— what's the secret?"

"All right. Sean's six years older than me, and he enlisted in the Marines straight out of high school. When he got out of the Marines, he went to work in El Salvador."

"Isn't that dangerous? There's a revolution down there."

"Sean's a mercenary. A soldier for hire."

"A mercenary? Really?"

"I'm the only one in our family who knows. I've always been close to him. The rest of the family thinks he's selling construction equipment in Central America."

"Wow."

"Now you know why you have to keep it secret. He could get in trouble."

"Was he hired by the rebels?"

"No, he was training government forces to fight the rebels."

"Doing what— training them how to kill nuns?" There had been stories in the news of government soldiers killing Catholic nuns who were helping rebels overthrow the military-run government in El Salvador.

"Sean's a good Catholic; he'd never kill nuns."

"I'm not saying he would, but I've read about the military killing nuns. If he's training them, he's guilty by association."

"That's probably rebel propaganda. I know Sean. He'd never get involved in something like that. End of discussion."

"Why's he coming back?"

"He finished his mission."

"Is he dangerous?"

"No, he's a pussycat. Just keep his secret a secret."

"No problem. I don't need mercenary troubles. I've got Barb Sigel."

"I can't wait for you guys to meet; you'll like him."

"I've never met a mercenary."

"Remember, not a word."

"He's a salesman."

"Right."

"Got it."

In Haverhill, they ate at O'Callahan's, returned to The Shamrock, made love, and fell asleep cuddling. Paul took her home just before midnight.

"Let's hurry," Katherine said, "before your carriage turns into a pumpkin."

"Right. Pumpkins are a bitch to drive."

The phone rang at six a.m. interrupting Paul from his dream of making love with Katherine on the beach as the Seabrook nuclear reactors billowed plumes of white smoke and protestors cheered. "Hello," he mumbled.

"You still sleeping? Wake the frick up!" Brian's voice blared.

"Brian?"

"The one and only. Don't you know the early bird gets the friggin' worm?!"

"I don't eat worms." Paul sat up and rubbed crusts of sleep from his eyes. "Where are you?"

"A crappy motel in Bangor. Want the phone number?"

"No. How'd you get my number?"

"Your girlfriend, Barb. How's it going?"

"Great. Made all my media buys, and I sold some promotions—"

"It's going super fantastic with me," Brian interrupted. "I'm nailing it. I worked the radio stations hard, and got tons of promotions. All half-cash half, half-trade, baby—"

"Same here."

"I told the stations I wasn't playing games. Told them I knew radio sales from the frickin' inside because I used to be a rep myself. That got their respect. Respect makes all the difference." Paul nodded, realizing the call was not about Brian checking in to see how he was doing— it was about him bragging.

"Sounds like you're doing great."

"Yeah. I think I'm going to have enormous sales. Probably break the Finnion, Barton & Powell record. I'm doing freakin' fantastic."

"You staying away from young girls?"

"Hey, if they're old enough to know better, they're old enough for me. There's plenty of sweet ladies here, and the Bri-monster is spreading himself like frickin' warm butter on hot toast. I'm getting my share of the ladies, don't you worry. How about you? Getting any action?"

"I met a terrific woman here."

"Big tits?"

"Grow up, Brian."

"If they're smallish, that's cool. Anything more than a mouthful's a waste. Am I right, or am I right?"

"She's perfect."

"Don't get tied down, Paulie. Us circus guys gotta love 'em and leave 'em. There'll be plenty more ladies down the road. You can't drop anchor, pretty soon it'll be sails up to your next town."

"I guess so."

"Is Barb coming your way?"

"Yeah, tomorrow or Wednesday."

"Then, she'll be checking on me. Barb will be impressed how great I'm doing."

"Good luck on your shows."

"Thanks. You too. Stay in freakin' touch, okay? Don't be a stranger."

"Sure."

"Us marketing guys got to stick together, right?"

"Right."

"And don't go back to bed, sleepyhead." Brian barked a laugh. "Catch that worm, early bird."

"Bye, Brian." Paul hung up, hoping Brian would find a new friend.

CHAPTER NINE
The Foleys

"Life is expectations fulfilled and celebrated, or expectations missed. You can accept failure, or blame bad luck or God's cruelty. It's easier to blame fate than yourself."

— *Paul Driscoll's notes, Bluefield, WV*

Carl and Wanda Foley had sawdust in their veins having worked thirty-one years for Finnion, Barton & Powell Circus.

He joined at age seventeen as a roustabout, doing manual labor, helping erect the big top, sideshow and mess tent.

Wanda was born into circus life. Her parents were The Flying Aces, Eric and Jessica Munnford, a husband and wife trapeze act, and a top attraction of Finnion, Barton & Powell Circus for twenty-seven years. The parents tried teaching their daughter trapeze artist skills, but a fear of heights, clumsiness, and gravity cursed Wanda.

Her parents were disappointed in their only child, but never spoke of it. They had hoped she'd join the act and continue their legacy. A child in a family act meant surefire ticket sales, and increased sales meant more leverage in negotiating higher performance fees. The Flying Aces were a popular act, but not a star attraction like Chuck Gund, The Wild Cat Wizard.

As Wanda grew, she was introduced to other acts as possible career paths. She was incapable of acrobatics, timid around animals, and clown greasepaint made her skin break out. With all avenues to performance exhausted, young Wanda was tutored in the business side of circus: selling tickets, concessions, and souvenirs.

Essential work, but not critical.

When she was sixteen, Wanda developed a crush on a roustabout named Carl. He was tall, handsome, with thick brown hair, and a muscular build. And he thought she was the most beautiful woman he'd ever seen.

Within a month, Wanda was pregnant. In two months, the couple married. Although The Flying Aces weren't happy a roustabout was marrying into their family— one they considered to be circus royalty—they hoped the performance gene would skip a generation and their grandchild would fly on the trapeze. They could teach the child, and call it their own. The Munnfords looked youngish and didn't like the idea of promoting themselves as flying grandparents— even if it might be a novelty draw.

But the grandchild never arrived. There were complications in Wanda's seventh month of pregnancy. In an emergency procedure, the child was lost, along with Wanda's reproductive equipment.

The dream of a future Flying Ace was forever grounded.

Soon after Wanda and Carl lost their baby, the circus lost Willie Ramsey, the "paperhanger" who for forty-two years had plastered towns with circus posters and circulars. Willie died in his small mobile home in an RV park outside Winchester, Tennessee. Neighbors had complained of "a God-awful stink" coming from his trailer. Police investigating discovered Willie's naked body on the floor, bound and gagged, with deep whip marks on his back and buttocks. His body was a gallery of garish mementos of sadomasochistic acts. There were no gunshot or stab wounds. The medical examiner estimated he'd been dead two to three days.

The cops declared Willie's death a suicide. It was easier than opening an expensive, time-consuming investigation into the death of a traveling carny. The circus was notified Willie committed suicide, and his remains were shipped to his brother in Dallas.

No one on the show was surprised by the news. Willie kept to himself and never seemed very happy. Suicide was plausible.

His RV, owned by the circus, was fumigated and became the home of the new paperhangers: Carl and Wanda Foley. After a few seasons working the job, the Foleys sold the death RV, and bought a used one. Wanda drove it, and Carl drove a small pickup they used for work.

Over the years, the Foley marriage deteriorated into a begrudging relationship steeped in bitterness and longing for paths never taken. Wanda felt she had married beneath herself, and Carl resented the fact he'd never hear the words "father" or "dad" thanks to her. Having only a sister, he was the end of the line for the Foley name on his branch of the family tree. Carl felt like a failure to his ancestors.

They were functional alcoholics who worked the work of the righteous by day, and at night, retreated into bottles of regret, anger, and superiority over all the foolish, idiotic people in the world. Carl held a special place of resentment for circus marketing directors. He had met many over the years, and he came to one conclusion, "They don't know shit from shinola."

Wanda agreed.

Carl called The Essex Mall office. "I'm looking for Paul Driscoll. He around?"

"May I ask who's calling?" Katherine said.

"Carl Foley, with Finnion, Barton & Powell Circus." Katherine put him on hold, and told Paul. He was not familiar with the name.

"Hello, this is Paul Driscoll."

"Carl Foley, here. Me and the wife are in town ready to start papering."

"Papering?"

"Putting up posters for your shows. Didn't Barb Sigel tell you about us?" Carl was agitated. He'd only been doing this job forever, and the history of circus posters was as old as mankind itself— so why was it always a mystery to dumb ass college kids how important papering a town was to the success of the shows they were supposed to be promoting?

"Right, papering the town. Now I remember. Posters and that," Paul said.

"Posters and that," Carl repeated in an annoyed, mocking voice. "Anything I need to know before we start hanging paper?"

"What do you mean?"

"Any city ordinances or restrictions? I don't want some local yokel cop throwing my ass in jail."

"Not that I know of." Paul wondered if he was supposed to have checked about papering ordinances with city officials. He didn't recall anything about that in his master plan. Maybe he should call Kirby Tooby. No, he knew Tooby would charge some fees. "I don't think so."

"I'll put in my report you said we're good to go."

"Your report?"

"You got your paperwork, I got mine. Part of my job's filing paperwork with the home office. That okay with you, Paul?" Carl thought this Paul Driscoll seemed like a new breed of idiot. He wondered where management found the nitwit.

"Sure. That's fine."

"Thanks, sonny boy. You know, I've been doing this goddamn

109

job thirty-one years, and I think me and Wanda know what the hell we're doing."

"Absolutely."

"I'll get you some window signs and posters for your mall sponsors. The more paper you get up, the better your chances for success."

"Right."

"We'll be there soon with your paper."

"Thanks. I appreciate it."

Carl hung up the phone and returned to the pickup. Wanda was lighting a cigarette. "Light me one, too," Carl said.

"What's the new guy like?" She handed him her cigarette.

"Another college-educated shit-head. But, he's got some manners. I'll give the bastard that."

Paul was talking with Katherine when the Foleys entered the office. "You must be Carl. I'm Paul Driscoll." Carl looked up and down at the smiling man, and shook his outstretched hand.

"Carl Foley. This is the wife, Wanda." Paul noticed Carl's large hands were rough and nicotine-stained. His breath smelled of acrid tooth decay, tobacco, and stale liquor. He was over six feet tall, with deep brown eyes and short, thick dark hair speckled with gray. Carl was a foot taller than Wanda, who had violet eyes and long graying hair pulled into a ponytail.

One or both of them had a sour body odor. Carl wore baggy gray pants, a wrinkled blue shirt, and an old plaid sports coat. His brown loafers curled up at the toes.

Wanda wore faded tight blue jeans, old black Converse All Stars, and a long-sleeved red shirt emblazoned with the Finnion, Barton & Powell Circus logo. She had a large heavy canvas bag slung over her shoulder.

"Pleasure to meet you, Wanda," Paul said.

"Hey," she gave no smile and a limp handshake. Her face was wrinkled into a frown; constant disappointment had marked its territory.

"Brought you some paper," Carl said, reaching into Wanda's canvas bag and handing Paul a stack of Finnion, Barton & Powell Circus poster boards and folded paper circus posters. "Plaster store windows. I always say, the more paper you post, the more paper money you'll get in sales."

"I will," Paul said. The posters had the colorful woodcut artwork of Randy Killinger, who in the 1920s and 30s was known as the da Vinci of circus posters. His clowns exuded pathos— sad eyes juxtaposed with funny facial expressions. His lion tamer scenes captured the ferocity of the wild jungle about to be whipped into shape by the courage of one brave man.

"Me and Wanda will start papering this morning," Carl said. "We've got a hell of a lot of ground to cover. Got your show, then we're headed to Salem and Bangor. Won't see you again until your next town. You know it yet?"

"No." Soon Paul would be told his next assignment and leave Katherine behind. He smiled at her.

"They'll tell you soon. You'll be seeing a lot of us down the road," Carl said, in a fog of bad breath.

"Looking forward to it." Paul wondered what kind of future conversations he'd have with the Foleys— advanced techniques for adhering paper to objects? Perhaps the hidden artistic statements of the human condition made by Randy Killinger? Did Randy's garish depiction of clowns represent man's intrinsic inhumanity to man, or something even more disturbing?

"We better get going. You have good shows. Nice meeting you." Carl shook Paul's hand. His long fingers were muscular sausages covered with hard calluses. He looked at Katherine and nodded, like the sheriff in a Western.

"Nice meeting you, Carl. You, too, Wanda," Paul said extending his hand. She looked at his hand hanging mid-air, smiled, and nodded.

"Good meeting you." She pivoted and exited with Carl.

The Foleys walked through the mall looking out of place among shoppers in clean, fashionable clothes.

"Not a bad kid," Carl said.

"He stunk of cologne," Wanda said. "Bet you dollars to donuts he's banging that office girl." She lit a cigarette and handed it to Carl, and lit another for herself.

"You should have been a detective, Wanda. You'd have been a good one."

"Damn right."

"So, those are your people, circus man?" Katherine asked.

"They're a couple of characters, aren't they?"

"They're characters all right. We may have to fumigate the offices."

"They were pretty ripe."

"Not exactly intellectual heavyweights, either."

"Probably not. But spending time with colorful people like them will help my writing."

"That's a tough way to get stories."

"Art is painful sometimes."

"Love is painful, too. I guess people pick their pain." The subject of love had been broached. She beat him to the punch, using the label for what he had been feeling.

"Please, Katherine, you know I really care about you, and I'll be back after the season ends." She pursed her mouth, her eyes began to water, and she went back to her desk.

He went back to his office, distracted by emotions.

Barb Sigel blew into Haverhill midweek, like a tornado touching down on a city of tissue tents.

"Your boss lady's on the phone," Katherine said, standing in the doorway of Paul's office. "You want to talk, or should I tell her you've quit your crappy job so you can be with me?"

"I'll take the call."

"I was afraid of that." She walked back to her desk, and he picked up the phone.

"Paul, I'm at a McDonald's twenty miles outside of Haverhill. How's it going?" she asked, in her high-pitched nervous voice. "Are you selling lots of promotions and working the master plan? Are all the radio stations at full throttle? I've been jumping around the dial and I haven't heard one of our spots yet. Are you blanketing the media?"

"It's going great, Barb. All the stations are running full schedules and the Foleys are papering the town and —"

"I want to see you. I'll be there in about a half hour. Keep working the master plan, Paul. Serve it, and it will serve you."

"I am."

"Great." She hung up. Katherine stood in the doorway smiling.

"How's our girl?"

"She's coming this way."

"Should I lock the door? Barricade the office? Borrow the security guard's gun and shoot her?"

"Silly girl— resistance is futile. She'd only break the door down and toss you around like a rag doll. Bullets only make her angry."

"Sounds like a charmer." Paul looked anxious.

"I've got to get organized." He began looking through his master plan, making sure his paperwork was in order.

Although Paul had described Barb to Katherine, the circus woman's appearance was still startling. She was larger than Paul described, and waddled in wearing skin-tight black polyester pants and a black top with red piping. Her face was heavily made-up, and her messy hair looked like shampoo hadn't touched it in days.

"I'm Barb Sigel, with Finnion, Barton & Powell Circus," she told Katherine in a nasal-y voice. "Is Paul Driscoll here?"

"Yes. I'm Katherine Flynn-Ryan, with mall management."

"Pleased to meet you." Barb shook her hand with a strong grip.

"Follow me." Katherine escorted her to Paul's office, where he appeared deep in thought, staring at his master plan. He looked up, stood, and put his hand out.

"Circus family doesn't shake," Barb said, engulfing his body into hers. She squeezed, and he felt her large breasts mashing against his ribcage, deflating his lungs. He looked at Katherine with a desperate, helpless expression. She smiled, winked, and walked back to her desk.

"The office girl's cute," Barb said.

"I guess so."

"You didn't notice?"

"I've been busy working."

"Right," she smiled. "Let's see what you've been up to." She reached for his master plan and pulled a ballpoint pen from her purse. She clicked it, and for the next forty-five minutes, grilled him. Her interrogation was intense, but he had answers that seemed satisfactory.

When she finished, she said she'd love to spend the night with him, but had to leave for Salem to meet another marketing director. Then, she had to go to Bangor and check on Brian.

"Hold on to your rain check for our night together," she smiled. "We'll cash it down the road. And, Paul, even if it's not raining, you won't need rubbers." She winked a mascara-laden lid, laughed, and he forced a smile.

He was relieved when Barb left. Katherine returned. "Well, I think her perfume means we won't be needing exterminators this summer. I'm not sure which was worse— her perfume or the Foleys' au natural bouquet."

Paul closed his office door, and embraced Katherine, and kissed her, hard. He was officially head over heels, dead on arrival in love. His chest ached with the thought of leaving her and seeing Haverhill disappearing in his rear-view mirror.

CHAPTER TEN
Blippo

"Circus is a celebration of humanity. We tame the wild, defy gravity, and cheat death. And let's not forget the dedicated people selling cotton candy and funnel cakes."

— *Paul Driscoll's notes, Brownsville, TX*

Blippo the Clown was the professional name of Henry Steven Huggins, a twenty-six-year-old closeted homosexual not committed to his sexuality, living between stages of sadness and anger, darting across their borders with rare bouts of contentedness.

Henry knew from an early age he was not like other boys. He was attracted to boys, but petrified to act for fear of rejection, ridicule or savage beatings. He faked an interest in girls, telling male classmates, "I'd like to get into her pants" or "I'd love to screw her."

Although Henry wanted to be a guy's guy, he stole glances of swinging dicks as young men walked to the showers after gym class.

He attended The University of Nebraska for two semesters, and drank his way to flunking out. He worked minimum wage jobs and thought about possible careers.

Nothing interested him.

His father gave him encouragement: "Get your shit together,

Henry, and make something of yourself!"

"Jesus H. Christ, life's not a goddamn dress rehearsal— find something you're good at, do it and make money! It's not that goddamn hard, Henry!"

The young man fell into an emotional quicksand of depression, self-loathing and low self-esteem.

One night, after his parents went to bed, he watched the movie "The Greatest Show on Earth" on TV. Henry was mesmerized by Emmett Kelly's performance. The legendary clown's sad face attracted attention, empathy, compassion, and love from adoring crowds. His face was a universal, irresistible invitation for adoring acceptance. Kelly made Henry smile. The clown looked on the outside the way he felt on the inside.

Henry decided to become a circus clown. It was as if God was speaking to him through the TV, telling him to turn his sadness into happiness for others. He felt confident; being a clown would stoke flames of joy within himself as he pleased people.

Finally, he had life figured out.

The next day, Henry went to the library and researched a clown career. He learned about Hennimen, Hurley & Fester Bros. Clown College in Clearwater, Florida, described as "the Harvard of greasepaint arts". The college sought people who were gregarious, had great senses of humor, loved making others laugh, and were athletic and acrobatic.

Henry had none of these, but knew he could learn.

That day, he began practicing acrobatics and learning how to juggle. He pretended to like humans, especially the small ones called children. It was a slow and arduous process, but he practiced and persisted. Henry completed his college application.

Within a week, he received a letter granting an interview at Hennimen, Hurley & Fester Bros. Clown College. He was thrilled and told his parents this was his destiny. They agreed to loan him the tuition money if he was accepted, but, if he didn't make it, he'd have to support himself in Florida. They would not support his life long distance. Henry agreed.

He packed, loaded his car, and drove to Florida.

Henry failed his first interview and audition because the clown college Dean didn't think he had the skills and advised him to keep practicing.

"Clowning is hard work, Henry," he said. "Many are called, but few can fill the big shoes!" The Dean barked a laugh and performed a comic walkaway, tooting a small bicycle horn.

Henry frowned.

The failed student clown found a job as a janitor in an elementary school and became more comfortable around children. He practiced acrobatics in the gymnasium at night, teaching himself how to walk on his hands, tumbling, pretending to step on rakes and doing pratfalls. After six months, Henry had another audition and was accepted into the college.

He practiced his craft religiously, and met other closeted homosexual men. One night, Henry was seduced by a classmate called "Giggles" who refused to give his birth name. The sex was awkward and painful. He lost interest in Giggles.

Henry engaged in more homosexual relationships with his classmates. None were satisfying. He felt nothing for women, and ambivalence toward men. The only emotions he felt after his sexual encounters were disappointment and anger.

He thought he might be asexual, and asexuality seemed the worst of all worlds.

A man with no country is a hard man to be.

By graduation, Henry had developed the character of Blippo the Clown. He auditioned for the legendary Hennimen, Hurley & Fester Bros. Circus, with two traveling squads, but didn't make it.

He was an unemployed clown with an expensive degree. There was nothing funny about that.

Pootah, a clown Henry had sex with, made it into the Hennimen show and told him about an opening with Finnion, Barton & Powell Circus. Henry auditioned and was offered a job.

He performed under the big top for five months, engaging in more unfulfilling gay relationships. Then, opportunity knocked.

The FB&PC advance clown, Maxxo Blaxxo, had a major gaffe in a radio interview with a Scranton disc jockey. Maxxo's job was to arrive before the show, do interviews and magic shows, whip up excitement, and create publicity.

During his interview, Maxxo thought there was a commercial break and tried to get a laugh telling the DJ that children were "little sticky fingered motherfuckers." The microphone was live, and the clown's joke was broadcast in 100,000 watts over Pennsylvania.

Maxxo Blaxxo got fired. There was an advance clown opening.

Henry told Randy Trumble, the circus boss, he loved children and would be a perfect advance clown. Randy gave him the job because he thought Blippo was a mediocre clown, and as advance clown, he would look good, wearing big shoes, tying balloons and doing menial magic tricks. Trumble thought any idiot could handle that job, and Henry Huggins was any idiot.

Good clowns wanted to perform in the show, not be on the road promoting the show.

Henry was paid a Spartan salary and reimbursed for gas. He paid his own living expenses. Blippo was given a quick advance clown training course from LuLu, the head circus clown, who stressed "watch your damn mouth at all times. Remember, you speak for the Finnion, Barton & Powell Circus. There's no such thing as off-the-record. Not ever! When in doubt, keep your goddamn mouth shut!" Blippo nodded, like an obedient dog.

On June 4, 1978, Blippo began his advance clown career and in his four-year tenure, he had never sworn at or about children, on the air, or in the press. For this accomplishment, circus management allowed him to fill the big shoes of advance clown.

Blippo came to a town after Carl and Wanda Foley had papered it. When he arrived, he contacted the marketing director who shuttled him to radio, newspaper, and TV interviews, magic shows for kids, and photo ops at old folks' homes and hospitals. The marketing director was responsible for scheduling events. Blippo resented the pittance he was paid in return for the free press he generated. He lived in a constant state of near poverty.

Unlike marketing directors, Blippo couldn't afford to stay in motels, not if he wanted to save the money he needed to pay his parents back for tuition. Marketing directors could afford luxuries like color TV, fresh linens, small personal bars of soap, and maid service. He had a beat-up 1971 Dodge Dart towing his small camper. He lived in rural camper parks; a lonely clown sequestered in cramped quarters on the outskirts of town.

Blippo hated most marketing directors. He thought they were college-educated morons who didn't know the pain and suffering performing artists endured in entertaining.

Traveling ahead of the show, he rarely saw performances. That didn't bother him since he disliked most of the performers, especially those in clown alley, where the clowns dressed and made-up their faces. He thought show clowns were cliquish.

Blippo never felt at home when he performed with the show.

Although he'd had relations with a few clowns, he felt ostracized and knew they talked behind his back because he was not as promiscuous as they. He suspected they were happy when he left the show. Although he was one of them, he was not "one of them." He thought show clowns were sexual deviates, snooty egomaniacs, and self-centered pricks, while he was a humble clown in the tradition of his hero, Emmett Kelly.

Other clowns were perverted silly goons.

Blippo wasn't in it for free love of clown quarters; he was in it for the love of a clown's life.

But there was little in his life that he liked, let alone loved. He had manufactured his mythology— he was a hero on the road, spreading good cheer to bratty kids, ignorant yahoos, and shit head D.J. entertainment wannabes on local airwaves.

After twenty-six years on earth, Henry Steven Huggins had not found his way to a happier place, only the outer fringes of misery.

❧

Blippo called Paul and told him to pick him up at The Winding Trails Camp Grounds.

The marketing director had never been in a trailer park before, and it seemed exotic— where road gypsies banded together living in nature.

As Paul drove through, he sensed these people relished living outside the mainstream. If there were ever nuclear hellfire, these hardscrabble people would survive and spread their hearty seeds.

Paul parked his car by Blippo's trailer. Across the way, two young boys were throwing rocks at a dog as a man drinking a beer sat in a lawn chair watching and laughing. It was 7:30 a.m.

A different breed.

He knocked on Blippo's camper's door. "Just a second," an

agitated voice yelled. Paul walked in the yard and noticed a variety of homes— from glistening aluminum Airstreams to RV mansions to tents pitched beneath the canopy of trees.

"You Paul Driscoll?" a voice spoke from behind. Paul pivoted and saw a short clown in comically large shoes, red wig, and a small blue top hat carrying a box suitcase with the words "Blippo the Clown" painted beneath the Finnion, Barton & Powell Circus logo.

"Yes. You must be Blippo."

"What tipped you off, Einstein?" Blippo gripped Paul's hand.

"Ouch! What the hell." He broke the grip.

"A joy buzzer." Blippo smiled. "Brings joy to everyone— except the sucker on the receiving end."

"That's not funny. That hurt."

"Hey, I know funny, and joy buzzers are definitely funny."

Paul had set five appointments: three with radio stations, a stop at the local newspaper for a photo op, and a magic show at the mall.

Blippo was not a great radio interview. His answers were concise, as if he were being interrogated and feared he might deliver incriminating information.

Fortunately, the disc jockeys were well-versed in circus show dates and ticket information and pimped the shows with enthusiasm, even if the tight-lipped clown did not.

At the newspaper offices, Blippo tried getting laughs, but the journalists were not amused. A recent warehouse fire was a juicier scoop than the circus clown.

As Paul chauffeured Blippo, he tried engaging in conversation. Paul asked which comedians he liked.

"They all suck."

"What about Steve Martin? Richard Pryor? George Carlin?"

"They're okay," Blippo said, as he looked out his window, sucking up all the happiness in the world.

Paul decided conversation attempts weren't worth the effort. They rode in silence. He stopped at McDonald's for lunch. Blippo refused to enter.

"Just bring mine out," he said. "Whenever I go into McDonald's, kids think I'm Ronald McDonald. I hate what that bastard did to our profession— shilling for goddamn burgers and fries. The sell-out asshole." This diatribe was the most passion Paul witnessed all day.

Blippo's mall magic show had cheesy gags like a long multi-colored handkerchief the clown pulled from his hand as he pretended he was about to sneeze. When he sneezed, he unleashed a flurry of tiny sparkles.

He gave kids cans of nuts loaded with spring snakes that sprung out and surprised them.

Blippo asked a child to hit him in the head with a foam hammer; then he stumbled about in pain.

Kids liked seeing him in pain.

He gave one boy a handshake with his joy buzzer. The kid jumped, others laughed, and Paul failed to see the humor.

Blippo spoke throughout the show:

"Are you kids coming to Finnion, Barton & Powell Circus?"

"I hope to see all of you at Finnion, Barton & Powell Circus."

"You won't believe how much fun you'll have at Finnion, Barton & Powell Circus."

"Tell your parents you want to go to Finnion, Barton & Powell Circus— and bring them along, to pay! Ha ha ha!"

"And please, please PLEASE don't try and steal an elephant from Finnion, Barton & Powell Circus. They'll eat all your peanut butter, and they're impossible to housebreak!"

Blippo cackled at his jokes. Most kids didn't.

Paul thought Blippo was lackluster. He got titters of laughter, easy smiles, and polite applause, but never connected with the audience. There were few belly laughs. People were more respectful of the clown uniform than the person in it.

At the end of the appointments, Paul drove Blippo to his trailer park. "That was a great day," the clown said. "Thanks. Want to get dinner later?" Paul looked at the soulful eyes in his made-up face and sensed his loneliness.

"Sure. But I'm supposed to take this girl to dinner—"

"If you have plans, I'll just have a can of stew or tuna. No big deal."

"No, it's fine. We're just going to a bar. Join us."

"If you're sure."

"Sure. Her name's Katherine, she works at the mall. You'll like her. She's probably never dined with a clown before. I know I haven't."

"I don't dress like this after hours."

"When do you want me to pick you up?"

"Seven?"

"Seven it is. And, Blippo—"

"Yes."

"Don't wear so much makeup tonight."

"Very funny. I never heard that one before." Blippo grabbed his suitcase and wobbled his way to the trailer.

Paul drove to the mall and asked Katherine if she'd mind having a guest join them. He told her about the lonely clown and his diet of canned stew. She said it was fine and smiled.

"And, Katherine," he said. "One other thing."

"What?"

"I told him we're just friends, so, let's not tell him about all the stuff we've been doing."

"You mean the screwing, sharing crabs, our romantic walks on the beach—"

"Please, don't take it the wrong way. I just don't want him knowing about my personal life."

"Don't worry. I won't tell your precious clown anything."

"You're the best." He kissed her.

"Yes, and don't you ever forget that, circus man."

O'Shannon's Pub was a Haverhill institution that began serving drinks and food to textile mill workers in 1935. It smelled like stale beer and fryer grease, with the lingering aroma of broken hearts and lost causes.

Paul, Katherine, and Henry were seated in a wooden booth. Henry, sans clown face, had a square chin, pointy nose, high forehead, and a thinning crop of reddish hair. A waitress delivered menus and took their drink orders.

"They're famous for their meatloaf," Katherine said. "It has beef, pork, and steel cut Irish oats."

"Yummy," Henry said. "Can't ever get enough steel cut Irish oats."

"I can't get over how different you look without makeup, Blippo," Paul said.

"It's Henry. I'm only Blippo in full clown face."

"Okay. Henry."

The waitress delivered their drinks and Henry downed half his gin and tonic in a single gulp. Paul sipped his beer, and Katherine her Guinness.

"What's it like being a clown?" Katherine asked.

"Like any job. Good days, bad days."

"It must be great making people laugh," Paul said, trying to brighten the mood.

"Yeah," Henry said, finishing his drink and waving the waitress for another. "Laughs make it worthwhile, I guess."

"What's life on the road like?" Katherine asked. "It must be terribly lonely." She glanced at Paul.

"I like the freedom, but it can get lonely. The adventure's good, seeing the country and being in show business. But, it is lonely sometimes." Henry stared off into space with sad moo-cow eyes. The waitress brought a fresh gin and tonic, and he brightened taking a thirsty sip. Katherine looked at Paul, who looked away.

Over their meatloaf dinners, they talked about their lives and Paul pretended he was hearing about Katherine for the first time. He peppered her narrative with, "Oh, really?", "That's amazing" and "Wow."

She didn't care if the lonely little clown knew about their relationship and wondered if Paul was weak, afraid to declare publicly his emotions for a woman he claimed to love.

She became sad. Her Guinness glass drained.

Paul thought the evening was going very well. Henry had opened up, and Katherine seemed to be enjoying their act of just being friends. She hid their romance well.

Henry had already guzzled five gin and tonics. Katherine asked him, "Did you like performing in the circus?"

"I liked the show; but didn't like the miserable fuckers in it," he said. "Pardon my French, but fuck, it's the truth— the other clowns were pricks. Like high school all over again, with their stupid cliques and shit. Most of them were mean. Hell, most circus performers are egomaniacal assholes. Don't get me wrong, I love the circus— the tradition, the art and craft of it. I just don't like the cruel fuckers in it."

Henry waved to the waitress for another drink. Katherine gave Paul a hard stare. He smiled and looked at his beer.

As Henry got drunker, he got darker, angrier.

"Look at that," Paul said, "it's almost nine-thirty. I have a big day tomorrow, and, Henry, I'm sure you do, too, so I'll take you back to your trailer, then, take Katherine home."

"Home sounds like heaven," she said.

"It's early," Henry whined. "Let's have a couple more drinks."

"I'd love to," Paul said, "but I'm sure Katherine needs to put her son to bed."

"Mom probably already did that."

"See?" Henry smiled. "The little rug rat's off to sleepy town."

"What did you call my son?" Katherine asked, her eyes narrowing.

"Little rug rat. I always call kids 'rug rats.' It's a joke, I'm a clown.
"

"Robbie's no rug rat. Take it back."

"Look, I'm sorry, I didn't mean—"

"Take it back, or I'll kick your sorry clown ass."

"All right, calm down. Your kid isn't a rug rat. Christ, maybe it is time to go."

"I'll get the check," Paul said.

"Let me chip in," Henry said, placing a five-dollar bill with three ones on the table. Paul picked up the money. It wouldn't cover Henry's bar tab, let alone the meal. He glanced at Katherine. She looked upset.

On the drive to the trailer park, Henry was silent in the back seat. Katherine was quiet. Paul turned up the radio. "You're Going to Lose That Girl" by The Beatles was playing. John Lennon sang as Paul listened, hoping it wasn't a prediction.

"I don't feel good," Henry said.

"We're almost there," Paul said. "Crack your window. Fresh air will make you feel better."

Henry opened the window, poked his head into the night and began heaving, throwing up everything he'd consumed at O'Shannon's. Some splattered on Paul's car. Katherine glared at Paul as the clown puked into the wind.

On the radio, Led Zeppelin began playing "Good Times, Bad Times".

"Good times," she said, looking straight ahead. Paul pulled the car to the side of the road.

"I'm fine," the clown said, wiping his mouth with his shirtsleeve.

"You sure?" Paul asked.

"I'm empty. I threw up everything but my kidneys. I must be allergic to the Irish oatmeal in that damn meatloaf."

"What else could it be?" Katherine asked. "Certainly not the twenty-eight gin and tonics you guzzled."

Paul continued driving. The little man groaned in the backseat.

When they arrived, Henry apologized for getting sick. He also apologized to Katherine for calling her child a rug rat. "See you down the road, Paul," he said, staggering to his trailer.

"Man, he got wasted," Paul said. "Do you want to go back to my place?"

"No. I want to go home to my rug rat and people who don't live angry, pathetic, lonely lives with their glamorous circus jobs, drinking until they barf their guts out."

"I told you he was a character."

"He's not a character, Paul. He's an asshole. A mean, drunk little asshole living in a shitty little trailer. That could be you, if you stay with your stupid circus job."

"Come on, you're overreacting. You can't compare me to him."

"Look at him, and those other people— the Foleys, and that

horrible Barb woman. Are those your people, Paul? Are they?" Paul stared into the night, then turned back to her.

"I don't know. They're not like you or me, or most people, but they are good people. And I don't have to crap all over them to make me feel superior. Be fair, Katherine."

"I am fair; I'm being more than fair. I was dumb enough to fall in love with a guy who gave me crabs, and will be leaving me soon, until God knows when, so he can run around the country having adventures to write about."

"You're not even sure you had crabs. And, yes, I'll be leaving you for my circus job because it's what I need to do for money, and to grow up, and learn how to live on my own, and get stories. A writer needs experiences, Katherine. You think James Joyce became James Joyce staying in one place? Look at Hemingway, with bullfights and fighting in wars and hunting and fishing and living in Paris. I'm doing what I have to do."

"And what about me? What am I— a chapter in your book?"

"I told you I love you. I do. I'll call you or write every day. When the circus season's over in November, I'll have money saved and update my resume. Then, I'll find a copywriting job in Boston, and we'll be together."

"And I'm just supposed to wait?"

"If you love me, you will. Think of me as a soldier off to war. A short war."

"I don't know, Paul." Katherine started crying. "I do love you, we have so much in common and being together feels natural, but honest to God, sometimes I wish I never met you."

"Katherine, meeting you was the best thing that ever happened to me. I feel like we're soulmates. Fate brought us together for a reason, and meeting you was the start of a new life for me. My adult life. I love you."

"Then why do I feel like shit?"

"It'll be hard for both of us, at first, but we'll make it work. We'll be back together."

"In November."

"Right, when the circus wars are over and your soldier boy returns."

"That seems like a long time." He leaned over and kissed her.

"It'll be here before you know it."

They ended up at The Shamrock and gave Paul's bed a workout, then fell fast asleep. At 3:15, he drove her home and they kissed goodnight.

As he drove back to his motel, Paul felt empty and lost. He wasn't sure he was ready to go off to war.

CHAPTER ELEVEN
Showtime

"Things always look their worst in the moment, and usually look their best in the rear-view mirror, where they're smaller."
— *Paul Driscoll's notes, Panama City, FL*

The days before the circus arrived were hectic. Paul worked his master plan: ordering thirty bales of timothy hay for the elephants, scheduling the cleaning of 'donikers' (toilets mounted on a truck trailer bed), and trying to get media coverage of the erection of the big top.

All buzz was good buzz.

He did not do master plan activities he thought were pointless—arranging a circus parade through town, or persuading the mayor to present the circus ringmaster with a key to the city. Given his experience with Haverhill politics, Paul knew arranging stunts like these would require money and free tickets. If Barb asked, he'd say he tried selling a parade and city key ceremony, but local ordinances prohibited them.

Hustling publicity was his primary responsibility. He had press releases printed on circus letterhead displaying the colorful Randy Killinger artwork logo masthead, featuring the big top, lions, horses, and clowns.

The press releases were written in an over-the-top, alliteration-laden style— "colorful clowns cavorting comically" and "ferocious fanged felines fighting for feeding." While Paul thought the press releases were cheesy, he sent them with glossy 8" x 10" shots of performers. Marketing directors were expected to milk free publicity.

As his shows got closer, Paul tried getting closer to Katherine. They worked together in the mall offices by day and spent nights at restaurants and bars. Afterward, they'd sit on her porch talking, or, in his motel bed communicating with animal passion. As he clung close, he felt her withdrawing.

"What's wrong?" he asked one night after they'd made love.

"Nothing."

"You seem distant."

"'Distant'— that's a good word coming from you."

"I'm not distant."

"Not now, but you will be after your circus comes. Then, you'll be nothing but distant."

"Not this again," he said, regretting his words immediately.

"Yes, 'this' again, Paul. I was an idiot to fall in love with you. I should have known better."

"I told you I'm coming back, and I'll be in touch constantly."

"That's not the same. I can't hug a phone or cuddle with a letter."

"Leaving you will hurt me, too."

"Then quit. You know what circus people are like—they're misfits and angry drunks. Do you want to become one of them? Quit now and start job hunting in Boston."

"Finding a job isn't a sure thing. I doubt there's much demand for aluminum siding copywriters in Boston."

"You won't know unless you try."

"Job hunting takes time and money. Besides, I don't want to be a copywriter forever. I want to write, get published, and get out of advertising."

"And I want you here, with me."

"I know this is hard for you. It's hard for me, too, but I need to learn to live on my own. Just think of this job like I'm going off to war. Like our fathers did."

"That's bullshit, Paul. Our dads went to war because they loved their country. You're going off to your circus wars because you want to."

"No. Because I need to."

"Do what you've got to do, Paul. I'll stay here, wait by the phone and the mailbox for my soldier boy to grow up and return home. Maybe I'll get a job with the U.S.O., and dance with other circus soldiers."

Katherine began crying. Paul felt awkward and helpless as he comforted her as best he could.

His stomach hurt.

～⌒う

Finnion, Barton & Powell Circus arrived in Haverhill just after midnight on June 14th. The circus traveled in a caravan of thirty-two trucks, RVs, and trailers.

At 6:00 a.m., a crew of roustabouts began the five-hour process of erecting the heavy canvas red-and-white striped big top tent.

Paul was at The Essex Mall parking lot at dawn, ready to greet the media people he'd invited to the tent-raising spectacle. He had called all the media, none had committed.

He was nervous. He'd worked his master plan for three weeks, now he'd see if it would work for him.

Advance ticket sales were $6,800. A decent take. He needed big 'walk-up crowds for the shows to be moneymakers.

The circus had fixed expenses of $10,000 a day. Once costs were covered, the cash cow gave milk. With advance sales, he was over a quarter of the way to covering expenses, or, making the nut, for the four performances over two days.

During his interview, Tom Burnett told Paul the expression 'making the nut' dated back to old England, when gypsy circuses roamed the countryside performing. They often took flight in the middle of the night before settling debts with local suppliers and taxmen.

A city sheriff came up with a safeguard. When the gypsies arrived, he removed a wheel nut on the largest circus wagon, making it immobile.

When the circus paid all its debts, the nut was returned.

It worked. Gypsy circuses were made honest.

Today, many people thought circus people were cheating gypsies and required invoices to be paid up-front or upon show arrival. Paul understood their apprehension of extending credit, but he resented being treated like a charlatan.

Marketing directors were responsible for placing local classified ads for roustabouts. The demand for fresh muscle was constant since the roustabout population was in continual flux. Some joined the show because they were on the lam from the law. Most were alcoholics or drug addicts, and many were uneducated, shiftless ex-cons looking for their next score. Being a roustabout was the modern equivalent of a hobo riding the rails. A way of getting out of one place, and on to another.

As Paul stood in the mall parking lot, he watched roustabouts measuring off and staking the big top. "How's the advance?" asked a bloodshot-eyed, beer-bellied roustie.

"Good," Paul said.

"Great. Last town fucking sucked. The marketing director shit the bed." Paul smiled nervously.

"We'll do good here."

"We need it." The roustabout shifted the sledgehammer from his left arm to his right. His muscles were the size of Paul's thighs. The team of men began driving stakes into the parking lot blacktop.

At 6:55 a.m., the newspaper photographer arrived with his old Pentax. He had graying hair in full retreat, and looked hungover.

"You the circus guy?" he asked.

"Yes. Paul Driscoll, marketing director with Finnion, Barton & Powell Circus. You must be the newspaper photographer."

"Yeah. Tim O'Leary, shutterbug with the Haverhill rag. So, this is it," he said, looking unimpressed at the sea of red-and-white striped canvas draped across the parking lot. "Not exactly a photogenic moment." His breath stank of booze.

"It'll get better," Paul said. "Elephants will pull and hoist the big top up over the main support poles. It'll make a great front page shot."

"Uh-huh. When's that happening?"

"I'm not sure, but I can find out."

"You do that. I'll run down to Dunkin' and get some breakfast. Be back in a half hour or so."

"Okay, Mr. O'Leary. You eat and I'll find out when the elephants go to work."

"Mr. O'Leary's my dad— call me Tim. Can I get you anything?"

"Maybe a cup of coffee."

"How you take it?"

"Black. Let me give you some money."

"My treat. Don't let the elephants do anything until I get back."

The photographer walked to his old Chevy Vega, with more rust than sheet metal, and Paul went to the ticket office to ask about the elephants. As he walked, he prayed.

"Oh, dear Lord, please let the circus be a hit and bestow large crowds upon this humble sinner. Bring Thy masses here to see the wonders Thou hast created. Thank you, Lord God, for Thy glory is great. Lead me not into temptation, and please grant me good show dates. Amen."

The ticket office trailer was the hub of Finnion, Barton & Powell Circus. It had three sales windows, each caged with open slots. Sellers sat behind a counter with cash drawers. Spools of tickets were suspended above each sales station. Behind the sales counter was a narrow table with two chairs and a vinyl-upholstered bench seat. This was the domain of T. Clancy Plumbar, nicknamed "Cronk", a short, sturdy fifty-seven-year-old man who cast a long shadow in FB&PC history.

Cronk had a crew cut of thick white hair. He could tabulate ticket sales in his head faster than the sellers could with calculators. He was the operating chief financial officer of the canvas-draped enterprise, and was consulted by circus boss Randy Trumble on all major issues.

Cronk joined the show at age fifteen as a roustabout.

"This circus saved my life," he'd tell newcomers. "My old man liked his booze, and liquor brought out his demons— and goddamn if they weren't angrier than he was. When he was drunk, he saw me as a miniature of himself. Since he hated himself more than anybody— except maybe his old man — who beat the hell out of him — my dad took it out on me. I guess kicking the shit out of your kids ran in our family. I was an only child, an easy target. Slaps, punches, shoves, kicks, belt whippings, yanking hair— everything was fair game. My mom's pleading and crying couldn't save me. She died of cancer when I was thirteen, and that only got the old man angrier. It was him versus me, no referee. I knew I had to get out of that house before he killed me, or I killed him, and ended up in prison. This circus was my salvation."

Cronk was the heart, soul, and brains of the show. During his tenure, he had worked in all circus departments, garnering respect and admiration.

When he was nineteen, he fell in love with a young woman in the horse act named Sally Jenkins, a petite beauty with blond hair, vivid blue eyes, and easy smile. He pursued Sally with flowers, candies and poems cobbled from infatuation and near rhymes.

His courting worked.

Within three months, Sally became pregnant, and they married, naming their daughter Charlotte— the closest city where she was conceived. Cronk was a loving father, determined that the anger in his family's bloodline stopped.

When Charlotte was six, Sally was diagnosed with cancer. She had felt a lump on her breast years earlier, but never sought medical attention, fearing what a doctor might say. By the time she saw one, the cancer was rampant.

She was dead four months later.

Cronk was a heartbroken widower at age twenty-five, determined that their daughter never lacked for love or attention.

Circus people helped raise Charlotte; she was schooled with children of performers and given chores. She grew into a beautiful young woman who inherited her mother's gift with horses— the animals responded to her every wish. By age eighteen, Charlotte and her horses were star attractions in Finnion, Barton & Powell Circus. Then, like her mother, she came down with an unexpected pregnancy.

The father was Earl Foxmire, a roustabout who had joined the show in Kentucky, after he'd served a two-year prison stretch for burglary. One month after release, he was wanted for assault and battery. Fortunately, the circus came and he joined.

Earl was handsome, charming, and funny. He watched Charlotte as she stood on a white steed and galloped around the center ring. She looked like a queen and he wanted to be her king.

He seduced Charlotte with sweet talk in his soft Southern accent. During a week of torrid lovemaking, Earl planted his seed. When Charlotte discovered she was pregnant, she told Earl he was going to be a father, thinking the news would bring him to the altar.

He seemed happy and said they'd marry and raise the child in the circus, with sawdust in their baby's veins.

That night, Earl blew off the show like a breeze through pines. Charlotte never heard from him again.

Although she refused to disclose the identity of her child's father, Cronk knew it was Earl. He had never liked him. "That bastard gives roustabouts a bad name," he told Randy Trumble. "God knows that isn't easy."

Cronk urged his daughter to get an abortion, he knew people who performed the procedure safely and discreetly. "Charlotte, you're too young to be a mother," he said. "You got your whole life ahead of you. The world is a hard place for the child of an unwed mother."

"No," she said. "I'm going to love my baby and raise it like you raised me."

"But, you're just a baby yourself."

"Dad, I'm almost the same age you and mom were when I was born."

"There was two of us raising you."

"And there's you and me. It'll be fine. You'll see." That was the last discussion held on that subject.

Cronk hoped the child didn't inherit anything from Earl.

Augusta Plumbar was born on June 16, 1960, in Greenville, South Carolina. Charlotte guessed the baby had been conceived near Augusta, Georgia.

⌒

As Paul Driscoll walked to the ticket trailer, he met a young woman with light auburn hair tied in a ponytail. She had a beautiful face with perfect white teeth and violet blue eyes. "You must be the new guy," she said.

"Hi, I'm Paul Driscoll," he said, putting out his hand. She shook it with her warm hand, and he felt a slight charge with her touch— an emotional joy buzzer.

"I'm Augusta Plumbar," she said, taking out a key and unlocking the trailer door. She walked inside and he followed. "Welcome aboard. Close the door so flies don't get in. Flies drive us crazy."

He smiled noticing her perfectly proportioned body packaged in tight jeans and a faded Finnion, Barton & Powell Circus logo tee-shirt. He imagined her naked and felt guilty. He scrambled to keep the conversation rolling. "I hate flies, too."

"No one likes flies. They're disgusting."

"Right." He realized they had entered a conversational cul-de-sac. "Next up on 'Fly Talk'," he said in a deep announcer voice, "we'll discuss keeping flies off food. Join us after this commercial break." He smiled, hoping she'd appreciate his wit. She stared at him.

"'Fly Talk'— what are you talking about?"

"I was pretending we were on a talk show about flies. It was a joke."

"A joke? I don't get it."

"It was stupid. Forget I said it."

"Has anyone ever told you you're weird?"

"Yeah," he blushed. "Sorry for the bad joke."

"That's all right. I guess a talk show about flies would be kind of funny. Stupid, but funny." She smiled, and he smiled back, feeling guilty about his attraction to her.

"I'm looking for Cronk. I'm not sure if that's his first name, or last."

"Cronk's his nickname and he's my grandfather. His last name's Plumbar."

"Grandfather?"

"My mother's father. She works on the show. She'll be here soon to sell tickets with me."

"Is Cronk around? I have to give him the advance sales and some bills."

"He's out, but should be back soon. Have a seat." She pointed to the small upholstered bench. "How's your advance?"

"Pretty good. About sixty-eight hundred."

"Not bad. We could use some good dates. Last few cities have been slow." Customers came to the window, and she sold them tickets. Paul glanced at her beautiful back draped with a seductive ponytail. There was something intoxicating about her. He begged his brain to forget her— and concentrate on Katherine or the show.

His brain refused.

Paul struck an easy friendship with Cronk, who counted his advance sales. "Nice work," he said. "It'll be good to make some money again."

Paul acted as the liaison between Cronk and the local media reps and suppliers who were suspicious of the circus and anxious to get paid.

He met Cronk's daughter, Charlotte, the mother of seductive Augusta, and performer in the horse show. He learned Augusta was in the opening and closing circus parades, and assisted with the animals in the horse show.

The Plumbar family was three generations strong, FB&PC royalty. Sawdust blue bloods.

Paul's master plan listed two pages of opening day duties and he scrambled to complete them all. In between activities, he stopped in the mall offices.

"Your people have invaded," Katherine said. "Soon you'll be off to your circus wars."

"I'll be back before you know it, and in touch constantly."

"So you've told me a hundred times. It still hurts."

He hugged her. "I've got your family great seats for the seven-thirty show. You're going to love it."

"Great." She sighed. "Can't wait."

He hugged her tighter.

On the midway, the crowd was corralled into walking past the sideshow tent where Stan Whootmoor, a veteran Barker held court. Stan was tall, with a glistening bald head, bushy white eyebrows, and a billy goat white beard thick as a whisk broom. He wore a plaid sports coat of many colors. His posture leaned— the result of decades spent perched on an elevated stage leaning down to the curious crowds below as he preached.

He held a microphone plugged into a small amplifier and punctuated the air with his arm as he spoke. Stan had a deep, bourbon-cured voice that lured crowds with evangelical zeal. "Come, enter our tent of unforgettable curiosities and unimaginable wonders. You will not believe the perverse imagination that God displays in these grotesque and wildly wondrous oddities of the human form. Witness sights that will mesmerize, enchant, haunt, and delight you. Stupendous sights you will cherish forever."

Inside his tent was Volta— an electric woman, Throaty— a sword swallower who also pounded long nails into his nostrils, Starbella— an Amazon snake temptress described as "a rambunctious rapscallion ruler of reptiles", and Little Pete The Prophet— who Stan called "The peerless peg-legged prolific prognosticator, short of stature but long on vision. He sees into the future and can tell you what your days ahead portend! You'll be astounded by the accuracy of his amazing predictions and prognostications! In fact, Little Pete knows you are about to see him. So, step right up, and buy your tickets before we're sold out! Hurry, hurry— all tickets first come, first serve."

The temptation of Stan Whootmoor's sideshow tent was irresistible to those who entered it excited and curious.

After the show, many departed deflated and disappointed.

Perhaps Stan oversold his show.

There was a crowd of 2,800 for the 4:00 p.m. performance, and, although the big top was over half full, Paul saw the 2,200 empty seats. He had arranged for Kirby Tooby, city bureaucrat/hustler, to be the honorary ringmaster welcoming the crowd. Barb Sigel suggested this to ensure he wouldn't hold up the circus for more money. Tooby took the bait.

One of Paul's duties for every performance was selecting twelve youngsters to get made-up in clown alley and participate in a clown magic show during intermission. He chose his kid crew and escorted them to and from clown alley, afraid they might get lost, eaten by a lion or trampled by an elephant. It all went smoothly— a dozen youngsters joined the magic show, and twelve were returned safely to their families.

The crowd loved the afternoon performance. Paul felt good. One down, three to go.

For the evening show, Paul walked Katherine, Eileen and Robbie to their third-row center ring seats. "You'll almost be able to touch the elephants," he told Robbie. The little boy squirmed, scared.

"You don't have to touch the elephants, honey," Katherine said.

"Smells like a jungle in here," Eileen said.

"You're going to see some incredible feats performed by jungle animals," Paul said. "You'll love the show, Mrs. Flynn, I guarantee it'll be the best circus you've ever seen."

"I hope I like what I see better than what I smell." She reached into her purse for a tissue and blew her nose. "It stinks to high heaven." She covered her nose and mouth with the tissue.

"I'll take Robbie just before intermission to be in the magic show," Paul said. He turned to Robbie. "You're going to meet some real circus clowns and get clown makeup. Then, you'll get to play with them! What do you think, Robbie?"

"I hate clowns."

"You only think you hate clowns. Wait until you meet them. They're funny." Paul remembered the hilarious sight of Blippo puking out of his car window.

"I hate clowns," the boy repeated.

Paul sat next to Katherine. Their hands clasped, and he felt secure. The lights went down.

In the big top entryway, mercenary Sean Kincaid watched his cousin Katherine place her head on Paul's shoulder. He walked and sat in the back bleachers across the ring to observe them.

Circus Ringmaster Billy Mansion announced, "Ladies and gentlemen, boys and girls, children of all ages, welcome to the fantastic, the fabulous 64th edition of Finnion, Barton & Powell Circus: Tops in Big Top Splendorama!"

During the opening circus parade, Paul was captivated by the sight of Augusta Plumbar's body in a skintight sparkling outfit. His greedy eyes ran a slalom course taking in all her curves, making pit stops at her beaming face, painted as pretty as a doll's, amplifying the electricity of her blue eyes. She smiled as naturally as she breathed. He forced himself to look away and squeezed Katherine's hand gently. She gave a forced smile.

The show began with the elephant act. A dozen elephants marched into the big top littering squirrel-sized turds in their wake. They stepped up on wooden platforms and rose on hind legs. They circled about. Their finale was forming a line as each elephant lifted its front legs, placing them on the back of the beast ahead. Only the lead elephant had all four legs on the ground. Applause thundered. Paul glanced at Katherine— her face had a vacant gaze. Eileen looked uncomfortable and breathed into her tissue. Robbie looked at the big top ceiling.

Next, was the bear act, then a high wire act, and the horse and dog act with Charlotte Plumbar showing her Rockettes' legs. She had passed her sexy legs genes on to Augusta.

Then, an acrobat and juggling act, followed by a clown act led by LuLu, "The Minister of Mirth!"

The last performance of the first half was two motor bikers zipping around inside a steel globe as it was raised high above the crowd.

Twenty minutes before intermission, Paul herded Robbie and eleven other children back to clown alley for makeup. Most of the children were skittish and afraid of the clowns, especially Shrimpy, a

Mexican dwarf clown who spoke little English. Paul did his best to ease their fears. "Don't worry kids, you'll have a great time."

"Yeah, great time," said Sparky, a bum-faced clown. "Loads of fun in clown alley. Nothing we like better than making up brats and babysitting." His delivery was deadpan, and he laughed. Paul wanted to smack the greasepaint off his face.

As the children entered the big top with the prat-falling clowns, Katherine and Eileen smiled when they saw Robbie in clown face. The children sat on the center ring as clowns performed magic tricks and told corny jokes. Some children liked it, Robbie and others watched with suspicion and terror.

Paul returned the kids alive safely to their parents, his duty done.

The second half opened with The Flying Perez Family trapeze act. The five-member Mexican fliers featured Juan Perez, an eleven-year-old who attempted a quadruple somersault. A triple somersault was the highlight of most trapeze acts, and although Juan didn't always achieve four rotations, he attempted the feat in every show.

That night, he achieved it, and the crowd went wild. Even Katherine, Eileen and Robbie were impressed and applauded and cheered. Paul smiled.

Rocket Baxfree, a daredevil shot out of a large canon, didn't get a rise out of Katherine or Eileen, but the bang of the cannon made Robbie jump.

Another acrobatic tumbling act received polite applause and served as an appetizer for the main event.

The star attraction was Chuck Gund, "The Wild Cat Wizard" who tamed a dozen ferocious felines— seven lions and five tigers, with a whip, chair, blank gun, and nerves of raw steel, and eyes projecting icy stares.

Gund made the big cats sit placidly on podiums, jump through rings— even one of fire, roll over and play dead. Chuck Gund was masterful in manipulating crowd emotions, and the roars of the wild cats stirred primal fear in all. Even Katherine appeared to enjoy his act.

The crowd cheered and applauded. As the wild beasts were corralled back into their cages, roustabouts dressed in bright red jumpsuits disassembled the cages as clowns attracted the crowd's attention.

Once the cage was cleared, the band struck up a fanfare, and all circus performers entered the tent again parading around the three rings as they waved to adoring fans.

Paul thought Augusta was waving at him.

After the show, Paul went to the ticket trailer. Cronk told him the first day's sales were good. "We grossed just over twelve grand. Made our nut, with a little extra. Good work, Paul." Cronk gave Paul a firm handshake. "You're off to a great start. Keep it up."

The show boss, Randy Trumbull, came into the trailer and told Paul his next assignment was Oneonta, New York. Paul had never heard of it, but then again, he had never heard of Haverhill.

And he had found true love there.

That night, Katherine and Paul went to O'Callahan's Pub with Colleen and Maggie, and held an Irish wake.

Raising pints of Guinness, Katherine proposed a toast: "Here's to the soon to be dearly departed Paul Driscoll, circus man, guilty of stealing this Irish lass's heart and leaving her. He's promised to God above, who he believes in from time to time, to return and reclaim said heart. In his travels, may he discover that what he's searching for is right here. Let's toast to his safe travels and rapid return." She choked back tears and drank, staring at Paul, who swallowed hard before taking his first sip.

"Katherine Flynn, come hug your kissing cousin," a deep voice said. All turned as a large man approached.

"Sean!" The man embraced Katherine.

"Christ, it's great to see you," Sean said, kissing her on the lips. She quickly turned away.

"Where have you been? I was worried."

"Don't worry about me." He released her. "I can handle myself. Introduce me to your friends."

"You remember Colleen and Maggie."

"Last time I saw you girls was at Katherine's wedding," Sean said.

"Wearing our sexy sea foam green bridesmaid dresses," Colleen said.

"The dresses outlasted my marriage," Katherine said.

"Those dresses will outlast a nuclear bomb," Maggie said.

"Very funny. They were fashionable at the time."

"Who's the young gentleman?" Sean asked.

"Paul Driscoll," Katherine said. "He works for the circus set up at the mall."

"I've never met anyone who works for a circus," Sean said, extending his hand. Paul tried matching his grip strength, but gave up. "Clown?"

"No. Marketing director. Nice to meet you," Paul said. The mercenary released his vise grip. "Katherine's told me a lot about you."

"All good, I'm sure." Sean smiled and looked Paul up and down. "Absolutely."

"So, you're the bastard who stole my beautiful cousin's heart."

"More like the other way around," Paul said.

"She does have undeniable charms," Sean said, turning to Katherine and winking. "Undeniable."

"We've got to get you a drink, Sean," Katherine said. "We're having a wake for Paul, he's leaving town soon."

"I thought you just got here."

"I have to go work in Oneonta, New York."

"Sounds exotic," Sean said, waving at a waitress. "Another round here, and shots of Jameson. Can't have a proper wake without Irish whiskey."

"Thanks," Paul said, "but I don't drink whiskey."

"You've got to drink when people are toasting you. Plus, I'm buying."

"Looks like I'm doing a shot."

Sean was not what Paul had imagined. He was expecting the mercenary to be physically fit. Sean was thirty or so, over six feet tall, muscular, but stocky, with a retreating hairline, pale blue eyes, and a dimple in his chin.

"Let's sit," Katherine said. "Sean can tell us about his adventures in Central America."

"Not much to tell. Sales were good. The countries are shit holes, and the people ignorant," Sean lit a cigarette. "I'd much rather hear about you and the family, Katherine. How is everybody?"

"Robbie's an angel, wait until you see how he's grown. Mom's fine, but she had to kick Tommy out— he's been drunk, angry, and destructive since dad died."

"When I get settled, I'll have a talk with him. What about your shitty ex?"

"He's the same. Working construction, chasing skirts. He hardly ever sees Robbie, and I never see his child support."

"I'll talk to him, too. I can be pretty persuasive." Sean smiled. "I'm in sales."

"Let's talk before you do anything," Katherine said. "I don't want trouble."

The drinks came, they toasted, and talked more. At eleven, Colleen and Maggie announced they were going home. Paul said he needed a good night's sleep, and Katherine asked him for a ride home.

"I can take you, Katherine," Sean said.

"No thanks. I only have a little time with Paul. I'll have lots of time with you."

"Affirmative."

"What'd you think of Sean?" Katherine asked Paul on the drive to the Shamrock.

"Nice guy. Not what I had imagined."

"What'd you imagine?"

"I don't know. Guess I was expecting a superhero type with rippling muscles."

"He used to be in great shape. You should have seen him when he went into the Marines."

"He's in good enough shape to be a mercenary."

"Please keep quiet about that."

"I will."

Paul and Katherine spent the night together trying to occupy the same body. For the first time, she spent the night by his side.

The next day, Paul arrived at the circus site to meet reporters. Although he'd sent press releases and invitations to the local media, no one came.

He walked the circus grounds behind the big top, where there were rows of trailers and RVs of circus performers. Young children practiced acrobatic tricks on mats as adults spoke to them in foreign languages. The children were fearless, thrusting their little bodies into the air, defying gravity to hold them back.

He walked by a tall young man with red hair smoking a cigarette outside a tent.

"You the new guy?" he asked.

"Yes. Paul Driscoll, marketing director," he said, extending his hand.

"You don't want to shake my hand," the man said, flicking his cigarette to the ground and stomping it. "I've been shoveling shit all morning. I'm Teddy Roskind, senior shovel technician in the elephant department, along with other shit jobs."

"Nice meeting you. How long you been with the show, Teddy?"

"Joined mid-season last year as a roustabout, and worked my way into the elephant department. My official title is bull handler. Sorry, I'm fresh out of business cards."

"How do you like it?"

"The job's shitty, pay's shitty, and some of the people are shitty. So, if you like shit, this is heaven." He smiled, Paul laughed.

"You paint a pretty picture."

"It's not so bad. A lot more interesting than working in a library."

"You were a librarian?"

"Yeah, in Gaffney, South Carolina. I'm a bookworm, so it seemed like a good job, and it was, for a while— then it got boring. The Dewey Decimal System isn't as interesting as you think. I saw a want ad for circus workers, and joined up."

"Sounds like my story."

"You were a librarian, too?"

"No, ad copywriter. I got fired, saw a circus ad, sent my resume, interviewed, and got hired."

"You running from girl problems, family problems, the law?"

"No."

"Then we might be the only two people here who aren't." Teddy lit a Marlboro. "I've heard lots of sad stories. Even the performers got drama."

"Really? I'd love to hear those stories. One of the reasons I joined was to become a better writer."

"What do you write?"

"Fiction, mostly."

"Don't fiction writers make up stories?"

"Yeah."

"Then why do you want to hear my stories about other people?"

"Grist for the mill. I want to absorb experiences and stories to feed my imagination. Plant seeds and see what blossoms."

"Guess that makes sense, as long as what I tell you doesn't end up in print and bite me in the ass. I don't need people thinking I'm a snitch."

"I won't write anything you tell me. Swear to God."

"Okay. You keep quiet, I'll tell you some stories." A short, muscular man in his late thirties wearing a baggy white tee shirt and blue jeans came out of the tent and stared at them.

"Goddamn it, Teddy, you going to do your fucking job, or stand around jawboning all day?"

"Just taking a smoke break, Joe."

"Hurry up, I could use some goddamn help." He went back inside the tent. Teddy took a long drag, and mashed the butt into the ground. "Charming guy, right? We'll talk some other time, Paul. Elephant bowels are calling, and until they start wearing diapers, I got a job to do. Ah, the glamour of show business."

"Can I buy you coffee later, Teddy? I'd love to talk more."

"I won't be free until two, and I won't have much time then."

"That's fine. We can meet here or at the mall food court."

"Let's do the mall. I need a break from this place."

Paul stepped into the tickets trailer, and Augusta smiled. She wore a blue tee, white shorts, and radiated beauty. She began making change for a customer as Cronk looked up from his table.

"We doing some business today?"

"I think so. Did any media people come by asking for me?"

"Nope. You expecting some?"

"Not sure. I sent out invitations, but no one confirmed."

"Invitations aren't the same as scheduling events," Cronk said. "Did you schedule an elephant race?"

"No."

"Elephant races are great for publicity. Didn't Barb Sigel teach you that?" She had mentioned elephant races, but Paul didn't think any media people would be interested.

"I think so."

"They're easy. Just have local media people challenge each other to an elephant race, and you'll get coverage. But you've got to schedule the race on opening day for maximum publicity in selling tickets."

"I'll try one in Oneonta."

"Do that. Oneonta's a podunk town, you'll need to do everything you can to scare up crowds. Let me know, and I'll schedule a race with Joe Parkett, the elephant boss."

"He a short guy with blond hair?"

"How'd you know that?"

"I was talking to Teddy, in the elephant department, and saw him."

"You're making the rounds, that's good. Get to know the people working the show. You're a first of May, so they'll keep you at arm's length, but eventually they'll warm up."

"What's 'first of May' mean?"

"A newbie. Doesn't matter when you joined, new people are always firsts of Mays. After a while, show people will treat you like family. Get to know them."

"I will. Thanks, Cronk. I've got to get back to the mall office." Cronk nodded and turned his attention to paperwork. Paul walked to the door.

"Hi, Paul," Augusta said.

"Hi." He glanced at her, afraid to look directly into her eyes for fear of losing himself. "Have a good show."

"You, too. Close the door so flies don't get in."

"Right."

"I don't want a fly talk show." She smiled, he blushed.

In the mall offices, Paul told Katherine, "I met a guy who works with elephants."

"That's nice."

"He said he'd tell me stories about the show. Said there's tons of them. People running from problems, and the law, you name it."

"And these are your people?"

"Until I come back to you."

"Um hmm."

"Do you want tickets for tonight's show?"

"No thanks, mom's having Sean over for dinner."

"I'll see you later, right?"

"Yes. Come over when you're done."

"I will, it's our last night together for a while."

"Don't remind me." She looked away. "Now, get out, I've got a lot to do."

"Joe's okay most of the time," Teddy said, taking a gulp of coffee, "but sometimes he can be a real prick. Long as I get my work done, he's cool."

Paul and Teddy sat in the food court— a young man in a cheap suit talking to one in jeans and a torn tee.

"What's his story?" Paul asked.

"Not sure. But I know Joe served some time for something. He doesn't talk about it, and I'm not about to ask, but he says he knows what it's like to live in a cage. He says if you've spent any time behind bars, you'll do anything to stay free."

"How'd he come to train elephants?"

"He joined the show in his early twenties as a roustie. He said he always liked elephants, and when he saw them up close, felt like he had a connection. Joe says their eyes are sad and knowing. He got to know the trainer, an older guy, who was a legend. Joe worked his way into the elephant department and learned all he could from the master. Joe says you've got to think like an elephant, and he does. It's amazing to see a seven-thousand-pound beast afraid of some guy who's barely a buck fifty in wet clothes. But Joe knows how to get those big bastards to obey."

"What happened to the old trainer?"

"He died in his late fifties. He'd been training Joe for a couple years, and one morning, he didn't show up. Joe bangs on his trailer door; there's no answer. He goes inside and the old guy's in bed, dead. People think he had a heart attack or something. Well, the show must go on, and Joe gets a promotion. To hear Joe tell it, he was long overdue to be elephant boss. He said the old trainer was coasting, he said he did all the work. Who knows? There's a rumor that some people think Joe killed him. They say there was bad blood between them, and they had a big fight the night he died. The rumor is Joe snuck in his trailer and snuffed him with a pillow. People on the show love to talk shit— but murder? I don't buy it."

"That's a great story."

"Story's right. There wasn't an investigation or anything. Look, Joe's got a healthy ego, but hell, he's very good. Not many people can get eighty tons of elephants to do tricks with nothing but big balls and a bull hook."

"Is Joe teaching you?"

"No. He's taught me how to feed them at one end, clean up at the other. But that's my fault because early on I told him I wanted to work in the big cat department. I didn't know it at the time, but I might as well have spit in his eye and cum in his coffee. Joe hates Chuck Gund and the cat department. He thinks they get all the attention and glory. Chuck Gund is definitely the star attraction."

"And Joe's jealous?"

"Hell, yeah. There's lots of jealousy on the show. Egos like you wouldn't believe. Every one of the performers thinks they're king or queen shit, and the rest of the acts are warm-ups."

"Even Chuck Gund?"

"Especially him. He has a huge ego and doesn't mingle much. He's in his own world."

"You want to work for him?"

"I'd give my right nut to learn from him. When I've tried talking to him, he nods, smiles, and moves on. But, I'll get to him. Eventually."

"Until then, you're stuck with Joe?"

"There are worse things. Lots worse. And if I don't get my ass back soon, I'll find out because Joe will shit-can me. I've got to get ready for the shows and striking camp. Thanks for the coffee."

"You're welcome. It's great getting to know you."

"Remember, what I tell you is strictly between us, right?"

"Right. By the way, Cronk said elephant races are good for publicity."

"They are, and they're also a ton of work for me. Where's your next town?"

"Oneonta."

"Where's that?"

"The middle of New York."

"See you there."

"Thanks, Teddy. Break a leg."

"Don't say that. It's bad luck."

"Then, take care."

"You, too."

The afternoon show had a half-full house. Paul wondered if an elephant race would have helped attendance.

As Joe led the parade of elephants in the opening spectacular, Paul imagined him poised over his sleeping boss, smothering his way to a promotion. He waved at Teddy walking alongside the elephants. He smiled, waved, then manned a shovel and cleaned up after his gray companions.

The crowd was enthusiastic, and the performers fed off its energy. Paul was mesmerized by the sight of Augusta in her sparkling costume highlighting her beautiful legs. She smiled as she gave the crowd a mechanical parade wave.

Paul felt as if she were greeting him alone.

The evening show was almost sold out. The performers and animals sensed the crowd's excitement and their performances were perfect. Even the ornery clowns were happy seeing the children Paul brought to clown alley.

"Great crowd," Sparky said to Paul. "Looks like we finally got a marketing director who knows what he's doing."

"Thanks." Paul felt guilty about wanting to punch him yesterday.

After the show, Cronk and Randy congratulated Paul in the ticket trailer.

"We're in the black both days," Randy said, smiling. "Keep up the great work."

"I'll do my best."

"You will," Cronk said. "I have faith in you."

"Thanks, Cronk." Paul's throat felt dry.

"You just missed Sean," Katherine said, from the front porch as Paul approached carrying a six pack.

"Sorry, I got here soon as I could."

"He said he had to meet someone. How were your shows?"

"The afternoon was about half full, but the night performance was almost sold out. Everyone's happy, the show made money both days."

"My hero," Katherine said, with a sad smile.

"Hello," Eileen said, stepping on the porch. "Katherine, you didn't tell me your friend was here."

"He just got here."

"I'll finish cleaning up and check on Robbie," she said. "Good to see you again, Paul. I heard you're leaving us soon."

"Tomorrow. But I'll be back at the end of the season."

"Be careful."

"Thanks. I will." She smiled, and returned inside. Paul opened two beers, handing one to Katherine. "I don't think she believes I'll be back."

"You can't blame her. My track record with men isn't great."

"But you know I'm coming back, right?"

"Yes."

"I will."

"Sean doesn't think you'll be back, either."

"Why? He doesn't even know me."

"I don't know. He didn't say. Maybe he thinks all men are shits, and since you're a member of the club—"

"He should talk— with his double life. God only knows what he's done for money."

"Sean's family, Paul."

"Right. And family can never do wrong."

"Are we going to spend our last night fighting?"

"This won't be our last night together. I'm coming back."

"Okay, our last night for a long while."

"We could go to my place."

"No. I want you to remember what you're giving up, and miss it dearly."

"I'll remember."

"You promise you're coming back, no matter what, circus man?" Katherine asked, teary-eyed.

"Absolutely. Nothing could keep me away. Not lions, tigers, bears, or even clowns."

"You damn well better, dink."

They talked late into the night. She begged him to quit the circus and begin their new life now. He said he was committed. They embraced, and he kissed her hard.

Their kiss left the salty taste of her tears on his lips.

As Paul drove down the street from Katherine's house, Sean watched from the front seat of his car. The mercenary lit a cigarette, opened a fresh beer, and drove to a bar.

Paul teared-up on his ride back to The Shamrock. He projected missing Katherine, while he missed his father. He felt lonely.

He was cut from his anchors, about to move out into open waters.

CHAPTER TWELVE
Oneonta

"Hormones trump intellect. Passion obliterates logic. Lust rapes love. Imagine what humans could accomplish without their sexual drives."

— *Paul Driscoll's notes, Oneonta, NY*

Paul's sleep was not restful. He woke early and left for Oneonta.

As he drove, he wondered if he should turn around and head back to Katherine. It was a romantic notion, one suited for a movie, but he knew he couldn't. Even if he returned, he'd have to earn a living. He was too poor and pragmatic to quit a sure thing for an uncertain one.

Finding a good job with ads and brochures about aluminum siding, hydraulic pumps, and industrial paint pigments would not be easy in a cosmopolitan city like Boston. His job hunting would take time, luck, and money to support himself. He'd have more of at least two of those at the end of his circus season, along with stories, maturity, and whatever wisdom the experiences taught.

He created a mantra for his journey: "You're born into this world alone, you'll leave alone. Get used to it. If you can be alone and be happy, the rest of life is gravy."

Growing up with five brothers and sisters and two parents, Paul was rarely alone. When family members didn't surround him, he surrounded himself with friends. He began his ad career in Akron, not far from home, and returned home most weekends. He was living alone with training wheels. If Paul was serious about being a writer, he had to learn how to be alone.

Writing is not a team sport.

He joined the circus to force himself into being alone and writing, not falling in love.

He imagined his ideal ad career, working and becoming the creative director of a large New York agency. He'd be famous for brilliant work, but pressures would take their toll and he'd have a nervous breakdown by age thirty.

Another gifted adman who went off the rails.

He'd retreat to a mountain cottage where he'd begin stage two of his life— writing novels and becoming one of the literary elite. He envisioned his books being read on college campuses worldwide.

Paul Driscoll would be another J.D. Salinger.

It was a good plan. All it required was talent, hard work, a nervous breakdown, and more hard work.

Perhaps he could fast forward his ad career. Maybe the circus experience would be rich enough for him to write his literary masterwork at a young age. That's what Hemingway, Fitzgerald, and Capote did.

Why not Driscoll?

He told himself he had made the right decision staying with the circus. The experience would be what he needed. He smiled with trembling lips as the radio began playing Eric Carmen's "All by Myself."

Paul turned up the volume, and sang along at the top of his voice.

❧

Oneonta is a small town nestled in the mountains of upstate New York. For his three-week stay, Paul rented a room at The MountainAire Motel, an L-shaped cinderblock structure with 22-units. Each room's door was painted red, flanked by a dark green wooden Adirondack chair. Inside was a bed, nightstand, phone, lamp, small desk and chair, open closet with a horizontal pole and hangers, and a bathroom with a small sink, toilet, and shower stall.

Paul met with ecstatic local media sales reps who fawned over him, until he explained the circus policy of buying media half-cash, half-trade with additional promotions. Then, their happy expressions fell.

Because there weren't many media outlets, his buy was simple. He got everything he asked for, including participation in an elephant race between a writer for the local paper and the star DJ of the top-rated station.

Paul felt in control.

He missed Katherine. Writing letters and calling didn't replace her company.

He practiced creative therapy— writing poems *("bitter years/ battered memories/ hiding, contemplating/ scared of scars/ warmed-over pains/ fresh fears/ festering from fallen tears…)*, short stories, jokes, and movie ideas. One plot involved an ambitious assistant elephant trainer who sneaks into his boss's trailer at night, suffocates him with a pillow and becomes the new head trainer— but the elephants know he's evil. As he leads them in a circus parade, one of the beasts knocks him down and stomps him to death.

Paul thought "Justice Underfoot" was a clever title.

He wrote whatever came to him, dumping raw emotions onto white pages.

Watching the typed pages pile up lifted his spirits.

One night, Paul craved human contact and went to a downtown bar called The Thorndike.

A dozen people were scattered throughout cigarette smoke and dim light. Paul sat at the bar drinking beer and smoking as he watched the New York Yankees playing his beloved Cleveland Indians, a team whose long-suffering fans were elated with a .500 season. Being an Indians fan taught one to have low expectations, and be thrilled if they were exceeded.

The Thorndike crowd was Yankee fans, used to winning. Paul cheered his team silently.

"You have a light?" a female voice asked. He turned to a woman in her late twenties with deep brown eyes, short blond hair, and a small mouth framed by pouty lips. She was attractive, with a pleasant smile and breasts dressed for grabbing eyeballs.

"Sure," Paul said, flipping open his Zippo. She exhaled seductively.

"That's heavenly. I've been trying to quit for two weeks."

"You're doing a lousy job," he said, smiling.

"This is my first cigarette all day. You ever tried quitting?"

"No. I like smoking."

"I love it. Mind if I join you?"

"No. Can I buy you a drink?"

"Thought you'd never ask." She smiled, and sat.

Her name was Betsy Darlene Carpstin and her friends called her "B.D." She was a Oneonta native and the assistant manager of the local department store. She was mesmerized by Paul and his circus job. He assured her it was not as glamorous as it sounded. "It's pretty lonely."

"Don't you meet lots of fascinating people? Circus people must be incredibly interesting."

"I don't spend much time with them. My job's promoting the show before it gets to town, then doing publicity while it's there."

"It has to be more interesting than working in a department store."

"I guess so," Paul said, feeling like a celebrity. They talked over many beers and cigarettes. He told her about Katherine and his quest to find himself on the road, and how he'd capture the soul of America and write about it in books and movies. She said she'd never met a real writer before.

Paul liked hearing "real writer."

She told him he was unlike any man she'd ever met— he had dreams and ambition. She said most men she knew were small thinkers. "Their world vision goes as far as the city limits. They're not worldly like you."

Paul found her eyes and smile captivating.

B.D. said she'd love to read his writing. Paul invited her to his place to read some work, and she accepted. He settled the bar tab, bought a six-pack, and offered to drive. She said she'd drive herself.

"I'm in room eight," he said. "Between rooms seven and nine."

"Very funny, smartass. See you there."

On his drive, Paul imagined Katherine was probably going to bars with friends, and he certainly wouldn't fault her if she talked to guys. Talking's what people do.

He arrived at his motel, placed the six cans of Genesee in the bathroom sink and covered them with ice. There was a knock.

"Hello, again," B.D. said.

He got two beers, opened one, and handed it to her. She sat on the edge of the bed as he opened his beer and sat at the desk looking through a file folder.

He shared a few love poems and humorous short stories. As B.D. read, he sipped his beer and pretended to leaf through a magazine.

He glanced at her and was proud when she laughed, smiled, or uttered "oh" or "hmm" or "ooh." He took these gestures as thunderous applause, standing ovations; roses tossed to the altar of his literary prowess.

"You're a really good writer, Paul," she said. "I mean really, really, really good!"

"Thanks. I appreciate that." He blushed. "Who are some of your favorite authors?"

"I haven't read much since high school. I read all those stupid books they make you read, like 'Catcher in The Rye' and 'Great Expectations' and stupid Shakespeare crap— I'm not even sure that's English."

"Oh." Paul took little pride knowing his new fan thought he was a better writer than Salinger, Dickens, and Shakespeare.

"But I know talent, and you've got it. Let's celebrate." B.D. opened her purse and took out a small black plastic Kodak film canister and rectangular vanity mirror.

"What's that?"

"Some fine nose candy." She laid the mirror on the desk, opened the canister and carefully distributed a small pile of fine white powder on the mirror surface. She reached into her wallet. "We'll need cash and credit to make this purchase," she giggled, as she took out a five-dollar bill and laid it and a credit card by the mirror. She diced the powder with quick vertical chops of the card, then took the mound and cut it in half, carefully shaping each small hill into a thin line of white powder. "You're going to love this," she said, licking her lips. "You've done coke before, right?"

"Not really." Paul's experience with drugs was limited. The few times he smoked pot, voices echoed, and his paranoia fed on itself making the experience awful. Once, at a concert, he smoked grass in the balcony and became convinced the drummer was planning to kill him by throwing his drumsticks and impaling Paul's heart. Because of his reaction to marijuana, he abstained from going up the drug food chain.

Paul stuck with beer. It was a familiar, friendly buzz and was easy to regulate.

"You've never done coke?"

"No. What's it like?"

"You are going to l-o-v-e this. Coke gives you a burst of energy and hyper-awareness. It makes everything sharper, and makes you smarter. Plus, it's dynamite for sex. Coke intensifies everything. It's fantastic."

Paul had stopped listening after the word sex. Coke was "dynamite for sex"— why would she mention that?

Everything about their evening was almost an engraved invitation for sex. Her fascination with him and her deep admiration for his writing. And now, enticing him with cocaine.

If they did end up in bed together, what could he do? He was drunk and under the influence of a drug he'd never experienced before, so it wouldn't be his fault if the coke made him have sex.

Paul anticipated his fall from grace and was cobbling together a defense of his future sin. Rationalization was a skill and art. He was master of both.

"You're the coke virgin, you go first," she said, handing him the rolled-up five.

"Ladies first," he said, passing the paper tube back.

"Don't have to ask me twice." She took the rolled bill into her hand, bent over, and quickly inhaled a line. She raised her head. "Ummm, that's primo shit. Now for dessert." She traced her finger over the powder residue on the mirror, and ran her finger over her inside lower lip. "Delicious," she cooed. She handed the rolled-up bill to Paul. "Come in. The snow's fine."

"Okay." He did what she did: bending, inhaling, and acting ecstatic. He mopped the powder residue with a finger and rubbed the inside of his lower lip. It tasted foul. He drank beer to erase the bitter taste, waiting for pink dragons or green snakes to appear.

Within minutes, they were on his bed, their tongues in a spirited shoving match as their hands explored each other. Paul was erect. The coke, or the idea of it, had made him horny.

As did oxygen.

He began trying to unbuckle her jeans. "Ummm," she said.

Paul continued working the denim, and her hands grabbed his. "No. Don't!" He stopped. "Let's just kiss."

He exhaled his sexual frustration. Maybe her coke needed more time to get her engine revving like his.

He began kissing, and she kissed back. Hard. Her tongue was a battering ram— poking, darting like a dental probe. Paul's hands found their way to her bra clasp, and fumbled with it like a nervous safe cracker. "Don't," she said. "Let's just kiss."

He did as asked, his hands retreating to reconsider a battle strategy.

Her tongue calmed down. They kissed passionately. It reminded him of Katherine. He felt guilty, but his libido told his brain he was high and not responsible for his actions.

Paul strategized options for advancing the runner and tried second base again.

She held him to first.

He tried going for third.

She threw him out.

He was stranded on first base, with nowhere to go. Then she called the game. "I've got to go." She disengaged herself, sat on the edge of the bed, and took a deep breath, her forehead slick with perspiration.

"Stay, it's early."

"If I stay, I may do something I'll regret later."

"It's okay."

"No, it isn't. I keep thinking about those beautiful poems you wrote your girlfriend. It's obvious you're in love, and I don't want to be the other woman."

"We have an open relationship," he lied. Cocaine was quick for the mind and tongue.

"I don't want to be part of an open relationship. I've been the other woman, and I know it's nothing but trouble. Plus, I have to get up early and open the store."

"You could spend the night." He reached for her, but she stood and stepped away.

"I've got to go. It's been a fun night, and I'm really glad we met, Paul." She adjusted her clothes as he sat on the edge of the bed. She bent over and kissed his cheek.

"Finish your beer, we'll just talk." He thought with more time and liquid encouragement, she'd reconsider being the other woman.

"No. I'll see you around; I'm sure," she said. She put her coke and accessories back in her purse, and left. He heard her car start and drive away.

Paul was wired and hard. He opened his orange luggage and found a centerfold who didn't mind being the other woman.

The next morning, the phone rang, startling Paul out of a dream where he was stranded on a boat in the middle of the ocean. "Hello?"

"I didn't wake you, circus man, did I?" Katherine asked.

"No. Just getting up."

"What have you been up to?"

"Working my circus magic, and missing you."

"I miss you, too." As they talked, the pieces of the previous night fell into place as Paul's guilt hung heavy. He told Katherine about his Oneonta activities, leaving out B.D., her coke, and making out.

Maintaining a long-distance relationship was going to be harder than he thought. He'd have to do better remaining faithful.

Or become better at living without a conscience.

Paul visited The Thorndike four more times during his Oneonta stay. Although he told himself he was not looking for B.D., he was disappointed she wasn't there.

He visited the department store where she worked and saw her behind the cosmetics counter. "Hi, B.D.," he said.

"Hey." She looked up from the register, confused, then aware. "Paul, right?" She smiled. "The circus guy."

"Right. How are you?"

"Good. What are you doing here? Buying a present for your girlfriend?"

"No, I wanted to see you."

"Why?"

"I thought maybe we could get together again."

"I don't think so. I'm back with my old boyfriend, Bobby—"

"Oh."

"Besides, you have your girlfriend, right?"

"Yes. I thought we'd just have a drink and talk."

"No, thanks. You're a nice guy and I don't want to get you in trouble. Bobby's real jealous."

"I see."

"Your girlfriend probably wouldn't like it either. But it's good seeing you again, Paul. Good luck."

"Thanks," Paul said, feeling foolish. "The circus is coming next week; I've got passes if you want to go."

"Thanks, but Bobby doesn't like animals. I enjoyed getting to know you. Keep writing. You're really good."

"Thanks, I'll do that. Take care, B.D."

"Bye, Paul."

He left the department store with no purchase.

On opening day, the Oneonta elephant race attracted a good crowd in an open field behind the midway. Jerry "Scooter" Stockton, the town's most popular DJ, was pitted against the newspaper's feature writer, Gary Marple. The station did a remote broadcast, and the paper had a photographer.

The combatants shook hands and mounted their elephants. Teddy Roskind stood by Sophie who carried Scooter, and Joe Parkett managed Maxie, carrying Marple.

Each elephant man had a bull hook to encourage and manage his beast, and each jockey was instructed to hold onto the reins and remain calm. Fifty yards from the starting line, a finish line was set up where Cronk, acting as the starter, held a blank gun. He shouted his countdown, fired a shot in the air, and each elephant was prodded to run. The crowd cheered.

Scooter was startled and tried standing up. He dropped his reins, slid off his elephant, and fell. When he tried breaking his fall, a sickening crack sounded, and he shouted in pain. The remote radio microphone broadcast his agony live. Marple trotted past the finish line on his elephant as Teddy wrangled Scooter's bareback elephant until it stopped.

People screamed, Scooter wailed, Cronk and Paul ran to the DJ.

"Don't touch him," Cronk shouted. "Paul, make sure no one tries to move him. I'll call an ambulance."

"Okay," Paul said. The DJ, who had been so cocksure on the air before the race, was sobbing in misery.

"I think I broke my goddamn arm and leg," he said, grimacing. "I'm going to sue the hell out of you fuckers." Paul was worried.

"We're calling an ambulance," Paul said. "Hold tight." He remembered that "hold tight" was the explicit instruction the DJ was given when he mounted his elephant.

"Where the hell can I go with a busted arm and leg?" Scooter asked.

As the ambulance left the circus grounds, Cronk put his arm around Paul. "Wasn't your fault. That was a freak accident. I've never seen anything like it."

"The DJ said he was going to sue us."

"Don't worry," Cronk said, with a laugh. "There's a reason we make riders sign waivers before they get on their elephant. He doesn't have a case—we're not responsible for his stupidity. He probably just broke a couple of bones and learned a lesson to obey instructions. We should get some great publicity, though. This will make big news."

Publicity. Paul felt better.

The opening day's crowds were light. Even with Paul's media blitz, both shows were barely half-full.

On the show, the accident was the hot topic. Scooter had a broken arm and a severely sprained ankle. The DJ would be in a cast and on crutches for a long time, but neither condition would affect sitting and blabbing into a microphone.

Paul invited Teddy to join him for drinks after the evening performance, his treat. The elephant man agreed.

"Any news?" Paul asked, on the drive to The Thorndike.

"I had to stop an elephant from stomping a dumbass disc jockey."

"I'll carry that scene to my death bed."

"Speaking of death," Teddy said, "Rocket Baxfree tried to off himself a week ago."

"The cannon guy? Why?"

"Because he's a nut. The moody bastard's always in the dumps. I heard he tries killing himself at least once every season."

"Really?"

"Yeah. Probably just wants attention. This time, he overdosed on sleeping pills. He wrote a suicide note and taped it on his cannon after the opening night show in Utica. A worker trying to screw a townie saw the note and took it to Cronk. They ran to Rocket's trailer and banged on the door. There was no answer, so the roustie busted it down. Cronk drove Rocket to the hospital and got his stomach pumped."

"Holy shit."

"The docs wanted to keep him under psychiatric observation for a couple days, but Cronk told them it was an accident. You know Cronk— the show must go on. Rocket played along. No one mentioned the suicide note. Cronk brought him back and chewed his ass out."

"Is he okay? He still depressed?"

"He's Rocket Baxfree— who the hell knows? I think the only time he's happy is the couple seconds after he's shot from the cannon— when he's in the air, knowing he might die."

"A depressed daredevil— sounds like a great story."

"And not one you're telling. Everything I say stays secret."

"Right." They arrived at The Thorndike and sat at the bar.

"Had your fill of elephant races?" Teddy asked.

"We'll see how our press is tomorrow. We might get bigger houses."

"That asshole DJ could have been killed. A guy slips at the wrong time; an elephant could take him out instantly."

"He should have obeyed you and held on to the reins."

"Yeah, but he didn't."

"Cronk said it was a freak accident."

"It was."

"You don't like elephant races, do you?"

"They're a pain in my ass."

"But if they get good publicity, they could mean bigger crowds."

"Anything for the show, right?"

"Right."

"I'm going to start calling you Cronk junior," Teddy said.

"Do you know much about Cronk's granddaughter, Augusta?"

"The ice queen?"

"Ice queen?"

"That's what guys on the show call her. She's a prime piece of ass, and she knows it, but she always has her nose stuck up in the air."

"She seems nice."

"Good luck getting anywhere with her. I heard she's dating the trombone player in the band." Paul was disappointed to learn she was in a relationship, not that he wanted one— he had Katherine, but he liked to imagine it might be possible to see someone else if life on the road became unbearable. He wanted to believe Augusta could be his circus woman, the rainbow that appeared every three weeks to brighten his gray days alone.

"Any other news?" Paul asked.

"Shrimpy got in some trouble with the law."

"The dwarf clown?"

"Yeah. The little perv got caught under the bleachers looking up dresses. Some lady saw his pumpkin head and screamed. Her husband was a councilman, and got the little bastard arrested.

Shrimpy's Mexican and doesn't speak a word of English, so Cronk had to bail him out. You don't need to talk when Cronk's your mouthpiece. He got the woman to dismiss charges, and promised Shrimpy would never come to town again. Cronk's a smooth mother, but one of these days Shrimpy's going to do some shit he can't get out of."

"That's another great story."

"Keep it to yourself."

"Done."

The next day's Oneonta newspaper had front page pictures of the elephant race. In one, both men were side by side on their elephants. In the next, Scooter was midair heading for the ground. In the final picture, Scooter was on a gurney being loaded into an ambulance. The large headline over the pictures read, "GIDDY-WHOOPS!"

Scooter's radio station played Henry Mancini's "Baby Elephant Walk" every hour in honor of its fallen hero. His fellow DJs gave "The Scoots" a good ribbing on air.

"Obviously, Scooter's a disc jockey, not an elephant jockey," said afternoon DJ Kip "Mad Dog" Murley.

Unfortunately, all the press did not create larger crowds. None of the shows made their nuts. Paul was sad, but no one blamed him.

"I don't know why we bother with piss-ant podunk towns like Oneonta," Cronk told Paul, as he tallied ticket sales. "There's hardly enough population here to make it worthwhile. You gave it a good go, Paul. Keep doing your best, things will turn around. Your next town will be better."

"Think I should try another elephant race?"

"Can't hurt," Cronk said. "Unless you're a stupid DJ."

CHAPTER THIRTEEN
Bluefield

"Your own mind is the scariest place in the universe."
— *Paul Driscoll's notes, Greenwood, MS*

Paul's next town was Bluefield, West Virginia, in the heart of coal country. Thick green forests lined the mountainous terrain, hoisting them to the sky. Generations of West Virginians had blasted and carved their way into these mountains, scraping out black rocks for money.

The United States had an energy tapeworm, and West Virginians broke their backs mining coal to keep it satisfied.

Paul sequestered himself in a motel called The Clairmont, owned and operated by an Indian couple. The motel office had a musk of curry and exotic spices, pungent aromas alien to Paul's Midwestern nose.

His windowless room contained furniture constructed of thick wood planks in utilitarian designs, with cushions made of rough-hewn plaid fabrics. One wall had a picturesque landscape of a South Pacific beach sunset, an odd juxtaposition to the mountains visible outside the door.

Paul placed his typewriter on the desk facing the setting sun wall, unpacked his clothes and toiletries, and placed his orange suitcase in the closet.

He was ready to work.

On his first night, he went to a restaurant called The Bluefielder. The waitress was a teen with a pale complexion, short strawberry blond hair, and ears leaning away from her skull, as if trying to escape. She took Paul's order of meatloaf.

"You're not from 'round here, are you?" she asked, in a thick West Virginia twang.

"No, I'm from Ohio. How'd you know?"

"You talk funny. You move here?"

"I'm here on business."

"Coal business?"

"Circus business."

"You're pulling my leg," she said, smiling.

"Seriously, there's a circus coming to town and I'm the marketing director."

"The what?"

"The advance man."

"What's that?"

"I'm in charge of promoting the circus."

"Isn't that something? A circus coming to Bluefield." The waitress put her Bic pen into her uniform pocket. "Does your circus have elephants, lions, and the like?"

"Yes. Elephants, lions, tigers, clowns, daredevils, everything. It's called Finnion, Barton & Powell Circus— tops in big top splendorama!"

"Splendorama, huh? Sounds special."

"It's a great circus. The best. I hope you'll come."

"I will. Not much to do in Bluefield, and your circus sure sounds like something to do."

"It is."

She smiled and left. He looked over his Bluefield master plan and wondered if business here would be better than Oneonta. Although neither city had a population as large as Haverhill, Paul wanted to make his mark.

He looked around the restaurant and guessed everyone was local. The people looked weathered from rough lives spent gouging livings out of rocks. Most patrons were seniors with deeply-lined faces forming perpetual scowls.

A lanky old man with a stubble of gray beard wearing faded jeans, a blue flannel shirt, and a John Deere cap walked across the restaurant.

"You looking for something?" he asked Paul.

"No."

"Then why you been gawking at me and everyone else? You a lawman? Government? I know damn sure you ain't from these parts, so what's your business?"

"I'm promoting a circus coming to town."

"What circus?"

"Finnion, Barton & Powell Circus. See?" Paul pointed to the colorful logo on the cover of his master plan binder.

"I ain't heard nothing about a circus coming."

"You will. In a week or so, you'll be hearing all about it on the radio and in the paper."

"I guess I believe you," the old man said, rubbing his chin with a muscular, veiny hand with long, dirty fingernails. "But let me give you some advice. Mind your own business. Don't go poking your nose where it don't belong, staring at people like they're monkeys in the zoo."

"Sorry, I didn't realize I was staring."

"You were, and I don't appreciate strangers looking me up and down. I making myself clear?"

"Yeah. I mean, yes. Sir."

"You go about your business, and I'll go about mine."

"Yes, sir."

"Good." The old man walked to the register, paid his check, and left in an ancient red Ford pickup. Paul was embarrassed he'd been caught observing people. His waitress brought his order. The meatloaf was mediocre, the green beans salty, and the runny mashed potatoes hid beneath a puddle of greasy brown gravy.

It was a plate of disappointment.

He ate what he could, not wanting any more trouble.

That night, Paul went to a small bar called The Mineshaft. A half-dozen cars and four motorcycles were parked out front.

When he walked inside, every head turned to see who had brought street light into their dark, smoky place. Paul sat at the bar leaving an open stool between himself and two young men wearing work shirts, jeans, and dirty baseball caps. "What'd you want?" the bartender asked.

"Do you have Stroh's?"

"No. We don't have fancy beers." Paul noticed the men next to him were drinking Budweiser.

"I'll have a Bud." The bartender nodded, reached into a cooler, pulled out a bottle, opened it, and set it down. Paul gave him a five-dollar bill, got change, and lit a cigarette. The two men seated to his left stared at him. "Hi," Paul said. They nodded acknowledgment they'd heard him and turned their attention back to their conversation.

Paul drank, being careful not to stare at anyone. He watched the

Cincinnati Reds game on TV. Across the bar, two middle-aged men stood and faced-off.

"Who you callin' chickenshit, motherfucker?" said a short, beefy man.

"I ain't callin' no one chickenshit," said a tall, skinny man.

"Hell, you ain't."

"Roy and Jay are at it again," the man closest to Paul said to his friend. The men smiled.

"I fought in 'Nam," the short man said, "and I ain't about to take shit from you." He threw a punch that glanced off the tall man's head. People pounced off barstools and formed a semi-circle around the men as they wrestled trading blows.

"Jesus Christ," said the bartender, reaching beneath the bar and grabbing a Louisville Slugger. He slammed it on a beer cooler. Everyone turned to the loud clang. "I'll clear this bar if you goddamn rednecks don't settle down! I ain't losin' my liquor license 'cause of you assholes."

The two fighting men disengaged and returned to their barstools. People dispersed and moseyed back to their seats. Paul was the only person who hadn't reacted to the fight. One of the men who'd been sitting by him stopped and looked at Paul. "What the fuck you looking at, boy?" he asked.

"Nothing," Paul said.

"Best not be, or I'll rip your fucking head off— boy!" He shoved his shoulder into him and walked back to his stool. Paul gulped his beer and left a dollar tip.

He went to a convenience store, bought a twelve-pack of Stroh's, and returned to his motel.

Paul spent the rest of his Bluefield nights secluded in his room with his beautiful beach at sunset view.

He worked his master plan and learned the Bluefield circus site location was too small to accommodate parking. Paul called Barb.

"You're shitting me," she said. "There's no parking?"

"The bookers had to know the site was too tight for parking."

"Unbelievable. I'll make sure someone gets ripped a new asshole."

Later that day, she called back. "You'll have to improvise, Paul."

"What do you mean?"

"Find a place close by where people can park, and make arrangements for transportation to the circus site."

"Arrangements?"

"Hire some buses and shuttle them."

"Buses?"

"Yes, buses, Paul. But don't blow your budget. It's summer vacation, rent school buses. Use tickets for trade. But not too many—we can't afford to flood the market with comps. We need big shows in Bluefield. Sales have been soft." Paul felt a knot tighten in his stomach.

"I'll do my best, but I didn't book a circus without parking."

"I know that. The bookers fucked up. Be creative, fix it."

"I'll try."

"Trying isn't good enough."

"All right, Barb," Paul said, getting agitated.

"Keep me posted."

She hung up, and he wondered if any new assholes had been ripped. He suspected not. It seemed once a show was booked, it was up to the marketing directors to sell it— no matter what.

Paul's steady diet of fast food and greasy spoon fare took its toll on his digestive system. He spent a lot of time on the toilet.

His evenings were spent drinking beer and writing letters, short stories, and poems. He iced his beer in the bathroom sink.

The more beer he drank, the higher his opinion of his writing. The alcohol tore down inhibitions and allowed his creativity to explore beyond consciousness. Much of what he discovered was sadness.

He called Katherine and wrote her long love letters. He missed her smile, laugh, and embrace.

Paul Driscoll was a social creature who began talking to himself. When he got bored with the sound of his voice, he spoke in accents. He developed a Liverpudlian accent, like one of The Beatles.

"Ringo, don't eat me cheese and crackers," he'd say in a lyrical lilt.

"Need more bass, Paul. A bit more bottom end, mate."

"George, be a love and pass me a rum and Coke."

"Who was the sexy bird you were with, John?"

In restaurants, when his check arrived, he'd glance at it and impersonate Desi Arnaz from "I Love Lucy".

"Too 'spensive, Lucy," Paul said, to no one.

After he'd been drinking, he talked to himself in his bathroom mirror in a Southern baritone.

"What the hell you lookin' at, boy? I oughta kick your ass just for the hell of it. Think I won't? Goddammit, I swear to God I will. You best believe I'll whip your sorry ass!"

These imaginary encounters and conversations kept him sane.

One Saturday, he took a coal mine tour. The guide was a short, stocky man with a plump, well-weathered face. He wore a miner's cap with light affixed, and told the history of West Virginia coal mining, dating back to 1742.

He was a sixth-generation miner and was proud only one of his family members had lost his life mining.

"Six generations and one dead is something not many folks around here can say," he said, with a sad smile.

A dozen tourists followed him into a decommissioned mine. Each person laid down on a flatbed contraption set on tracks and was pulled deep into the tight confines of a coal mine shaft.

Paul took his ride noticing the shaft walls were tight, slick with dripping moisture. He felt claustrophobic. After a short journey, he was delivered to an open area and stood.

The tour guide explained when miners tried to unionize, the mine bosses hired goon squads to fight them. Blood mixed with coal dust, but, in 1902, unions secured a foothold and working conditions improved.

"But," the guide said, "coal mining's still awful dangerous. Death's your constant shadow."

Paul concluded West Virginians were like their mountains— but rather than reserves of coal, they had veins of sorrowful anger buried within.

"Paul, how are you doing?" a nervous voice asked over the phone one morning.

"Hi, Barb. I'm good. How about you?"

"Not too good. I thought I'd come see you Thursday, but I can't. Something's come up."

"Oh," Paul said, relieved.

"My grandfather died and I have to go to the funeral."

"Sorry to hear that."

"He was sixty-six, had a good life."

"Was he sick?"

"Had some nasal trouble, but died of a heart attack."

"I'm sorry."

"Me, too. I was looking forward to seeing you."

"That's too bad," Paul said, smiling.

"But everything's good? You've got the parking under control?"

"Yes, we're good." Barb had called him every hour last week until he had secured parking at a closed drive-in theater near the circus site and arranged for school buses to shuttle people. She pushed him to negotiate hard. Although he asked, he did not get the ridiculous price Barb wanted. But, she reluctantly blessed the deal.

"Keep working your master plan," she said.

"I will."

"We need great dates."

"I'm working on it. How's Brian doing?"

"Great, according to him. I don't know."

"His best promotion is for himself."

"You're my stud, Paul. My star stud student."

"Thanks."

"I wish I didn't have to go to this stupid funeral."

"Family's important."

"I know, but I miss seeing you." There was a long silence. Paul stared at the sunset wall and imagined walking the beach as Barb chased after him. "I won't miss your next town, I promise."

"I'll do my best here."

"I know you will— my stud." He imagined his beach scene and running into the ocean, swimming in hopes of sharks eating him.

"Thanks, Barb."

When Carl and Wanda Foley came to town, they invited Paul to their trailer for dinner. He was happy to go.

The Foleys were staying at an RV park on the outskirts of Bluefield. Paul brought a twelve-pack and a bottle of Riunite red wine. When he pulled up, Carl was bare-chested with a cigarette drooping from his lips. He wore jean cut-offs and flip-flops as he tended a charcoal grill.

"Hey, Paul." Carl stopped fanning the coals with a newspaper.

"I brought some beer and wine."

"Thanks, but we're liquor people. But, you can't ever have too much." Carl smiled. "Wanda!" he shouted, to the trailer. "We got company! Come say hello, and bring me another drink."

"I hear you! I'm not deaf," Wanda's agitated voice came from the trailer. "Be out in a minute."

"She's lying," Carl said, in a confidential tone. "She's deaf as a doornail." Paul opened a beer. From Carl's unstable posture, Paul suspected he was drunk. The trailer door opened, and Wanda came out with a tumbler of brown liquid in one hand, and a glass of clear liquid in the other.

"Hi, Paul," she said, handing Carl the brown liquor. "Here's your drink, cranky butt."

"I ain't cranky."

"Shouting at your wife when there's company ain't exactly polite."

"Jesus, Mary, and Joseph, I wasn't shouting."

"How you doing, Paul?" Wanda asked.

"Good."

"Beautiful country," Carl said.

"Yes, but the people aren't too friendly."

"West Virginians can be hard," Carl said.

"You had trouble?" Wanda asked.

"A little, but I've mostly been keeping to myself."

"Smart," Carl said. "Few years back, one of our guys got the shit kicked out of him by hillbillies. Poor guy tried picking up the wrong girl in a bar and locals nearly killed the son of a bitch." Paul thought of Brian's experience in Bridgeport with the young waitress's brother.

"I didn't want to take chances," Paul said, "so I've kept to myself."

"Better safe than sorry," Wanda said, taking a long drink of vodka.

"Pace yourself, Wanda," Carl said.

"You should talk, mister guzzles."

"For Chrissake, I'm not trying to be your father here. I'm just saying slow down so you can enjoy the whole evening."

"Good thing you're not trying to be my father, because you're not half the man he was. And don't worry— I can handle myself fine without any goddamn advice from Mr. Carl Foley." She fumbled for her cigarette pack in her pants, and lit one.

"Whatever you say," Carl said, in a tired voice. "I'll leave you be since you know every goddamn thing." He drank his whiskey.

"Goddamn right you will," she said, exhaling smoke. She drained her glass and stumbled back into the trailer. Paul began chugging his beer. He had some catching up to do.

Carl cooked sirloin steaks, and Wanda tossed a salad of iceberg lettuce with thick chunks of cucumbers and tomatoes doused in Kraft Italian dressing. A loaf of soft Italian bread and a brick of cold hard butter was passed around. They ate at the small kitchen table inside the cluttered trailer. Wanda was calm, and Carl mellow as he sipped Jack Daniel's. Paul drank his Stroh's.

"We looking at some big dates here, Paul?" Carl asked, with a cud of half-chewed steak in his mouth.

"I think so. There aren't many people around here, though."

"That's what you think," Wanda said, in a slight slur. "There's hillbillies all over. They drink moonshine and fuck like jack rabbits. You get the word out, Paul, and watch these mountains come to life."

"I'm getting the word out everywhere."

"We'll paper the shit out of the town," Carl said, shoveling another hunk of meat into his mouth. "If it ain't moving, we'll paper it." Carl winked at Paul and smiled.

After dinner, Wanda served vanilla ice cream drizzled with canned Hershey's syrup. They went outside, sat in frayed lawn chairs, and watched the sun set.

"The show needs some goddamn business," Carl said.

"It's the bookers," Wanda said. "They're booking any shithole."

"The site they booked here doesn't even have parking," Paul said.

"What?" Carl asked.

"The site's too small for parking. I made parking arrangements at a drive-in down the road for school buses to shuttle people."

"That's the most asinine thing I ever heard," Wanda said. "A circus lot with no parking. Those booking bastards should be shot, castrated, hung, then shot again."

"That's too good for them. Un-fuckin-believable," Carl said. "We're paying a drive-in and buses for hauling people to and from the show?"

"Yes." Paul finished his beer and opened another.

"Jesus H. Christ. Next we'll be paying to wipe their goddamn asses." Carl gave himself a generous pour of Jack, and Wanda refreshed her Smirnoff. "Business is in the shitter and now there's extra expenses. Why don't they fire those booking assholes?"

"You know goddamn well why," Wanda said. "Because they're related to Randy Trumble, king of the circus. They can do whatever they goddamn want— including running this goddamn show into the goddamn ground!"

185

"You're talking out of school," Carl said. "You don't know they're related."

"I don't know for sure, but they must have something on Randy or why would he tolerate them?"

"I don't know. But you shouldn't start rumors."

"Don't tell me what I should and shouldn't do, Carl. I come from circus; I know circus. If anyone has a goddamn right to talk circus, it's me."

"You may know circus, but you don't know for a fact the shit you're spewing in front of this youngster. Keep a lid on it, unless you know for certain."

"Everyone knows those bookers are shit-heads, and I'm going to speak my piece. Don't worry about protecting Paul's virgin ears— he's a man, Carl, he can take it."

"Jesus Christ, Wanda, you're missing my whole goddamn point."

"Which is what, Carl? That I should shut the fuck up and be bullied by a goddamn roustabout?"

"No. That you shouldn't say shit you don't know to be a hundred percent true."

"Nothing's a hundred percent true."

"The sun rises in the east, and sets in the west. That's a hundred percent true."

"Not if your compass broke."

"What the hell does that mean?"

"It means east and west are only directions if a compass says so."

"Oh, for Chrissake, you're drunk and talking bullshit." Carl looked disgusted and lit a cigarette.

"I'm drunk?! What time this morning did you start drinking, mister temperance?"

"Enough, Wanda, this conversation's getting old. Let's talk about something pleasant."

The night wore on with Carl and Wanda ranting at one another like a scene out of "Who's Afraid of Virginia Woolf". Paul finished eight beers and told his hosts he had to leave.

He left the bottle of Riunite. Carl told him to take his remaining beers.

"They'll keep," Carl said. "And don't worry, Paulie— we'll paper the shit out of this town so you have some good dates."

"Goodbye, Paulie wallie doodle," Wanda slurred, waving from the trailer door as Paul walked to his car.

"You can spend the night here if you like," Carl shouted. "Got plenty of room."

"No thanks." He didn't want to hear what Foley pillow talk sounded like.

On his show dates, Paul had the added duty of directing traffic.

He stood in front of the drive-in and held-up traffic as the school buses loaded with patrons made the half-mile journey up the mountainside to the circus site. As the sun beat down, Paul sweated in his polyester suit, shirt, and tie. He thought about the esteemed life he was living— in cheap motels, dodging bar fights, and directing traffic.

His four-year college degree wasn't paying off the way he'd hoped it would.

Due to the space restrictions, Paul didn't schedule an elephant race. Teddy was happy about that.

Cronk was disappointed advance ticket sales weren't stronger, but understood.

"Bluefield's hardly a prime circus market," he said. "These

hillbillies wouldn't cough up two bits to see Jesus juggling and riding a unicycle. Maybe we'll get decent walk-up business."

They didn't. Business was soft both opening day shows. Paul sensed disappointment from the performers—it seemed they were going through the motions, receiving polite applause.

After the evening performance, Paul and Teddy sat outside the elephant tent and shared a twelve pack.

"Any news?" Paul asked. "Rocket try killing himself again?"

"No. He's back to his usual depressed self. Sparky got in some trouble, though."

"The bum-face clown?"

"Yeah. He pushed a kid."

"He's an angry bastard," Paul said, recalling how Sparky acted when Robbie was being made up.

"He almost got his ass kicked by the kid's father. The guy went looking for Sparky after the show and threw a couple punches. Rousties broke it up, and saved Sparky's ass. He got a nice shiner, though. You can't tell because of his makeup, but the dad landed a good one."

"Wish I could have seen it. How's Augusta? Any news with her?"

"Nope. The ice queen continues her reign. Why are you so interested? I thought you loved some girl in New England."

"I do. Just curious."

"Uh huh. Stick with your girl. Augusta wouldn't give you the time of day, even in a clock store."

"I was just curious."

"Right."

The morning of the second show day, Paul's motel phone rang at eight o'clock. "How's it going, circus man?" Katherine asked.

"Opening day was slow, but I'm hoping today makes up for it."

"Always the optimist."

"I've got to be. What's up with you?"

"My ex is in the hospital."

"What happened?" Paul sat up in bed.

"Sean went to talk to him about the importance of paying child support, and he used fists to emphasize his advice."

"Is your ex alright?"

"Couple broken ribs, broken arm, black eyes. He'll heal. Eventually."

"Did Sean get arrested?"

"No. Patrick Ryan said he fell down some stairs. He can be smart when he wants to be."

"So, Sean got off?"

"Sean always gets off— he's a professional, remember?"

"Damn."

"I think my ex will finally start paying his child support."

"That's good. Everything else okay?"

"No— I miss you."

"I miss you, too."

"Then it's settled. You'll quit that crappy job and drive here. You can make it by sundown."

"You know I can't. I'm saving money. I'll be back in a few months."

"I'm not sure I can wait that long."

"You've got your family, you'll be fine."

"You've fallen for a cute clown, haven't you?"

"I wish."

"I love you, Paul."

"Love you, too."

On the second day of the Bluefield stand, the circus got good publicity but attendance was mediocre. The show didn't make its nut either day. Paul had low shoulders walking into the ticket sales trailer after the second show. Cronk sat at his table sipping whiskey.

"Pour you one, Paul?" he asked.

"No thanks. I feel like I let the show down."

"You did your best," Cronk said. "Some places aren't circus towns. Bluefield's one of them. Your next town will be better."

"Where's that?"

"Greenwood, Mississippi. Deep in Dixieland."

"Is that a good circus market?"

"We haven't played there in a couple of years, but we usually do well in the South." Augusta opened the trailer door and walked in wearing her sparkling circus costume clinging to every curve, accentuating her long, sexy legs.

"Hi, Paul."

"Hi, Augusta. Great show."

"Thanks. I wish more people had seen it."

"You and me both."

"This isn't circus country, sweetie," Cronk said. "Why haven't you changed? We're jumping soon."

"I forgot something," Augusta said, reaching into a drawer at her sales station. "I'll be ready in no time, grandpa. Bye, Paul, hope to see you soon."

"Bye, Augusta." She smiled, and left.

"Get over your Bluefield blues, and make us some green in Greenwood," Cronk said, smiling

"I will. Thanks, Cronk."

Paul exited the circus trailer and walked to his car. He thought of Augusta.

Somewhere, she was undressing.

CHAPTER FOURTEEN
Greenwood

"When a man starts thinking life would be better if his woman was there to share it, that's when you know he's DOA in love."
— *Paul Driscoll's notes, Haverhill, MA*

The next morning, Paul began driving to Greenwood. The car radio was playing "Staying Alive" by the Bee Gees, and he wondered if Brian was faring better than he was.

In Alabama, he picked up a young hitchhiker. "Where you headed?" Paul asked.

"Quinton." The teenager had peach fuzz whiskers and wore a Lynyrd Skynyrd tee-shirt, dirty jeans with holes, and mud-caked Nikes.

"I don't know where that is," Paul said. "Tell me where to drop you off." The young man nodded and looked out the passenger window. There was a long silence. "So, where is Quinton?"

"Not far from Birmingham," the hitchhiker said, to his window and the passing landscape. A road sign read Birmingham: sixty-four miles.

"I've never been to Birmingham," Paul said, thinking it might seed a conversation. The young man was quiet. "It's my first time in the South." Silence. "You originally from Alabama?" he asked, turning his head to the hitchhiker staring out the window.

"Yeah."

"From Quinton?"

"Yeah."

"You going home?" Silence. "Going home to Quinton?"

"Yeah."

"Been on the road?"

"Yeah." Paul waited for him to elaborate, but he didn't. "Where were you?"

"At a friend's," the passenger said, in a bored voice. Paul waited for more. The hitchhiker was mute.

"Friends are good." Paul realized how stupid that sounded. "I mean, it's good to have friends."

"Uh-huh."

Paul drove in silence. He felt like the young man was judging him for his idiotic remark. He also felt betrayed and cheated since the only reason he risked picking-up a stranger who could be a homicidal maniac was for a conversation.

This hitchhiker was as talkative as bread.

After five minutes of silence, Paul took another stab at conversation pointing to the kid's tee shirt. "You a Skynyrd fan?"

"Yeah." Paul waited for him to talk about his favorite album, song, or concert.

Nothing.

"I never got into Skynyrd or southern rock," Paul said. The rider was quiet. "I'm more into British rock— The Beatles, Stones, Zeppelin, Elvis Costello, Springsteen." He stopped, realizing he'd classified Springsteen as British. He waited for his passenger to pounce on the mistake. Silence. "Of course, Springsteen's from New Jersey."

No response.

Paul drove, stewing in anger for having the bad luck of picking up the world's quietest hitchhiker.

After ten minutes of silence, Paul tried again. "What's Quinton like?" There was a long pause.

"Ain't hardly but one red light," the kid said. Paul waited for him to say more. He didn't.

"It's small?"

"Yeah." His passenger stared out his window.

"I'm from a small town, too. There's more than one red light, but, it's pretty tiny." Nothing. "It's in Ohio."

In his peripheral vision, Paul noticed the young man was a seated statue, staring out the passenger window as the world flashed by. Paul turned and made a funny face at the back of young man's head, then turned his attention back to the road. The hitchhiker didn't react.

For the remainder of their ride, Paul made quick funny faces at his quiet passenger and never got caught.

After fifty minutes, the young man spoke. "You can drop me off up here."

Paul pulled to the side of the road, and the kid got out without saying anything. He closed the door and began walking, relieved to be away from the crazy guy he'd seen making faces at him in the reflection of the passenger window.

Paul floored the car, catching rubber as he got back on the highway. "Fuck you," he said in a Liverpudlian accent. "And the bleeding horse you rode in on, you tight-lipped bastard."

The road was taking its toll.

Greenwood billed itself as "The Cotton Capital of The World." The old city was in the heart of lush green Delta country, rich with cotton fields and the new cash crop of catfish farms.

Paul went to a drugstore phone booth, opened the Yellow Pages and began calling hotels and motels for weekly rates. He selected The Huntington, a large hotel built in 1914, when Greenwood was the epicenter of the cotton universe.

The hotel had fallen on hard times. Its vast lobby had well-worn furniture from the 1950s. A man in his eighties, with a shiny bald head lined with a crown of white hair, sat sleeping in a lobby chair with a newspaper on his lap. His head rested on his chest as he snored.

An elderly man with a ruddy complexion and bent wire frame glasses melded into his pudgy face looked up as Paul approached the front desk.

"Hello. I called about a room."

"Called about a broom?" the desk man asked, in a slow Southern drawl. "Don't know nothing about no broom. You spilt something, did you?"

"No, not a broom— I called about a room. Do you have a room?"

"Of course we got rooms. We're a hotel. Got lots of them. You want one?"

"Yes. I was quoted sixty-dollars-a-week."

"You want a room for a week?"

"Three weeks."

"Three weeks? Guess you'll be living with us a spell," he said, sliding a clipboard with registration papers and a pen across to Paul. "Fill this out, I'll get you a room key." He completed the registration and paid cash for one week. The manager shouted at the sleeping man in the chair. "Willie, we got a guest. Show him his room." The sleeping man didn't respond. "Wake up, Willie! We got a guest!" The old man slowly roused himself and turned toward the registration desk.

"You say something, George?"

"I said we got a guest. Show him to his room— three-seventeen. Got that? Three-one-seven."

"Three-seventeen. Third floor, right?

"Yes. Third floor."

"Got it." The old man pulled himself out of the chair as the newspaper fell from his lap to a stained old rug. Willie didn't notice. "Follow me, young man." He began walking toward the elevator with a manually operated sliding metal cage door.

Room 317 had light pink plaster walls, a cracked ceiling, two lumpy beds, a large wooden desk, a lamp with a translucent yellowed lampshade, and an old black dial telephone. There was an enormous closet with sliding doors, an ancient black and white TV, Venetian blinds covering large windows facing a view of downtown, and a bathroom with an old tub, sink and tile floor— all spotted with yellow water stains.

The room was musty and reminded Paul of his grandparents' house. It smelled like old people clinging to their lives.

But, for less than ten bucks a night, the room was a palace. Paul tipped Willie a dollar. The old man looked confused. He blinked twice and shoved the crumpled bill in his pocket.

"Thanks," he said.

The Greenwood Moose Club was sponsoring the circus, and its president was Bill Thomas, the chief of police. Paul's first order of business was meeting him at city hall and discussing arrangements.

The chief was six-foot-two, middle-aged and weighed almost three hundred pounds, much of which was blubber draping over his belt. Beneath his brown mustache were multiple chins. He was balding and had a pasty complexion the sun had scorched. The chief had a bone-crushing handshake Paul tried to reciprocate.

"Glad to meet you, Paul Driscoll," the big man said, in Southern drawl. "It's great having y'alls circus coming to town."

"Thanks, Chief Thomas." The cop sat behind his desk, as Paul sat in a heavy oak chair facing him.

"Enjoying our Mississippi weather?" Thomas asked, taking a handkerchief from his pocket and mopping his brow. "Hot enough for you?" The chief laughed.

"Yes, sir," Paul said.

"Gets awful toasty here in the summertime, so I was glad when the boys booking your circus told me about your air-conditioned tent." Thomas pulled a pack of unfiltered Camels from his pocket and lit one.

"I'm sorry, would you repeat that?"

"Said I was glad when your bookers told me about your air-conditioned tent. After a hot day, it'll be nice to cool down and watch your circus."

"I think they were mistaken."

"What's that?" the chief said, leaning forward.

"Our big top isn't air-conditioned."

"What do you mean?"

"It's a big canvas tent. There's no air-conditioning."

"They lied to me?"

"I'm sure it was a miscommunication."

"Miscommunication, my ass. They sat right there and lied to my damn face."

"I don't know what to tell you, Chief Thomas," Paul said, feeling guilty.

"Goddammit," Thomas said, taking an angry pull on his cigarette. "I oughta issue an arrest warrant for those boys."

"Our big top gets a nice cross breeze."

"Cross breeze ain't exactly refrigerated air, now, is it?" Chief

Thomas asked, with narrowed eyes.

"No." Paul reached for his cigarettes in his pocket and fumbled with the pack. He took one out and lit it, noticing the cigarette was trembling.

"So, Paul Driscoll— what goddamn lies you going to tell me?"

"No lies, sir. I promise." The cop glared at him. "I'll be here through the show dates to make sure everything goes perfectly. I'm staying at The Huntington."

"Then I know where to find you, and if anything gets fishy, it'll be your sorry ass on the line. You understand me, son?"

"Yes, sir. Everything will be great."

"Shake on it," Chief Thomas said, reaching his huge paw across the desk and crushing Paul's hand again. "Your word, your ass, Paul Driscoll. Understand?"

"Yes, sir." The chief released his grip. Two of Paul's fingers were numb.

That evening, the day's heat had been absorbed by the streets and buildings and radiated it back as Paul walked to a small restaurant. He enjoyed the best fried chicken he'd ever eaten.

That night, he called Katherine.

"Hello, dink," she said. "What's up in the Deep South?"

"I had to defuse another bomb planted by the booking agents."

"No parking?"

"No. They told our sponsor we have an air-conditioned big top."

"Wow, that's good."

"The sponsor's also the chief of police, and he's mad as hell. He said my ass is on the line if there are any more lies."

"Quit, Paul. Come here— we'll put you up until you find a job."

"I have to see this through."

"Cleaning up more lies?"

"Probably."

"Does your Catholic guilt make you think you have to do this?"

"Let's not get into this again, please. How are things there? How's Sean— he sent anyone else to the hospital?"

"No. But my ex came through with some child support."

"Impressive. Maybe Sean could negotiate for our circus."

"He'd be excellent. He's persistent and always gets his way. That's how he gave me my first kiss."

"You never told me that."

"I was a wide-eyed thirteen-year-old Catholic school girl, and he was a worldly nineteen-year-old going into the Marines."

"Sounds creepy. A young man kissing his kid cousin."

"It was creepy, when he wanted it to go further. But I shut him down, fast."

"He tried seducing you?"

"No. He tried persuading me that it'd be a good idea if he taught me about men and their moves. He said it would be better coming from him than a stranger."

"That's statutory rape creepy. Incest creepy."

"Rape? Incest? Come on, Paul, nothing happened. He was like an older brother giving me helpful advice."

"You sure about that?"

"Why are you so judgmental of everyone, Paul— everyone but yourself?"

"How's this my fault?"

"I'm telling you an innocent story, and you turn it into rape and incest. Meanwhile, you're living like a gypsy with a bunch of lying, cheating, carnies because you say you have to grow up."

"That's not fair. It's a legitimate circus, not carnies, and you know why I'm doing this."

"Well maybe there's more to Sean than you think. People are complex. Not everyone is guilty."

"I think a nineteen-year-old man trying to seduce his thirteen-year-old cousin is wrong, and I think the Pope and Catholic church would agree."

"I confessed those sins long ago," Katherine said. "God knows where I stand. How about you, mister high morality— are you ready for judgment day?"

Paul looked out his window into a clear night of lights dotting the flat landscape of Greenwood, trailing into a horizon of dark sky, peppered with stars and a half moon. He thought of B.D., and his attraction to Augusta.

"I guess so," he said.

"Let's not fight, Paul." There was silence. "I wish you were here, circus man."

On Sunday, the Greenwood newspaper had a feature article on the retirement of Father Brian Murphy, a Catholic priest with St. Michael's parish since 1928. The Catholic Church was established in Greenwood in 1912, and had floundered until the arrival of the young Irish-American priest fresh out of the seminary.

Father Murphy worked diligently to build a Catholic congregation in the heart of Baptist country. Over fifty-four years, he had built a stable parish. The article had a picture of the smiling seventy-eight-year-old.

Paul decided to attend Fr. Murphy's swan song service.

The church was a ten-minute walk. Paul wore dress slacks and a short sleeve shirt. Parishioners dressed in suits, ties, polished leather shoes and well-pressed dresses. Paul sat in a back pew, feeling like a fashion leper.

St. Michael's was compact, with statues of saints, stained glass depictions of Christ suffering at the hands of mortals, a statue of the Virgin Mary on a small altar, an elaborate main altar over which hung a large Jesus Christ figure nailed on a crucifix, and murals of miracles Jesus had performed. Paul felt at home. He knelt on a thinly-cushioned kneeler and prayed as he looked up at the sad face of Jesus bleeding on His cross.

"Oh, dear Lord Jesus Christ, my Savior and Redeemer, who is merciful and eternally generous with His love and mercy, please forgive me my many sins. Help me be strong and do Your will so I won't have to beg Your forgiveness. Please bless my family, and Katherine and her family, and allow us to live in the glory of Thy love. Keep us safe and bring us together again so we might do Your will as good Christians and receive Thine many blessings and grace. Help me resist Satan's temptations of the flesh, and stay true to Katherine. Please give us large circus crowds, for Thy people need entertainment. And please provide cool breezes under the big top so we don't suffer the ravages of a hell-like atmosphere. Forever and ever, amen."

Paul made a sign of the cross. He thought this was like placing a stamp on an envelope of prayers.

The Mass began.

Father Murphy moved slowly, flanked by two young altar boys. Paul had been an altar boy and enjoyed assisting the priest. It was like being a magician's assistant. The old priest was good, making the ceremony momentous but accessible. His sermon was blessedly short, concise with a strong call to action— love thy neighbor. He was the only Catholic priest Paul ever heard who had something to say, and said it well.

The best part of the service was Father Murphy's transubstantiation, the transformation of wheat wafers, wine and water into the Body and Blood of Jesus Christ.

Unlike most priests, Father Murphy knew his lines cold. He did not have to glance at the open book or turn its pages. He spoke with sincerity and conviction. When he raised the host and chalice, the action was accented with tinkling bells played by an altar boy. The mood was magical. Paul was transfixed and inspired. Miraculously, like an angel from heaven, his muse delivered an idea for a novel— the imagined interpretation of Father Murphy's life called "The Perfect Host".

After Mass, there was a ceremony. Paul shook hands with Father Murphy, wished him well, and hurried back to his room and began jotting notes.

His novel opens in the future, 2010. An old priest named Donald Moran is in a Catholic retirement home, feeling like a prisoner. The priest begins writing his memoir.

His father sold insurance policy machines to airports in the early 1950s. His mother was a zealous Catholic who doted on her only child, Donald. When Donald is fifteen, his father dies in a plane crash. He has no insurance, not even a policy issued by an airport vending machine.

The family is left with bills, and memories.

The mother goes to work at the parish rectory, and attends church daily, praying for her husband's soul and her son's future.

The boy grows up, dreaming of being an actor, but he's not attractive. Donald is overweight, slightly cross-eyed, with a large nose, thin lips, and cabbage leaf ears.

Hardly a marquee face.

The mother worries about him. Every time she asks about his career pursuits, he says, "I don't know. I'll figure something out." He doesn't tell her about his acting dream.

The mother urges him to talk to Father Keith, the popular priest who heads their parish. After weeks of begging and pleading, Donald speaks to the priest in the confessional.

He confesses his dream of being an actor, entertaining others and bringing joy. "But," Donald says, "I'm pretty ugly. What should I do with my life, Father?"

The priest is shocked and tells Donald that his coming to talk must be a miracle because when he was his age, he faced a similar dilemma. Father Keith wanted to be a comedian, but he was terribly shy. His mother urged him to talk with a priest, so, young Keith opened his heart in the confessional and the priest advised him to become a priest.

The priest said he could pursue his comic dreams daily, with a rapt audience. There was no need to be shy or nervous since parishioners are a captive crowd. Although the Mass script was set, he could write homilies and perform, making jokes, telling stories, entertaining and moving people.

All in the glorious name of God.

Young Father Keith questioned his faith, not sure he was 'called' to the priesthood. The elderly priest told him God does not call all men. Many pursue the vocation and later receive calls. Regardless, priests were doing it for the right reason— an expression of self as creatures made in God's glory, through the unique talents he had blessed them with. And, if Keith brought people to Christ in the process of exercising his God-given talent, wasn't that a priest's primary objective?

Serve yourself, serve the Lord, and serve others— all at the same time. It was God's plan, albeit an indirect one.

Father Keith advises young Donald to pursue the priesthood. He does, attending seminary, working hard, getting ordained.

And it was good.

His first assignment is in the boonies— Greenwood, Mississippi, a single-A club for a Catholic priest in 1960. The Deep South was Siberia.

He takes his assignment in good cheer, inheriting a parish from a retiring priest who says he's done his best, but his flock is only a couple dozen strong. He tells young Donald that Southerners are afraid of the Holy Mother Church and its leader, the Pope— who wears a funny big hat, and claims to never be wrong, and has a direct line to God.

"Baptists think Catholics have too much pageantry and magic," the old priest says. "These people like their traditions more sedate. They like a celebration of themselves and the successes they've achieved by their own hard work. They rejoice in the empires they've built, and like to believe they did it all themselves, with blessings from God."

He explains that Baptists love choirs, getting dressed up for services, showing off their possessions, and social activities like potlucks. Donald listens carefully. From the sound of it, Greenwood people are like him— they like the show of religion more than the spirit of it. He decides this insight is the rock upon which he will build his church. He'll use the lure of being a star to nurture his parish's growth.

Father Donald assumes the reigns of St. Michael's and tells parishioners he wants to assemble the best choir in the city. He says his flock will wear the most fabulous choir robes in the state. Word quickly spreads.

Those already in Protestant choirs mock the silly Catholic priest. They believe the papists are notorious for their lack of musical talent and off-key singing.

But there are others whose interests are piqued. Those who did not make the Baptist choirs and are filled with envy and bitterness.

They audition for the Catholic choir.

The young priest selects a musical director, and charges him with finding the best voices, and designing special choir robes with many gold embellishments and tassels. He builds a choir of singers with more egos than talent; those who couldn't cut it in a Protestant choir are stars in the Catholic brigade.

He assures people he'll make it easy for them to convert to Catholicism, and does so by taking liberties with the rules. Although it will be a while before they can receive Holy Communion, he allows them to participate in all other aspects of the mass. Of course, with an adult choir member, their families come along for support.

Pews begin filling.

Father Donald builds his congregation and the diocese takes notice.

He eventually ascends to become a Bishop.

Paul wrote the bones of the story— a Catholic priest's tale inspired by Fr. Murphy's retirement mass. The premise was dark and cynical, a reflection of Paul's grappling with faith. He liked the conceit— what if one doesn't necessarily believe what one preaches, but still succeeds in giving others faith?

Does it matter?

Paul would spend the rest of his circus days working on "The Perfect Host", looking forward to sharing it with Katherine on his return.

He had found his whale to pursue.

CHAPTER FIFTEEN
Willis & Rumor

"I imagined circus personalities would be huge, like Macy's Thanksgiving Day balloons, tethered to Earth by humanity. But most of the performers have petty egos that whither when cast into the shadows of spotlights.
Ta-da quickly turns to wah-wah."

— *Paul Driscoll's notes, Panama City, FL*

The Huntington Hotel had twenty ancient residents. Paul was sure he was the only guest. Greenwood in the summertime was hardly a tourist attraction.

The hotel and its gloomy shadows permeated Paul and inspired him. He imagined stories of past crimes and tragedies in The Huntington. He felt if its walls could talk, they'd talk themselves breathless.

He bought black and white film and used his camera's timed shutter to create a photo mini-drama in which he played an out-of-town salesman. Paul dressed in a suit and smiled for the camera in his room.

He placed the camera on the hallway floor, set the timer, and took a shot of himself on one knee looking terrified, as if something evil was approaching.

He took a shot of himself running away.

Then, a close-up of his frightened face reacting to impending harm.

Next, a long shot of Paul's lifeless body on the hall carpet.

Then, a shot of his arm draped over the bathtub, his body within.

The pictures told a mysterious tale. What had happened to this traveling salesman?

Something. Something evil.

Another casualty of The Huntington Hotel.

〰〜

In his second week, Paul was invited to the home of Willis Hargrain, a member of the Moose Club, to see his hobby.

"Mr. Driscoll," the petite, slender man said, in a high-pitch Mississippi accent, "I am doubly delighted to make your acquaintance." He thrust out his arm and shook his hand.

"Please, call me Paul."

"Seriously, Mr. Driscoll?"

"Yes."

"Then, Paul it is. I will do as you command," he smiled, "Paul!" Willis took a deep breath. "I cannot believe I am on a first name basis with the official representative of the Finnion, Barton & Powell Circus! I am about to burst with pride!"

He gave Paul a small ice-cold bottle of Coca-Cola and led him down the basement stairs.

"I'd ask you to close your eyes, but I don't want my honored guest tumbling down my stairs. That wouldn't be very hospitable." Willis laughed nervously.

The small basement had a large sheet of plywood laid across a large table. On its surface, Willis Hargrain had constructed a complete miniature world. "Paul, welcome to the 1938 Finnion, Barton & Powell

Circus." He waved his arm across its landscape. "I made it with models, and what I couldn't find, I made with papier maché. Each piece is hand-painted. Look-here, Paul," he said, pointing to painted train cars. "I have all the attractions of the day— The Burkov Brothers & Bears; The Amazing Dunkirk, the Flying Aces, the best trapeze act in FB&PC history, the Death-Defying Danny Broman, who could turn a passel of angry lions into pussycats. Look here— I even have Sad Sandy, the clown with a heart bigger than the big top. They're all here, Paul, all the acts and attractions. Every last one! I even created the sideshow, with Wilbur the Wonderful, Garfield the Geek, Toby the Terrible, Peter the Pinhead and Elma the Electric Lady. It's the entire show— exactly as presented in the year of our Lord, 1938."

Willis was rightfully proud. Paul noticed each person in the crowd was distinctive. A man held his daughter's hand as she clutched a cone of pink cotton candy. Two parents led four children along the midway. Elderly couples held hands. A boy licked a chocolate ice cream cone. A young woman kissed a soldier behind a tent. Roustabouts unloaded cargo from the train. Elephants paraded down the midway as clowns juggled. People lined up at ticket windows. He had captured a circus universe.

"This is amazing," Paul said, finding it hard to believe a grown man would devote his time and energy to such a frivolous task.

"I'm glad you like it, Paul. I truly am."

"I love it." He did not want to crush the little man's spirit by asking why the hell he would do it.

"I always wanted to be in the circus," Willis said. "And here I am." He pointed to the figure of a little boy holding his mother's hand. "That's mother and me. We attended this very show when it came to Greenwood on September 6, 1938— five days after my dear daddy died in a car accident. He was hit by a cotton truck. Daddy had promised me the week before he joined our Lord that we would go to the circus. And Mother kept his promise. I will never forget that day, no sir— the most special day of my life."

"Wow," Paul said, feeling guilty for questioning Willie's motives in building his circus model.

"And do you want to know something, Paul? That day, I had the feeling my daddy was there with us. He was at the show, with me and mom, just like he promised," his voice cracked with emotion. "But enough about silly old me. Tell me about you, Mr. Paul Driscoll, working for Finnion, Barton & Powell Circus. It must be magical. I cannot even imagine."

Paul did his best to muster enthusiasm for his work and the glories of traveling the country, living in cheap motels, and spreading the word about the wonders beneath the big top, but it wasn't in his heart. He wanted to talk about the problems caused by lazy, lying booking people, but he couldn't— not to this circus zealot.

Paul spoke about the satisfaction of bringing people to the show. He tried recalling Tom Burnett's impassioned speeches from their Philadelphia interview. Willis cocked his head and looked captivated as Paul spoke, but the young advance man suspected this circus fanatic detected the ugly truth— Mr. Paul Driscoll had little sawdust in his veins.

Paul fumbled through the next hour as Willis Hargrain relayed stories about the history of Finnion, Barton & Powell Circus. Finally, Paul said he had to leave for an appointment. Willis was sad and gave him a warm handshake.

"I cannot begin to tell you what a pleasure it has been to make your acquaintance, Paul. I truly appreciate it greatly." His eyes glistened and his sincerity pierced Paul's cynicism.

He left the home suspecting that the Willis would quickly return to his miniature-fabricated fantasy.

When Paul got back to The Huntington, the desk clerk said he had a message, and handed him a pink slip. "Was long distance, I think. Sounded far away."

"Thanks," Paul said, glancing at the message. The name scratched on the paper read: "BAR SEAGULL."

"Was a woman," the desk clerk said. "Kind of pushy. Didn't leave a number. Said you had it."

"Yes. Thanks."

"If it is long distance, you'll have to dial one before you dial the number. It's not like a local call, you got to dial one or the call won't go through."

"I'll dial one."

"Long distance costs more, you know."

"I know. Thanks."

"Don't forget to dial one."

"I won't."

Barb Sigel spoke with her usual anxiety tinged with impending doom. "Is Greenwood going to be big, Paul?"

"It's too early to tell, but I think it'll be okay."

"We need better than okay. The show's bleeding money. We haven't made our nut in weeks. You've got to hustle, Paul. We need big sales."

"I'm doing my best, Barb."

"Do your best, then a little better. You can do it, Paul. I know you can!"

"I will, Barb."

"Good. I'll see you tomorrow. I should be in around five. We can go to dinner and you can show me your master plan. You are working your master plan, right?"

"Absolutely. Working it hard." Paul had barely looked at it in recent days. His media buys were locked, there were no more promotions to sell, and it was too early to order hay and show services.

"Good. Serve the master plan, it'll serve you. That's what I always say."

"Yes, you do."

"Do what?"

"Say that. And I do always serve the master plan, and it always serves me."

"Good. See you tomorrow."

Barb Sigel looked frazzled as she sat across from Paul in the red vinyl booth of a diner. Her makeup looked as if it was applied by paint rollers. Her perfume reeked of funeral home flowers. She was in full war paint.

"Did you try selling retail promotions?" Barb asked, looking up from his master plan.

"There aren't many advertisers here."

"What about the department store down the street?"

"I tried," Paul lied. "They weren't interested."

"What about hardware stores, feed stores, or wherever local yokels shop?"

"Like I said, no one really advertises. It's a pretty small town."

"Then we'll have to rely on media promotions, I guess."

"I've got good promotions and all radio buys were half-cash, half-trade."

"I wish there was more we were doing."

"Trust me Barb, the town's covered. And we're getting papered on Friday. Carl said they'd blanket the town. That'll help."

"What about Blippo?"

"He's booked for three radio interviews on Monday."

"Take him to the newspaper, too. He's a good photo op. Hick town papers are dying for news, and it's not every day they get a professional clown. Get Blippo on the front page."

"I'll try."

"Definitely. What about school shows?"

"It's summer. School's out."

"Goddammit. Mall shows?"

"The mall's not a sponsor. They won't do it."

"Fuck. We've got to make Greenwood a blockbuster."

"I'm working the town hard, Barb."

"I know, Paul— but we need big shows. Business sucks."

"How's Brian doing?" Paul asked, wanting to get the spotlight off himself.

"You didn't hear?"

"Hear what?"

"He quit. He got jumped by a bunch of rednecks outside a bar in bumfuck, Kentucky two weeks ago."

"Really?"

"Yes, and he got beaten pretty badly. Spent a couple of days in the hospital. His family came down from Philly, and he quit and went home. It's pretty sad, really," Barb Sigel said, lighting a cigarette. "Very sad," she said, exhaling. Paul couldn't tell if she was sad about what happened, or sad for his leaving the show.

"Has anyone heard from him?"

"No." She took a long drag on her cigarette. "I guess Brian didn't have sawdust in his veins."

"Guess not. If he had, the sawdust might have stopped his bleeding." Paul reached for his cigarette pack and Barb raised her eyebrows. Brian's story was depressing, even though Paul didn't like him.

"Are you all right, Paul?"

"I'm fine."

"I didn't think you guys were that close."

"We weren't, really."

"Brian was okay. But he could be obnoxious."

"Yeah."

"I'm sorry he got hurt. I warn marketing directors to be careful. The road can be dangerous—" Barb leaned in and lowered her voice, "especially in these hick towns. Are you being careful, Paul?"

"Yes." He rarely went out after the bar fight in West Virginia. His routine was buying beer, making phone calls or writing letters, working on his novel, and watching TV— until he passed out and woke to "The Star-Spangled Banner" playing at the end of another broadcasting day.

"I know the road's lonely," Barb said, reaching over and placing her hand on his, "but I can help." Paul looked at her as she stared into his eyes. "You do know I'm attracted to you, Paul."

"Uh, thanks." He rescued his hand from hers.

"I didn't get a hotel room yet. I thought we'd spend the night together and I'll make sure you're not lonely." She smiled her large white teeth and winked.

"Barb, my room's small, and the bed's a twin—"

"All the better for cuddling."

"No, I mean, I—"

"Then, I'll get a room with a double bed." Paul thought of the acres of vacant rooms in The Huntington.

"I think the hotel's pretty full."

"I'll talk to the manager. He'll find me something." She placed her hand on his again. He pulled away.

"The thing is, Barb, I'm seeing someone."

"Really? Who?"

"A girl I met in Haverhill."

"You have a girlfriend in Haverhill?"

"Yes. We fell in love."

"Haverhill was months ago. She means so much to you that you can't play around?"

"Yes."

"That's pretty unbelievable," she said, snubbing out her cigarette and reaching for another. "Paul, I've been doing this job a long time, and I can tell when someone's lying. I think you're making up this girlfriend story."

"It's true, Barb."

"Level with me," she said. She lit her cigarette and leaned forward, exhaling a plume of smoke. "You're gay, aren't you?"

"Gay?"

"You're not the first one, Paul. It's pretty common in the circus."

"Why do you think I'm gay?"

"It's pretty obvious. When we were training, you resisted me by saying you were in love with a girl in Ohio. So, I gave you a rain check for the road. Now we're down the road, and you say you have a new girlfriend in Haverhill. You're refusing free sex again. It doesn't make sense, Paul. It all adds up to one obvious conclusion, you're gay. Wait a second— were you and Brian lovers?"

"Brian? No."

"But you were roommates."

"We roomed together to save money. Jesus, Barb— Brian!"

"Okay, so Brian wasn't your type. You don't have to have a hissy fit."

Paul put out his cigarette and Barb placed her hand on his. "Look, I don't care if you're gay. Whatever floats your boat. I've learned it's impossible to turn a gay leaf. I'll quit trying."

He thought about what she said. Barb could only take 'no' for an answer if the answer had some extenuating circumstance behind it. The only way a male subordinate could refuse her sexual advances was if he was gay. It was the only explanation her egotistical mind would accept. So, if by being gay, Paul could avoid the nauseating thought of getting into bed with her, so be it. Let her think what she wanted. What did he care? His circus tour would be over in a couple of months, and he wasn't returning.

"Barb, don't take this personally," Paul said, quietly. "But, for the last time, I'm not gay."

"Okay, Paul. I've come to accept that all the best men are gay. It's God's practical joke. But I'm still getting a room at your hotel."

"Pleased to have you, Miss Sigel," The Huntington desk clerk said, reading the name from her registration form. "We don't get many Jews in these parts."

"Really? Most Jews love pork, and it looks like there's a lot of swine around here," Barb said. She glanced at Paul and smiled. He stared at his shoes. "I'll tell all my Jew friends to come visit you," she told the clerk. "I'll let them know you run a Jew-friendly hotel." The old man gave Barb a puzzled look and slid a room key to her.

"Enjoy your stay, Miss Sigel."

"I will. And speaking for all Jews, sorry about the whole Jesus thing. Shalom."

That night, Paul and Barb shared drinks at a bar. She played matchmaker, telling him about the many gays in the circus. "Paul, is Blippo light in his size thirty-eight loafers? He's gay, right? Most clowns are."

"I don't know, Barb." Paul had no idea if the advance clown was even human, let alone homosexual. Blippo was an angry life form in greasepaint.

"Bet you he's gay," she said, draining her rum and Coke, clinking the ice to get the bartender's attention. Paul ordered another beer and wondered when the evening would end.

When Carl and Wanda Foley arrived, Paul could tell something had changed. In the past, the couple was friendly, in their gruff, hungover way. They'd tease him about his circus inexperience and school him in the importance of broadsheet advertising for show success. But as Paul sat with them in a coffee shop booth, the talkative couple was quiet. Paul tried tugging the conversation along.

"How's it going?" he asked.

"Another day, another buck," Wanda said, pouring a stream of sugar into her coffee.

"Been busy?"

"The usual," Carl said, staring out the window.

"I'm glad you're here. This town needs paper."

"Uh-huh," Wanda said, stirring her coffee. She joined Carl and looked out the window.

"I think with your help, this town will be a success." Neither Foley responded. "And I'd love lots of paper to give our sponsors."

"Look, we know how to do our goddamn job, all right?" Carl said, snuffing-out his cigarette. "We're goddamn professionals."

"Is something wrong?"

"No. Nothing. Except we're not even sure we know who the hell you are, Paul."

"What do you mean?"

"We heard you're a closet queer," Wanda said.

"Who told you that?"

"We got our sources." She reached for her cigarettes and lit one. Carl did the same.

"That's not true."

"Uh-huh," Carl said.

"Even if I was gay, what difference would it make?"

"It don't make two shits of difference what you do with your pecker," Carl said. "Except we thought we knew you. Hell, we broke bread with you and shared our home, and all the while you were a goddamn stranger."

"Circus is about trust," Wanda said. "And we can't hardly trust you if you're keeping secrets."

"I thought we were friends," Carl said. Paul realized they were lonely; the Foleys sought friendship, loyalty, and trust.

"We are friends, Carl, and I'm telling you, I am not gay."

"Then why'd you say you were?" Wanda asked.

"I suppose you heard that from Barb."

"Doesn't matter where we heard it," Carl said.

"Barb was upset because I wouldn't sleep with her. I told her I'm in a relationship with a woman in Haverhill."

"Haverhill," Wanda said, "that was months ago."

"I met a woman there I like a lot, and I'm trying to stay faithful. Barb thought I was making up the girlfriend story because I was gay."

"You're serious?" Carl asked. "You got a long-distance relationship and you're staying true on the road?"

"Why's that so unbelievable?" Carl looked at Wanda, she looked at Paul. "And I don't find Barb attractive, so I said no to sleeping with her. Now she's telling everyone I'm gay."

"You really aren't gay?" Carl asked.

"No. I'm in a relationship."

"You never struck me as queer," Wanda said. "But why'd you fall for some woman on the road when you knew you'd be leaving?"

"And why stay true to her?" Carl added. Paul looked at each Foley.

"Because I guess I'm in love."

"Love? That's about the stupidest goddamn thing I ever heard," Carl said, laughing. Wanda and Paul joined him. As their laughter died, Carl said, "Hell, Paul, even if you weren't in love, I wouldn't fuck Barb— not even with your dick."

They laughed again.

Blippo arrived, and Paul sensed their relationship had changed. The sad, bitter clown now seemed cheery.

"Are we going to have great show dates, Paulie?" he asked when Paul picked him up at the trailer park. It was the first time Blippo showed interest in the box office.

"I think so."

"I hope you have a big one," he said. "I'll bet you have a huge one." The clown laughed— he rarely laughed. It dawned on Paul he was flirting. Barb Sigel must have told him the gay story.

"Look, Blippo, there's a rumor going around about me, and if you heard it, it's not true."

"What rumor?"

"A rumor that I'm gay." Paul clenched the steering wheel. "I think Barb Sigel's spreading the rumor, and I want to nip it in the bud."

"Barb's saying you're gay?"

"Yes."

"Why?"

"Because I told her I was in love, and she thought I was lying to cover for being gay."

"You're in love?"

"Yes. With a woman. Katherine, that girl who worked at the

Haverhill Mall. We went out together, remember?"

"The angry lady with a rug rat?"

"Yes. We fell in love and I'm being faithful."

"You going to marry her?"

"I don't know. When the season's over, I'm going back and we'll see where it goes."

"What about the circus?" Paul sensed an air of desperation in Blippo's voice. He didn't want to confess he had no intention of coming back, but he'd already told him too much. Announcing he was leaving would not serve him well for the remainder of his tour.

"I'll be back."

Blippo was quiet. Paul could feel the dark clouds of Blippo's normal personality returning— depression mixed with a foreboding of doom and gloom. The two spent their day together talking to caffeinated happy-talk radio disc jockeys.

Blippo muddled through his interviews. He seemed heartbroken.

The day before the circus arrived, Paul met with Police Chief Bill Thomas at the Moose Club Lodge to discuss ticket sales and sponsorship settlement. Paul reviewed the Moose Club's ticket receipts, and calculated its percentage of sales. The chief stared at him.

"Congratulations, your club earned eight hundred forty-two dollars," Paul said, smiling.

"That's all? Those boys booking your show told me we'd make a couple thousand bucks— easy as falling off a log."

"I'll double-check the numbers." Paul felt queasy. He worked his calculator again, and the answer repeated: eight hundred forty-two dollars.

"Those boys lied to me about your air-conditioned tent and about how much money we'd make. When they opened their mouths, bullshit just naturally came out."

"I'm sorry, Chief Thomas, I don't know what they told you, but my numbers are here in black and white. If your members had sold more, we'd be happy to pay you more."

"You saying we didn't sell enough tickets?"

"No, I'm just saying that if the club had sold more tickets, it would make more money. Sponsors get a percentage of member tickets sales."

"So, your show's going to be a bust?"

"It depends on how sales are on show days."

"And since we don't get a percentage of those sales, that don't mean shit to us, does it?"

"You'll get eight hundred forty-two dollars for your sales."

"Eight hundred forty-two dollars ain't exactly a couple thousand. Maybe we shoulda sold tickets for your other circus— the one with the goddamn air-conditioned tent." Chief Thomas glared at Paul, snubbed his cigarette out, and lit another. "It's unbelievable I fell for their line of shit, but I did. Go on and pay us our money."

"I don't have your money. Circus management will pay you tomorrow."

"Tomorrow? When?"

"First thing in the morning. We'll settle up at the ticket sales office at nine."

"We'll settle up all right. And I'll make damn sure you cheating carnies pay every penny you owe us and everyone else in my town." Paul's lips trembled. "Mr. Driscoll, I feel like you've taken advantage of us, and I don't like it. Not one goddamn bit."

"I'm sorry you feel that way, but we'll settle all accounts first thing tomorrow. I promise."

"Your promise ain't worth shit. I've seen what circus promises are worth. I'll see you at nine, and once your goddamn circus finishes, I hope I never see any of you lying cheats again." Paul slid his calculator into his canvas briefcase and looked him in the eye.

"I'm sorry, Chief Thomas." He turned and walked out the door, feeling the angry fat man's glare on his back.

⟿

Paul called Katherine that night. He didn't tell her about the gay rumor. He didn't want her to know Barb Sigel was putting moves on him. He told his encounter with Chief Thomas.

"Have you had enough sleazy circus life yet?" she asked.

"Once I save enough, I'll find a job in Boston in the off-season."

"I miss you."

"Miss you, too. God, I miss you. I'm tired of being a stranger in town."

"This was your decision, Paul."

"Remember, if I hadn't joined the circus, I wouldn't have met you."

"You remember where the people who love you are."

"I do."

"Sean asked about you the other day."

"How is the mercenary?"

"Shhh."

"No one's listening. I don't think the old fart at the front desk can even operate this newfangled telephone contraption."

"It's best to be quiet, Paul. You'll never get in trouble for the things you don't say."

"How is Sean?"

"Good. He got a job working construction. It's good money and he likes it."

"Tell him I said hello, and that kissing his cousin is creepy."

"You're hilarious, circus man."

"Thanks."

"I miss you, dink. Be safe. Don't get shot by a cop."

"I'll try not to. Love you."

"Love you, too." He heard a dial tone.

His signal to open another beer.

Paul arrived at the circus grounds at seven a.m., ready to coordinate press coverage of the tent-raising. There was an elderly man from the newspaper with a Nikon slung around his neck. Paul introduced himself. They watched roustabouts pound thick spikes into the ground and pull the large canvas tent across the field.

"Pretty soon the elephants will raise the big top," Paul said. "It's amazing. You're going to love it."

"Uh-huh. Elephants make a good shot."

The elephants arrived. Joe and Teddy led the beasts in raising the big top. The photographer snapped away.

"Nice light," he said. After he'd shot a film roll, Paul gave him circus passes for the afternoon show.

"Bring lots of film. You'll get tons of great shots."

"Thanks." The photographer left. Paul felt confident he'd score a front-page photo and prove to the circus that he was a marketing dynamo.

"How's the gate?" asked a tattooed roustabout with long greasy hair.

"Pretty good. I think we'll do some good business here."

"We need it. Sales have been softer than an old man's dick." He spat and swung a sledgehammer down on an anchoring spike.

Paul knocked on the circus ticket wagon door, and Cronk opened it. "How are you, Paul?" He gave him an automatic handshake and brief eye contact.

"Good, Cronk. I think we'll have good shows."

"We need them." Paul was used to the never-ending whine of slow sales and was convinced the circus was making money— but that narrative wouldn't motivate the troops. Talking about losing the war got soldiers to fight harder.

Paul brought in his sponsor receipts, unsold tickets, and paperwork. Cronk tallied the numbers.

"Not bad," Cronk said.

"The Moose Club President will be coming at nine to get their cut. He's pretty pissed, which is bad because he's also the chief of police."

"What's he pissed about?"

"The bookers told him they'd make a couple grand in ticket sales."

"Eight hundred forty-two bucks isn't bad."

"The Chief thought they'd make a lot more. He thinks the bookers lied."

"Christ, the greed of some bastards." Cronk opened his cash box and began counting bills. He counted twice, and placed the wad of currency into an envelope.

"The bookers also told him our big top was air-conditioned." Cronk looked up and laughed.

"The rube believed that?"

"Yes. When I first arrived, I had to tell him our tent wasn't air-conditioned. I've been on his shit list ever since."

"This guy sounds like he was born disappointed," Cronk said, licking the envelope and sealing it. "He'll feel better when he gets his money." Cronk locked the envelope in the cash drawer.

"I doubt it." Paul tried small talk with Cronk, but the circus guru seemed distracted and excused himself, saying he had things to do.

"Is Cronk all right?" Paul asked Charlotte, Cronk's daughter, setting up her sales window.

"He's got a lot on his mind, I guess." She smiled and went back to counting bills in her cash drawer.

"Going to check for media people, I'll be right back." Paul walked the circus grounds. He didn't recognize most of the roustabouts. The crew had turned over, again. A fresh pool of possible murderers, boozehounds, druggies, and thugs on the run.

Just another day.

Stan Whootmoor was sipping coffee and smoking a cigarette at his sideshow pulpit.

"Hi, Stan," Paul said. The old Barker looked up and squinted. "Who's that?"

"Paul Driscoll, marketing director." Stan smiled.

"Right. Sorry, Paul, didn't recognize you. Still got too much morning in my head. How we looking here? Got a good advance?" Paul wondered why Stan didn't just ask 'Lil Pete the Prophet about sales, after all, he could forecast the future.

"Pretty good. We should do well."

"Been slower than hell lately. It'll be nice to separate the locals from their legal tender." Stan smiled, Paul smiled back. There was an awkward pause. "I'd better go. Take care, Paul."

"Sure, Stan." Paul continued walking the midway, sensing something was wrong. Stan and Cronk weren't their usual chatty selves.

"Well, if it isn't our dashing young marketing director," said a tall young man in a blue knit shirt and tight jeans.

"I'm sorry, do I know you?" Paul asked.

"Silly goose, it's me— LuLu."

"LuLu?"

"The clown!" He sighed. "I see I've made an unforgettable impression."

"Sorry, I've never seen you out of makeup before."

"It is I. Portrait of the clown artist as a young man."

"You look so different."

"I hope you like what you see." LuLu struck a model's pose.

"You look like a regular guy."

"I was hoping for better than 'regular.' Perhaps gorgeous, or handsome."

"You're a nice-looking man."

"Can't we do better?" LuLu asked, leaning in and batting his eyelashes. Paul stepped back and laughed.

"You look like a model."

"For the Sears catalog, or something a bit more stylish?"

"More stylish, I suppose."

"Damn, I wanted to be a Sears model— wearing nothing but a tool belt," he smiled. "Would you like to see me in a tool belt, and nothing else, Paul? Just LuLu and his Craftsman tool?"

"Very funny," Paul said, nervously. "Look, I've got to get back to the ticket trailer to see my sponsor. He's the chief of police and I don't want to keep him waiting."

"Oh, my, an angry cop! I hope he doesn't put you in handcuffs and hit you with his big stick. Although that does sound sexy." LuLu smiled, and winked. "Run along, little angel. We'll talk later."

"Right." Paul walked back toward the ticket sales trailer as Augusta was exiting it. "Hi, Augusta."

"Hi, Paul." She walked past him.

"How are you?" She turned and looked at him.

"All right, I guess. How about you?"

"Good," he said, walking toward her. "I think we'll have strong sales."

"We can use them. Been slow."

"I heard." Paul looked at her faded University of Florida tee-shirt.

"I like your shirt." Augusta looked down at it, then at him.

"It should be a rag, but I haven't done laundry in a while."

"It's nice." Paul felt warm. "You wear rags well."

"Thanks." She glanced at his eyes, then at the ground. "I should get going. I'm working pretty soon."

"You sure you're all right?"

"Yes. Why?"

"You seem like you're mad or something."

"I'm fine. I just don't know why some people can't be true to themselves, is all."

"What do you mean?"

"I mean you. I thought you liked me, Paul, and had a crush on me, which was sweet. Then I heard you don't even like girls, which is fine, that's your business. But you should be up-front with people."

"Where'd you hear I didn't like girls?"

"There's no secrets on the show, Paul."

"Did Barb Sigel tell you I was gay?"

"It doesn't matter where I heard it. Just be true to yourself, that's all."

"I'm not gay, Augusta, I swear."

"Then why are people saying that?"

"It was a rumor started by Barb. She wanted to spend the night with me, and I told her I'm seeing someone."

"Seeing who?"

"A girl I met in Haverhill."

"What girl?"

"She works at the mall and we got to know each other, and, well, I like her, so I'm trying to stay faithful."

"If you have a girlfriend, why'd you act like you liked me?"

"I do like you. But I know you have a boyfriend."

"Do you like me more than the girl in Haverhill?"

"No. I mean, I don't know. I think she might be the one."

"But you like me, too, and you like playing the field— is that it?"

"No. And what's it matter since you're in a relationship?"

"That's what I don't understand. If you like this girl, why were you flirting with me? And if you're gay, why act like you like girls? It doesn't make any sense, Paul."

"No, I guess it doesn't."

"Be who you are, Paul. Whoever that is."

"You're right."

"It's okay if you're gay." She smiled. "And it's okay if you're not."

"I'm not gay, Augusta."

"I'm glad to hear that. I've got to run."

"Okay." She walked away and Paul bathed in the wake of her fresh aromas of shampoo and flowered soap. He wondered why he pursued her while loving Katherine— what kind of a sleazeball was he? A large hand slapped him on the back.

"Just the guy I'm looking for," Chief Thomas said. "It's payday!"

Paul took the cop to the ticket trailer, and Cronk gave him a thick envelope of cash. The Chief opened it, and counted the bills twice.

"Thanks for your support, Chief Thomas," Cronk said. "We appreciate it and look forward to great shows in Greenwood."

"You'll do good, folks here are starved for entertainment. I just wish the bastards booking your show weren't such lying sons of bitches."

"I'm sorry there was a misunderstanding," Cronk said.

"Wasn't any misunderstanding. It was lies, bold ass, brass lies. An air-conditioned tent, sponsors making a couple grand, easy as pie. All lies."

"Of course, we don't have an air-conditioned big top," Cronk said, chuckling. "That would be impossible."

"I don't know nothing about possible or impossible in the circus business. But I do know two slick bastards sat in my office and told me straight to my face you had an air-conditioned tent, and that our club would make a couple grand selling tickets."

"I'm sorry your cut isn't more. We're always happy to pay our sponsors. More for you means more for us. I'm sorry your club didn't have better success."

"Uh-huh. Well, I'm going to make sure you pay every last bill you owe. And you'd better leave these grounds cleaner than when you came, or I'll personally see to it someone pays the price with their ass behind bars. I making myself clear?"

"Yes. We always pay our debts and leave a clean lot." Cronk gave the cop a firm handshake. "Can I give you some free circus passes for your family and friends?"

"I got enough passes to wallpaper my goddamn house," Chief Thomas said. He exited the trailer, slamming the door.

"Told you he was mad," Paul said.

"I've seen worse," Cronk said. "He'll get over it. He's just greedy. Everyone wants easy money. And if his club had busted ass selling tickets, they would have made a couple of grand. It's not our fault they're lazy." Cronk sat behind his desk and began counting money. Paul asked the question that had been on his mind all morning.

"Cronk, are you mad at me?"

"Mad?"

"Upset, or something. I sense you've been avoiding me."

"Paul, it's none of my business what someone does in his personal life. You're a good guy, and I like you. Always thought you were a straight shooter. But I've heard you're not the person you're pretending to be."

"You heard I was gay."

"That doesn't matter to me. It's your business."

"But I'm not gay."

"Really?"

"Yes. I swear it."

"I didn't think you were, Paul. You always looked at my granddaughter like she was a ribeye steak and you were a hungry dog."

"I do like Augusta. This gay rumor was started by someone because I wouldn't spend the night with her because I'm trying to stay faithful to someone else."

"That's a lot of someones."

"I know it's confusing, but that person thought I must be gay because I didn't want to sleep with her."

"Because you like someone else?"

"Yes. Someone I met in Haverhill."

"Haverhill? Where's Augusta fit into all this?"

"She doesn't. Not really."

"But you like her?"

"Yes."

"So, you're in a long-distance relationship with someone in Haverhill, but you're sniffing around the chicken coop close to home with my granddaughter, is that it?" Cronk gave him a stern stare. "Sounds to me like you lead a very complicated life, Paul. I suggest you decide what you want, and stay focused on whatever the hell that is. Otherwise, you'll die from exhaustion running in circles and pissing off people."

"That's good advice. Thanks, Cronk."

"Concentrate on your next assignment."

"Where?"

"Brownsville, Texas, a stone's throw from Mexico."

"That'll be a drive."

"It will be. Pack up after today's shows and hit the road first thing tomorrow. We'll take care of everything here."

"I can sneak out of town before Chief Thomas knows I'm gone?"

"Yes. It doesn't seem like he wants to throw you, or us, a farewell party. We'll just pack up our air-conditioned tent and move on." Cronk smiled and patted Paul on the back.

It was good to have his mentor again.

Greenwood was a success. All shows made money, and the circus people were happy. Paul didn't get to bask in the glory. He began driving to Texas on the second day.

He later learned from Teddy that Chief Thomas was sitting with his family in center ringside seats of the afternoon show. As the elephants performed their elephant chain— each one raising its front legs on the back of the elephant ahead, one of the elephants let loose a stream of urine on the front row, and Chief Thomas got drenched. His wife and children were left dry.

Cronk later told Paul, "I've never seen anyone mad as that fat cop. He swore we made the elephant do it on purpose. I think if he'd had a jail cell big enough, he'd have arrested that elephant."

The story became circus legend.

CHAPTER SIXTEEN
Brownsville

"When the voices in your head start coming out of your mouth, it's not good."

— *Paul Driscoll's notes, Bluefield, WV*

Another circus had played Brownsville a month ago. Paul had his work cut out— how many circuses did people want to see?

Brownsville is a border town on the Rio Grande River. Paul didn't think the streaming dirty puddle was very grande. Matamoras, Mexico, a poor, vibrant market sat on the other side. Trucks with speakers drove down city streets blasting pre-recorded Spanish advertisements.

He would pimp his circus bilingually.

Paul met with a young Mexican woman in his motel room to negotiate the media buy for the sound trucks. She had an olive complexion, long black hair, a perfectly curved, fit body, and an angelic smile. She spoke as little English as he spoke Spanish. She pointed to a sales sheet showing the number of spots with the respective cost in pesos. Sound truck commercials seemed cheap, and she agreed to accept half-trade in tickets, but she wanted half-cash up front.

Paul slowly explained circus policy of settling payment on opening day. She was insistent. He wasn't sure if she didn't understand him, or, if she was being a tough negotiator. He said he would get her a check.

The negotiation was difficult, not just because of the language barrier, but also the beauty barrier. Paul was entranced.

They agreed to terms, and he signed the contract written in Spanish. After she left, her sweet scent lingered. He called the home office and requested payment.

Two days later, she returned to his room wearing a low-cut dress positioning her breasts center stage. Paul handed her the check and as she looked at it, he glanced at her cleavage. She looked up, smiled, and shook his hand.

"Muchas gracias, Senor," she said. He gave her the circus radio script for translation and broadcast.

He fantasized taking her into his arms and locking lips. Their animal instincts would run wild as they worked out their sexual energies on the lumpy bed. She'd confess her love for him. He wouldn't understand her, but as she began ripping off his clothes, he'd catch her drift. And then—

After she'd left, Paul felt empty. Their torrid relationship was over.

Adios.

　　　　　　　　　　　　⌒

He worked the local media reps making his buys with lazy, efficient professionalism, without pestering people to get the most for the least.

He worked on his priest novel. As he searched for his voice, he found many voices in his head that needed exorcising. Voices rooted in insecurity and immaturity, many echoing back to childhood.

He learned writing is an ordeal if one doesn't like his own company.

Paul procrastinated, wrote, procrastinated, then, wrote some more. By and by, blank pages filled, and his black humor priest novel came to life.

～

One morning, as Paul watched "The Andy Griffith Show", the phone rang. "How's it going?"

"Good, Barb. I have sound trucks broadcasting in Mexico, and my Brownsville media's running. I'm blanketing two countries." He watched Barney Fife lock-up Otis the drunk, and waited for Barb's sob story about poor ticket sales and the need for blockbuster sales because the future of the circus and civilization itself rested on his shoulders.

"I've never seen business this bad, Paul."

"I get it, Barb. I'm working my ass off here." He surprised himself with the sharpness of his voice. "It's not my fault we're playing a town another circus just played."

"Calm down. I know you're doing your best. I just wanted you to know business is bad."

"Barb, business is always bad, and your pressure doesn't help. Neither does spreading rumors."

"What are you talking about?"

"Why does everyone on the show think I'm gay?"

"I don't know."

"Seems funny that right after you visit me and I say I don't want to sleep with you, everyone suddenly thinks I'm gay."

"Paul, I don't care if you're gay. It's none of my business."

"That's right, it is none of your business. But I'm not gay."

"You're in love with a Haverhill girl."

"Right."

"So you won't be cashing my rain check?"

"Right again."

"And you're not gay?"

"No. For the hundredth time, I'm not gay." Paul's voice was cold. "And I'd appreciate you not spreading that rumor."

"It wasn't me, Paul, but fine. I just called to let you know Chuck Gund has agreed to do press interviews for publicity."

"Really?"

"Yes, and he never does interviews, but Cronk talked him into it. So, you need to get all the media coverage you can the morning or early afternoon of opening day— TV, newspapers, radio, everything."

"Okay."

"The show needs this."

"I'll do my best."

"Keep me posted."

The moment they hung up, Paul began contacting his media reps pimping interviews with the show's star, Chuck Gund— the world famous "Wild Cat Wizard."

In a 1980 "Pittsburgher" magazine profile, Ray and Kathleen Gund said their son Chuck, at age seven, chased the neighbor's cat, a tabby named Tiger.

"He hated that cat," his mother recalled. "We had an apple tree out back, and he'd chase Tiger, throwing apples. Now we tease him to use apples to tame his tigers and lions. Chuck doesn't think that's funny. I guess he's getting a big head these days."

Charles Raymond Gund was born on June 12, 1947, in Pittsburgh, Pennsylvania. He was an only child indulged by his mother. His father worked at the Homestead Steel Works, the temple that forged Andrew Carnegie's fortune and fame. Young Chuck saw what working in a mill did to his father, breaking his spirit, and causing him to settle and "not make waves" so he could collect paychecks and bank on his pension.

Chuck wanted to make waves.

When he was ten, his parents took him to see the Restford Bros. Circus, featuring Terrence McGuintry, "The Jungle Master". McGuintry, recognized as the greatest lion tamer in the world, faced six lions and four tigers with only a whip, wooden chair, and a pistol filled with blanks. The Jungle Master made the wild cats perform tricks— jumping through rings, chasing their tails, rolling over and roaring on command. Little Chuck Gund was mesmerized and decided he wanted a career taming wild animals. His parents laughed when he told them, and their laughter fed his determination and desire.

Chuck wrote fan letters to Terrence McGuintry, including pictures he'd drawn. He was persistent, asking for advice on becoming a lion tamer.

McGuintry ignored the child, but the letters and requests continued for months. One day he wrote the boy.

"Dear Chuck,

I'm happy you want to be a lion tamer when you grow up. Study hard in school and work hard to make your dreams realities!

Thanks for your kind words and good luck!!!

Sincerely,

Terrence McGuintry

"The Jungle Master"

Although the letter said little, young Chuck was thrilled the grand master wrote back. His father framed the letter and hung it on Chuck's bedroom wall. The boy cherished it.

He continued writing letters to McGuintry, but never received another reply. He was determined to be a lion tamer, but the only professional track he found close to that was zoology and veterinary medicine, both required scientific knowledge.

In high school, Chuck had trouble with math and science.

The summer of his sixteenth year, he worked in the steel mill with his father and hated it. He'd rather face hungry lions than a blast furnace.

He made a plan.

In his senior year, Gund dropped out of high school and ran away to become a roustabout with Peppermill, Monstone & Woorly Circus, a small circus that seated eight hundred. The show had a lion tamer, an elderly alcoholic named Chester Mapleton. Chuck befriended Mapleton, telling him he had dreamed of becoming a lion tamer since seeing Terrence McGuintry.

"McGuintry's a bum," Mapleton said, in whiskey breath. "I'll teach you how to be a hell of a lot better than that egotistical asshole."

Over the next two years, Chuck Gund worked as a roustabout and assisted Mapleton with his act taming four lions, long in their teeth.

After hours, Mapleton taught Chuck the tricks of his trade. "You know why I have a whip and a chair?" he asked the young man.

"To beat the lions back if they attack?"

"A whip and chair won't stop a charging lion."

"That's why you have a gun."

"My gun's filled with blanks."

"Then what's your protection?"

"Distraction. A lion is four hundred pounds of savage fury. He's king of the jungle, but not king of my cage. When lions are in my space, they have to believe I'm tougher than they are. And I do that with distraction."

"I don't get it," Chuck said.

"Animals don't think like people. They're simple creatures, with a one-track mind. A lion looks at me like I'm lunch— if he wants to attack, my only defense is distracting him from that thought. So, I put my chair with four legs in his face, the lion looks at one of those legs, or a couple of them, and he backs off. I scattered his thought of attack."

"What about the whip?"

"Same thing. I lead their attention by dangling it in front of them, or snap their thought pattern by cracking the whip."

"And then," Gund said, "if they still want to attack, you pull out your gun and they back off because they think you'll shoot them, right?" Mapleton laughed.

"Chuck, you think lions know anything about guns? You think they grew up watching westerns? Big cats don't know shit about guns. But they sure as hell know about loud noises. My last resort distraction is firing my gun in the air. Bang! Whatever was on their mind is gone. The only thing they're thinking about is running away."

"Oh."

"Being a wild cat trainer is like being a magician— you got to sell yourself through misdirection. There's only one thing you have to remember when you're in the cage with them. Never, ever, ever let those cats sense you're afraid. Once they get a whiff of fear, you're done. Understand?"

"Yes, sir."

⌐~⌐

Mapleton continued mentoring him. Gund learned how to handle the whip, chair, pistol, and read a lion's eyes. When he saw a cat preparing to attack, he learned how to distract and diffuse it.

Through practice, he remained calm and in control. Mapleton was impressed and proud.

Chuck watched Mapleton perform his act in Wooster, Ohio. Chester began strong and confident, and the lions did his bidding. Then, the old man doubled over, dropped his whip and chair, and clutched his side. His face showed pain and panic. The lions looked on expectantly. Chuck told roustabouts to get Mapleton out of the cage while he distracted the lions. The rousties looked at him as if he were crazy.

Chuck entered the cage and closed the door. He picked up the whip and chair, and began cracking the whip by the lions. They retreated and sat on their perches. Gund stepped forward and stood between four lions and Mapleton writhing in pain on the sawdust floor.

"Get him out," Gund shouted to the roustabouts. They looked scared. "Do it! Now! I've got the lions!"

Two men quickly opened the door and dragged Mapleton out of the cage, slamming the door shut. The lions roared. Gund poked the chair in their direction and cracked his whip. The lions settled.

Chuck took a deep breath and completed Mapleton's act.

The audience gave Chuck Gund a standing ovation. Afterward, he learned Mapleton died. He had bought his liver one too many drinks.

The newswire services picked up the story of the young protégé who bravely saved his mentor from wild lions.

And the legend of Chuck Gund was born.

Gund took over Mapleton's act, adding more lions, new tricks and theatrics. Every show was a sellout— everyone wanted to see Chuck Gund.

Soon, larger circuses came to watch Gund perform. He was courted and recruited to leave Peppermill, Monstone & Woorly Circus for more money, opportunity, and artistic freedom to create the act he wanted.

Chuck Gund felt an obligation to Peppermill, Monstone & Woorly, and worked the rest of the season. In the off-season, he decided to join Finnion, Barton & Powell Circus. The show fired Larry Kimpert, its animal trainer. FB&PC had five lions and two tigers. Gund began working with them, earning their respect and fear. Then he constructed a new act.

When the new season began, an ambitious young marketing director named Tom Burnett capitalized on the young wild animal trainer. He hired a professional photographer to shoot publicity shots of Chuck in action. Burnett wrote sensational press releases: "Gund fearlessly leaped into a cage filled with ferocious lions and saved his beloved mentor's life, before the ravenous jungle beasts made the helpless man their tasty dinner…"

Burnett arranged media interviews for Gund, and came up with the moniker "The Wild Cat Wizard."

It stuck.

Chuck Gund was charismatic and talented, a natural circus performer who knew how to engage audience empathy, build drama, and milk it for all it was worth.

As Gund's star rose, so did Burnett's. The circus promoted Tom into management. Over the years, "The Wild Cat Wizard" changed his act, swapping younger wild cats for older ones and adding more lions and tigers.

When Terrence McGuintry, The Jungle Master, hung up his whip and chair following an accident requiring 246 stitches, Chuck Gund was the undisputed best animal trainer in the game, and the star attraction of Finnion, Barton & Powell Circus.

Then, he withdrew from the public eye when not performing. He refused doing publicity.

～⌒つ

When the show arrived in Brownsville, Cronk thought it would be good for Paul to introduce himself to Gund before his media interviews.

"Chuck can be aggressive," Cronk warned. "A byproduct of being around wild cats."

Paul found Gund's trailer, a large RV that looked brand new. There was a star on the door reading "CHUCK GUND, THE WILD CAT WIZARD!" Paul knocked, and dogs barked from within. The high-pitched yaps increased in speed and intensity.

"Who's there?" a man's voice yelled.

"Paul Driscoll, marketing director."

"Who?"

"Paul Driscoll. Cronk sent me. I arranged some media interviews for you."

"Shit," the voice said. "All right. Just a minute." Paul heard the man trying to silence his dogs, and failing. The door opened, and Chuck Gund stood, wearing a bathrobe and holding a small yapping dog in each arm.

"I'll tie them up," Gund said, passing by Paul with his yapping dogs. He tied them to long leashes in the yard and led Paul into his trailer. "What's your name again?"

"Paul Driscoll."

"Have a seat, Paul. Sorry about the mess." Paul sat on a built-in sofa. The trailer had clothes — male and female, empty snack packages, an empty vodka bottle, and a few crushed beer cans. Gund scooped a pair of woman's underwear from a seat opposite the sofa, stuffed it into his bathrobe pocket and sat facing him.

"Cronk thought I should brief you before your interviews."

"Fuck, that's right. When are they?"

"There's a newspaper reporter and photographer at eleven, and a TV interview at one-thirty." Gund shook his head.

"Shit, then let's make this quick so I can get ready. What'd you want to tell me?"

"The newspaper reporter is a woman who writes feature stories."

"She pretty?"

"I don't know."

"Print reporters are usually dogs. If they're sexy, they're on TV."

"The TV interviewer is with a guy named Mike Cowell. He's one of the news anchors. Very popular."

"A guy. Great. Some pretty boy. Can't understand why more stations don't hire hot chicks— that's who I want telling me about death and destruction, not some goddamn Ken doll. Anything else?"

"Ticket sales are slow."

"You think I don't know that? Christ, I've been playing crowds the size of a kid's birthday party. I don't know what the fuck you marketing people are doing, but it sure as shit ain't filling my goddamn big top."

"I've been working hard, Mister Gund—"

"Call me Chuck."

"Another circus played here a few weeks ago, Chuck."

"Right. 'Another fucking circus.' How long you been working the show, kid?"

"A few months."

"Uh huh. You seen many circuses?"

"No."

"Fantastic. It's great having an experienced hand like you on the team. If you had seen many circuses, you'd know only one goddamn show has an act with seven lions, five tigers, and one man training them with just a whip, chair, a pistol with blanks, and big brass balls."

"Your act's the best I've ever seen."

"It's the best anyone's ever seen. That's my fucking point. Don't tell me sob stories about another circus played here— wah-wah-wah! Big shit! Another circus doesn't have The Wild Cat Wizard. Only this one does!" Paul could feel the anger as Gund reached into his pocket, pulled out a pack of Winstons and lit one.

"Right, and your interviews should get more people coming."

"I know that. The only reason I agreed to do interviews is to put some asses in seats. Since I get a percentage of the gate, I'm dying here, too. But I hate doing these goddamn things."

"Interviews?"

"That's what we're talking about, isn't it? Yes, interviews. Talking to shitheads who don't know circus from their ass. I did so many goddamn interviews coming up, I swore I'd never do another." Gund took an angry drag on his cigarette.

"Thanks for doing my interviews today."

"What's your attack plan?"

"Attack plan?"

"Are you bringing the reporters to my trailer, or am I meeting you at the sales trailer? Tell me where and when I'm supposed to be. I have other things to do, you know."

"I'll bring the reporters here."

"Great," Gund said. "Now I have to clean this goddamn place."

"We can meet at the ticket trailer if you like."

"No, it's too cramped, and Cronk will try running the goddamn show. We'll do it here; then I'll take them to see the cats. That's a good photo op. I know the drill."

"Great. Thanks, Chuck," Paul said, rising from his seat and reaching forward to shake hands. "Your interviews will be great." Gund gave him a quick handshake.

"I know that. I'll have them eating out of my hand. Someone's got to get some fucking people into my big top."

As Paul walked back to the midway, he saw Teddy exiting the elephant tent.

"How's it going, Paul?"

"Fine."

"Got a good gate?"

"Advance sales are weak, but Chuck Gund agreed to do some interviews, so that should get some buzz."

"He never does interviews."

"I just met with him."

"How was he?"

"Kind of a prick."

"At least, he talked to you. He never talks to me."

"He was pretty pissy. I'm not sure what kind of interviews he'll give. He's very sarcastic. He might do more harm than good."

"Don't worry, he loves attention. He'll be fine."

"I think he scored last night. There were women's clothes all over his trailer, and Gund stuffed some panties into his pocket."

"That's interesting," Teddy said. "Gund's married, and I heard he's totally whipped. Pretty ironic, right? Coincidentally, his wife left yesterday to visit her sick mother in Florida."

"It didn't look like wife underwear."

"What's wife underwear look like?"

"I don't know, frumpy. These panties were lacy. Sexy."

"Interesting," Teddy said. "How's the road treating you?"

"Okay, I guess."

"Still in love with that girl?"

"Yeah."

"Too bad. I heard Augusta broke up with her trombone player."

"Really?"

"Yeah. Apparently, he was banging someone. Girlfriends don't usually like that."

"Is Augusta heartbroken?"

"Who knows what the ice queen feels? What do you care, you're in love, remember?"

"Just curious."

"Curiosity got the cat's balls cut off."

"I never heard that one."

"You should have. Good luck with your interviews. Put in a good word to Gund for me."

"I will, if he'll even listen to me."

Chuck Gund was charming, humble, polite, and captivating in his interviews. He was respectful to reporters, and cooperative with photographer requests.

He gave tours of the wild cat cages and explained the difference between his American style animal act— with whip, chair, and pistol, and the European style, training animals at early ages, and rewarding them with food as positive reinforcement for good behavior.

"My act treats big cats like the wild jungle animals they are. It's me versus them. European trainers want to make the wild mild. I don't fight Mother Nature. I figure she knows better than me."

He said the show spends fifty thousand dollars annually on Grade B meat to feed his dozen cats.

"It's not prime rib. Not fit for human consumption. It's a mixture of chicken, beef, beef by-products and vitamins. Our cats eat better than lions and tigers in the wild," he said, with a proud smile. "And as long as they don't eat me, I'm happy," he laughed.

He regaled them with his history, the tale of a young boy mesmerized by a wild animal trainer at his first circus.

"I knew then, it's what I wanted to do."

He humbly told the tale of saving his mentor when he collapsed in the cage during a performance. "It was my natural instinct," Chuck said, recalling it with teary eyes. "I did what anyone would do."

Chuck Gund delivered sound bite after delicious sound bite, and the reporters ate them up. Although first day Brownsville ticket sales were soft, Chuck Gund's publicity brought almost sold-out crowds on the second day.

Paul met with Cronk in the trailer after the second day's shows.

"I'll be damned," Cronk said, as he tallied receipts for both days. "We actually made some money. Good work, Paul."

"Thanks, but I think Chuck Gund is the real hero."

"Don't let him hear you say that," Cronk said, pouring a drink. "That son of a bitch doesn't need his head getting any bigger."

"Will he do interviews from now on?"

"Doubtful. But I'll try."

"He was great."

"He's a P.R. pro. Unfortunately, he got burned-out." The trailer door opened, and Augusta walked in, wearing tight jean cut-offs and a tee. Her hair was tied back in a ponytail.

"Hi, Paul," she smiled.

"Hello, Augusta." Cronk looked at Paul, then at his granddaughter.

"You need something, honey?"

"No, I just wanted to see when you thought we might get to our next site."

"It's only a thirty-four-mile jump. We should get there around eleven."

"Thanks, Grandpa."

"Where's your next city, Paul?"

"Port Arthur."

"I'm sure you'll make them great dates. See you down the road." She smiled and walked out of the trailer. Paul shifted in his seat and Cronk looked at him.

"Still in love with that girl up north?"

"Yes."

"Keep it that way."

⌇

Augusta approached Paul as he walked to his car. "Hi, again," she said.

"Hi." Paul looked over his shoulder to make sure Cronk wasn't watching.

"Thanks for getting good crowds. We needed the business."

"I can't take credit. It was Chuck Gund's interviews."

"But you arranged them, right?"

"Yeah."

"Then take credit." She smiled.

"Thanks."

"Are you still seeing someone?"

"I don't see her. She's in Haverhill."

"Doesn't sound too serious."

"I mean, yes, we're still together."

"Oh." She looked to the ground. "Because if you weren't," she looked back up at him, "I thought maybe we could do something."

"I'd like that, but I can't, Augusta. I think she might be the one."

"I'm glad for you. At least you're not a cheating scumbag like most men."

"Thanks. I think."

"You're one of the good guys. There aren't many left."

"Thanks."

"Take care, Paul," Augusta said, leaning in and kissing his cheek. "See you in Port Arthur." He blushed.

She walked away and he watched, her soft fragrance lingering.

CHAPTER SEVENTEEN
Port Arthur

"Others viewed my travels as a great adventure, but it was a sentence of self-seclusion. An exploration of who and what I was. And it was no vacation."
— *Paul Driscoll's notes, Panama City, FL*

Port Arthur is called "The Energy City" because of its many oil refineries.

Paul worked the phones to find his local home. The motels were expensive, capitalizing on the oil trade. He booked a week at an expensive motel downwind from an Exxon refinery. The noxious aromas of petroleum being refined gave him splitting headaches and made him nauseous. He suffered through the week and escaped.

He went to an old hotel downtown. Center city was dreary and economically depressed. Port Arthur was the birthplace of Janis Joplin, and Paul quickly understood why she sang with such sorrow and pain.

The hotel lobby had derelicts and dope addicts. Skeletal humanoids clutching to life, reclining on worn furniture. The lobby smelled of decay, dried sweat, cooked cabbage.

The front desk was situated behind a barred window with a curved counter and slot for sliding money. Behind the fortress sat an old black man whose voice sounded like Louie Armstrong with a severe cold.

After Paul paid for his room, the old man slid him a room key and croaked, "You're on the second floor. Gotta take the stairs; elevator's busted again." Paul trudged up the stairs with his luggage.

His room had shiny green walls with peeling paint. There was no television. The mattress had a canyon, and the cramped bathroom had a yellow and brown-stained toilet and sink. The towel was thin as toilet paper; the toilet paper like thin sandpaper.

Paul decided the room was not worth the $18 he had paid. He took his luggage and walked downstairs to the desk clerk's cage. The old man was doing a Jumble puzzle in the newspaper. Paul noticed a large sign on the wall: "NO REFUNDS. NO EXCEPTONS!" The old man looked up. "Help you?"

"There's no refunds?" Paul asked, pointing to the sign.

"Nope."

"But there's no TV in my room."

"Ain't no TVs in any rooms. TVs kept getting stolen."

"You didn't tell me there wasn't a TV."

"You didn't ask. You come here to watch TV, or to sleep?"

"Sleep, but I like watching TV, too. Most hotels have TVs."

"Guess we ain't like most hotels. Help you with anything else?"

"No." Paul would withstand one night in this hellhole, just for the experience. "By the way, your sign has a misspelled word.

"Oh, yeah?"

Paul pointed to the "NO REFUNDS. NO EXCEPTONS" sign. "There should be an 'i' in 'exceptions'." The clerk looked at his sign.

"You sure about that?"

"Yes."

"Guess watching all that TV taught you something." He returned to his puzzle.

Paul spent a sleepless night swatting cockroaches away and listening to the doppler effects of police, fire truck and ambulance sirens.

The next day, he found an affordable cinderblock motel twenty miles away, on the outskirts of Beaumont. His room had a television and no toxic refinery fumes outside.

Paradise.

Paul found little pleasure in life. The Texas Summer heat, the stench of oil refineries, the scrambling to make the best of poor business conditions, and the loneliness of the road were taking their toll.

He talked to himself constantly, in accents, dialects, and gibberish. He'd look at his reflection in the fluorescent-lit bathroom mirror and ask, "What the fuck are you doing with your life, then?" in a John Lennon accent. "Have you gone mad, you silly git?"

He traveled roads of regret. He thought of his first real love— Wendy, a petite brunette. When they met in college, she had a boyfriend who had beat her, so her father forbade her to see him. Paul had an opening.

He fell hard, attending to her every wish, proving not all men are uncaring brutes. She fell for him, and they became passionate.

There was a pregnancy scare; she was three weeks late. She said if she was pregnant, she'd keep the baby. Paul said he'd marry her, with no idea how they'd manage. He was living at home, going to school studying advertising, and working part time at an electronics store. But if he was to be a father and husband, he'd find a way somehow.

She went to the doctor and discovered she wasn't pregnant. He thanked God. She suggested they get married but Paul said they needed to finish college and start careers first. Then, they'd marry and eventually start a family. She agreed.

A week later, on a hot July day, she met him outside the business school at noon.

"I can't see you anymore," she said, with tear-filled eyes. "I'm sorry, but I can't. Goodbye, Paul." She walked away.

It was the day before his twentieth birthday.

Surprise.

It took him months to get over her. She avoided him, refusing to answer his calls or letters. He'd drive past her house late at night, drinking beer, smoking cigarettes, listening to Elvis Costello and screaming along with the angry lyrics.

He wallowed in misery and martyrdom. He had done everything for her— he was nice, compassionate and loving. And he lost her.

He learned she was back with her abusive boyfriend. It made no sense and the injustice ate at him.

After his first love, Paul went through a series of relationships with neurotic women; he was attracted to their fragile psyches. Paul thought he could cure them.

Instead, the women brought him down, piling their troubles onto his shoulders, submerging him into their despair.

His attraction to them was not a reflection of their weakness. It was a reflection of his.

Paul Driscoll's history with women was disastrous. He was either romanticizing his first love, or aimlessly looking for relationships in hedonistic affairs like he'd had with Amy.

Then, he met Katherine. In his fragile, depressed state, he had to remind himself that she was his reward. She could raise his spirits. She understood the pain of losing one's father. She was strong and independent, a transformative figure who loved him for who he was.

Katherine was the one worth waiting for. Augusta, barflies, and beautiful Mexican saleswomen were temptations, but Katherine was salvation.

He turned to the Bible during his dark days in Texas.

After months living in rooms with Gideon Bibles, Paul finally read one of them. He had no interest in the Old Testament. That God was angry, carried hellish grudges, and was vengeful.

He read the New Testament— Luke, and his tales of the sweet, loving, generous, and merciful Jesus Christ.

Paul read about Jesus and the devotion of His disciples and followers. He read about His miracles, the ones he'd heard many times in church.

There was something compelling about reading the verses at night with a belly full of beer. This Bible-reading fed his imagination for his priest novel.

He turned his pain into art, writing his way out of low spirits and dreaming of the end of his circus journey.

The beginning of his new life with Katherine.

Paul never knew what to do when a woman cried, especially when she was crying long distance.

He and Katherine had been having a pleasant phone conversation when she said, "I wish you were here," and began sobbing.

"I wish I was there, too."

"I mean now." She broke down and began sobbing harder, in short breaths, making sorrow-filled noises.

"What's wrong?"

"I want to be with you," she said, composing herself.

"I'll be there soon. The season's almost over, and then I'll go home, get my portfolio, pack, return to you, and start job hunting in Boston."

"We could go somewhere else, too."

"I thought you loved Boston."

"I do. But I'm open. If you want to go somewhere else, I'll go."

"What about your family?"

"I could use a break. Some distance might be good." Paul was quiet. It wasn't like her. "You're my family now. You and Robbie."

"Is something wrong?"

"No." She gave a heavy sigh. Silence. "Sean's been a jerk lately."

"How?"

"It's nothing."

"He's not beating people, is he?"

"No. Forget I said anything."

"Is he killing for fun, or, out of habit?"

"Not funny, Paul. He's family."

"Sorry."

"I'm just tired. Tired of being lonely. I'll be better once you're here."

"I'll be there soon."

"Promise?"

"Right hand to God."

"I'll take that as a yes."

Paul met the Foleys at a greasy spoon outside Port Arthur. They stunk of stale liquor and B.O. They sat and lit cigarettes.

"How're sales?" Carl asked.

"Soft. I'm hoping they'll pick up."

"Good fucking luck," Wanda said.

"I'm waiting to hear if Chuck Gund will do interviews."

"Fat chance," Carl said.

"He did interviews in Brownsville, and it worked great. We got huge crowds the second day."

"And that success went straight to his head," Carl said. "He hasn't done publicity since. Word is he's shopping his act."

"Fenterman Brothers, I heard," Wanda said, with disgust.

Fenterman was the most popular circus in the world, an arena circus that had two units playing large venues in major cities.

"Shit," Paul said.

"Shit's right. If Gund leaves after this season, we're sunk," Carl said.

"Doesn't he get a percentage of ticket sales?" Paul asked.

"Can't be much, or he'd do more publicity," Carl said.

"He could just be negotiating," Wanda said. "Playing poker with management."

"Pretty shrewd, if that's his game," Carl said. "Business is in the shitter and the season's wrapping up—"

"His contract's probably up, too," Wanda said.

"Gund's got management by the balls," Carl said.

"I'm sure Randy and Cronk will figure something out," Paul said.

"Maybe, maybe not," Wanda said. "No one likes getting pushed around. And Finnion, Barton & Powell made Chuck Gund who he is."

"This shit couldn't be happening at a worse time," Carl said.

The mood didn't lighten when the advance clown arrived.

"Did you hear?" Blippo asked, after getting into Paul's car to go to his first interview.

"Hear what?"

"Chuck Gund's leaving."

"What?"

"That's the rumor. I heard he won't be back next year. He's going to Fenterman Brothers." Paul began driving.

"You sure?"

"Not a hundred percent, but it's what I heard."

"Barb said he won't do any interviews in Port Arthur."

"See?"

"But he never gave interviews, except for Brownsville."

"I don't know if the rumor's true," Blippo said, "but I've got some feelers out, just in case."

"Feelers?"

"If Gund's not returning, neither am I."

"You've been with the show forever."

"Yeah, but Gund is the show."

Paul caught himself caring about the future of Finnion, Barton & Powell Circus.

<hr/>

The Foleys blanketed Port Arthur with paper. The local newspaper's front page featured a photo of its editor shaking hands with Blippo. And, circus advertising and promotions blitzed all media.

Still, advance ticket sales were poor.

When Paul arrived to handle media coverage for the tent raising, he sensed the bad mood of the show.

"How's sales?" asked a short roustabout with a scarred cheek.

"Not great," Paul said. "But we might get good walk-up traffic."

The roustabout's belly rolled out from under his tight tee. He spat on the ground and lifted his sledgehammer. "Heard that before." He resumed pounding stakes into the ground.

The local newspaper sent a photographer who took shots of the tent raising, and a TV station sent a man with a video camera for news 'b-roll' footage.

Maybe that would spark interest.

<hr/>

"How're we looking?" Cronk asked Paul in the ticket trailer as the marketing director handed over his paperwork.

"Advance sales were pretty slow."

"Been slow everywhere," Cronk said, with a smile. "But that'll change. Chuck Gund has agreed to do interviews from here on out."

"That's great. Should I try and get some interviews later today?"

"Don't bother. We just struck the deal last night, and I promised Gund he didn't have to work this market."

"The newspaper and TV covered the tent raising, so we might get some good walk-up business."

"We'll take it." Augusta walked into the trailer.

"Hi, Paul," she said, smiling.

"Hi, Augusta."

"Do you have anything to say to your loving grandfather?" Cronk asked.

"Good morning, Grandpa."

"Morning, honey." Cronk began counting the advance ticket money.

"How're sales?" she asked Paul.

"Not great, but we should get some strong walk-ups."

"I'm sure you did a fantastic job."

"Publicity was great."

"Thanks to you," Augusta said. She smiled again, warm and inviting. Paul felt nervous.

"I better see if there's any media people out there."

"Bye, Paul," she said.

Walk-up business was poor. The afternoon show was not half-full. The evening show was little over half-full. The shows didn't make the daily nut.

After the evening show, Paul and Teddy went to a bar called The Texan Star. Two guys in jeans and white tees were shooting pool. At a table, three men in cowboy hats drank Lone Stars with whiskey bumps. The circus men sat at the end of the bar and ordered beers.

"Here's to better days," Teddy said.

"I'll drink to that."

"You heard the big news, right? About Gund doing interviews."

"Yeah, Cronk told me."

"He tell you how it happened?"

"No, just that Gund agreed to do interviews through the end of the season."

"Thanks to me," Teddy said, smiling and taking a long sip from his Lone Star bottle.

"You?"

"Yes, me. And you."

"What are you talking about?"

"Remember when you told me about meeting Gund and him stuffing panties into his pocket?"

"Yeah."

"Well, since his wife was out of town then, I figured the panties weren't hers. Gund was playing around."

"So?"

"Well, I heard Gund's contract was up for renewal, and when I found out he wasn't doing interviews, I figured he was making a power play."

"So?"

"I told Cronk about Gund and the mystery panties."

"You didn't mention me, did you?"

"No. I just said I had it on good authority that Gund was playing around while his wife was away. Cronk wanted to know more. I told him I didn't know more, but I'd be happy to do some snooping if he'd do me a favor."

"Favor?"

"I told Cronk I wanted to get on the cat crew next season."

"You sly dog."

"Cronk said he'd make it happen if I got hard evidence of Gund's affair. He gave me his camera and said I had to get pictures of Gund in the act."

"That's secret agent shit."

"Gund's wife returned for a couple weeks— her mom got better, so Chuck was playing good hubby. But a couple nights ago, Gund's wife went back to Florida. Her mom's sick again."

"And Gund was back at it?"

"Hold your horses. After the night show, I took Cronk's camera and camped out by Gund's trailer. Then, I see a woman sneaking across the backlot. I can't tell who she is. And there were flashes of heat lightning. A storm was brewing."

"I'll say. This is like a damn movie."

"The mystery woman knocks on Gund's door. It opens; she goes in. I'm thinking, this is my break. I had stashed a ladder in the bushes behind the trailer and I set it up quietly by his open bedroom window. The curtains are flapping in the breeze. I see old Chuck and the woman making out on the bed. They start ripping off each other's clothes, like they're in a stag film."

"Don't tell me Gund had his whip and chair."

"You want to joke, Paul, or hear the story?"

"The story."

"Then, shut up. The action's heating up, and so is Mother Nature. There's more heat lightning flashes in the sky, which is a great. It's dark in the trailer, so I'm going to have to use the camera flash, but they'll just think it's lightning."

"Smart."

"Gund starts getting it on with the lady, and she's really into it. That trailer's rocking. I zoom in on the action and snap a shot. They don't let up. I take more shots. Suddenly, Gund looks up, and the lady looks up. I snap one more. 'Who the fuck's out there?' Gund yells. I jump off the ladder and run like hell to my trailer."

"Who was the lady?"

"Couldn't tell, but I found out later. The next morning, I tell Cronk I've got the goods on Gund and hand him the roll of film. Cronk smiles like I've delivered him the holy grail. He says good work, he'll handle everything from here. I ask him not to mention me working on the cat crew until after the season's over, so Gund won't connect the dots."

"Nice."

"So, Cronk develops the film, and I ask to see the pictures. He won't show them, but says they're really good. He says I did a great job, and he has what he needs for negotiations. I ask him who the woman was. He smiles, and says she flies— and fucks, with the greatest of ease."

"Mrs. Perez?"

"You didn't hear that here."

"Holy shit."

"Then, this morning I hear Gund's signed a multi-year contract and will do publicity again."

"He had a change of mind."

"And a fear of his wife finding out where his dick's been hiding."

"Or, Manuel Perez finding out."

"That, too."

"What a story, Teddy," Paul said, draining his beer and ordering another round.

"That story ends here and now. Understood?"

"Absolutely."

The next morning, the phone rang as Paul was getting out of his shower.

"Rise and shine, circus man," Katherine said.

"I am shining, I just showered."

"Don't try seducing me long distance. How was your opening day?"

"Pretty bad," Paul said, sitting on the bed. "But I heard some good news. Chuck Gund, the lion tamer, is going to do interviews and signed a long-term contract. He's our star attraction, so everyone's happy."

"I guess that's good news for people who want to work for a circus the rest of their lives." There was a long pause. "But that's not you, right, Paul?"

"Right. I have one more town until my season wraps, and then, I head back to you."

"Good, I need you. I love you."

"Love you, too. Any news?"

"My ex is missing."

"Missing?"

"He hasn't shown up for work in a week. No one's heard from him."

"That's weird."

"I wouldn't put it past him to blow town to avoid paying child support."

"That seems extreme."

"You don't know Patrick Ryan. He may have run away after Sean's little talk with him—"

"The talk that sent him to the hospital?"

"Sean scared the hell out of him, so maybe he decided to bolt."

"What about Robbie?" Paul asked.

"Patrick wasn't involved in Robbie's life, even after we separated.

He was never much in the father department."

"Has his family heard from him?"

"No. I talked to his mother yesterday. She's worried and filed a missing person report. But it could be a cover. A mother will do anything to protect her child. Patrick's younger brother, Michael, told the cops to look into Sean."

"Does the brother know Sean's a mercenary?"

"No one knows that, except you and me."

"Are the cops investigating?"

"They talked to Sean. He told them Patrick's a deadbeat, he probably ran to get out of paying child support."

"How is Sean?"

"He's Sean. A stubborn hot head. He got fired from his construction job for slugging his boss."

"And you say he's harmless?"

"He is, for the most part. He wants what he wants when he wants it. And he's not patient."

"But you forgive him because he's family."

"Yes, Paul, and I don't want to talk about him. I want to talk about you, and getting you back into my life. I'm sick of phone calls and letters."

"I'll be there before you know it."

"Hurry back. I'm anxious to start our life together."

"Me, too."

"Please. Hurry."

⁓

Business on the second day of the Port Arthur stand wasn't any better than the first.

Paul noticed the clowns were flirting with him. When he brought the children back to clown alley to get made up for the intermission party, LuLu said, "Between shows, I'd love to show you some new tricks." The clown traced his long finger down Paul's suit lapel.

"Thanks, LuLu, but I can't. I have things to do."

"I'd love to do things with your thing," LuLu said, chuckling. "Would you like that?"

"Cut it out. There are kids around." He gave him a cold stare.

"I adore your passion, Paul," the white-faced clown said, batting his eyelashes. "It's very hot."

The rumor of Paul being gay was alive in clown alley.

After the first show, Paul went into the ticket trailer to get his next assignment from Cronk. Augusta was selling tickets at her window and smiled at him.

"Sorry business wasn't better," Paul told Cronk. "I think Gund interviews would have helped."

"You'll have Gund in your next town," Cronk said. "You'll wrap your season on a high note."

"Where am I headed?"

"Panama City, Florida. We can't get out of Texas soon enough. We haven't played here in nine years, the show's not well-known, and business tanked. But people know and love us in Florida. And Panama City's always been big for us."

"I'll make up for Port Arthur, Cronk."

"Don't worry about it, you've done great this whole season. You're a real keeper." Paul felt a swell of pride. Augusta turned and smiled at him.

"Thanks, Cronk," Paul said, feeling flushed. As he left the trailer, Augusta looked up at him and mouthed the words "a real keeper." She smiled.

CHAPTER EIGHTEEN
Swan Song

"No one's more dangerous than a lonely man. Except perhaps a lonely man with a gun."

— *Paul Driscoll's notes, Kissimmee, FL*

Paul's Florida home was The Beach Bliss Motel on the "Miracle Mile" of Panama City Beach. The room had a kitchenette, large living area, and a bedroom with two beds. It was the nicest and roomiest housing of his travels— fitting accommodations for the swan song of his circus career. A balcony overlooked the pristine beach and its calming blue-green Gulf waters lapping soft white sands.

It was off-season, and the motel had few guests. His room only cost $230 a month.

Paul procrastinated most days, doing minimal work. He sat in a chair on the balcony watching flocks of birds scour the beach for food.

He updated his resume in preparation of his New England job hunt. It was difficult describing his circus job, but with some wordsmithing, he sounded critical to the success of the American economy.

❧

In his third week, Billy Burdeck, a marketing director Paul had met in South Texas, called. Billy wrapped his season and was driving home to Nashville. He wanted a place to crash, and Paul was happy to have company.

A drunk driver killed Burdeck's girlfriend in February, and the twenty-four-year-old joined FB&PC to cope with his grief. Like Paul, Burdeck was working the circus for an adventure, to escape, and to find himself.

He was tall, had long brown hair and an easy smile. Billy liked to drink and philosophize.

The young men enjoyed barhopping and swapping circus stories. Billy had heard the rumor of his being gay, and Paul detailed Barb's advances, and his intent of staying faithful to Katherine.

"You must be serious about her," Billy said.

"I am."

"If it doesn't work out, you can come back next season and marry Barb."

"Or, marry LuLu. He's cute." They laughed. "Are you coming back?"

"No, I'm going to get a job selling cars. Life on the road gets old."

"I know. Have you met many of the other marketing directors?"

"A few. James, Ken, Christine."

"I've only met you, Gary, and the guy I trained with. He left the show mid-season. What did you think of the marketing directors you've met?"

"They were okay, I guess. Loners who drank or did a lot of drugs. I doubt they'd ever be able to work a real-world job."

"Gary's been with the show four years. He's a lone wolf. I can't imagine him working in an office around other people."

"I think most of the marketing directors are lifers. They've got sawdust in their veins."

"And once you've got it, you're hooked, like a junkie. Pretty soon, you turn into a Foley."

"That's scary shit. Screw that," Billy said, raising his beer and clicking Paul's can, "here's to escaping."

"To escaping."

They talked late into the night and drank. Paul realized the depth of his loneliness and depression. He looked forward to getting home, then, starting a new life in New England. He wanted to assimilate back into society.

Billy left the next day, and Paul continued casually working his master plan. Most afternoons, he quit early, drank beer and stared at the Gulf of Mexico, monitoring its progress. At night, he drank, tapping his IBM keys writing sad poems and sappy love letters. He'd call Katherine and talk about seeing her soon.

He was excited.

"Shit-for-brains got a DUI last night," Wanda Foley told Paul as they sat in the booth of a diner. She heaped sugar into her coffee and stirred angrily. "I can't get him out of jail until eleven because that's the soonest the show can wire bail money."

"Sorry to hear that," Paul said.

"I've been telling him for years to knock off the sauce, but what the hell do I know— he's the great and mighty Carl Foley, mister goddamn know-it-all."

"Will he get any jail time?"

"I hope not. This is his second DUI; the other was five years ago. He'll probably get a fine and probation, but we might have to come back for a trial date."

"I'm sorry."

"You and me both. If we do have to come back, it'll have to be after the season. Cronk's mad as hell, and he's not going to limp back to Winter quarters without full paper along the way."

"Is there anything I can do?"

"Not unless you can you talk some goddamn sense into Carl."

"I can try."

"Doubt you'll have much luck, but come over tonight at six-thirty and we'll have a nice home-cooked meal."

"Sounds great. Can I bring anything?"

"Whatever you want to drink," Wanda said. "We can celebrate Carl getting sprung."

Paul arrived at the Foley's trailer park with a six-pack and flowers. Carl was manning the grill, fanning encouragement to the coals with a newspaper.

"Hey, Paul," he said. "You shouldn't have brought me flowers." He laughed. "Go inside and give them to Wanda. Say they're from me."

Paul entered the trailer. "Got some flowers." She looked up from chopping vegetables.

"That's sweet. Thanks. I'll find something to put them in, you go and keep the jailbird company." Paul returned outside and opened a beer. "Sorry to hear about what happened."

"Yeah. Shitty luck," Carl said, taking a sip from a tumbler of brown liquor. "I don't have to come back for trial until next month, so I can end the season."

"That's good."

"My lawyer thinks he can get me off with probation and a fine. Could have been worse."

"Right."

"How you been? Survived Texas, I see."

"Barely."

"Show should've never gone there. It was stupid to have circus wars in a state we haven't played in forever. But, on the plus side, Chuck Gund signed a multi-year contract and is doing publicity again."

"That's great news," Paul said, resisting the urge to tell him the story of how Gund's negotiations came to pass.

"Hope you're hungry. I got pork chops thick as a baby's thigh."

They ate their dinners at a wooden picnic table by the Foley trailer.

"So, Paul, what'd you think?" Carl asked, with a mouthful of pork.

"Think about what?"

"Circus life. The season. Think you're coming back?" Both Carl and Wanda looked expectantly at Paul.

"Sure. Yes."

"What about that girl of yours up north?" Wanda asked. "This job's hard on ordinary relationships."

"You saying our relationship ain't ordinary?" Carl asked. He sipped whiskey.

"You know what I mean, Carl. We travel together. We couldn't be married if you were on the road and I was back in Orlando."

"It'd make my life easier. I wouldn't have to hear your constant nagging."

"Nagging? You got your nerve, Carl Foley. Spending the night in the drunk tank, while I'm hustling to get your bail money, and now, I'm a nag!"

"All's I'm saying is if you're not riding me about something, you don't have a whole hell of a lot to say."

"I ride you because I see you killing yourself with a bottle."

"You drink as much as I do, Wanda."

"And how many DUIs do I have?"

"None. Because I do all the goddamn driving." Wanda turned to Paul.

"Go on, Paul, you tell him."

"Me?"

"Tell him he needs to cut back on his drinking."

"Well, Carl," Paul started, "it might be a good idea if—"

"You're both full of shit if you think I'm going to listen to someone dumb enough to fall in love on the road." Paul felt embarrassed.

"I just think if you cut back on your drinking—"

"Jesus Christ— now I'm getting goddamn lectures in stereo." Carl crumpled his paper napkin and threw it on the table. He stood up. "I'm a grown man, and I don't need a nagging woman and a shit-head kid telling me how to live my life. I'm getting another drink, if that's all right with you two." He went into the trailer.

"There's no talking to him," Wanda said. She drank her vodka.

Carl returned, and they acted like the scene never happened.

"Glad to hear you're coming back, Paul," Wanda said. "Every season gets easier."

"Yeah," Carl said. "Before you know it, five years, ten years, twenty have passed. Circus life's good, Paul." He took another slurp. "Real good."

"Thank God you're not driving tonight," Wanda said. Carl shot her an angry look.

By the end of the evening, Paul and the Foleys hugged and wished each other well.

"See you next season, Paul," Wanda said.

"Be safe," Carl yelled, as Paul backed his car out. "Watch out for Johnnie law. Those goddamn bastards are everywhere."

Barb Sigel was the most relaxed Paul had ever seen her. She sat in a restaurant booth and was reflective.

"I think we'll have big show dates," Paul said.

"That's nice." She smiled.

"You all right?"

"I guess so. I don't know." She lit a cigarette. "I just have the end of season blues."

"Aren't you happy the season's almost over?"

"It feels like we've finished a marathon, so there's a sense of accomplishment. But it's sad because it's over. The show goes into Winter quarters, we head home or wherever, collect unemployment, and wait until we go out again."

"You can rest and do something you've wanted."

"I suppose," Barb said, in a sad exhale of smoke. "Don't worry. I'll be all right."

"Good."

"What will you do in the off-season? You're coming back, right?"

"Sure," Paul lied. "I'm going back home, maybe do some freelance copywriting."

"What about your girl in New England?"

"I'll see her, too."

"But you are coming back, right?"

"Probably." Barb looked concerned.

"Yes, I'll definitely be back."

"Good. You're one of my favorites, Paul. You know that, right?"

"Yes. Thanks."

"And my rain check is still open. Twenty-four hours a day."

"Thanks, Barb, but I have to stay faithful."

"And you're still not gay, right?"

"No, Barb. Don't start."

"Just checking. Next season, we'll get together, okay?"

"Maybe. We'll see."

They finished their meal. Barb said she had to go to Fort Walton and meet with Gary, the marketing director working that market. They shared an awkward moment standing in the parking lot.

"I guess this is goodbye then— until next season," Barb said.

"Guess so."

"You take care of yourself, Paul."

"I will. You, too."

"Don't worry about me." She leaned in and clutched his face, then kissed him on the lips. He pulled away.

"Please, Barb—"

"Sorry. Your rain check's always open and will collect interest. And I promise it will pay handsome dividends." She got in her car and drove away.

Paul watched, relieved.

When Blippo arrived, he was more melancholy than usual. His radio interviews were flat, and his mall magic show bordered on hostile. The little clown was a knotted ball of sad rage.

"Is something wrong?" Paul asked.

"I've been thinking a lot lately."

"About what?"

"About life. I've been an advance clown for years, but I'm not sure it's what I want to do anymore."

"Do you want to go back on the show?"

"I don't know. I'm not even sure I want to be a clown."

"What else would you do?"

"I'm not sure. That's what I've been thinking about."

"Maybe you just need some rest."

"Yeah, maybe. What about you? You coming back?"

"Sure."

"You're not going to marry that girl in New England, are you?"

"I don't think so."

"Good. She's wound pretty tight." Paul said nothing. "You can do better. I like you, Paul. You were a good hire."

"Thanks, Blippo, I appreciate that."

Blippo's lower lip quivered, and he looked away.

Paul had been drinking beer and watching a PBS documentary about Auschwitz when his motel phone rang.

"I got your letter and poem today," Katherine said. "I loved them."

"I meant every word. How are things? Your ex ever surface?"

"No. It's been over three weeks. It's not like him."

"Are the cops still looking for him?"

"They say they are, but I doubt they're looking hard. I think everyone's convinced he left the state."

"How's Robbie?"

"He asks about daddy. I told him he was away on business."

"What's Sean think?"

"He thinks Patrick ran because he's scared Sean will talk to him again."

"I don't think anyone likes conversations that end in the emergency room."

"Are you excited to pull the plug on your circus career?"

"Yes. I'm a popular guy, everyone wants me back."

"They can't have you. You're mine. All mine."

"Good. I've updated my resume so I'll be ready to job hunt in Boston."

"I'm open to other places, too."

"I thought you loved being close to family."

"I do. But sometimes family gets too close."

"Is everything all right, Katherine?"

"It's fine."

"Sean's not asking to give kissing lessons again, is he?"

"Shut up, Paul. God, I wish I never told you that story."

"Sorry."

"Finish your stupid job, dink, and get here soon. I mean it."

"Yes, dear."

Teddy was excited to see Paul walking the backlot the morning of the Panama City show opener.

"I got big news," Teddy said.

"What?"

"We're short a clown. Short a very short clown. Shrimpy got arrested in Dothan, Alabama."

"What happened?"

"The little perv hit on the wrong woman. He asked her if he could crawl up her beaver, and unfortunately, the lady's husband was a cop. They hauled the little bastard away in handcuffs."

"I didn't think Shrimpy even spoke English."

"He speaks enough to get arrested."

"Didn't the show bail him out?"

"They tried, but Shrimpy has a history of pervy offenses. Not even all Cronk's horses and all Cronk's men could put Shrimpy back together again. He'll probably do some jail time."

"Making a crude remark isn't a serious offense."

"It's serious if you tell the wrong person and you have a history of wrong behavior."

"Will he be back?"

"I don't know if Cronk wants him back. The guy's more trouble than he's worth. His only talent is being short. He almost got arrested in Texas— caught in the bleachers looking up dresses."

"The poor horny little guy."

"He won't be horny in his jail cell. He'll get lots of action."

"You want to get beers tonight?"

"Absolutely. I'll buy the first round."

Paul arranged Chuck Gund media interviews. Gund was his usual surly self with Paul, and gave his "aw-shucks-I'm-not-so-brave" act for the press.

His act played well.

The first day's business was spectacular; both shows were packed houses. The performers fed off the crowd's energy, and Paul felt proud.

Even the roustabouts seemed to be enjoying themselves.

After the second show, Augusta approached Paul as he waited outside the big top for Teddy.

"Sorry I didn't get a chance to talk earlier," she said. "I was swamped selling tickets."

"That's okay. We had great shows today."

"Thanks to you." She smiled, her eyes reflected the overhead lights.

"I just did my usual job. This is a great circus town. Tomorrow should be good, too. Chuck gave some interviews."

"Are you doing anything tonight?" She smiled.

"I'm going out for a beer with a buddy. You want to come?"

"I don't want to be a third wheel."

"You won't be."

"No, thanks. My grandfather doesn't like me leaving the grounds at night. He says there's too many ways to get in trouble with townies." Paul wondered why she asked him what he was doing. She had something in mind. He'd traveled far being true to Katherine—was he now being tempted by a siren call to the rocks?

"You sure you don't want to join us?"

"Some other time." She looked directly into Paul's eyes with her full moon pupils. "Paul, you're coming back next season, aren't you?"

"Yes, I think so."

"Great." She gave a relieved smile. "I'd really like to get to know you better."

"That'd be nice." Paul felt guilty he didn't answer her honestly.

"Goodnight," she said. "We'll talk tomorrow."

"Goodnight, Augusta." He smiled, and she walked away. Teddy approached.

"Was that the ice queen?"

"Yes. And I think I'm melting her a little."

"Right. Keep telling yourself that. Let's go, I need a beer or twelve."

A mile down the road from the circus site was a bar called The Beachcomber, a wooden structure with festive Christmas lights strewn across its front, and neon signs flashing beer logos into the night. Paul and Teddy sat at the bar and ordered beers from a bartender who seemed bothered by customers. There were a dozen men in the bar and a few women.

"Here's to the new cat man," Paul said, clinking his bottle against Teddy's.

"It's not official yet," Teddy said. "Cronk said he'll break the news to Gund at the end of the season."

"You're almost there, Teddy."

"It's amazing how blackmail can advance your career."

"Here's to blackmail."

"To blackmail." They drank.

"Hello, boys," a voice said, from behind. It was LuLu, out of make-up, in jeans and a tight knit shirt, with Rocket Baxfree, the suicidal canon daredevil, and another man, short and slight with a complexion that made Andy Warhol look tanned.

"LuLu," Paul said, "good to see you."

"Hi, Rocket," Teddy said.

"Hey."

"Rocket, do you know Paul Driscoll?" Teddy asked. "He's our marketing director working Panama City."

"Nice to meet you," Paul said. "I love your act."

"Thanks. Terrific crowds today."

"Should be good tomorrow, too."

"Great. Crowds make all the difference."

"This is my friend, Michael," Lulu said. "He's a townie who gave us a ride." Paul shook the small man's hand— four limp fingers, a thumb, and moist palm.

"Nice meeting you," Paul said.

"Michael was in clown college with me," Lulu said. "He was smart enough to get out of clowning."

"What do you do now?" Teddy asked.

"I sculpt hair," Michael said, in a high-pitched voice. "A hair artist. Stylist." He smiled.

"Can we join you?" Rocket asked.

"Sure," Teddy said. The three men took seats to Teddy's right, lining the bar parallel to the hallway to the restrooms. They ordered drinks, and the grumpy bartender complied.

"Here's to bringing this miserable season to an end!" Rocket said, raising his gin and tonic.

"Amen," LuLu said, raising a Rum and Coke. The men drank.

As the night wore on, the bar got crowded. The circus men discussed the troubles in Texas. Michael listened, amused and relieved he'd chosen a different career path. As Lulu told a story of trying to pick up a townie in Temple, Texas, Michael leaned back and laughed. "Watch yourself," a deep voice said, from behind him.

"Sorry," Michael said, turning to see a six-foot, forty-year-old man with a three-day beard.

"You better be sorry, faggot."

"Hey," Lulu said, "where's your Southern hospitality? He said he was sorry."

"It was an accident," Michael said.

"Your boyfriend's sticking up for you," the man said. "I'll kick both your faggot asses."

"We're not looking for trouble," Paul said. "It was an accident. He apologized. End of story."

"And who the hell are you?" the man asked, stepping toward Paul and leaning in. "Another queer?" Paul smelled liquor and onions on his breath.

"I'm their friend."

"A friend of a fag is a fag."

"I'm not," Paul said, "and it's none of your business. Leave us alone."

"This is America, asshole," the man said. "I'll do whatever the hell I want."

"Hey, buddy," Teddy said, standing up. "Back off."

"Well, you must be the queen bee." The man turned his head toward a table of men. "Hey, guys, we got us a pack of queers over here."

"Our sexual preferences are none of your business," Lulu said. "And it's none of our business what species you mate with."

"You little cocksucker," the man said, stumbling toward Lulu with a cocked fist. "I'll beat your ass." Rocket stood and shoved the man. He tumbled backwards as his friends rose from their table and rushed forward. The four circus men and Michael began fighting the drunk man and his six friends, as the bartender and others tried breaking up the brawl.

～

When he came to, Paul felt a tightness cutting into his wrists. A plastic band pressed into his flesh. He heard the clicking sound of it locking on itself.

"What's going on?" he said, lying on the dirty bar floor. Barstools and chairs were turned over, beer bottles and broken glass were strewn across the floor. The scene was illuminated by the bar's interior lights and flashing red lights outside.

"You're under arrest," a young cop said, helping Paul to his feet.

"For what?" The short cop led him outside.

"Inciting a riot, starting World War Three, assault and— hell, I don't know. We'll figure it out at the station."

"But we didn't start anything," Paul said.

"Right, you guys are a bunch of innocent carnies."

"We're not carnies. We work for Finnion, Barton & Powell Circus."

"Tell that to the judge," the cop said, opening the back door of a police car and tucking Paul's head under the doorway. Paul slid in next to Teddy, who had his arms cuffed behind his back.

"You're alive," Teddy said, smiling. The cop slammed the back door.

"What happened?"

"You were kicking some serious redneck townie ass, Paul, and you got cold cocked, I guess. I'm not sure, I was mixing it up pretty good myself."

"Where's everyone else?"

"In another cop car, headed to the station. Lulu and his pal got beaten pretty badly, but Rocket held his own."

"What about the drunk idiot who started the fight?"

"Cops let that asshole go. The guy's connected. Townies never get prosecuted. Once the law finds out we're circus, they assume we're at fault."

"What are we going to do?"

"What else? Call Cronk. The show must go on, right?"

The police station smelled of stale coffee, cigarettes, and damp mold. It was old and built like a sprawling ranch-style home, parts of which had barred doors and windows.

Paul and Teddy got fingerprinted, had their mug shots taken, and were placed in a holding cell where Rocket and Lulu sat by a drunk old man mumbling to himself.

"Where's Michael?" Teddy asked.

"The hospital," Lulu said. "He might have some broken bones. He was on the ground and some prick kept kicking him."

"The whole thing's bullshit," Paul said. "That drunk guy started it, calling us fags."

"That's life on the road, Paulie-dear," Lulu said. "We're strangers, they're locals. Strangers are always guilty."

"Christ, Lulu, you're going to have a black eye," Paul said.

"Not my first, and nothing greasepaint can't hide. Looks like someone tagged you, too."

"I'm all right."

"Thanks for sticking up for us," Lulu said. "You're quite the fighter, Paul."

"What about me?" Teddy asked.

"Both of you. It was sweet."

"We've got to stick together, especially when hicks think circus people are carnies," Paul said.

"They're idiots," Rocket said. "We need to get the hell out of here." He stood and walked toward the bars and shouted, "I want to make my call!"

"Make my call," the drunk stranger mumbled to himself, he then turned his head and puked on his feet.

Paul, Teddy and Lulu stood, and walked over to stand by Rocket.

"Jesus," Cronk said, getting into his car, "you bastards are going to be the death of me." Rocket sat in the front passenger seat, Teddy, Paul, and Lulu squeezed in the back. Cronk began driving.

"We were minding our own business, Cronk," Rocket said.

"How many times do I have to tell you guys that doesn't matter? Townies see strangers, and you're bait for trouble. Couldn't you just get drunk on circus grounds?"

"It gets claustrophobic, Cronk," Lulu said.

"Claustrophobic my ass. Lulu, you're lucky you didn't end up in the hospital."

"Sorry, Cronk."

"You guys should know better. Circus people and civilians don't mix. Never have." There was silence as Cronk drove along a rural road. The sun was rising. Paul felt a hangover waking up. He was tired, but felt at ease.

Cronk dropped Paul at his car in the bar parking lot.

"Come by the trailer at eleven, Paul," Cronk said. "Tom Burnett's blowing in and says he wants to see you before you head home."

"Okay." Paul wondered what Burnett wanted. He hadn't heard

or seen anything from the marketing maven since his job interview. Paul went to his hotel room and found a couple hours sleep.

When Paul arrived at the circus grounds, roustabouts smiled.

"Heard you kicked some townie ass last night," a tall man with crooked teeth and greasy hair said.

"A little, I guess." Paul didn't recognize the man.

"Someone gets in your shit, you gotta shut 'em the fuck up," the man punched his fist into his hand four times rapidly. "Show the bastard who's boss."

"Right."

"Can't let 'em get away with nothing, or they'll think you're a pussy."

"I guess so."

"I know so! Good work," the man said, slapping his dirty hand on Paul's shoulder. "Keep kickin' ass!" The roustabout walked away, whistling a happy tune.

Joe Parkett, the elephant boss, came walking toward Paul.

"Good job, kid," he said. "We got to stick together, no matter what." He shook Paul's hand. It was the only time he had been addressed by the elephant man.

As Paul approached the ticket sales trailer, he heard Augusta shouting. "Wait up, Paul." He turned, she was running toward him wearing tight shorts, a blue tee, and white sneakers. Her hair was pulled back in a ponytail exposing her tanned face. "I heard about what happened last night," she said.

"Seems everyone's heard."

"It's big news when townies jump us. I heard you stood up for Lulu and his friend. You beat up some locals." Paul felt like Gary Cooper in a western, with Augusta playing the doe-eyed school teacher who admired his heroics.

"Yeah, until I got knocked out."

"Are you all right? Your face is bruised."

"I'm fine. I just have a little headache."

"I have aspirin."

"Thanks, I already took some."

"Will I see you before you leave?"

"Sure."

"Let's meet after the last show at the ticket trailer. I want to say goodbye."

"Okay."

"Great." Augusta walked away, and Paul watched, lost in her seductive wake and wading into his lust-filled imagination.

Tom Burnett met Paul at the ticket trailer wearing a pressed gray suit, crisp white monogrammed shirt, and deep blue necktie tied in a full-Windsor knot. His black shoes were at high gloss.

"Congratulations, Paul," he said, shaking his hand. "Your first season's under your belt."

"Thanks, Tom."

"Let's celebrate at the cookhouse, grab some grub and talk." Paul had never been to the cookhouse, the tented area reserved for show personnel.

They stood in the serving line, and a tall man with a balding head and easy smile said, "Morning, Mr. Burnett. What can I get you?"

"Hi, Bill. Any breakfast left?"

"Got scrambled eggs, toast, and bacon."

"Perfect."

"How about you?" Bill asked Paul.

"I'll have the same. Thanks." They took their plates and coffees, sat in a secluded area, and began eating.

"What did you think of your first season?" Tom Burnett asked.

"It took some getting used to, but it was good."

"That's normal. Life on the road takes practice. Most people can't fly solo, they'd rather travel in packs."

"I had some troubles with the bookers," Paul said, uncertain about how much truth he wanted to tell. "They told lies I had to fix."

"Par for the course," Tom said, laughing. "Sometimes they'll do that to first of Mays. It's like your initiation." Paul didn't say anything; he knew there'd be no arguing with the slick circus man. "And what about your writing?"

"I started a novel."

"A novel, that's great! What'd I tell you, Paul? This job gives you the freedom to write what you want, while seeing things few people ever see, and having experiences others only dream about." Paul thought of his experience directing traffic because the bookers secured a lot with no parking, and telling the chief of police there was no air-conditioned big top, and denying he was gay to the circus community.

"Right."

"I'm sorry I didn't see more of you," Burnett said. "It was a crazy season for me, scouting other shows, recruiting talent, and managing our way out of Texas. I would have liked spending more time together, Paul. Sorry I wasn't around much."

"That's okay. I found my way."

"Yes, you did. Barb told me you did great. And Cronk loves you. I heard you even got into a scrap last night with some townies. Looks like you got some souvenirs on your face."

"Yes, we got arrested, too. My first time."

"It happens. Don't worry, there's no paperwork on your arrest. No record. You're circus family, and family always looks out for family. Right?"

"Right."

"Cronk wanted to garnish wages to cover your bail, but I told him the show would handle it. It's an end-of-season-blowing-off-steam expense. He papered the cops with comp tickets and some legal tender."

"Thanks."

"Paul, when you've got sawdust in your veins, you get benefits. I hope you'll be returning to us next season." Burnett looked into Paul's eyes as if they were playing poker and he was reading the strength of his hand.

"Absolutely," Paul said, uncertain if Burnett bought his bluff.

"Fantastic. Then go home, take it easy, rest up. We'll call you a few weeks before we head out and we'll do it again."

"Sounds great."

"The second year's a lot easier than the first, Paul. And every year after's even easier. Trust me." He smiled.

"Did you know what happened to Brian?"

"Brian, who?"

"Brian Munyard, the guy I trained with."

"Oh, the fat guy from Philly."

"Right."

"No. I just heard he made a move on a townie and paid the price. Got his fat ass kicked, then he ran squealing home. He was obviously not suited for life on the road. Like I said, Paul, things happen. Brian was tested, and he failed. The job was bigger than the man. He had no sawdust in his veins."

"Right."

During the opening spectacle of the afternoon show, Paul watched Rocket wave, and smiled at him. Lulu blew Paul a kiss. Teddy smiled as he led the elephants past. And Augusta smiled and gave him an enthusiastic circus wave. Paul waved back, and felt warm.

Both shows were packed. The crowd applause was thunderous. Paul ended his career on a high note.

After the second show, Paul stood by the ticket trailer waiting for Augusta.

"Great job," Cronk said, as he approached Paul. "Fantastic business both days."

"Thanks, Cronk."

"You're coming back next season, right?"

"I think so," Paul said, wondering if Burnett's story about Cronk wanting to garnish his wages was true.

"What about your girl?"

"We'll see where it goes," Paul said.

"And if it doesn't work out, you'll be back?"

"Absolutely," Paul said, getting good at lying.

"Then we'll leave it up to the love gods to see if a circus man can be domesticated."

"Thanks for everything, Cronk. I appreciate all your help."

"No problem, Paul. You're a good advance man, and they're hard to find. Follow your heart and see where it takes you. If it's to that girl, so be it. If not, come back, we'd love to have you. I heard you're also a good scrapper in bar fights. We always need those."

Cronk shook Paul's hand and walked into the trailer. Augusta walked down the midway, smiling. She wore tight white shorts and a bright orange tee shirt. "Great crowds, Paul."

"Thanks."

"Want to go for a walk?"

"Sure." They walked across an open field where patrons had

parked, and crossed a two-lane road to the beach. A full moon illuminated the water merging with the sky on the horizon, as surf lapped the shore. They stopped and stared at the vista.

"I love the beach at night," she said.

"Me, too."

"I think it's as close as heaven gets to Earth."

"That's nice. Very poetic."

"Thanks." She turned toward him. "Paul, are you still staying true to that girl?" He took a deep breath. His bar fight and relationship seemed to be the talk of the circus.

"Yes. I need to see where our relationship goes." Augusta nodded.

"I respect that. I do. Not many guys are that strong."

"Why did you ask?"

"Just curious. I like you and thought maybe we could get to know each other better. To stay in touch between seasons." He stared into her eyes. "Are you planning on coming back?"

"Maybe. It depends on how it goes in New England."

"I hope you find happiness, Paul, wherever it is. I just wish we'd gotten to know each other better."

"I didn't think you liked me much."

"I'm shy. People think I'm standoffish. I know they call me 'ice queen' behind my back, but being cool is my shield against getting hurt. I've found out the hard way that most guys only want one thing, so I'm careful about getting hurt."

"Do you think we would have had a chance?"

"I don't know. I think so. You seem sweet and genuine. And the fact you're staying true to your woman proves you're different."

"I'm a romantic, I guess" Paul said. Her face was beautiful in the moonlight, luminous, her eyes shining.

"Me, too." She stared at the sea. "I think the world's harder for romantics. We don't take things as they are. We're always dreaming of something better."

"Wow, that's deep." She turned and punched his arm.

"You don't have to act surprised." She smiled and kissed him on the cheek. "I hope you find what you're looking for, Paul."

"Thanks. You, too."

"We'd better get back. I've got work to do before we jump."

They returned as the show was being disassembled; roustabouts were undoing what they had done the previous morning. The circus city was being packed into trucks and relocated.

Augusta and Paul stopped outside her trailer and she held his hands. Her hands were warm, he felt a tingle up his spine.

"Goodbye, Paul. Drive safely. Be careful, please." She kissed him softly on the lips and smiled. "I'm sorry. I couldn't help myself. I've been wanting to do that. Don't tell your girlfriend."

"That's all right," Paul said, blushing.

Augusta broke their grip and walked to her trailer door. "And, Paul—"

"Yes."

"Please don't get in bar fights. I like your face the way it is." She smiled, opened the door, and vanished.

Paul stared at the door, feeling the sting of newfound loneliness and a dull aching in his chest.

CHAPTER NINETEEN
The Return

"What kind of man kills, and what kind kills for money? 'Mercenary' is a polite way of saying hit man. But it doesn't make him any less dangerous."

— *Paul Driscoll's notes, Akron, OH*

The return of the prodigal son was joyous. Although no fatted calf was slain, the Driscoll family enjoyed a roast beef dinner prepared by Paul's relieved mother to celebrate his return.

He signed up for Ohio unemployment and researched Boston ad agencies at the library. Paul wrote letters to creative directors requesting interviews and later phoned them. He scheduled four meetings. His sales experience was paying off.

Paul had resumes printed and prepared his portfolio of ads. He had nothing to show for his circus experience since it was sales, but he thought agencies would find his promotion, publicity, and public relations experience valuable.

Or at least interesting.

He talked to Katherine daily. He was bringing the novel he was writing with a copy for her. She said she'd begun working weekends as a bartender to earn extra money for Christmas shopping, and that her ex-husband was still missing.

Paul had his week-long New England trip planned. The night before his flight, he'd stay with Frank, who would drive him to the Cleveland airport. Katherine would pick him up at Logan. He'd stay at The Shamrock Motel in Haverhill, and use Katherine's car for interviews.

His mother kissed him goodbye and looked worried. Her eyes broadcast the same concern they showed when he left for the circus.

Paul drove to Akron. He and Frank shared beers and pizza at a place called Gino's, with plastic red plaid tablecloths, and empty chianti bottles holding candles.

"Guess who I saw at the mall the other day?" Frank asked.

"Who?"

"Amy Jepson— looking like she stole a basketball under her sweater. She'll be dropping a kid soon."

"Really?" Paul began doing math in his head. "You just noticed she's pregnant? Doesn't she work for you?"

"No. She left the agency a couple weeks after you did. Said she was burned out and wanted to do something else. The other day was the first time I'd seen her in months."

"Did you talk to her?"

"No. She was across the mall. She went out the door, a car pulled up, and she was gone."

"Did you see who was driving?" Paul wondered if it was Greg Cartwell or Jack Lunkorm.

"No. And I didn't get the license plate number, either. Jesus, why are you so curious about Amy?"

"After I started my job, she called and said she might be pregnant. She said it was mine."

"Yours? Didn't you use rubbers?"

"Yes, usually. But I don't know how she could be so sure. You said the rumor was she was sleeping with Cartwell, and I saw her flirting with Jack Lunkorm— it's anybody's guess who the father is."

"She's a popular girl."

"A couple of days after she told me she might be pregnant, she left me a message saying that she wasn't."

"Then, you're in the clear."

"But you just said she's pregnant."

"Oh, she's pregnant all right, and if she already said it's not yours, don't worry. It's someone else's bundle of joy."

"I hope it's not mine."

"Take it easy. God, why do you have to be so Catholic?" Frank filled Paul's mug from the pitcher. "Let's toast to Katherine, the woman who might be the one."

"Amen."

That night, he crashed on Frank's sofa and dreamed he was running down an empty street with an infant in his arms.

He awoke and had trouble getting back to sleep.

The next morning, Frank drove him to the airport.

When he landed at Logan, Katherine was waiting for him. They hugged and kissed, and headed to her car. Paul observed a different Katherine Flynn-Ryan than the one he'd known months earlier.

This one was heavier and looked exhausted. Her eyes had lost wattage and she'd been biting her fingernails. The carefree woman he'd met in the mall offices now seemed stressed and distracted.

"Happy to see you, dink," she said, lighting a cigarette and starting her car. "You look like you've lost weight."

"I did. Greasy road food goes out faster than it comes in. It takes vital organs with it. They're just dead weight."

"Nice conversation, circus man. I'm bartending tonight, so we'll get you checked in, then you drop me off at work and pick me up later. My shift's over at one. Come earlier and keep me company."

"Sure. Any word on your ex?"

"No. He's still M.I.A."

"How's your brother?"

"Tommy's still out of the house, drinking his life away."

"How's Sean?"

"I haven't seen him lately. We got into a big fight last week."

"About what?"

"Nothing."

"You fought over nothing?"

"He was acting like a jerk. He said you were just using me and he didn't think you'd be coming back."

"Where'd he get that idea?"

"Who knows? Sean sees the world his way."

"You told him I was coming, right?"

"Yes. And that you're job hunting to be with me. 'We'll see,' he said. I got pissed, and we argued about that and other stuff. It got pretty ugly."

"It's not like you to argue with family."

"All families fight, Paul." Katherine gave him an icy look. "Let's drop it, okay?"

"Sure." Paul lit a cigarette and looked out his window at the gray New England sky. He sensed something was bothering her. Maybe she had been overeating out of anxiety, and the extra weight made her feel self-conscious.

Maybe.

Paul checked into The Shamrock. They entered the room, he dropped his luggage and they grappled each other on their way to the bed, shedding clothes and transitioning into a natural rhythm of emotional and hungry lust.

They cuddled afterward.

"Not bad— for a circus freak," Katherine said. "You didn't bring me crabs again, did you?"

"Hilarious. Want to hear some mercenary jokes?"

"Lighten-up." She tickled him.

They showered, dressed, and went to her house. Paul reintroduced himself to Robbie as "mommy's circus friend." The little boy hugged his mother tightly, treating Paul like a stranger. Katherine's mom, Eileen, was cordial, but cool. She seemed surprised he had returned.

Paul would adapt to his new family.

All in good time, he thought.

Buster's was an old single-story building in downtown Haverhill, with exposed brick walls and large wooden crossbeams. It was cluttered with neon beer signs, Boston sports pennants, road signs, and a spinning barber pole. Paul thought it was like a TGI Friday's— a place trying hard to be cool.

Katherine kissed him on his cheek.

"I don't want any trouble out of you tonight, circus man. No picking up women. Especially not bearded ones. Understand?"

"I'll try."

"And tip your beautiful bartender well. She needs the money."

"If I tip generously, can I pick her up later?"

"You better. You have my car." She smiled. "I'll get you a beer."

Paul watched college football highlights on TV. "Here you are, sir," Katherine said, placing a beer in front of him. He slid her a twenty.

"I expect change."

"First one's on the house. Once you're hooked, I'll start charging you. Big."

"You pushers are all the same. Thanks." He sipped as she served customers. Katherine was a perfect bartender— attentive, funny, personable.

The bar continued filling up. Paul took a notepad and pen from his coat and wrote notes for his novel. Drinking, observing bar life, and writing felt comfortable. He finished his beer.

"Want another?" Katherine asked.

"No thanks. The evening's early, I don't want to get trashed. How's the food here?"

"I'd order off-menu— any menu that's not here."

"Then, I'll grab something to eat, go back to the motel and rest, and come back later."

"Great. I'll be charming and earn big tips."

"You can be charming?"

"Beat it, dink," she said, waving a bar rag. "Let a girl earn a living."

When Paul returned at 11:30 p.m., Buster's was crowded and noisy. He found a barstool.

"Want a beer?" Katherine asked.

"If you insist." She poured a draft. "It's a busy night."

"Usually dies down after midnight. Oh, no," Katherine said, looking toward the door.

"What?"

"It's Sean. If he bothers you, ignore him."

"Okay."

Katherine went to serve a customer as Sean walked to Paul and slapped him on the back.

"You returned to the crime scene," he said.

"What crime?"

"Where you stole my cousin's heart." He laughed and gave Paul a firm handshake. "Good to see you, Paul." Sean looked larger and stouter than he'd remembered, and his eyes were glassy.

"You, too."

"Let's get a table. Talk man-to-man." Paul looked around.

"It looks pretty full."

"I'll find something." Sean walked to a booth with three young men and talked to them. The men grabbed their drinks and left. He waved Paul over.

The waitress brought Sean a draft and two whiskeys, Sean slid one to Paul. "For sipping."

"Thanks."

"I'm surprised you came back." Sean stared intensely into his eyes.

"I always planned on coming back."

"For Katherine."

"Yes."

"Then you love her?" Sean took a gulp of beer.

"I guess so." Sean gave a cold stare. "I mean, yes, I love Katherine— whatever love is."

"You don't know what love is?"

"Yes, I know. And, I do love her."

"Good," Sean smiled. "I want to make sure my cousin's happy. She deserves a prince after the asshole she married." He lowered his voice. "You're not an asshole, Paul, are you?"

"No."

"Good. I hate assholes. Assholes make me want to kill." He smiled, and raised his shot glass of Jameson. "Here's to not being an asshole." He shot it down. Paul took a sip of whiskey. Sean leaned in and whispered. "Katherine said she told you about my past. Is that right?"

"Yes. But I haven't told anyone."

"Smart." Sean leaned back. "So, tell me about yourself. Did you ever consider joining the military?"

"Not really. I mean, if I was drafted, I'd serve. Like during Vietnam— I would have gone." That was a lie. Had he been drafted, he would have fled to Canada. Vietnam seemed like a stupid war. Had he lived during World War II, he probably would have enlisted, like his father. That war was different. The country was attacked. He was glad he wasn't alive then because he wasn't sure he was soldier material. He sensed Sean was measuring him, and Paul was probably failing.

"I served in 'Nam. Lost lots of buddies. A lot of good men died there. I'll tell you something. Honor and country are everything. What makes America a country worth living in is what makes it a country worth dying for. Never forget that, Paul." Sean took a sip of beer and seemed lost in thought. Then he changed the subject to Boston sports.

Their freeform conversation continued. As Katherine worked, she was happy to see they were getting along. Sean left before last call, and gave Paul a bone-crushing handshake while staring into his eyes.

"You treat my cousin right. Treat her like the queen she is. I mean it."

"Absolutely. I'll always treat her right." Paul was buzzed, but the demeanor of the mercenary was sobering.

"You better, or I'll come looking for you." Sean broke his vice-like grip. "And you don't want that."

"No, sir." Sean waved to Katherine and exited into the night.

As they left the bar, Katherine asked Paul what he and Sean talked about.

"War, sports, weather," Paul said. "And you. My feelings for you."

"Was he nice? What'd he say?"

"He thinks you're a queen and said I'd better treat you like a queen, or he'd come looking for me. It sounded like a threat."

"Sounds like he was drunk. You're pretty plastered, too. Give me the keys, I'll drive."

"Sure." Katherine drove to The Shamrock, and asked more about Sean's conversation.

"It was like the Spanish inquisition," Paul said. "Without all the torture."

They got into the motel bed and began making out. Paul fell asleep and Katherine joined him.

∼⌒

The pounding on the door was loud. The bedside clock read 3:12. The pounding grew louder, angrier.

"Open the goddamn door," a male voice shouted. "Or I'll kick it in!" Katherine woke up.

"I think it's your cousin," Paul said.

"Go away, Sean," she shouted.

"Open the door, Katherine, or I'll bust it in!"

"Should I open it?" Paul asked.

"Leave us alone!"

"Not until you open this goddamn door. Now!"

"I think we should open it," Paul said.

"He's drunk. Open it, and let's see what he wants."

"Are you opening the door, or, do I have to kick it in?"

"Coming," Paul said, slipping on his underwear. He unlocked the door and it flung open. Sean stepped inside, his large body backlit by the parking lot light.

"Out of the way, Paul," he said, shutting the door. He stepped into the dark room, lit only by light seeping through the cheap curtains. "I need to talk to my cousin." Paul sat on the edge of the bed and Katherine sat up, clutching the sheet and bedspread to her neck.

"Get out, Sean. Leave us alone."

"Get dressed, Katherine. I'm taking you."

"I'm not going anywhere."

"Yes, you are. You're coming with me. He doesn't love you— he told me he doesn't even know what love is."

"That's not what I said."

"Shut up, Paul!" Sean pointed at him. "This little shit's using you."

"That's not true. I came back to find a job to be with Katherine."

"I said shut up. This is family business."

"But I—"

"Shut up! Get dressed, Katherine. You're leaving."

"I don't want to."

"You stupid bitch. Can't you tell he's using you? He'll fuck you and forget you."

"That's not true," Paul said.

"Don't you understand orders?" Sean took a wobbly step toward Paul.

"Sean," Katherine said, "if you don't leave, I'm calling the cops."

"You're leaving, goddammit!"

"No, I'm not."

Sean stepped toward her side of the bed, grabbed the covers and flung them back. She covered her naked body with her arms.

"Don't play innocent," Sean said. "I've seen it all before." She grabbed the bedspread from him and covered herself.

"Get the fuck out of here, Sean, or I'm calling the cops. I swear to God!"

"Katherine's told me a lot about you, Paul," Sean said. "She said you like doggie-style best."

"What?"

"Is that your favorite position, Paul?" Sean walked toward him. "I'm asking you a question, you little shit! Did you screw Katherine doggie-style last night? Answer me, goddammit!"

"We didn't do anything last night."

"She said you were lonely on the road. Were you a lonely boy? Did you miss your mama? Are you a little mama's boy?"

"Sean, get out!" Katherine said. He looked at her and walked toward her.

"Leave this mama's boy and come with a real man."

"Sean, do you want to get arrested for breaking and entering, public intoxication, and whatever illegal shit you have in your car? Do you?"

"I'm trying to protect you, Katherine."

"Leave us alone. Please."

"You want this little shit? Fine. Fuck you, Katherine. Fuck both of you!" Sean turned, stumbled out of the room, and slammed the door. They heard a car engine starting and tires peeling.

"Holy shit," Paul said. "What's his problem?"

"He's drunk, and wanted to put on a show."

"Some show. Jesus, he's a madman." Paul crawled under the covers and wrapped his arms around her.

"I hope he doesn't kill someone driving home. I've never seen him that drunk."

"Where'd he get that stuff about me liking doggie-style and being lonely?"

"Who knows? He's crazy."

"Did you tell him that?"

"God, Paul, forget about it. He'll forget it. He'll sleep it off and when he wakes up, he won't even remember being here. That's how he is. And if he does remember, he'll say he's sorry. That's Sean. He gets drunk and blacks out. It's what he always does. But he's family, and blood is thicker than water. Or alcohol."

"Right. He's family, so it's all fine." She broke his embrace.

"Paul, I told you before I'm willing to move away from my family. Get a job in Chicago, Denver, L.A., wherever— I'll go."

"It's too late. I have Boston interviews lined-up. And even if I did find a job in another city, what about Robbie— is he ready to move?"

"You and I would get settled, then, maybe mom could come out with him for a transition period."

"So, we'd just transplant your family. And when would Sean come? Would he have his own bedroom?"

"Not Sean! Absolutely not." She turned away.

"Look, Katherine, I understand your family's important, but I don't have money to job hunt all over. I've got interviews here. You're settled, we just have your crazy cousin to deal with. Maybe if he stays sober—" She turned back to him.

"Fat chance. He has the Irish curse. If there was no liquor, the Irish would rule the universe."

"Is he dangerous?"

"Not sober. And even drunk, his bark's worse than his bite."

"That's a pretty damn vicious bark. But you don't think dangerous?"

"Not unless he has to be. He keeps two loaded carbines in his trunk. They're modified to be automatics."

"So the angry, drunk mercenary has machine guns? Nice."

"They're for his protection."

"Protection from what?"

"He made enemies in El Salvador. He needs protection in case they come looking for him."

"The first night I met your brother Tommy, he threatened me. Now your cousin threatens me. It must be a family tradition." Katherine punched his chest.

"Stop it! They're family."

"Maybe we'll get lucky and Sean will get hired to train troops overseas."

"Maybe."

"He's very protective of you, but when he sees I'm committed and staying, maybe he'll back off."

"Maybe. Let's get some sleep."

"Okay."

"Just know I am open to moving."

"It's a little late for that."

She cuddled with him. "I'm so glad you're back."

"Me, too. It's a hell of a homecoming, though."

"It'll be better, tomorrow." She kissed him, retreated to her side of the bed, and rolled her face away from him.

Paul was wide awake and thinking about Sean. He soon heard Katherine's gentle snoring, like the purr of a contented cat.

He wondered if they'd ever find their previous easygoing relationship.

Paul woke at 10:25 a.m., and heard the shower. His head was throbbing, his brain foggy with memories of Sean in their room.

He sat up and smoked, thinking about what Sean said. The comments about his liking doggie-style and being lonely on the road were true. She must have told him. His remark about having seen

Katherine naked was probably gamesmanship to get under Paul's skin.

"You're awake," Katherine said, walking into the room, wrapped in a towel. Another towel served as a turban.

"I just woke up."

"I'm sorry about Sean last night."

"It's not your fault. But, where'd he get that stuff about me liking doggie-style and being lonely?"

"Who knows? You want me to explain a drunk maniac?"

"He didn't get it from you, did he?"

"He was plastered, Paul. Doesn't that explain it?"

"It's weird he knew those things."

"Right, you're the only guy who likes doggie-style."

"No, it's just that—"

"Can we just drop it? I don't want to fight. Not now, not ever."

"Sure. It's dropped."

"Good," she walked toward her purse and pulled out a hairbrush. "Have you seen my wallet?"

"What?"

"My wallet, it's missing."

"I haven't seen it."

"It was in my purse."

"Maybe Sean took it."

"Why would he take my wallet?"

"Why would he have a shouting match in the middle of the night? Sean's capable of anything."

"Maybe I left it at Buster's. We'll stop by later and check, okay?"

"Sure."

She kissed him. "Let's not fight. We should be celebrating."

"I was celebrating— until Sean showed up."

"He was drunk, you were too. Problems were bound to happen."

"I'm not a mercenary with loaded machine guns in my car, who breaks into rooms and threatens people."

"He was being dramatic."

"It was an Oscar-worthy performance."

"Enough. I'll finish up in the bathroom then it's all yours. Then, we'll take mom and Robbie to the 12:15 Mass. Sound good?"

"Mass?"

"We all need redemption, Paul. After Mass, we'll drop Robbie and mom back home and head to Busters. When I find my wallet, I'll buy you lunch, then we'll go to Boston for the day. And tonight, we can celebrate properly in the pubs."

"No Sean?"

"Absolutely not."

"I'll drink to that."

꙳

St. Patrick's was beautifully lit. Sunlight filtered through stained glass depictions of pain, anguish, suffering and glory heralded from Heaven. Candles and low-wattage bulbs provided warm fill lighting. The faint scent of incense and beeswax candles transported Paul to warm childhood memories of a comfortable environment.

A safe cocoon for shame, guilt and redemption.

He genuflected before entering the pew, then knelt with three generations of Flynn's. He took his cues from Eileen, following the mother's lead on when to sit, stand, kneel, make the sign of the cross, etc. She attended church daily and had the script and stage directions nailed.

The priest was young and pious. His homily grazed across a variety of subjects: the importance of sacrifice, the need for forgiveness, the never-ending grace of God and the demands He has for us to demonstrate our Christian love for one another, the ever-present temptation of Satan that must be refused at all costs and, even though there is pure innocence in children, we all carry the sins of Adam and Eve rejecting God's will, and so we must work hard to clean our slates if we have any hope of earning our eternal rewards in Heaven.

The sermon was like a pinball hitting theological bumpers in the machine to rack up points; none of it adding up to anything parishioners could take away or use for inspiration.

It was a minefield of dogma. Paul thought it was standard priest drone.

He fought heavy eyelids throughout the homily. Katherine noticed him nodding off and nudged him, and he survived all twenty-six excruciating minutes.

As the priest changed wafers and wine into the Body and Blood of Christ, Paul was unimpressed. The father had no stage presence and little familiarity with his lines. For the transubstantiation ceremony, he referred to an open book on the altar, reading with mechanical precision and zero passion.

His performance had the energy of a bored man reciting a shopping list.

Paul thought about Father Donald, the main character in his novel, who builds a thriving Catholic church with charisma and theatrical flair in the heart of Mississippi. He felt good about what he had written so far, and looked forward to sharing it with Katherine. Maybe after they got back from Boston, he'd show her the manuscript in progress.

Paul got into the Communion line with Katherine and Eileen. Robbie held Katherine's hand. It was a training-wheel trip to the altar since he was years away from his first Holy Communion.

"Body of Christ," the priest said.

"Amen," Paul replied. The priest delivered the Host to Paul's cupped hands. He placed it in his mouth, savoring the yeasty flavor as he walked back to his pew and knelt. He prayed Sean would leave them alone, and that he'd have success in job hunting.

When Mass ended, the congregation said they would "go in peace to love and serve the Lord." Just like they always did— until they returned next week begging forgiveness for the fresh evils they'd done.

After Mass, Paul sat at the kitchen table talking with Eileen as she prepared lunch. Katherine was upstairs packing her bag. Paul felt awkward sitting at the table talking with a devout Catholic woman while her daughter prepared a sleepover kit for a night of unmarried sex with him in a cheap motel room.

He hoped Eileen and God would understand and forgive them.

If they did get married, Paul wondered, would their premarital sex still be a sin? Would it receive a reduced sentence?

Eileen was curt but polite. Paul thought he was growing on her.

Robbie ignored him; the boy's attention was absorbed by a spaceman coloring book. Paul tried talking with him, but the youngster was unresponsive.

When Katherine came downstairs, she kissed her mother on the cheek and scooped Robbie into her arms, smothering him with kisses.

"Mommy has plans tonight, little angel. I'll be back tomorrow. Be a good boy for Grandma, okay?"

"Where are you going?" he asked.

"We're going away for a little."

"Are you seeing daddy?"

"No, honey. Daddy's still on his trip. Mommy's going with Mr. Driscoll to Boston."

"Can I go?"

"No, honey. Maybe another time. I'll be back tomorrow. I promise, angel."

"Okay," Robbie said. Katherine rubbed his hair and put him back in front of his coloring book. Eileen looked at the sad little boy.

"Don't worry, Robbie, we'll have a wonderful time. And after lunch, we'll go on an adventure." Katherine kissed Robbie and gave her mother a kiss on her cheek.

"Thanks, ma." She picked up her bag, grabbed Paul's hand, and they headed out the back door.

Paul felt guilty but was relieved to be leaving.

Buster's was crowded with people watching football. Katherine didn't find her wallet. She and Paul sat at the bar and ordered burgers, fries, and soft drinks. Then, she called her cousin with the bar phone.

"Uh huh, yes, Sean. You're always sorry. Uh huh. Look, I want you to leave us alone. I mean it. Well, make sure it never happens again. Right. Remember your sober promises when you're drunk. Okay. Listen, the reason I called was to see if you saw my wallet last night, it's missing. No, I'm not accusing you of stealing it, I'm just asking if you saw it— in the bar, in our room, anywhere? Okay. Fine. Yes. Yes, I believe you. Yes, Sean, I swear to God I believe you," Katherine rolled her eyes. "No, I'm not working tonight, Paul and I are going to Boston. No, we're coming back tonight. Okay. Remember your promise. Right. You have a good night, too. Uh huh, okay. Goodbye." She hung up.

"Let me guess, he's sorry and didn't see your wallet."

"Good detective work, circus man."

"Did he really sound sorry?"

"Yes. He kept apologizing. I told you he'd be sorry."

"Maybe your wallet will turn up."

"Hope so. I'd hate to deal with the DMV for a new driver's license."

Katherine and Paul explored Boston like tourists, visiting Newbury Street, Beacon Hill, the financial district, Faneuil Hall and the waterfront. They found the buildings where Paul had interviews scheduled.

"You'll own this town," Katherine said. "I prayed for that in church today."

"From your lips to God's command."

They had an early dinner and headed to The Limerick Pub. A band was setting-up in the corner, and Paul bought pints of Guinness.

Katherine went to the bathroom. He stared at the creamy cloud of Guinness swirling up to a head in his glass, like the overview of a hurricane. Paul tried pinpointing what was different about Katherine and their relationship. She seemed preoccupied. Their conversation wasn't flowing like it used to. Maybe they were still growing back into each other, working to ignite the relationship they once had.

When she returned, they toasted and drank.

Paul began feeling better. Katherine smiled. He kissed her. Maybe the distance in their relationship was his imagination. Maybe everything was fine. Maybe it was just the change of seasons, the difference between a New England spring and a New England winter. Perhaps it was the nature of change itself— nothing to be feared, just accepted and understood.

Every sip of Guinness brought relief. He felt more at ease.

They stayed at The Limerick for three pints and a set of Irish music. The songs juxtaposed the misery of living under the oppressive rule of cruel English bastards, with the joys found at the bottom of whiskey bottles.

The pub got packed. They left and went to The Blarney Stone, a dark pub smelling of smoke and spilled ale. They sat in a booth, and stayed for two pints. With mellow Guinness buzzes, they headed back to The Shamrock Motel.

On the drive back, they talked about Paul beginning his new life in New England. Everything had led to this moment. Fate and God had dealt this hand. It felt natural and right.

At the Shamrock, Paul wanted to show Katherine his novel. He checked his canvas briefcase, but the envelope with his original and the copy was missing.

He looked in the flaps of his luggage. Nothing. He searched the dresser drawers.

"Don't bother," Katherine said. "I'll read it tomorrow. Your brilliance deserves sober eyes."

"They're my only copies."

"Don't worry, they'll turn up. I've got a better idea."

She took Paul by the hand and led him toward the bed. She kissed him, and they fumbled onto the bed, stripping one another, and made passionate love like they used to.

The couple snuggled and was fast asleep by 12:30 a.m.

CHAPTER TWENTY
The Passenger

"If you want to tax your imagination, try understanding why people do what they do. You'll soon go bankrupt."
— *Paul Driscoll's notes, Boston, MA*

They woke early. Paul felt good, a little foggy, but not hung-over. He went to McDonald's and brought back breakfast.

Katherine was dressed, sitting on the bed watching TV. He handed her coffee and an Egg McMuffin, and they heard a car drive up. Katherine went to the window and drew back the curtain.

"Oh, no. It's Sean."

"Not again." There was loud knocking.

"Leave us alone, Sean!" she shouted to the door.

"Don't make me break this down," Sean yelled. "Open the door— now!" Katherine unlocked it.

"Get out of the way," he said, pushing her aside. "I want to talk to lover boy." He looked angry, drunk, and exhausted.

"Don't talk to him, Paul," she said. "If he doesn't leave, I'll call the cops."

"You're not calling anyone," Sean said. "I'm talking to Paul."

"Get our coats, we're leaving," she said. Paul began walking toward the closet. Sean stepped and stood in front of him.

"Excuse me," Paul said.

"Don't try getting by me, if you know what's good for you." Paul looked at Sean's piercing bloodshot eyes— they were empty, soulless. He stepped back. Sean turned to Katherine.

"Wait in the car, Katherine. I want to talk to him. Alone."

"Please, Sean, leave us a—"

"I said, wait in the goddamn car, Katherine! Now!" His face was red; his jowls twitched.

"This isn't fair."

"Katherine," he said, in a low voice, "if you care for this little shit, you'll do what I say. Now."

She grabbed her coat, took her car keys and left. Paul sat on the bed. His breaths were shallow, his hands shaking.

"You're going back to Ohio," Sean said. "I'm taking you to the airport."

"My flight's not until Saturday."

"No, it's today. I changed it. Start packing."

"But I have interviews in Boston—"

"You're not going to Boston, you son-of-a-bitch."

"Why do I have to leave?" Paul stood up.

"Because I said so." Sean pushed him in the chest, knocking him back on the bed.

"But, I've made plans."

"Fuck you and your plans." Sean curled his meaty fists into taut sledgehammers. "I want to kill you so bad right now it's ripping the shit out of me. You're not going to use my cousin, and you're not working in Boston. Hell, you'll be lucky if you live long enough to make it to the goddamn airport." He stepped forward and looked down at him. "I'm going outside and telling Katherine the plan. So, start packing, now. Understand?"

"Yes." Paul hoped Katherine could talk some sense into her cousin. Sean walked outside.

He stood. His lips trembled. He felt as if he was in a movie. Paul thought if he were directing, he'd have a wide-angle camera in the corner of the ceiling across the room tilting down, the shot depicting a small man trapped by insanity.

He began packing hoping Katherine would walk in and tell him Sean had gone home to sleep it off. Then, they'd resume their lives as planned.

But Katherine Flynn-Ryan never entered the room again.

After five minutes, Sean returned. "You packed?"

"Yes."

"Good. Listen carefully." Sean stared at him. "We're loading your stuff in my car. Say goodbye to Katherine. Nothing else, just goodbye. No touching, hugging, kissing, or fucking. Just goodbye, then, I'll take you to the airport. Understand?"

"Yes."

Sean grabbed Paul's suitcase and went out the door. Paul slung his briefcase over his shoulder, grabbed his portfolio case and followed. Katherine was crying in her car. The engine was running. Paul walked to her window and she rolled it down. Her eyes were red.

"Goodbye, Katherine." He waited for her to give him a sign, a plan of how they'd escape.

"Goodbye, Paul," she sobbed.

She took a deep breath, rolled up the window and backed her car out, never looking at him. She drove away.

Sean stood by the open trunk of his 1976 Chrysler Cordoba, caked with road salt and dirt. He grabbed Paul's bags and tossed them into the trunk littered with tools, dirty blankets, crumpled newspapers, and empty Gallo wine bottles. Paul thought somewhere in this mess are two loaded semi-automatic carbines.

For protection.

Or, maybe the guns were inside the car.

Sean slammed the trunk lid shut. "Get in."

The interior was messy. At Paul's feet was a quarter-full half-gallon bottle of Gallo white wine. An empty large Styrofoam cup was in the cup holder. Sean started the car and handed the cup to Paul.

"Fill me up." Paul poured and handed the cup back. Sean took a gulp, then began driving.

At a stoplight, he handed Paul a pair of eyeglasses with the left lens missing. Sean reached into his coat pocket and gave him a smudged lens.

"Put that back in the frame." Paul slid the lens into the cracked plastic frame and handed the glasses back. Sean put them on. "That's better." He drank. Paul tried being invisible, wondering if Sean could hear his heart pounding. It was loud in Paul's ears.

As he drove, Sean sipped and occasionally wiped his nose with his coat sleeve.

"Listen carefully," he said. "If you ever call Katherine again, or write her, or contact her in any way, I will kill you." Sean looked at Paul. "You understand me?"

Paul nodded, afraid to talk. Sean's tone was cold, sharp. "You want to know something, Paul Driscoll?"

"Yes."

"I am one bad motherfucker." He smiled at him, then, turned his attention back to the road. "There's nothing I'd like better than to beat the living shit out of you." He turned, his beady red eyes behind smudged glasses. "Do you understand me?"

"Yes." Paul's vocal cords were tight, his voice weak. "Yes, sir," he

310

said, louder. He noticed Sean's fists clenched tightly around the steering wheel.

"You're never going to use Katherine again."

"But I didn't use her."

"Are you going to marry her?" Sean shouted. "Are you going to fucking marry her and move to fucking Ohio?" he turned toward Paul with a red face, and quickly turned back to the road.

"No. I mean, yes, I think so. I came back to be with her and find a job in Boston. We were going to take it from there."

"Take what from there?"

"Our relationship." Sean pulled the car off the side of the highway, hit the brakes and slammed the car into park.

"You're not going to work in Boston, you little shit. If you ever even go to Boston, and I find out about it, I will kill you. I swear, I'll fucking kill you if you ever set foot in Massachusetts again." he punctuated his words with clenched fists. "Do you fucking believe me, Paul Driscoll?"

"Yes, sir."

"Good. I told you, I'm one bad fucker. You do not want to find out how bad I am."

He shifted the car into gear and drove. There was silence. He exited for Lawrence. Paul knew this wasn't the way to Logan Airport.

The passenger looked at the gray winter sky and a dreary landscape of closed businesses, leafless trees, and rundown homes. He wondered about Katherine. Was she at her mother's house? Or, at the police station rounding up a cavalry to rescue him?

The car turned right at a sign that read "Hillside Cemetery" and began descending a hill. A cluster of people gathered beneath a tent for a burial.

Sean drove past, down the road, and parked.

"Get out," he said. Paul was scared— would Sean shoot him in a cemetery? "I said, get out. Now!"

Paul opened the door and stepped onto the wet dead grass.

"Start walking." Sean's shoes crackled on the cold gravel road. "Down there." He pointed down a row of gravestones. Paul walked with the mercenary behind. "Keep going."

Paul thought through his options. He could run, but if Sean had a gun, he'd be dead after a few steps.

No.

He thought of shouting for help to the people at the funeral. Maybe they'd hear him before Sean shot him dead. Maybe not.

Too risky.

He thought of clasping his hands together, quickly turning, and hitting Sean in the head. A surprise attack might work, but in the Panama City bar brawl, Paul only held his own for a short time before he was knocked-out. With a trained soldier, if his surprise attack didn't knock him out, he'd have an angry, and possibly armed drunk mercenary to deal with.

Not a good bet.

If Sean were planning to kill him, maybe Paul could use his circus sales skills to talk his way out. Begging for his life was a gamble worth taking.

The only option.

Paul thought of his mother and family. If he was killed, they'd never know the circumstances. His body found in a Lawrence, Massachusetts cemetery would be a mystery.

Yes, authorities would interrogate Katherine, but what would she say? As much as he thought Katherine loved him, Paul was not family.

Didn't she just leave him alone with her drunk maniac cousin?

Would Katherine keep Sean's mercenary past a secret from the authorities?

Or, would she strike her "blood is thicker than water" philosophy and protect him?

Paul wasn't sure. He prayed for God's help.

He noticed all the gravestones read "veteran" and had military markings. He would die among fallen brave soldiers. His death would be either poetic or ironic. His breaths were shallow; he exhaled white puffs of fear into the cold air.

"Okay, shithead, stop!" Paul stopped, and closed his eyes. He had to decide if he was ready to die, or plead for his life. He thought of his father, gunned down in a convenience store. A random act of violence. Wrong place, wrong time. Would his son receive a similar fate?

Was bad luck hereditary?

"Turn around," the mercenary said. Paul turned, expecting to see a gun.

Sean stood by a gravestone and descended to one knee. He placed his right hand on top of it, bowed his head and spoke.

"I swear to you, if Paul Driscoll ever writes or calls Katherine Flynn-Ryan, or contacts her in any way, or, if she contacts him and he talks back— if he ever sets foot in this state again, I swear I will kill him. I swear this upon my brave father's grave. And, sir, killing him will be my honor, and pleasure."

Sean rose, kissed the gravestone and stared at Paul. "Get back in the fucking car. Move!" They walked and got inside the Cordoba. "Now, do you think I'm serious?"

"Yes."

"Swearing on a soldier's grave is the strongest promise any soldier can make. It's an unbreakable bond. My father died a soldier's death, dying for his country. He died for duty, for honor. My swearing on his grave is a sacred pact. Some people swear on Bibles. Fuck that! The Bible don't mean shit. It's a book. A bunch of stories. The only thing that matters is country, duty, and honor. You understand?"

"Yes sir," Paul said, his heartbeats thumping in his eardrums.

"You'd better. You goddamn better because I'm not fucking around here." Sean started the car and began driving back through the cemetery. Paul looked again at the funeral ceremony taking place and thanked God he was still on the right side of the soil.

Sean drove back to the highway and told Paul to pour him another cup of wine.

The drunk madman was wired. Even though the car's interior was cold, Sean was perspiring. Paul tried staying out of his peripheral vision by looking out the passenger window. He smelled Sean's body odor and heard his raspy breathing.

"You want to go ten minutes with me, hand-to-hand?" Sean asked.

"No. Sir."

"Goddammit! I want your ass!" Paul turned and saw his red face. Sean's fists gripped the steering wheel. "Five minutes, you pussy. Give me five fucking minutes, hand-to-hand."

"No thanks."

"You're chickenshit."

They rode in silence. Sean turned the car onto Interstate 95 South toward Boston.

"Paul," he said, "did Katherine tell you we're lovers?"

"I'm sorry— what did you say?"

"Did Katherine tell you that we're lovers?" Sean looked at him and smiled.

"No." Paul wondered if Sean was trying to provoke him into a fight, or, if it was true. He remembered Sean's comment in the motel room about having seen her naked.

"We're lovers. She needs a man, not a boy. Give me a cigarette." Paul reached for his pack. "And light it."

Paul passed the lit cigarette trying to still his shaking hands. Sean worked keeping the car between the highway lines.

"Did Katherine tell you about the guy I killed in Lawrence?"

"No."

"The bastard was sent from El Salvador to kill me. But I got him first. Fucker blindsided me outside a bar. He had a knife, and I kicked it out of his hand. We wrestled, fell into the canal, and kept fighting. I held his head underwater, strangling the son of a bitch, kicking him in the balls." Sean took a long drag on his cigarette, as if recounting a tender memory. "I kept strangling him until I felt his lifeblood leaving his body. I killed that fucker because I had to. For preservation. But you, Paul, you— I'd kill for sheer pleasure. You think I'm serious?"

"Yes, sir." Paul looked at the floor, afraid to expose his eyes to Sean.

"I've killed lots of people. Most of them for country, duty, and honor. But you? I'd kill you for fun. And if you ever contact Katherine again— it doesn't matter how sneaky you are, I'll find out, hunt you down, and kill you. You can't hide. Trust me. Got that?"

"Yes, sir." Paul's hands were clammy. He clasped them together and swallowed; his throat was dry and constricted.

"Goddammit, say something smart ass and give me a reason to kill you."

Paul looked over and saw Sean's left hand restraining his right, holding it onto the steering wheel. Sean's forearm muscles were tense. He thought the mercenary might fling his right arm across the front seat and strike his face. Paul grimaced, closed his eyes, and turned his head.

"Relax, chickenshit. I'm not going to hit you. Pour me another drink, then tell me everything you've done here." Sean passed the empty cup, Paul filled it and passed it back.

"What do you want me to tell you?"

"Tell me every fucking thing you've done since you landed. Everything."

Paul recounted meeting Katherine at the airport and driving to The Shamrock Motel.

"What'd you do after you checked in?"

"What do you mean?"

"I mean, shithead, what the hell did you do at the motel? Did you fuck her?"

"Yes, sir, we made love."

"'Made love' my ass. That's pussy talk. You fucked her— you fucked my cousin. The other night, you told me you didn't."

"But I didn't, not that night. We did it in the afternoon."

"Are you a goddamn lawyer looking for loopholes? You're using her. She's just an easy piece of ass to you, isn't she?"

"I'm not using her. I came back here to find a job and be with her."

"You're not getting any fucking job, and you're not going to be with her ever again. Didn't I make myself clear?"

"Yes sir." Paul noticed Sean's cup was empty again.

"You know what I'd like to do to you?"

"No."

"I'd like to tie you up, castrate you with a dull knife, then stuff your cock and balls down your lying fucking throat. Would you like that, mister loophole?"

"No, sir."

"I guess you're not as dumb as you look."

During the ride to Logan, Sean repeated his threat if Paul contacted Katherine, or returned to the state.

He had Paul repeat the warning.

Paul wished Sean would drive faster. He was relieved when he noticed aircrafts flying at low altitudes. He wanted out of the car and to be in public, where he'd have a chance of safety.

At the airport, Sean parked and took Paul's luggage from the trunk.

"I'm coming in to make sure you get on the plane."

They headed to the American Airlines counter and stood in line, Paul in front. He looked for his ticket in his briefcase, but couldn't find it.

"I've got it," Sean said, waving a ticket jacket. He must have bought him a new ticket, Paul thought.

The counterman served a customer and hoisted a bag on to the luggage scale. Paul stepped forward.

"Please wait behind the line until I've finished with this customer," the counterman said.

"Get back here," Sean shouted, grabbing Paul by the shoulder and pulling him back. "Now, soldier! You're disobeying a direct order!" The counterman was startled.

"I didn't order you," he said.

"We do not disobey orders, mein capitan!" Sean said, standing at attention, crisply saluting and clicking his heels together. The counterman smiled, thinking it was a joke. He placed the bag on the conveyor belt, gave the passenger his ticket and asked Paul to step forward.

"Move, soldier," Sean said. Paul went to the counter and Sean handed his ticket to the clerk. He typed on his keyboard.

"Because you're changing to an earlier departure date, there will be a $59 charge, sir." he said. Paul was confused. He thought Sean had purchased a new ticket, but the clerk showed Paul a ticket with his original departure date. Sean must have stolen his ticket at the same time he took Katherine's wallet.

"Pay the man," Sean said.

Paul handed the clerk a credit card. He completed the transaction and gave him his boarding pass.

"We've got some time before your flight," Sean said. "Let's get a drink."

They sat at the bar. "Bring us tequila," Sean told the bartender.

"I don't drink tequila," Paul said.

"Then get what you want, pussy," Sean said. He turned to the bartender. "Give me a double shot of tequila." Paul ordered a draft. The bartender took Paul's credit card and started a tab. Sean gulped his shot and ordered another.

"I drink tequila by the bottle," he said. "I love tequila, but my constitution's a lot stronger than yours, chickenshit." Sean was perspiring heavily. His breath reeked of tobacco and liquor. It mingled with his body odor creating a fog of sour funk. The bartender brought another double tequila and walked away. Sean stared at his shot glass and spoke quietly.

"I could have easily killed you at the motel. Katherine would have sworn you attacked me, so it would have been self-defense. I could have killed you and she'd have given me an airtight alibi. You believe me?"

"Yes," Paul said, not sure she would give her cousin a murder alibi— even if he was family.

"You better believe it." Sean hoisted the shot glass and downed the tequila. He flagged the bartender and ordered a beer. When it arrived, he leaned in to Paul.

"Does Katherine think I killed her ex?"

"She didn't say anything about that."

"Then, she thinks the deadbeat just ran away?"

"I guess so."

"Good. Light me a cigarette." Sean took sips of beer and smoked as he told Paul about his exploits in Central America, training troops, leading missions, and "killing for duty and honor."

Sean recited his hierarchy of the things worth dying for.

Country, first— being a patriot.

Duty, next— obeying orders.

Then, honor— doing what was right.

Fourth was love.

And a distant fifth was money.

"But killing you, that'd would be for kicks." He smiled, and drained his glass.

Paul nursed his beer. His throat was tight. He lit a cigarette. Sean grabbed his pack and lighter and clumsily lit one. He regaled Paul with more ways he wanted to kill him. Paul hoped the bartender would overhear him and sense danger.

The bartender was more interested in TV sports, and ignored them.

As the clock pushed past noon, Sean waved to the bartender for the check. "Settle your tab, Paul, we got to catch your flight."

Paul signed for the $21 tab. The madman was no cheap date.

Sean wobbled as he escorted Paul to his gate. The flight was boarding.

"Do you understand everything I said?" Sean asked.

"Yes, sir."

"Good. Then for your sake, I hope I never see your pussy ass again." He stared with bloodshot eyes. "Because if I do, Paul Driscoll, my ugly face will be the last fucking one you see."

The big man stepped forward, dropped Paul's suitcase, embraced him, and said something in a foreign language. He kissed him on each cheek, turned, and stumbled away.

Paul watched as the drunk mercenary did his best to walk sober.

When the plane landed at Cleveland Hopkins Airport, Paul called Frank and asked to be picked up.

"What are you doing back? Frank asked. "You just left."

"It's a crazy story. I'll tell you when you get here."

Frank met him outside baggage claim. In the car, Paul told him what happened. He realized how unbelievable it sounded. Frank listened, punctuating the story with "You're kidding!" and "No!" and "Really?"

When Paul finished, Frank took a deep breath. "Holy shit."

"Yeah."

"What are you going to do?"

"What can I do?"

"You going to call her?"

"Hell, no. I'm not giving that maniac a reason to come kill me."

"You think he would?"

"Absolutely. He swore on his dead daddy's grave, for Christ's sake. He told me lots of different ways he wanted to kill me. The guy's insane, and Katherine knows it. If she wants me, she knows where to find me. If it's meant to be, it'll work out. If not, so be it. She's there, I'm here. Alive."

A Zen approach was the only way Paul could process what had happened.

Frank shook his head "What a way to break up. That's one for the books."

They stopped by a grocery store and bought two 12-packs of Molson's, went to Frank's apartment, and began drinking. Paul's throat loosened, and beer never tasted so good.

He spent the night there. He told Frank about his bar fight and arrest in Panama City, and stories about Brian, Barb, The Foleys, Blippo, Cronk, Augusta, Teddy, Chuck Gund, a police chief in Greenwood, and an elephant that gave him a golden shower.

They laughed. Laughter eased his pain.

CHAPTER TWENTY-ONE
Homecoming

"Don't live for today, live for tomorrow's memories of today."
— *Paul Driscoll's notes, Kissimmee, FL*

When he returned home, Paul didn't tell his family the complete story of what had happened. Instead, he told them and his friends that his relationship went sour and he probably wouldn't be moving to New England.

No one seemed surprised or inquisitive. He sensed relief from his mother.

His memories replayed. Katherine's missing wallet, his missing manuscript, her interactions with Sean, the mercenary's threats and his murder and lover confessions on the ride to the airport.

❧

"Amy Jepson came by the office today with her bambino," Frank said, over the phone. "A little boy named James."

"How old?"

"I don't know, baby-age. Anyway, Greg Cartwell and Jack Lunkorm both seemed pretty interested in the kid. One of them might be the proud papa."

Paul thought about Amy and their pregnancy scare. The calendar put him in the potential daddy lottery.

"Who's the baby look like?"

"You. Looks exactly like you."

"Really?"

"No," Frank laughed. "I mean, yes. He looks like you, me, Greg, Jack, any guy. The kid looks like a baby. Jesus, Paul, you still don't think you're the father, do you?"

"I don't know. I could be."

"Give your guilt a rest. She gave you a get out of jail free card. If it was your kid, she'd tell you."

"I guess you're right."

"Anyway, I thought you'd like to know."

"Thanks."

"Anything happening on the job front?"

"Unemployment."

"That's steady work," Frank said.

"I'm good at it."

Paul called the Boston ad agencies he had interviews scheduled with and said he was cancelling due to an emergency. No one asked to reschedule; the agencies would somehow survive without the Paul Driscoll magic.

He collected unemployment, went to the library researching ad agencies, and drank in bars with friends waiting for his psyche to heal.

Sean's warnings replayed in his head. He wondered what was happening in Haverhill. He tried putting his future with Katherine into the past.

Paul wasn't sure what he wanted to do. Whether to look for a copywriting job close to home, in Cleveland or Pittsburgh, or try a major market like New York or Chicago. He knew it'd be hard to break into larger markets with the quality of his work, and he didn't have money to fly around searching.

Twenty-nine days after his return, his mother shouted upstairs he had a call. "I think it's that New England girl," she said. "It's someone with a funny accent." Paul's hand shook as he lifted the phone receiver.

"I got it, mom," he shouted. He waited until he heard the downstairs phone disconnect and the soft static of a long-distance connection. "Hello?"

"Paul," Katherine said. "What happened? Why didn't you call?" He felt blood rushing to his head.

"Remember your crazy cousin, Katherine? He abducted me, you remember that, right? Then he took me to the airport and threatened to kill me if I ever contacted you. Sean doesn't know you're calling me, does he?" His pulse was racing.

"No."

"Christ, Katherine, how could you let him take me? The guy's a—"

"Sean's dead," Katherine said. She began sobbing. "He was shot in the head last night outside his apartment."

"Who did it?"

"No one knows. The cops are investigating."

"Did your ex-husband ever turn up?"

"No."

"When Sean took me to the airport, he asked me what you thought happened to him. I said you thought he ran away so he wouldn't have to pay child support. Sean seemed happy about that."

"So?"

"So, maybe Sean killed your ex."

"Or, maybe he did run away, and returned yesterday and killed Sean."

"You said your ex's brother suspected Sean. Maybe the brother did it."

"You think Michael Ryan did it?"

"Him, or someone from Sean's mercenary days."

"My God, Sean's dead and you're playing Sherlock Holmes."

"He had a lot of enemies. Sean told me he killed a guy from El Salvador sent there to kill him. He said he strangled him in the canal and you knew about it. Is that true, Katherine?"

Silence.

"Let's not play detective. I miss you, Paul, come back."

Long silence. "No."

"I thought you loved me." He thought about all he'd invested in their relationship, the miles of loneliness fueled by the expectation of reuniting— exploded because of an insane relative she protected.

He thought about Sean saying he and Katherine were lovers. His quote about having seen her naked.

Paul recalled her last-minute openness for him to job hunt in other cities. Was that to ease her guilt and complicity in knowing how dangerous Sean was? Was Paul her escape plan?

It was complicated, but added up to one unavoidable truth: he didn't trust her.

"Katherine, I'm not sure how I feel, but I know Sean was a maniac."

"Please, don't speak ill of the dead."

"'Ill of the dead?' Christ, Katherine, the guy threatened my life. The crazy bastard took an oath on his father's grave saying he'd kill me if I ever contacted you. So, I didn't. I've been waiting for you to contact me. Now it's four weeks later and—"

"He threatened me, too, Paul. The night you left, I was working at Buster's, and he told me to take a break and meet him in the alley. Then, he handed me some papers he said you wrote. He said it was sacrilegious bullshit, and he told me to rip it up."

"Was it my novel?"

"It was dark, I couldn't tell. Probably."

"He stole it, like he stole your wallet and my airplane ticket."

"Sean told me to rip up the pages or he'd kill me. Then, he'd find you and kill you, too."

"Did he have a gun?"

"I don't know."

"What happened?"

"He had a crazy look in his eyes. He shouted for me to rip up the pages, so I did. Then he had me throw the scraps into the dumpster. And he said that on the ride to the airport you told him you were just using me."

"That's bullshit."

"He said I should test you. That if you really loved me, you'd call. But I couldn't call you first. He said if he found out I contacted you, he'd make both of us pay. When I didn't hear from you, he said it was proof you never loved me. I kept thinking you'd call, but you didn't."

"Sean told me you two were lovers. Is that true?" Silence. "Is it?"

"You can't believe everything he said. And besides, what's past is past. He's dead."

What if he weren't dead, thought Paul. What if Sean was still alive, and listening in on the phone call as a test?

"I have too many bad memories about the crazy shit Sean put me through. I'm done, Katherine."

"But he's gone now."

"It doesn't matter. I've moved on. You should, too." She began sobbing.

"Did you ever really love me, Paul?"

326

"I came back, didn't I? Don't you think my actions proved I did?"

"Do you still love me?"

"I don't know. Maybe. But you didn't protect me from him."

"But, he's gone. We can get back to our plans."

"No, Katherine. I can't forgive and forget. You were my reward at the end of the road. My anchor. But instead, I got insanity because of your maniac cousin— who you protected because you said blood is thicker than water."

"Blood is thicker than water."

"I guess I'm water. You made your choice."

"I want you, Paul."

"I'll never know the real story about Sean, if he was really your lover, threatening you, or whatever the hell else he was doing, like maybe killing your ex. I'll never understand why you didn't call the cops on him— the guy was obviously dangerous. But it doesn't matter, it's too late. Like you said, the past is past. I'm done."

"I'd love to see you again, Paul."

"No. Let's keep the good memories and get on with our lives." She began sniffling sorrowful convulsions. "I wish the best to you and your family."

"You, too."

"I've got to run, I'm late for an appointment," he lied.

"I guess this is goodbye then," her voice cracked.

"Goodbye, Katherine, and good luck." He placed the receiver on the hook and lit a cigarette with shaking hands. He breathed deeply, calming down enough to smoke.

He wondered if perhaps she had killed Sean. She certainly had motive. He tried purging that thought.

He'd never know the true story; he only knew his side of it.

Over the next two months, Paul interviewed for copywriting jobs in Akron, Cleveland, and Pittsburgh. He thought his circus experience would be viewed as an asset, showing his depth of character, adaptability, and understanding. How many copywriters traveled and took the pulse of America? He thought his adventure would be valued by a creative industry.

It wasn't.

His interviewers questioned his motives for taking the job, and made bad jokes— "This place can be a real circus sometimes" or, "Did your position require a shovel?" Paul forced smiles and laughed.

He noticed the ad agency offices displayed award show trophies— "attaboy" and "attagirl" hardware reminding creative people of their worth. Proof of their incredible talents.

On his resume, Paul had listed the Akrie Award he had lifted from Greg Cartwell's office the day he was fired. It didn't seem to warrant respect or notice in an industry congested with accolades.

Paul saw framed ads hanging on agency walls. Clever headlines with snappy copy, leading readers through a labyrinth of logic, ending with a summation demanding action to buy the featured product or service. The ads strove to persuade, smug in the assumption a sale had been made. Paul thought the writing was formulaic and anemic compared to his fiction— words so powerful they enraged a maniac to threaten death to his beloved cousin, unless she destroyed the pages.

His interviews yielded mild interest, but no offers. Agency creative directors asked him to stay in touch and keep them posted on what he was up to. But there were "no openings right now."

He collected his unemployment checks and contemplated the future.

Paul turned over in bed and looked at the alarm clock: 8:02 a.m.

He scanned the room. On the wall was a painting of two men in a boat, fishing on a serene lake as the sun rose. The bathroom door was open, and sunlight streamed through a small window. A television sat on a table, and a desk and chair were off to the side.

Paul rubbed crusts from his eyes, sat up, and stretched. Although he had never awoken in this room before, it felt familiar.

He remembered he was in Kissimmee, Florida, and he'd be meeting Augusta Plumbar in an hour and twenty-eight minutes for breakfast.

It was going to be a good day.

~~~

Paul was early to the circus grounds, and walked the midway toward Stan Wootmoor, setting-up his microphone perch in front of the sideshow tent. He looked down at Paul and squinted.

"You came back." He smiled and climbed down from his pulpit. Paul could tell the barker didn't remember his name.

"Hi, Stan. I'm Paul Driscoll, remember?"

"Right— Paul. Sure, I remember. Good to see you again."

"Good to see you, Stan. Do you have any new attractions this season?"

"Nope. Got the same collection of human oddities and natural wonders." He winked.

"Is 'lil Pete predicting a good season for us?"

"Yes, but that little bastard always predicts a good season. Hell, even a broken clock's right twice a day. We'll be fine— as long as we stay out of Texas."

"Great."

"What's your first town?"

"I don't know yet. I came down to see a preview show and say hi to some friends."

"Go enjoy yourself. It's good to see you again, Paul."

"Thanks, Stan. It's good to be back."

"Welcome home, son."

He walked into the big top and noticed a team of roustabouts assembling the three rings. He didn't recognize any of them. Fresh muscle for a new season.

Across the big top, Paul saw Augusta enter the tent. She was backlit by warm morning sunshine, an angelic vision. She saw him and began running toward him. He smiled.

The smell of sawdust and hope filled the air as he jogged toward her. He tried keeping pace with his racing heart.

He was confident maybe she was the one.

Acknowledgments

My eternal gratitude to my wife for being the one.

Thanks to David Norton for his support and smart ideas, Anya Moss for her encouragement, Kitty O'Keefe for her cheerleading, Ann Fisher for her editing skills, and George Weinstein for his wisdom.

And thanks to the talented, passionate souls who brought circuses to glorious life, providing cherished memories burnished for lifetimes. Take a bow and give a circus wave!

About the Author

PD (aka Patrick) Scullin is a writer who created some famous advertising campaigns, started a successful ad agency and sold it to write more entertaining words. Early in his career he worked as an advance man for a circus. It was inspirational.

PD is married with two sons. He lives in Atlanta and at pdscullin.com

You Have Great Influence—Please Help

If you enjoyed SAWDUST, please let the world know. Post a star rating and review the book on Amazon and your social media channels.

It will only take you a minute and will make a world of difference to me. Thanks.

Made in the USA
Columbia, SC
12 September 2021

45324129R00202